The Melforger Chronicles

BOOK 1

DAVID LUNDGREN

First Printed, 2012
Revised Edition, 2014

Cover Design by David Lundgren
Title font and logo by George Watson (jiggerflea.wordpress.com)
Interior Design by David Lundgren

ISBN-13: 978-0615719603 (MELFORGER)
ISBN-10: 0615719600

www.melforger.com

For the diaspora

TABLE OF CONTENTS

1. <u>COLORS</u>

Wesp coughed into his sleeve and then spat over the side. Shivering, he peered up angrily at the threatening swirls of grey cloud that could just be made out through the foliage high above. Rain was coming, and lots of it.

The wagon wobbled its way along a worn path that curved around the base of one of the enormous trees that the locals called *Ancients*. Apparently, the ground here was actually *on* the branches of these scattered forest giants. Another trader back in Miern had once tried to explain it to him, how the huge branches that grew out from the trunks had been cemented together by vines and plant roots over the centuries until they formed this natural, compact layer that ran above the actual forest floor. Wesp was dubious. And yet, perhaps it was possible; despite having traveled here before, he still found himself bewildered by the sheer, *staggering* size of the *Ancients*, soaring upward to form a distant canopy a hundred yards above the other normal-sized trees. Nowhere else in the world had he ever seen anything like it, and he'd traveled more than most.

A clap of thunder pounded through the forest, bouncing between the towering trunks and then fading into silence. An eerie silence. Instead of the usual cacophony from countless birds and insects, there was this muffled stillness with only the occasional ominous creaking of branches. It was as though the heavy skies had taken a deep breath and it seemed only a matter of time until they burst.

Automatically, he reached under his coat and brought a battered, leather bag to his mouth, taking a long, noisy swig before recapping it in a practiced motion. It wasn't the potent whisky he drank in the gambling pits back in Miern, but some sort of mead from Three Ways, the main forest town. It was dwindling fast though. Hopefully, he could stock up on more at the main village in the south before looping back up to the Pass for the long trip home.

There was also one last crucial item on his list still to find: a local delicacy they called vinehoney. If he could get some, it would justify the entire wretched journey from Miern. There was a craze in the city for the jasmine-tinted syrup that could only be found in the Aeril forest and Wesp had managed to strike a deal with the chief cook at the Gerent's Palace. He was desperate to obtain a few jars for some royal function in a few weeks' time, and willing to pay a fortune for it – enough that Wesp could perhaps even think about retiring.

He had a good feeling about this last village, and if they had some vinehoney, it would be easy enough to do some trading for it. They were keen on trading, these foresters. Wesp smiled. Keen, but not particularly good at it; whereas he had cut his teeth in Miern. If you could say anything about Wesp Tunrhak, it was that he knew how to haggle with the best. He reached down to pat the leather case that was stowed under the bench and there was a familiar clinking of coins in response.

Taking another disapproving look at the darkening skies, he turned to spit over the side again and then poked his sandal into the back of the young boy sleeping on the wagon floor.

"Get up."

The boy grunted in pain and then sat up, rubbing his eyes and scratching the tangles of blonde hair that fell around his freckled face.

"We're stopping here for the night." Wesp pointed at the three burly goats. "Get 'em fed and tied up before this rain sets in."

2

"Why? Where are you g-"

Wesp whipped his hand down to flick his shoulder. "Just do what I tell you!"

Quickly climbing out of the wagon, the boy untied the animals and led them away toward a clump of blackberry brambles further down the lane. He cast one sulky look back at him but wisely kept his mouth closed.

Wesp jumped down and pushed his way through the dense undergrowth that bordered the path nearest him. Drawing a small axe from his belt, he began hacking at the foliage until bushes and vines fell to the ground where he kicked them to the side. He moved further and further into the brush, carving up branches that stood in his way and kicking over young saplings until he had a decent-sized patch cleared. To one side, he spotted a short, gnarled trunk wrapped in thick vines that would be perfect for his fire. Stepping up to it, he lifted his axe and then hesitated as a sudden whiff of something repulsive filled his nostrils. Covering his mouth and nose with a sleeve, he poked the axe blade tentatively into the trunk – and grimaced when it pushed through as if the wood were made of butter. On the outside it seemed healthy, but on closer inspection, Wesp saw that the inner pulp was a dark moldy color. Spitting on the ground in disgust, he left it alone and moved to search the other side of the clearing.

. . . .

Raf curled his toes up in his sandals and poked at the leaves that lay scattered around him in a thick mat. It wasn't an *Ancient*, but the hollowed section half way up this dead oak was still big enough for him to stand in. And surrounded by leafy strangler vines, it was well hidden from the path below.

He combed his fingers through his shaggy hair and tried to brush out some of the dust from the climb up the inside of the tree. Probably time to get a haircut soon, really. While most

3

foresters let theirs grow, Raf had inherited his father's thick, almost black hair, and unless he had it cut every month or so, it turned into an unruly mess that seemed to just attract dirt.

Leaning back with a contented sigh, he smiled to himself. He'd just managed to escape from a tedious music lesson with Madame Ottery while all of his classmates were still trapped there. He just wasn't in the mood for school after the incident that morning. His friend Nedrick had overheard someone saying the Festival might not happen, and when Raf had asked his parents about it during breakfast, his mother had *completely* hit the roof and banned him from mentioning it again. It wasn't like *he'd* started the stupid rumor! Sometimes, having two parents who were on the village Council - and therefore supremely uptight all the time in the case of his mother - was a huge pain.

Why was everyone so stressed, anyway? The Festival wouldn't be cancelled; it was far too important. This time last year, the whole village - the entire Aeril Forest! - had been fired up about the Festival; and that was when it had been hosted way up north. Now, for the first time in many years, it was Eirdale's turn, and you could almost taste the excitement in the air. Well, until the rumor, anyway.

As long as it doesn't mess up my sojourn plans, he thought.

Sojourns happened at the end of school for every forester. For a few weeks or even months, school-leavers would travel and experience life outside of their village. Raf wanted to go somewhere outrageous. Somewhere far. The furthest he'd ever traveled was up north to Three Ways - and that was still in the Forest! The Foreman himself had said sojourns were good for 'broadening your perspective', so why be boring and go somewhere close or similar to home? Cisco's older brother had spent seven months way south of Sayenham on the coast where he had apparently managed to get work on a fishing boat. His tales about the turquoise sea and whale music were fascinating. Proper stories, those.

Raf looked up at the ledges around the hollow chamber that gave him somewhere to prop up his recent attempts at carving. There was a short, rough pipe he'd carved out of rosewood, a hollowed gourd that was the start of a lute, and an attempt at making some panpipes that could've been decent if he hadn't made such a hash job of cutting the holes into the bamboo pieces. Sighing in frustration, he reached up to retrieve the piece of soft cherry wood that he'd picked up on his way from school and ran his fingers over it.

"All right, here we go again," he muttered. "Some sort of pipe, maybe. And I think I'll name you…Orfea."

He pulled out his knife and, giving it a quick wipe on his shirt, set to work whittling away at the wood, his grey-green eyes squinting in concentration. Shavings fell to the floor as he scraped and cut, but only a few minutes later, he sighed again and put his knife back in its sheath.

"Rubbish."

He held the stick up and grimaced at the mess he'd made of it, before throwing it down on the floor in disgust.

The wind whistled softly through the cracks in the bark around him and, as he relaxed against the trunk, there came the soothing rustling of leaves, the subtle creaking and groaning of the dead tree, and of course, the never-ending backdrop of birdsong. Two young marmosets sprinted past the window, chasing each other excitedly and he smiled to himself as their chatter faded away. They had far too much energy. As if on cue, a sudden yawn sent his jaw creaking. From nowhere, a tune sprang to his mind and he found himself humming it quietly. It was soft and lilting, and after a few moments his eyes grew heavy and then closed. An instant streak of colors lit up the darkness behind his eyelids.

What…?

His eyes shot open and he straightened his head, but the colors were gone. He frowned and rubbed his eyes before closing them, and waited curiously to see if anything would

5

happen. But when nothing did, he felt himself slowly relax again. After a few moments, he started humming the same tune. There was no mistaking it this time when a wave of colors washed across his eyes, so he kept them tightly closed and peered blindly forward, still humming.

He waited for them to fade, but instead, the colors lingered in front of him, flittering aimlessly like feathers being buffeted by the wind. The tune he was humming moved to his favorite part and as it drew more of his attention, the colors grew in intensity. Then they suddenly started moving with purpose, red and purple patterns spinning and spiraling through each other – right toward him! He gasped in astonishment, hands raised defensively as he flung his eyes open, expecting something to be crashing into him. But there was nothing. Just the inside of the tree. The colors were nowhere to be seen – nor any cause for them.

Okay... he thought. *So now there's something wrong with my head. Great. I better go see Dr. Ferrows and find out if I'm going crazy.*

He pursed his lips. *As long as she doesn't go and tell mom. If she finds out I'm 'seeing things' with everything* else *that's stressing her out at the moment...*

He lay back, gloomily shaking his head, and closed his eyes. The tune had an annoying way of lurking just beneath his thoughts and he soon found himself humming it once more. When the strange colors emerged into view again, he forced himself to ignore them, humming louder and turning his thoughts back to the pipe he'd been trying to make. He focused hard on imagining himself carving the instrument - anything to draw his attention away! - picturing the shape he wanted in such minute detail that he soon forgot about the weird colors.

....

Fergus yawned and stared blankly into the distance as the three goats munched their way through yet another bush laden with berries. Although he'd come to adore the Forest with all its animals and birds and trees, working for Mr. Wesp was hard, and he was sometimes really horrible. Aunt Firda had said that he was an important, rich man and Fergus should try to learn how to become a trader, but if having money meant you had to act - and smell - like Mr. Wesp, then he thought he'd prefer to live more like the Forest people.

A bright green lourie shrieked in the leaves above and made him jump. He giggled with delight as it spread its wings, showing off the hidden feathers of fiery red underneath, and soared away around one of the trees. The only birds he had ever seen in Miern were crows; big, black birds that lived near the waste dumps that always squawked loudly and stalked around on their funny wire legs trying to steal bits of food.

He suddenly felt his mouth flood as a delicious smell of roasting meat drifted past. He realized what it meant, though and with a worried gasp he scrambled to the wagon and climbed up on top. Peering over the bushes nearby where he'd last seen Mr. Wesp, he spotted a big clearing had been cut away. Broken vines and branches littered the ground and in the middle of the mess was the old trader sitting by...a huge fire! You weren't allowed to make fires in the middle of the Forest! Even Fergus knew that. It was the first thing you were told when you came into the Forest. What was Mr. Wesp *thinking*? There was another rolling boom of thunder and Fergus looked up hopefully, urging the heavy clouds to hurry.

Wesp lifted his mead bag to his mouth and took a long draft. Under his free arm rested the leather case, his hand stroking the straps that held it tightly closed. He stared into the flames, watching as they crackled and danced next to the roasted peacock carcass which he'd set to one side.

The breeze was strengthening and growing more damp and cold as the evening set in, so he stood up and made his way to the wagon. He seized the thick pine branch that was propped against it and, dragging it back, up-ended it onto the fire. He stepped back as it crashed into the flames, embers flying up in a small storm. The locals would erupt in conniptions if they knew about his little bonfire, but he was well hidden here and the rain was on its way, anyway.

He turned to sit down again, but as he did there was a strange movement under him, a shifting sensation that stopped him in his tracks. He stared around trying to determine what it was until, with a soft tearing noise, several tiny cracks appeared in the ground around him. He edged backward, staring curiously as the splits spread out under the fire and across the clearing in a web - when the center suddenly buckled and collapsed. With a great, smoky puff of sparks, the entire bonfire disappeared. A jagged hole appeared out of the debris, widening rapidly as large chunks of ground gave way and fell through.

Wesp fled, stopping only when he reached the edge of the clearing where he clung to a tree trunk. Embers that had caught on hanging vines were still flickering away along the sides of the hole, illuminating the inside. He peered over the edge, which was only a few feet away, and was just in time to catch sight of the bulk of the fire tumbling down in a glittering cloud through the darkness below.

He jerked himself backward, fighting dizziness. It was so far down! The flaming logs had been bouncing down the side of a trunk like tiny rag dolls when he spied them - a hundred yards below at least! - before they disappeared into the darkness. He'd had no idea this platform was so high above the forester floor...

Panting, he stared around - and then flinched in shock as he saw where he had been sitting.

"No!" he rasped, his eyes darting around the broken ground.

A sound behind him made him jump but it was only the stupid boy who had skidded to a halt next to him, a shocked expression on his face as he took in the hole.

"Where *is* it?" hissed Wesp, spinning to stare in dismay again at the gaping hole where he had been sitting. A tight groan escaped from his throat. "It can't have..."

"Sir?" quavered Fergus.

"My leather case!" Wesp crouched down at the hole's edge, squinting through the smoke. "No! It can't..." He clutched at his face with dirty hands. "My money..."

Fergus crawled carefully around to the opposite side of the clearing, peering down into the dusty darkness until he pointed excitedly at something. "Mr. Wesp, sir!"

"What? What is it? Can you see it?"

"Sir, there's a small tree hanging upside down and your bag's stuck on it!"

"Where?" Wesp nervously leaned over and spotted the bag twenty feet down, hanging from a branch.

He tilted his head back to yell in despair before pausing as a thought struck him. He slowly turned to look at the boy. "You...can climb, can't you?"

9

"Uhh, yes, sir. I'm the best in the whole of the Docks."

"Time for you to earn your way then," said Wesp. "I think you're going to fetch my case, yes, Fergus? When you get it, your aunt will find out how good you've been when we get back. Think how proud she'll be."

Fergus looked over the edge. "But what if it falls? And it's started raining now, too, s-"

Wesp clenched his fists in rage and marched around through the bushes to the boy. "You're lucky I let you travel with me for the last two weeks! And feed you! Any of 'em other good-for-nothing orphans like you in Miern would kill for the chance!"

He took hold of Fergus' neck in a tight grip, and walked to the edge, forcing the boy in front of him. "Now get down there and fetch my case!"

. . . .

Fergus rubbed his neck and sat down at the jagged lip of the hole, his legs dangling over. It wasn't *that* different to climbing around back in Miern, really. He just needed to be careful – especially with the drizzle starting to come down quite hard. He moved forward and then paused as something rotten filled the air, stronger even than the damp smoky smell. It seemed to be coming from through the hole, though, so he shrugged – Mr. Wesp wouldn't want to hear any more excuses - and, breathing through his mouth, eased himself over the edge.

Gripping ripped branch ends and vines, he lowered himself until he reached the trunk of the hanging sapling, its roots splayed and stretched taut, securing it to the solid ground above where Mr. Wesp was crouching. It should have been completely dark underneath, but the dim light spilling through from the newly created opening revealed a landscape of formless shapes; the nearest ones dull brown and ocher, fading

10

into sullen greys and charcoals as they stretched into the gloom.

The case was snagged on a small branch jutting out about half way down the dangling tree, so Fergus wrapped his arms and legs around the trunk and shimmied his way down, inch by inch. It was a strange sensation hanging over this dark emptiness. Everything was undefined and murky, although he could see hundreds of rain drops shooting down in front of him, crystal-bright as they entered the hole, and then disappearing as they sailed downward.

"Come on, hurry up!" The trader had slid on his stomach to the edge and was looking down at him.

Fergus rubbed the rain from his eyes with a sleeve and then gripped a branch, edging his feet down to another branch below. Heart pounding, he got closer and closer to the case until it was only a few feet away. Slowly, slowly, just a few more inches. There was a ripping sound and the whole tree shuddered, dropping a few feet before jolting to a halt again. Fergus' hands slipped off the trunk to send him falling downward for a split second, before he crashed into a branch lower down. He frantically circled the trunk again with his legs, and stayed in that position, breathing hard and shaking.

"It's getting wet with the rain, sir," he whimpered.

"Oh, come on! You're almost there," came a feverish hiss. "Think of your aunt!"

Fergus sniffed and looked up at the case hanging just above his head. Reaching up carefully, he took hold of the strap and tried to pull it off, feeling the coins shift awkwardly. There were a lot of them inside.

"It's heavy!" he shouted, eyes half closed to avoid the rain that was falling fast and hard. "I don't think I can do it. I'm scared, sir... I want to come back up."

"You useless gutterpig!" screamed the trader. "You stay right there, don't move!" With that, his shadowy shape disappeared from above the hole.

Fergus tried to blink the rain out of his eyes, and as he clung tightly to the tree, things started to come into focus in more detail. Around him, huge round trunks materialized slowly out of the musty blackness, rising up smoothly from the depths below. They were almost like the pillars of the Gerent's Palace, but these were much, *much* bigger. Even the smallest one he could see was thicker than a house – maybe as thick as the Palace itself, even.

Looking up along the underside of the path they walked on, he could make out the massive branches that grew out from the trunks. Wrapped around them and between them were millions of vines in a kind of thick, natural weave. A few hundred yards away, another eerie beam of light pierced the darkness. It was beautiful, and the rain that was falling twinkled like tiny crystals through the light. Fergus stared in wonder at it, forgetting for a moment where he was. But his reverie was quickly shattered by a hard, wet smack across his head, and for one brief moment he thought that Mr. Wesp had climbed down to beat him. Flailing around his head with one arm, his hand brushed against what turned out to be a slender length of coarse rope.

"Tie up the case to the rope!"

Fergus shuffled the rope through his fingers until he reached the end of it and then threaded it through the case handles before looping it over and through itself a few times.

"All right, Mr. Wesp, I think I've tied it," he called, when the makeshift knot was tight.

"Make sure nothing falls out of it! If you lose anything, anything at all, you'll regret it, boy!"

The rope snapped taut as the trader pulled on it and then, with a few rattles and clinks, the case slowly lifted in jerks upward. Fergus followed it as best he could, carefully unhooking the bag every time it got caught on something. He could see Mr. Wesp's face above, stretched tight with the effort as he hauled on the rope - when the hanging tree suddenly tore away completely from the path above and plummeted.

Feeling himself dropping with a sickening rush, Fergus threw his arms upward and somehow managed to hook his fingers in the open side-pocket of the case. It stretched to breaking point but held and, with a jerk, he swung wildly through the air. Above him, there was a shriek as the trader was pulled toward the edge with the sudden extra weight.

The tree tumbled down past Fergus and the last of the roots whipped his legs painfully as it fell away into the deep darkness underneath.

"Help!"

Dangling helplessly, he looked up and saw the trader's torso, crouched at the edge, fighting to regain control of the rope. He was clenching his teeth as the weight of the boy and the moneybag pulled him closer and closer toward the lip of the hole.

"Let go!"

"Sir, please, I don't want to fall!" wailed Fergus.

"Let go of the bag!" yelled the trader through clenched teeth. His left foot slid forward in the mud and for a split second he lost control of the rope. The case lurched downward, stopping with a jolt as he regained his footing. But not before there was a small tear in the seam, and from the top-most pouch a couple of shiny coins glittered as they tumbled downward.

"No! Don't let them drop!"

The trader heaved back as hard as he could, his heels digging into the ground, and Fergus saw the rope and then the case strap slide up over the edge. And then he found himself within reach of the edge, so he quickly threw a hand up to seize a thick vine. With the sudden reduction in weight, the trader staggered backward out of view. Fergus hooked a leg up over the side and levered himself onto the ground, rolling away from the edge where he sat up against a tree trunk. He hugged his knees and tried to catch his breath, quiet whimpers escaping each time he exhaled.

"Enough of that."

Mr. Wesp was also leaning against a trunk, panting. He looked down at the leather case clutched to his chest and then added, "I don't want to ever hear you speak about this." He nodded back at the hole. "Else you'll learn exactly how far down it goes in that hole there. And next time you won't find me there to save you."

Raf sat up in his hidey-hole and yawned, rubbing his eyes groggily after taking a long, refreshing nap.

Better sleeping here than sleeping in Ottery's class, he mused. Skipping her class could probably come back and bite him, but that was a worry for another time. It had been a *great* nap. He needed to get back, though. That evening, he was meeting up with Cisco and Nedrick to go tracking. Apparently someone had seen a leopard a mile or so east toward Emborough, which was pretty rare.

Blinking sleepily, he started climbing down the hollow trunk, but then hoisted himself back up to get the stick he'd been whittling. It was there, lying in the same place he'd thrown it.

"Yup, that's about the most rubbish carving I've ever seen. Orfea is way too pretty a name for you."

He whipped his arm back and turned to toss the mangled stick out the window. But then he paused, his arm suspended in mid-air. Above where he had been sleeping, there was a thick net of branching vines and something was in the middle of the leafy mass. Something very out of place.

He stepped forward, staring in stunned silence. Poking out was a wooden pipe about two feet long with a flared end like a horn; only, it wasn't haphazardly stuck in there, it was actually growing from the vine. A surge of dizziness rocked him as he realized that it was very similar – no, *identical* – to the instrument he had been thinking about carving when he had drifted off to sleep!

What? How...? He rubbed his temples. *Come on, what's going on here? That's not possible...*

Leaning forward, he grasped it and twisted it carefully. With barely a sound, the tiny green stalk at the end snapped. Raf could feel his heart throbbing in his chest as he gently held the pipe and felt the uncanny familiarity of its shape and weight. It fitted his hands perfectly. He lifted it to his mouth, his fingers slotting automatically into position and blew softly through it. The soft woody note sent goose-bumps storming over his body and, with a whimper he flung the pipe away. It bounced against the knotted bark and sailed out the window.

He turned away, slowly rubbing his hands over each other. "Right," he whispered. "Right. Probably best to...to go home."

He scrambled toward the opening and almost threw himself down it in his eagerness to get out. Dropping the last few feet to the floor, he tore off down the path toward the village.

. . . .

A few days later, a troop of marmosets escorted the wagon as it rolled along the path. Fergus was sitting on the bench, his eyes scanning the trees around them, giving the occasional click of his tongue to keep the goats moving. At the back of the wagon, sitting sprawled against the wooden beams, was the miserable figure of Mr. Wesp, hair messy and eyes bloodshot. Every movement of the wagon made him flinch.

He squinted up into the bright, late-morning light and, giving Fergus a dark look, shuffled onto his side to lie down. Before closing his eyes though, he reached inside his coat to quaff from a mead bag. The wagon lurched over a particularly deep rut as he took a second gulp and a slop of liquid spilt down his tunic.

"Watch it!" he growled.

Fergus ignored him, absorbed in watching the foliage above them. There seemed to be even more birds since the storm from two days ago had passed, with every bush a flurry of multi-colored squawking and chirping. The marmosets were his favorite companions though. All they seemed to do was scamper around having fun. And they were quite friendly, too. Having got up early as usual that morning, Fergus had left the trader fast asleep and crawled all the way up an old knotted olive tree to the canopy above where a small troop of the little monkeys were grooming each other. They had eyed him warily at first, the thick tufts of white hair quivering where it stuck out from their ears, but they soon accepted him and went about their morning activities. Once they had finished their cleaning, it mostly consisted of chasing each other frantically from branch to branch. Fergus was *so* jealous. He had spent the first few hours of the day sitting happily with them, the colors of the sunrise making the tree-tops change color around him.

It was almost as if the whole incident with Mr. Wesp's bag and the hole hadn't happened.

Over the creaks of the wagon, a new noise brought his attention back to the path. There was something in the distance: a regular knocking sound, like someone hammering.

"Whoaaa." He pulled gently on the goats' reins. Standing on tip-toes, he peered forward to where the noise was coming from.

"Why have you stopped? Are we there?" came a mumbling from the back of the wagon.

"I heard something, sir! A kind of knocking or something, I think."

He heard the trader scrambling to his feet and then the smelly man was suddenly beside him, peering eagerly up the path. "Where?"

"Listen," said Fergus. They stood there, still as statues for a few moments.

"I can't hear anything." Mr. Wesp turned away and then

pointed at something on the seat next to Fergus. "And what's that?"

"Those little monkeys were playing with it this morning and dropped it, sir. I think it's an instrum-"

"Of course it's an instrument, you fool," snapped the old man, snatching up the wooden pipe. "I'll have that."

Fergus slumped on the bench and scowled as he flicked the reins to get the goats moving again. The wagon shook as it took off and the trader moved back to stow the pipe in a large chest.

Fergus felt his lip trembling and sniffed as they made their way down the bumpy path. Why was he so *mean* all the time? He threw occasional angry looks back at Mr. Wesp as they traveled on. Eventually, mouth tightening more and more in irritation, the trader cursed and then darted forward to grab hold of Fergus' shoulder, yanking him around.

"Now listen here, you."

Fergus tried to twist his head so he wasn't directly in front of the trader's horrible breath, but Mr. Wesp moved up close so that their faces were almost touching. "I'm getting a little bit sick of your atti..."

A faint knocking noise echoed again through the trees and the trader's eyes suddenly seemed to sharpen. He snatched the reins out of Fergus' hands and pulled on them to bring the wagon to a halt.

"Right. You listen to me, boy. This is my last chance to get some vinehoney and I'll not 'ave you interfering with so much at stake. I think it'd be best if you didn't say a single thing, you hear?"

Fergus tried to move away. "Y-yes, Mr. Wesp."

"No talking to anyone, no playing with their filthy children. And most of all, don't mention a single thing about the vinehoney, understand?"

"Yes, Mr. Wesp."

"Are you sure I can trust you to do that? This could be the trip that gives me my well-earned retirement and I won't have my contract ruined by you. You remember that little hole in the ground?" Fergus nodded. "Someone could have a serious accident there. So easy to fall in. Wouldn't your poor aunt be sad..."

The trader stepped down into the back of the wagon and Fergus flicked the reins with shaking hands, biting down on his bottom lip.

....

Raf moved back from the thick leaves in front of him, considering what he had just witnessed. While they did get visitors in these southern parts of the Forest, it was still quite startling to see foreigners come casually traveling down into Eirdale. Especially a bizarre little pair like those two. And what was all that about a hole?

He crawled back into the trunk and sat thinking for a bit. If the old man really was a trader, and that's certainly what he must've been with that laden wagon, then this could be a lucky break for the villagers. Odd that this trader also seemed so anxious to get vinehoney. The last trader who had passed through Eirdale a few weeks' back had only stopped here long enough to buy some vinehoney and a few supplies for his return trip before rushing off.

He got to his feet to leave but, for the hundredth time, the memory of what had happened with the pipe flickered into his thoughts. He moved next to the opening in the wall and squinted down at the path in frustration. After two days of scouring the bushes below the window it had flown out of, he'd never found the strange pipe. He was almost convinced the whole thing had been a strange dream.

At the sound of the wagon creaking away toward the village, he quickly tucked his knife in his belt and climbed down through the hollow trunk of the snag using the knotted bark for footholds.

The Eirdale commons was a large open area between some *Ancients* that served as the main location for most village meetings and events. By the time he reached it, there was already a crowd by the wagon, burbling enthusiastically as the trader stood surveying the reception grandly in an elegant cloak. Raf looked across from the back of the crowd to the group of children who were being conducted by Madame Ottery as they sang through the *gretanayre*.

The duty often fell to the youngest school kids when visitors arrived, and Raf was vastly relieved he didn't have to sing anymore, being in his last year of school. A gaggle of kids screeching at visitors didn't seem the best introduction to Eirdale. He cringed as he caught sight of his young brother, Rio, in the front row, belting out a harmony enthusiastically.

There was a disturbance on the other side of the crowd and they parted, still clapping and singing heartily, to reveal a stately procession. Raf stared in surprise as no less than the entire village Council came marching out to meet the trader.

This guy must be more important than I thought…

At the forefront was Eirdale's barrel-chested Foreman, his massive strides making it hard for Raf's mother, Leiana, to keep up. But she did, her legs pumping furiously and her shoulder-length mahogany hair, normally so immaculately groomed, bouncing erratically around her sharp eyes. Behind came the other Council members, Raf's father Tarvil included, his hands loosely clasped behind his back, wearing his usual calm smile. They sang along with the crowd, and then halted at the front to let the Foreman approach the trader.

"Welcome to Eirdale," he declared.

Then, drawing a breath, he sang the *gretanayre* in a rich and deep voice that sent notes booming out and echoing off the nearby trees.

Barely started, he was interrupted by the trader who held up his hand. "Please don't feel obliged to sing on my behalf."

"It is only proper to honor you with the song of greeting,"

said the Foreman, and he gestured to the other Council members standing behind him to join in.

"There's absolutely no need, really. I've already heard enough music from you foresters to last a lifetime of... happy memories."

The Foreman looked taken aback. "I...I'm sure you understand it is our way. We would not want to disrespect you by not -"

"No disrespect, Foreman. None whatsoever!"

"Only, we don't receive many visitors here in the south and the opportunity to share -"

"- will surely come up many times in the future," finished the trader. "But for now, I have traveled far and if you have some accommodation where I could clean and refresh myself, then perhaps you might be interested in some trading? I must leave early tomorrow morning to get back to Miern where I am awaited by the Gerent, you see. Little enough time to conduct trading as it is; so if you don't mind declining what I'm sure you'll agree is a tedious ritual..."

"We will at least put on a banquet tonight in your honor."

"I'm not quite sure -"

"Nonsense," said the Foreman. "Miern must be a noisy nightmare these days and the voyage down the Pass must have been grueling, so we will treat you to a feast and some entertainment before you return - and *before* we conduct any trading. I insist." The Foreman lifted his chin slightly. "Mr.?"

"Err... Wesp," the trader replied, before swirling his cloak around his shoulders. "My name is Wesp Tunrhak, Miern's most reputable trader. And personal friend of the Gerent himself."

"Of course you are, Mr. Tunrhak, and it is a delight to have such important company in our midst. We are simple rural folk, but will do our best to leave you with an enduring impression of our lovely village for when you return to Miern." The Foreman nodded at Raf's younger brother. "Rio here will

21

show you to the guest quarters down by the school enclosure. I hope you find them comfortable."

Wesp grunted and spun on his heels, his cloak billowing outward. "They will probably do."

4. <u>SOJOURNS</u>

Raf stood idly as the wagon rolled down the path, the excited burbling of the villagers washing over him. From behind, there came the sound of footsteps, and he turned to see his father approaching.

"Tired?" asked Raf when Tarvil sat down, rubbing his eyes.

"Exhausted. We've been at it non-stop for days now. It'd be the first time that there hasn't been a Festival. As unlikely as it seems, this trader may be our last chance to make enough coin to finance it." He sighed. "Funny thing really. It used to be about the music when I was your age. All you needed were a few people with instruments, and the rest took care of itself."

Raf looked down at the floor. He knew what was coming.

"I'm assuming you're still not interested in playing if the Festival goes ahead?"

"Dad, I don't mind getting up there with the others to do something, but there's no way I'm going to stand there singing by myself or pratting around on an instrument."

His father shrugged. "Your mother will be disappointed. You know how she wants you to be the next musician journeyman."

"Probably the next Foreman as well," muttered Raf.

"You can't be too angry with her. She only wants the best for you. And she has a lot of pride; remember, your grandfather's a Foreman. The bar was set quite high, unfortunately."

"But I'm not interested in it all."

"You used to be so confident with singing when you were Rio's age. What happened?"

"Nothing happened. It's just, well, I don't enjoy it anymore. Not really. Nobody does. Except for the old villagers, and they're probably all deaf anyway." He scowled. "Ned has the same thing when he plays the lute."

"Tovier?"

"Yeah. Everyone laughs at him when he plays. He hates it, but with his dad being in the Council, too.... The second he finishes school, he'll probably take that stupid lute and throw it down a burial chute."

"It's a pity; he's very good."

"Maybe, but playing a lute isn't exactly... I mean, did you know that some guys our age in Miern are already in the Guard? Some of them are even journeymen. And Cisco's brother met a boat captain in Sayenham who was only fifteen! Eirdale's...well, it just seems so lame."

"Raf, our lives are different. For a start, we don't have an army - or a need for one, thankfully. And, strangely enough, boats are a little hard to come by up here in the tree-tops." Tarvil paused. "Do you even know what you'd like to do?"

Raf shook his head and threw a stick at the ground. "Not really. I'm not really that good at anything. I was thinking maybe a canopy-farmer?"

"Harvesting? It's hardly ambitious, Raf."

"But it's important, right? We need the food. And we need people who are good at getting it. It may not be high-ranking in mom's book, but someone has to do it, right?"

His father laughed out loud. "Tell you what, son, I'll let *you* tell her you're giving up the dream to be a woodsmith or Foreman so you can pick mulberries all day."

"It's not *my* dream."

"True." His father looked fondly at him, patting his shoulder. "So, what about your sojourn? Given any thought to that yet?"

"Yeah," said Raf. "I was going to ask you about it, actually. I think I'll skip the redwoods up north. Trent Brunnow went last year and I'd like to do something different. The amount he's talked about it, I feel like I went with him, anyway."

"So you're thinking of a trek south? The mountains? I hope you're ready for the cold. You've never seen snow. It's colder than you can possibly imagine! And someti-"

"No, not south. Or west."

Tarvil opened his mouth and then closed it. Clearing his throat with a quick cough, he turned to face Raf. "I'd just like to make this plain and clear. Firstly, personally, I think it's a terrible idea. Sure it may be where I did *my* sojourn, but that was a long time ago and things were completely different. It was smaller than it is now, and the old Gerent was still in power. He seemed much friendlier than this new one." He held up his hand to cut off Raf who was trying to butt in. "Secondly, I'd like to know where I can buy tickets to watch you tell your mother." He laughed loudly, genuinely, and then, mimicking Raf's voice, said, "Mom, not only am I never going to be something as good as you want, but I'm also going to go to Miern."

"Dad," moaned Raf, "it's my choice. I think it'd be brilliant to see a city. You said it was amazing!"

"Absolutely true," replied Tarvil, grinning wolfishly. "But I didn't have your mother to tell."

"Can't *you* tell her?" begged Raf.

"Hah! Not on your life, boy. You're on your own. If you want to be the first sixteen year old to be killed in Eirdale, you go ahead."

Raf reluctantly smiled. "So, you don't mind?"

"It's your trip, Raf. A sojourn is each person's own decision." He paused, pursing his lips pensively. "What I will say though, is that we'll need some help getting you there."

"What do you mean?"

"Miern is at least ten days' travel from here, sometimes more depending on the weather. You can't do it alone. We need to find out when there'll be a caravan down the Pass. The

Forest I know you'll be fine in, but once you get to the Pass, you've got to travel with company and spend the nights in communes for safety. Supplies are essential for the trip as well, and obviously you'll need some coin for food and accommodation while you're there."

"How long is the Pass?"

Tarvil chuckled. "I see you've done all your research on this." At Raf's glum expression, he continued, "Oh it's a decent distance: probably about a hundred and fifty miles all told. And it's unimaginably hot. It follows a canyon that cuts right through the middle of the desert and although it's shaded to some extent by the cliffs on either side, they also trap heat in it. When the sun's right overhead, you have to rest in the shade or under cover or risk getting burned to a cinder. Us foresters just aren't able to deal with that sort of open-air experience. Even the canopy-farmers would struggle."

"Oh."

"Once you're on the other side of it though, the landscape turns beautiful. Sand dunes, and little lakes everywhere."

"It sounds amazing," said Raf, smiling. He looked up. "Nobody else is going there. They're all too worried about what happened to those guys from Three Ways last year. People think they died, or maybe were even killed."

"Sad to say, but as they haven't heard a thing from any of them, it seems likely. So, with all the dangers and expenses and hassles getting there, you're still keen to do it?"

Raf thought about it, his eyes flickering around the ground in front of them. Then he nodded firmly. "Definitely."

"Right," said Tarvil, slapping both hands down on his thighs and standing up. "Then what we need to do now more than ever is get this Festival up and running."

"Why?"

"Firstly, we need to make a little money for you to spend on your sojourn. Also, people come from all over to see this, and if we're going to find a company for you to travel with back to Miern, there's no better place to search than in the crowds at the Festival."

Raf's face lit up. "Of course!"

"Small problem though. The only way we're going to get the coin to rescue it at this late stage is from this Miernan trader. Mr. Tunrhak, it seems, is our last hope; but a trader and his coin are tightly joined, as they say."

Raf tapped his mouth with a finger thoughtfully.

"What?" asked Tarvil.

"Well, funny that you mention it, but, I skipped Ottery's lesson earlier on today -"

"*Madame* Ottery. And why did you ski-"

"I think I may have overheard something rather interesting, Dad."

The afternoon was well under way by the time the village chimes were rung for the second time. Bonfires had been built and fed in the ironwood fire-pits until they were roaring, with three large, golden-brown boars suspended above the dancing flames. They crackled with the intense heat and emitted a delicious aroma that tantalized the throng of villagers seated on the commons' benches. Wandering between them were young children delivering bowls of food and filling rapidly emptying mugs with frothy mead.

Raf strolled down from his home and paused as he came across a cluster of peacocks on the path. One of the males had its tail spread out, a stunning metallic rainbow of colors. Raf stood and watched it strutting for a while, rapt – until his trance was shattered as one of the brown peahens suddenly let out a screech. They scurried away, bobbing their heads furiously as Raf grinned at them. A flock of tiny green parrots had taken off in fright at the noise, soaring off through the trees in a shimmering cloud of green. With a glance up at them, he set off again, and as he reached the commons, he was greeted by a blare of noise from the hundreds of villagers already there. Raf decided not to find his family at the Council end and instead, joined Nedrick and Cisco at the back, digging into a bowl of plump grapes. At the front, where he could see his parents and the rest of the Council sitting next to the trader, the Foreman said something to Raf's mom and then got to his feet.

"Here we go," he murmured, popping another grape into his mouth. "My last chance…"

Tarvil spotted Raf at the back of the crowd and gave him a fond smile. Next to him, Foreman Manyara called to a young boy sitting on one of the benches right in front of them. He stood nervously, drawing a shaky breath, and started to sing the *metanayre* in a beautiful treble voice. A wave of silence immediately swept through the villagers, rolling down the throng of people toward the benches where Raf was. It was one of Tarvil's favorite pieces, and it didn't matter that it was sung at every mealtime in every single home in the whole Forest, it still moved him every time he heard it. The first verse came to an end and he prepared himself to join in for the next part, when there was a sudden noise from the side. The trader was clapping loudly – rather obnoxiously, too, Tarvil thought, but then he stopped at the onslaught of surprised looks he received.

"Oh, I thought he'd finished." Wesp shrugged and grabbed his mug, raising it to the choirboy.

The Foreman looked across at the young boy who stood fidgeting nervously. "That was beautiful, lad."

Dipping his head, the boy quickly made his way to a bench and sat down with his family.

"I s'pect you're jealous, really."

Leiana tilted her head at the trader's comment. "Jealous?"

"Of the northern villages of course. They're much closer to the Pass, obviously. They get most of the attention from Miern."

"Oh, I don't know. We're quite happy here in Eirdale. What we miss out on we can probably do without." Leiana sniffed and took a sip from her mug.

Wesp covered what could have been a smile with his mug. "Of course you do, of course you do."

Tarvil coughed softly to attract the trader's attention. "I visited Miern in my youth and remember the old Gerent as a talented musician and an enthusiast of Miern's musical traditions. I wonder if you're aware of the new Gerent being equally supportive?"

"Ha! I doubt it. It's true that not too long ago the Gerent's Festival would attract thousands from all over the world to see it, but times change and move on. It's only yourselves here," he looked briefly upward, "living in the trees, who cling to the past." He turned back to the table in front of him to take hold of a large chunk of golden-brown crackling on a platter. He sank his teeth into it and the fat trickled down his chin and into his scraggly beard. "The Gerent's now more interested in trade and growing Miern. Not to mention sorting out the problems up in 'em Ka'toan mountains. Things have changed drastically since the kidnapping, of course."

"The what?"

Wesp looked up, surprised. "You 'aven't heard? Surely you've heard about his son being taken by raiders?" The Council looked at each other questioningly and all shook their heads. "There've long been problems with the Ka'toan raiders stealing cattle and sheep from the outer farming districts, something the old Gerent had tried to sort out diplomatically. Fat lot of good it did. So, the new one tried being a bit more aggressive with 'em, sent soldiers in to warn 'em to step in line. Then, a few months ago, we found out that a group of raiders had snuck into the city and managed to abduct the child – from right inside the Palace!"

"That's terrible!" muttered Tarvil. "Has he been found yet?"

"Not by the time I left. I 'spect he'll be safe, though. They won't kill 'im; they'll keep 'im to make sure the Gerent backs off. Those filthy raiders have always wanted their own space to do their ritual killings and whatnot."

The Foreman shook his head irritably and stood up. "The

Ka'toans are a peaceful people who, if anything, are less violent than most."

Wesp made as if to argue, but the Foreman cut him off with a raised hand. "Let us get to business, Mr. Tunrhak, as I suspect you would like to get some trading in before you return."

"Abuniah!" he shouted, his deep voice rising above the general hubbub to where a small group of people sat laughing and eating. A tall, smiling man dressed in a plain white tunic and with a great sprouting bush of curly black hair on his head stood up and stepped forward slowly into the bright orange light of the bonfire. He performed a ludicrous bow that ended with a flourish of his hands. "You beckoned, Foreman?"

There were a few laughs from the people sitting around him.

"I did, you pompous fool," said the Foreman, chuckling. "We are in for a treat with our guest tonight as he has come from Miern to do trade with us." There was a small half-hearted cheer from the crowd. "But what would a night like this be without an introduction befitting such an important occasion?" He raised a huge hand to point at Abuniah, who was posing dramatically. "Let there be music!"

The lanky man sprang backward to stand beside a colossal wooden drum. Seizing the sticks on either side, Abuniah started beating out a wild rhythm. A few of the foresters behind him grabbed tambourines and beat them animatedly, while others pulled out flutes, wood-whistles, lutes and pipes to play. Within seconds, the commons was awash with music, guided by Abuniah's steady beat.

Tarvil watched as Wesp's face fell, particularly as he noticed some elderly women start wiggling their bodies to the beat, clapping enthusiastically. He got up and started walking back to his quarters.

"Mr. Tunrhak?"

"My wagon needs setting up," replied the trader. He spat on the ground and marched off, hooking a finger angrily at his young assistant to follow.

The slightest hint of a smug grin touched the Foreman's face and he turned back to face the commons. Abuniah was putting on an astounding show of dexterity and coordination, pumping out a rhythm on the drum that one could barely follow it was so complex. The Foreman crossed behind him to one of the storerooms and re-emerged, dragging out a wooden marimba, huge hollow gourds hanging pendulously underneath the carved pine keys. Once in place, he unhooked two heavy beaters and, with a shout, he hit the large bass note of the marimba, giving off a low, earthy pulse that was felt rather than heard. Everyone stopped what they were doing immediately. Then the Foreman started a solid rhythmic pattern of notes, the beautiful woody sound echoing around the trees. Abuniah joined back in with his drumming, the two slowly working together to create an intricate, but powerful beat. Then the Foreman began to sing, his powerful voice rising above the music, and on cue, the whole village joined in to create an exhilarating blend of voices and instruments in harmony that shook the Forest to its roots.

. . . .

When instruments were put away and a small crowd remained, milling around expectantly, Wesp reappeared with his assistant and stood beside his wagon.

Spitting into the ground, he turned and nodded. "Now."

His young assistant quickly stood up and fiddled with a few levers around the side. With a click and groan, the bottom half of the side of the wagon swung down to the ground unveiling rows of merchandise, and the villagers clapped as they eyed the colorful array.

Raf stood toward the back of the crowd, trying to observe everything inconspicuously. He was also immediately annoyed with himself for being impressed at a beautiful shiny blue wrap flapping gently in the wind. It had waves of darker blue running along its length and glittered as it moved in the fading sunlight as though there were thousands of tiny flecks of silver in it.

"Um, Master trader?" An elderly lady called Maritha stepped forward from the crowd holding a wicker box in her hands, a rather embarrassed expression on her face. "I can't help but notice that you have a rather lovely garment; the blue one just there." She lifted a spindly hand to point at the blue wrap. "I wonder if I might have a closer look?"

The boy started to reach across to unhook the garment and Wesp shouted, "Stop!" The crowd collectively drew a breath. "Don't touch it! You'll ruin it."

He carefully put his flask of whisky down on a table and then moved closer to his wagon. "What you've spotted there is a rare siminutrian garment called a *tso'be*. You're very lucky that I have one left, as the other three were snapped up at the very first village I visited. This particular color is the height of fashion in Miern as we speak. Why, Mesathinia, the Gerent's wife, has one herself."

Maritha's eyes opened at bit wider at this, her mouth forming an 'o' shape as she nodded. "Is it very expensive?"

"In Miern you would struggle to find a *tso'be* of this quality for less than twenty bronze coins." There were some gasps from the crowd and Wesp raised his hands to quieten them. "And although I'm sure you'd agree it's easily worth that, I completely understand that it may be difficult to find that sort of coin all the way out here." He stepped back and raised his voice. "However, this is my last stop before I return to Miern and I have one last item left to acquire. Something of little value, I'm sure. Certainly less than this *tso'be*. I understand it is called vi-"

"Only," interrupted Maritha, "I have this box of some lovely old jewelry I don't wear anymore. Would that be of interest, maybe?" She opened the rather tattered wicker box to reveal an assortment of wooden bead necklaces.

Wesp stared at her. "Don't be ridiculous, woman. I'm overflowing with bracelets and necklaces. No, what I'm really interes-"

Raf could've sworn that the trader's eyes flickered oddly for a split second as he glanced at the box before he lifted up a hand and stroked his chin. "Uh…your jewelry in there – all of it – for the *tso'be*? Is that what you're offering?"

Maritha's face broke into a hopeful smile and she nodded eagerly.

"Done!" Wesp snatched the box out of her hands. Then he unhooked the wrap and tossed it to her, but it fell to the ground and she had to quickly stoop down to lift it off the dirt. Behind her, some of the crowd moved forward eagerly to see her new purchase.

Raf watched as Wesp opened the box, reached inside and then let the whole thing drop to the ground, the necklaces spilling out. He held something shiny up and blew on it, scrutinizing it carefully in the light. Raf peered forward to see what it was but then spun around as there was movement behind him.

"Wait!" Maritha's husband, Alfred, hobbled past urgently toward Wesp. "My ring! My grandfather's signet ring!"

The crowd went silent as the trader moved a step backward and raised an eyebrow at him. The Foreman looked up from the sidelines where he had been sitting and then quickly got to his feet as he took in the aghast look on Maritha's face.

He moved up to put a hand on her shoulder. "Didn't you know it was in there, Maritha?"

"No, I had no idea! I didn't know he kept it there; it's always been *my* box." She covered her mouth with wrinkled hands.

"It's obviously been a misunderstanding. And easy enough to sort out," he said. "Mr. Tunrhak?"

"It *is* rather a nice ring," the trader said, rubbing the gold band in his fingers. "Of course, the deal's been made now. No way back. Should prob'ly keep better track of their possessions."

"Now see here," said the Foreman, "they didn't know that was in there. It was a simple mistake. Can't you just give them back the ring and keep the other jewelry?"

Wesp laughed. It was a loud, unpleasant laugh that sent bits of spittle flying from his mouth. "Keep the other items? Don't be absurd! They're worthless." He casually slipped the ring onto one of his fingers. "*This,* if I'm not mistaken, is pure Ka'toan gold, and it would fetch a decent price from a dealer I know in Miern." He removed it again, gave it a kiss and inserted it into his belt pouch.

"The deal has been made and we are bound to it," he said looking up with a smile.

Alfred hobbled quickly round the shoulder of his stricken wife to wave his walking stick in Wesp's face. "You give me my ring back, trader!"

Wesp smiled and opened his arms in a gesture of friendliness. "The nature of trade is to lose something and gain something else. Perhaps you can recover what you've lost if you have more to trade? If you 'appen to have any vi-"

"No." The Foreman moved forward to stand between the trader and the crowd. "I am disappointed with you, trader; that was a cruel thing to do." He waved an arm above his head. "Trading is finished."

Wesp looked at him frostily. "A foolish decision. I am not an unimportant man in Miern, and when I tell of what happened here, you'll find a distinct lack of *any* trade in the future comin' your way." He sneered and then spat on the ground at the Foreman's feet before climbing up onto his wagon.

The Foreman turned his back on the trader, his face stony with fury, and motioned with his hands for the crowd to move away.

6. <u>**VINEHONEY**</u>

Raf stood there, his heart pounding. The opportunity was slipping through their hands. "Wait!"

The Foreman, along with the rest of the crowd, turned around and stared at him.

"Err...we can't...I mean, surely it doesn't have to.... I..."

"What are you on about, Raf?" asked the Foreman.

"I...was just thinking that...the trader said he wanted something..." His mind went blank at the sudden barrage of eyes focused on him from everyone and all he could do was stutter, his mouth half open.

"Foreman," came the quiet voice of Tarvil, "what I think my seemingly witless son is trying to say, is that it seems such a waste to...to..."

"Oh come on, Tarvil," muttered the Foreman. "Can anybody speak properly?"

"I was just thinking that we shouldn't completely discount dealings with the trader."

"Oh but we should," said the Foreman. "No more trading."

"But, Foreman," insisted Tarvil, "it doesn't *have* to be trade, surely?" He tilted his head staring pointedly at the Foreman. "Maybe Mr. Tunrhak would be interested in spending some coin here."

"Not likely," said Wesp from the top of his wagon. "I trade to make money, not spend it."

The Foreman walked away, shaking his head.

"There *must* be something we have that is valuable, surely," Raf said desperately.

Tarvil joined in. "We have many rare things here: orchids, vinehoney, coffee. And not just any coffee, but a rich and strong local blend."

The Foreman glanced back to see the trader suddenly sitting straighter, an attentive look on his face. Raf bit his lip nervously as Wesp climbed down slowly from the wagon, his eyes flickering from the Foreman to Tarvil.

"As one last attempt to leave things amicably, perhaps...I might be interested in something you just mentioned."

"Wonderful news," said Tarvil. "Some coffee, perhaps?"

"I was wondering more about this vinehoney."

"Vinehoney?" replied Tarvil. "Well, the kind we harvest here is sweet and wonderfully thick." He paused and looked up at the trees, pursing his lips. "It's been a very difficult season though and the pickings have been unusually slim."

The Foreman stared at him. "Tarvil? What are you talking about? You know that we have pl-"

"Of *course!*" said Tarvil quickly, staring intently at the Foreman. "Of course I know we do have a limited reserve set aside for the annual Council meeting."

"The annual -"

"- the annual meeting, Foreman. You know, the one you're hosting next week?" Tarvil rolled his eyes comically, slapping the Foreman on his shoulder.

The Foreman stared at Tarvil. "Silly me. To forget such an important thing... The annual meeting. Vinehoney..."

Tarvil turned to Wesp. "I hope you understand that this is highly irregular and will leave the Foreman in a bit of a predicament at the meeting?"

"I see," said Wesp, frowning.

"And for that reason, as the village's accountant, I'm afraid we can't ask for less than five silvers a jar."

"But I need four jars! Are you telling me it'd cost me *twenty* silvers?" spluttered Wesp.

"And the ring returned."

"That's absurd!"

"I understand completely and apologize for wasting your time, Mr. Tunrhak. Perhaps you will find a better deal on your way back to Miern."

Wesp closed his mouth and a sour look appeared on his face. "Fine. Four jars and the ring returned. Done. They better be absolutely full to the brim, you hear!"

Tarvil shouted over his shoulder to Raf. "Fetch them from the Foreman's office, would you?"

Raf turned and sprinted past the school and under the chimes. When he reached a storage room in an official *Ancient*, he barged in to find Nedrick waiting.

"Did it work?"

"I think so."

"How many did he want?"

"Four jars."

Nedrick turned to pass him two from the pile of jars behind him that reached to the ceiling and then took two himself, holding one under each arm. Together they walked back to the wagon where the crowd moved to let them pass.

Tarvil nodded at Raf and turned to Wesp. "The silvers?"

Wesp stood grinding his teeth so that the tendons in his cheek stood out. "Boy!" he snapped.

The youngster scrambled up to the driver's area and dug around underneath the bench for a bit.

"Hurry up!"

"Yes sir!" called the boy, pulling out the leather bag and climbing down off the wagon. He held out the bag to Wesp, but as he did so, his thumb caught on the side-latch, unclasping it and the bag tilted downward, tipping out mixed coins all over the ground.

"Idiot!" shouted Wesp, and he swung his hand around to cuff the boy hard on the back of his head. He bent down and counted out twenty silver coins from the ground and put them into Tarvil's hand before scooping the rest back into the bag.

Tarvil waited until Wesp took out the ring and dropped it into his palm as well.

"Done," said Tarvil. "Or is it 'deal'? I'm not sure what the exact wording is; we're seldom so formal with guests." He chuckled self-deprecatingly and held out a hand for Wesp to shake.

The trader snorted, spitting on the ground. "Twenty silvers... It's robbery! You may think you've done well today, but let me warn you, forester, I'll not be quiet about this. I have friends in Miern. Don't be surprised if no trader comes within a mile of you in the future." He walked toward the wagon.

Raf made himself exhale slowly as his pounding heart started to calm down in his chest. There was a rush of wind behind him and suddenly his mother was standing there.

"I understand you've bought some vinehoney from us, Mr. Tunrhak?" she said brightly. "This is splendid news. Do make sure you strap them on carefully; they're not the most stable containers as we discovered."

"Mom..." hissed Raf. She was going to ruin everything!

"I'm just saying, it's very easy to knock one of these silly jars over. Not that that poor trader minded too much."

Wesp's lifted his head from packing. "What?"

"A trader was here a few weeks back and my husband -" she tilted her head back toward Tarvil who tried to subtly shake his head at her, "- managed to knock a jar all over him." She gave a half-hearted chuckle. "I told you, these jars aren't the b--"

"He bought vinehoney?" interrupted Wesp.

"Well... yes."

"He was from Miern?"

"Yes, like most traders who visit. He was very complimentary about the vinehoney, actually. He wanted some for his trip back to the city. He said it was for a party, I think. Or a banquet, maybe."

Wesp hit the side of the wagon with a fist and growled furiously.

Leiana tried to placate him, saying, "That's right, yes, a banquet. Nothing to do with trade or anyth-"

"The *Gerent's* banquet! The same banquet I bought the honey for! I've bought it for nothing! This other trader will be there before me! You said -" His eyes suddenly narrowed and he raised a finger to point it at Raf and then Tarvil. "You knew! You knew all along." His eyes stared around. "I've been tricked... Give me back my money, forester!"

Tarvil shook his head. "The deal is made and we are bound to it. Isn't that how you said it, Mr. Tunrhak?"

"No!" hissed Wesp. "I must have that money back. I have items here to sell, rare and beautiful objects. Tools from the famous smithies of north Almia, books and medicines." He rummaged desperately through his chests as the villagers watched him.

"I'm afraid the trading for today has come to an end," said the Foreman. "Come, Council, let us depart and discu-"

"No! I have more! Things you have never dreamed of. Weapons of Miernan steel th-"

"We have no need of weapons here."

"Maps? Dyes?" Wesp was frantically throwing things out of trunks onto the wagon floor. "Wait! I have something you will most certainly be interested in. It's an instrument made of a rare, fine wood, a piece of art of such intricate beauty you will hardly believe it real!" He whipped his hand up in the air, holding the instrument. Madam Ottery, who was standing at the rear, murmured in appreciation.

"Orfea!"

Every set of eyes swiveled to rest on Raf who covered his mouth as soon as the word left it.

"Raf?" asked his mother.

"Uh... nothing, sorry," replied Raf, blushing furiously.

"Who's this Orfea?"

"Her name... I mean, it's the name of the instrument."

"Really?" puzzled Tarvil. He turned to Madame Ottery.

"Have you heard of one of those before, Resma?" She shook her head.

"Yes, that's right! An *orfea!*" said Wesp.

"How do you know that, Raf? Where have you seen one before?" asked Tarvil.

"Well…I…I think I made it," stuttered Raf, feeling the heat rising in his cheeks.

"Ha! *Made* this? *You?* This beautiful piece of artwork?" Wesp sneered.

Tarvil approached him, frowning. "None of your pranks now, Raf."

"I'm not lying, Dad, I did make it. I lost it a few days ago on the northern path. The trader must've found it."

"Can you prove it's yours?" asked the Foreman. "Have you carved your name on it or anything like that? Do you have another one like it? Anything that would stand as proof? I want to believe you, but I must be fair."

Raf looked down nervously. "No. I mean, I could…maybe play it for you?"

"That might do," said the Foreman with a nod.

Wesp snorted and held the instrument out, sneering at Raf with a withering look. Raf took Orfea and held her in his hands, smiling faintly.

"Well?" came the harsh voice of Wesp. "What are you smiling about, boy? Called your bluff now, have I? This is no simple forester pipe; this takes a master musician to play."

Raf shook his head as he covered the holes with his fingers, drew a breath and lifted it to his mouth. A soft, sweet, mellow note flew out of Orfea, followed by more as he trilled a fluid reprise of the *farwelayre.*

"Well, I think that's settled," said the Foreman, giving Raf a quick approving look.

"What do you mean settled?" said Wesp. "That proves nothing!"

"I believe him."

"I don't care what you believe, I want that pipe back!"

"As Foreman of Eirdale, I'll gladly look into the matter further but it will take some time." He looked up at the branches above them, his fingers moving as he counted under his breath. "My estimate, bearing in mind that the Festival is just around the corner, is that it will probably take a month or so to come to a satisfactory conclusion."

"A month?" chirped the young boy from the wagon top. "Mr. Wesp, can we stay?"

"Shut up!" Wesp leaned up and smacked the boy's dangling foot hard so that it crashed into the wagon rail. The boy scrambled backward, cowering against the back railing rubbing his bruised leg. Wesp growled and turned back to the Foreman. "You're nothing but thieves! The first thing I'm going to do when I get back to Miern is report this!"

"I understand your frustration, trader, but my decision is made."

"How dare you!" sneered Wesp, drawing himself up. "I am Wesp Tunrhak, personal friend to the Gerent!"

Tarvil smiled faintly and then, cupping his chin with his thumb and forefinger, said, "Yes, quite so." He turned to the young boy. "Perhaps we should hear what this young lad has to say about it? I imagine he would have been there when you first obtained the instrument. Were you, boy?"

Wesp lunged to the wagon, pointing a finger at the boy. "Do you remember what I said about that hole?" The boy's face went white and he shrunk against the wagon side. "If you say another word…"

The Foreman frowned and said, "That really is enough now, trader. Go easy on the kid, will you? You may stay overnight, but I think it would be best if you left at first light."

He gave the young boy in the wagon an uneasy glance and then walked away, gesturing to the other villagers to follow suit.

The village was painted with the muted half-light of evening as the lanterns' orange glow filled the commons. The stream of birdsong that accompanied daylight had diminished now, to be replaced by the soft calls of nightingales and larks. And behind it all, the incessant vibrating rasp of cicadas.

Raf stood awkwardly by the trunk of the sequoia *Ancient* that served as the Council chambers as his parents and the Foreman followed the other Council members inside, and then he tried to surreptitiously nip around the corner.

"I don't think so, young Gency. We have one or two things to clear up first," said the Foreman wryly, indicating for Raf to enter.

"Yes, sir," said Raf glumly.

The Foreman pulled the door closed behind him and then strode to the back of the room where he sat down and swung his boots up to rest on the table-top.

"So, what did you think of that trader then, Raf?"

"I...I'm not sure, sir," muttered Raf, feeling a flush rise again on his face under the stare of the Council. "But it *is* my pipe, sir, I promise!"

"And how is it that you've hidden this ability to craft what is an incredibly intricate instrument? And with no training?" asked Madame Ottery. "I know you haven't been trained because I am the only person within miles who knows anything about the craft and even I couldn't make a perfect flarehorn like that." She stared at him.

"I don't know," said Raf shrugging. "I honestly don't know how I did it, exactly. But I did."

"Well, let's leave that for now," said the Foreman, looking over at Raf's father. "What I want to know is what sort of game you two were playing there, Tarvil."

"Well," said Tarvil, "Raf overheard the trader speaking about wanting vinehoney. He brought the information to me and -"

"- and you didn't think to share it with us?" said Leiana.

"- *and*, bearing in mind our current financial difficulties, it seemed wise to maximize the situation. It's unfortunate that he found us out, though."

The Foreman grunted. "A fine line to tread, Tarvil. As much as we need the money to fund the Festival, we also need to build ties with Miern. I'm sure he was mostly full of wind, but bad news travels twice as fast as good news, and it could be grim for us if he follows through with his threats." There was a general mumbling of agreement. "Still," he added, "it seems that against the odds, we now have the money to get the Festival back on track, which is certainly something to celebrate!"

Raf was making his way for the door when the Foreman called out, "Well done today, master Gency. I don't imagine things would've turned out quite so well for us if it wasn't for you."

The other Council members added their appreciation with a few pats on the back. His mother sat looking slightly bemused and then broke into a reluctant grin.

Then the Foreman stood and walked to hold open the door. "When you return from your sojourn, perhaps there might be a junior Council role on offer? A third Gency, perhaps?" The Foreman winked at him, and as Raf stepped out into the night, the last thing he saw before the door swung shut was his mother's glowing face.

. . . .

Junior Councilman? Not likely, fumed Raf. *I'd rather spend every day doing theory with Ottery than sitting in Council meetings and dealing with all* that *nonsense. No, thank you.*

He wound his way back through the school area, deep in thought as the cicadas buzzed around him. The usual evening hubbub had died down to a calm silence throughout Eirdale, and most homes were pitched in darkness with only the occasional voice that drifted through the fragrant air.

What a day...

He walked around for what felt like hours and did an entire loop of the center of the village as he pieced together all that had happened during the day. When he got back to the commons, he stopped for a while as he ran through the ridiculous situation that had arisen with the trader. Again and again his thoughts went back to what the Foreman had said. What if the trader *did* spread the word that Eirdale was a bad place to go? It would probably result in even less traders than usual visiting, which would be devastating. What if he ruined it for all the future Festivals, too? It was the biggest – and sometimes only - opportunity for the villages in the Forest to do trade. Not to mention somewhere to stay, food to eat, and entertainment for the thousands of people who journeyed here. They'd buy cartloads of local goods and in return, the villages would get essentials that they depended on like medicine, clothing, books and other things - especially metal. Raf himself was the proud owner of an excellent knife that his grandfather had given to him years ago: a foot-long, slim, sharp blade made of high quality steel. It was his most treasured possession and one of only about twenty in the entire village. As the canopy platform they lived on was high above the actual Forest floor, mining was physically impossible and you could only get metal from traders. Some types of wood that they used here were very hard, like ironwood, which was a pretty good substitute for metal, but there were some things that you simply couldn't do without metal for – like carving the ironwood itself. If trade were to stop, it would cause massive problems in every part of their daily lives.

He stopped walking. The idea that he might be responsible for that sort of problem was awful.

Maybe I can convince Wesp that it was my fault, or something. I have to try. If he follows through with his threats and tells people not come here, it'll ruin everything.

He picked up his pace and, shooing away another cluster of peacocks with Orfea, moved swiftly toward the guest quarters. Once he had made it through the last small tract of coffee bushes that bordered the school rooms, he crept up to the back of the guest quarters where Wesp was staying, keeping a wary eye on any movement from the paths in front.

Working his way around the base of the oak tree, he peered up toward where the trader's wagon was kept. Panning his eyes around the small commons in front, he suddenly spotted a light. A small fire! And three men sitting around it. It was Wesp and two foresters. They seemed to be having a good time, and were very drunk from the sound of it. He moved to lean against the trunk's wall, lifting his elbow up to rest it on the ledge of the window.

"Who's there?" said a voice right in his ear.

Raf leaped backward, gasping in surprise, and tripped over a root to fall heavily onto the ground. He scrambled onto his hands and knees, and stared at the window. "Who's that?" he whispered.

From the darkness of the window came a soft, "It's only Fergus, sir." Wesp's young assistant moved forward so that his face came into the dim light.

"You nearly scared me to death, you idiot," whispered Raf through clenched teeth.

"I'm sorry, sir. I didn't mean to. You scared me too. I woke up just now when I heard a wolf. I think it was a wolf, anyway. Do you get wolves here, sir?"

"Not in the southern Forest," said Raf. He tilted his head

46

and stared at the boy in the dull lamplight. "So your name is Fergus, huh? Did you travel all the way from Miern, too?"

"Yes, sir," Fergus replied. "Aunt Firda asked Mr. Wesp to take me on his trip so I could see the world."

"Well, I'm kind of jealous, Fergus," said Raf wryly. "What do you think of the world you've seen so far?"

"Oh, sir, it's amazing! The Pass was so hot and dry and horrible, but then we arrived at the Forest and... I love trees, sir! And they're so big! Everyone's really friendly here. And there are peacocks!"

Raf laughed out loud.

"Shhh, sir! He'll hear you and then he'll come back. I'm supposed to be asleep. He'll be so angry with me."

"Stop calling me 'sir'. My name's Raf." He peered at the boy's dimly lit face and saw a slight swelling on his cheek. "Was that Wesp? Did he do that?"

Fergus nodded.

"He doesn't seem to be a very nice person, Fergus," muttered Raf. He suddenly had a thought and turned back to the boy. "Why don't you stay here with us? Oh, but then I suppose your family back in Miern would miss you, wouldn't they?"

Fergus' eyes opened wide and his face lit up. "Stay with you? Here in the Forest? That would me amazing, sir! I mean, Raf. It's only me and my aunt, and she'd think it was fine, I'm sure, 'cause she works all the time, anyway." His face dropped. "But Mr. Wesp would never let me stay."

Raf pursed his lips. "We had someone once who was visiting with his family and he wanted to stay here. He asked the Foreman for sanctuary - that's what it's called - and he's lived here ever since. But I don't think you're old enough, Fergus. Maybe the Foreman can speak to Wesp in the morning, I'm s-"

Fergus shook his head violently. "Oh no, sir, please don't do that! Mr. Wesp wouldn't like that. He...he'll probably take me back to...to..."

"To Miern? Is it really that bad?"

Fergus shook his head and lifted his eyes. "To the hole."

"The hole?" Raf looked puzzled. "What h-" He was interrupted by a huge crash as the oak door swung open inside the room and smashed against the wall.

"Boy!" shouted the drunken voice of Wesp. "Why are you awake? And who are you talking to?"

"No one, sir," replied Fergus. He sounded terrified.

Wesp stumbled over to the window and stuck his head out to peer around into the murky night, eyes searching the darkness. "I heard you talking, you brat! Have you found a friend here? Even when I told you not to?"

He was slurring slightly and as he stood there breathing heavily, a line of spit ran down his chin and dripped - right onto the shoulder of Raf, who was cowering under the window. He held his breath, staring upward at the trader's looming head.

With a grunt, Wesp suddenly withdrew into the room and Raf heard a dull slap followed by someone falling down.

"Don't lie to me! Get up."

There were further noises and Raf clenched his teeth. This was his fault! He should never have talked to the poor kid.

"We're leaving earlier than expected. I've found out some useful things from those two idiots. Can't hold their liquor, these thieving foresters." There was a wet spitting sound. "I'm leaving for a bit. Have the wagon ready to leave immediately, hear me?" There was a whimper of pain from the boy. "When you've done that, wait for me here. Understand? One word to anyone and I promise you I'll drag you to that hole right now and throw you down, yes?"

"Y-yes, sir! Please let me go..."

There was a scuffling of feet and the door slammed, leaving the young boy crying softly. Raf peered carefully around the side and saw Wesp walking away along a path at the edge of the commons boundary.

He jumped up quickly and hissed, "Fergus? Are you all right?"

"Yes," came a quavering voice.

"I have to follow him and find out what he's up to. Are you going to be all right here?"

Fergus stepped up to the window nervously. "I need to get the goats ready, sir. Otherwise..." He broke into sobs again and, muffling his mouth with his hands, disappeared back into the darkness of the room.

Raf hesitated, not knowing what to do. "Fergus, I need to follow him, but I'll be back, I promise. I'll try to help you, all right?" There was no reply, only the continuing sound of boxes being moved. He thought quickly and then had an idea.

"Fergus?"

"Mm?"

"I want you to have this."

He held Orfea up to the window.

There was a gasp. "It's very pretty. Are you sure, sir? I don't have any money to pay for it."

"Absolutely sure," said Raf quickly. "And, for you, it's free. I made it. Well, as a matter of fact, it's actually a 'her'."

"Her?"

"Yes, her name is Orfea."

"Orfea? Oh, thank you, sir!"

"It's Raf."

"Sorry, Raf." Fergus emerged into the light again and his tear-stained face spread into a look of delight as he reached up to gently take Orfea from Raf's outstretched hand.

"Thank you!"

"You're welcome. Now, I have to go."

Raf sped off in a low crouching run. He slowed down briefly as he neared the fire, looking around for the other two who had been drinking with Wesp. They were both lying on the ground by the embers, snoring loudly.

Scanning up ahead, Raf saw the central path that Wesp had

turned down, and followed it until he caught sight of something white flapping a hundred feet or so ahead. Immediately, he stepped into the brush on the right side of the path and crept forward.

Wesp was peering intently into the dark patch of central *Ancients* that included the Council chambers. Raf crept forward inch by inch toward the trader. Whatever he was doing – and it surely couldn't be good - he'd picked a clever time; late enough that everyone was asleep, but not so late that the canopy farmers were already getting up.

He crept out of the brush and kept on Wesp's tail, moving from trunk to trunk and hiding behind smaller trees. He watched him walk up to the chambers and stop for a second, staring up the length of the *Ancient's* trunk. In the northernmost Forest, there were many of these imposing redwoods, but here in the south this sequoia was somewhat of a unique spectacle. And a spectacle it was at over a hundred feet wide, rising in one smooth, reddish column to disappear far above through the canopy. It was magnificent, and for that reason had housed the Council headquarters as far back as village history went.

Raf watched curiously from behind a small maple tree as the trader took a quick look around the commons and then crept inside. What was he doing? Nobody was in there. The sequoia *Ancient* just had empty meeting rooms in it.

Suddenly Raf gasped; there was also one *other* smaller room above the rest: the village vault.

. . . .

Wesp looked across the room. He'd stayed in many of the foresters odd tree-houses before on his previous trips to the forest, but he'd never been in one quite as big as this. There wasn't much light see by, but he could make out a large table in the middle of what was probably an office. What had they said? A ceiling entrance to a room above the others? He could see over a counter ledge to the adjacent room and in the middle of that, he spotted a set of winding wooden steps leading up. He walked across and carefully ascended, hoisting himself up through the small trapdoor into the storage room.

The vault was square in shape and surrounded by shelves set in the walls. There were some long, very thin windows cut into one wall which were probably for ventilation. He snorted and spat on the ground. These foresters simply wouldn't be able to handle the gambling Pits. Hundreds of people at all hours of the day trying to win some coin, rooms filled with the aroma of sweat and thick smoke, untarnished by so much as a breath of fresh air. He missed them!

On a pitch black night like this, the slits also let in a tiny bit of welcome light from outside and he began snooping around. Time was pressing. Moving to the closest shelf, he opened a velvet-lined box and discovered a set of dusty parchments. It was too dark to read them so he closed it and moved over to a small sturdy chest. He unlatched it carefully – no lock, the idiots! – and smiled immediately as the dim light revealed a neat pile of coins inside. More than they'd taken from him, for sure, but he'd consider it a fee for inconveniencing him. Not to mention lost future earnings; there was no way he'd be returning to this place again. He picked the box up and held it to his chest, sighing as he looked around at the other potential treasures. If only he had more time. But he needed to be well on his way by the time they got up.

Raf stayed absolutely still. He had climbed up into the tangled branches of a young maple and hidden himself behind a screen of leaves. As Wesp came creeping out of the chambers into the slightly less murky light of the commons, Raf saw that he was carrying a chest.

The trader walked out scanning the commons and then suddenly stumbled on a root, jerking forward before regaining his balance. The chest shook loudly, and the coins inside gave a metallic clinking sound that cut through the stillness. There was a commotion right above Raf's head and a night-ape took off in fright and bolted up to the top of the tree. Fluidly, it jumped across to another one, emitting a plaintive squeal before disappearing along a branch. Breathing heavily, Raf mentally cursed and lowered his eyes again - to find Wesp staring straight at him. A tense scowl was on his face and he had one arm stretched out toward Raf, a strange object in his hand.

"I didn't realize I 'ad company," he said. "Why don't you come down?" He motioned with the object in his hands as Raf slowly moved down the branch. "Come on, come on. Do anything funny and you'll find yourself full of holes, understand?"

Raf climbed down the last branch, his heart pounding, and stared at the object Wesp was holding. It was made of metal and had a curved handle; definitely some sort of weapon. The trader threw a few uneasy glances around the commons and then looked back at Raf who was fidgeting, an icy sweat beading on his forehead.

"Not so chatty now that you're by yourself, hey? Now that you're face to face with my little friend here from Miern. You seen one of these before?" Raf shook his head. "Nothing to say? All quiet suddenly? You couldn't keep your mouth shut earlier on, I seem to remember." Wesp spat on the floor.

Raf swallowed and looked down at his feet. "I...came to ask you not to tell anyone bad things about us."

"Did you, now?" Wesp sneered and took a step closer to Raf.

"Mr. Tunrhak." They both looked up. Out of the darkness emerged the towering figure of Foreman Manyara. "Perhaps we should all just calm down a bit," he said, walking up to stand in front of Raf.

Wesp swung the weapon around to point at him. "Stay right where you are!" he snarled, backing up toward the chambers. "I'll shoot you! You know I will!"

"Actually, you won't," said the Foreman, folding his arms across his chest. "Well, you might. But it would be a bad idea because you'd then find yourself full of arrows. Not as impressive as the bullets from your pepperbox there, but equally fatal. Possibly quite a lot more painful as well."

"You bluff," said Wesp, swiveling his head from side to side as he squinted into the darkness. "There's nobody else here."

The Foreman smiled calmly. "I don't wish for any violence tonight. I think the best thing is for you to put that chest on the ground and leave. Right now. Just go. Take your vinehoney. And we'll forget all this happened."

"You must be mad. This money's mine!" Wesp started edging sideways along the sequoia. "I'm leaving right now - that much I'll do. But the coins come with me."

The Foreman sighed softly. Then he tilted his head back over his shoulder and said, "Orikon."

There was a faint whistling sound in the air, and two arrows suddenly sprouted, vibrating, in the trunk behind Wesp. The trader instantly stopped, peering nervously into the darkness.

"Why don't you just put the chest down and leave, Mr. Tunrhak? Your pepperbox only has a few shots in it. We have many, many arrows. I'm afraid the odds are very much against you."

The Foreman stepped forward, his bear-like frame seeming to grow larger in the flickering lamplight. Behind him, a line of villagers appeared out of the darkness. Orikon and a few other hunters armed with bows moved to the front. Raf spotted his parents and grimaced. There would be words about this later.

Wesp's face took on a dark look and then he let the chest drop to the ground where it sprung open, ejecting its cargo of coins.

"I'll have to retrieve my wagon," he said sourly. "Unless of course you plan to steal that like you've stolen everything else from me."

"I hope you don't mind that I've taken the liberty to have it brought here already." The Foreman gestured at the south path behind them where, appearing out of the dark, was the wagon driven by Abuniah. Raf could just make out Fergus sitting next to him on the bench looking very nervous.

Wesp scowled and walked up to it as Abuniah jumped to the ground. He climbed up to the driver's bench and gave Fergus a rough shove. The boy caught hold of the wagon's side railing and then climbed down to take hold of the goats' reins.

"You haven't heard the last of this, forester," snarled Wesp. "I'll have the Guard on you as soon as I get back. Your thieving days are numbered."

With a flick of the whip, the goats started pulling the wagon forward again. As it rolled past, Fergus stalled, staring back mournfully at the villagers.

Raf thought quickly. There was no time left and he had to

do *something*. Waving to catch Fergus' attention, he mouthed the word at him.

"Hurry up, boy, blast you!" shouted Wesp, leaning down to hit the boy across his back with a long whip. Fergus didn't seem to even notice as he stood staring intently at Raf, his lips moving silently.

Ignoring the questioning look he was getting from the Foreman, Raf nodded urgently, appealing to Fergus with a desperate look.

"San..... s....s..."

"Oy!" snapped Wesp. "You shut up, boy!" He cracked his whip against the boy's back again. "Keep walking!"

Fergus flinched and then, slowly lifting his clasped hands in front of him, he looked at the Foreman. "Sanctuary, sir?"

A silence fell among the crowd who had gathered behind them, and Raf saw the Foreman's face tighten. With a creak, the wagon pulled up and Wesp started clambering down, growling furiously.

"Please," said Fergus. "S-sanctuary."

"Foreman?" Madame Ottery stormed up to him.

He looked at her, took in the other anxious expressions around him, and then, with a quick glance at Raf, he nodded. "Accepted."

The word cut through the silence like a knife and suddenly from behind them came an outburst of cheering from the foresters. Fergus sprinted forward just ahead of Wesp's grasping fingers to wrap the Foreman in a tight hug. Madame Ottery broke into song and started clapping, patting the boy on his back - when suddenly there was an enormous explosion above them. Wesp stood with his arm in the air, the pepperbox pointed upward with a thin wisp of smoke trickling out of the end.

"What do you think you're doing?" he yelled. "Boy! Come back and get on this wagon. Now! *Fergus!*"

The boy held to the Foreman, refusing to look up.

"The boy has requested sanctuary and we have accepted. You heard him, trader," said Madame Ottery.

"I don't care what he said! Either he gets back on this wagon or I start shooting."

Gasps of fear echoed through the crowd and people scampered backward. The Foreman lifted his hand to stop them and then disengaged the boy from himself, pushing him across to Madame Ottery.

"According to our laws, the boy has been welcomed as a member of our village now, trader."

Wesp snarled savagely and suddenly fired the pepperbox again, a second deafening explosion that made them all jump. "I don't care about your laws, you fools! I will shoot someone if he isn't back on the wagon in three seconds!" He waved the weapon wildly at them. "One!"

Raf thought desperately. *What do I do? This is my fault!*

"Two!"

The Foreman was trying to say something to Wesp, appealing to him, but the trader wasn't listening, just wildly swinging the pepperbox from left to right at the crowd. There were screams as people ducked and tried to scramble away.

"Thr-"

It happened so slowly in Raf's head. Wesp swung the pepperbox to point at the Foreman and in one smooth motion, Raf grabbed the hilt of his knife, whipped his arm backward and then flung it at the trader. He watched in slow motion as the knife spun through the air. There was a bright spark as the knife blade hit the pepperbox and knocked it out of Wesp's hand to clatter to the ground.

The trader screamed in pain. He held his hand to his chest and Raf saw a line of blood run down his right arm. One of his fingers looked like... Raf gagged as he realized half of the finger was *gone*. It had been sliced off.

There was silence as Wesp moaned through clenched teeth, his face screwed up grotesquely in pain. He stumbled to the

56

wagon, shrieking at the goats as he crawled on board. The animals - already nervous from the shots - took off in terror, and the wagon skidded and reeled as it tore off down the path, bouncing over roots. Wesp turned around once, face contorted in agony, to give them a last, venomous look, before he disappeared into the night.

As the wagon noises faded, the only sound left was a soft whimpering. Madame Ottery looked down to stroke the hair of a shaking Fergus who was standing with tears streaming down his face.

"It's all right, dear. He's gone now. You're going to stay with us here in Eirdale." He looked up at her, eyes red, tears still flowing, and gave her a half smile.

The Foreman gazed in the direction of the vanished wagon. "Orikon."

The hunter nodded once at him before jogging down the path after the wagon.

The Foreman walked slowly up to where Wesp had been standing and stooped down to pick up both the pepperbox and the knife. Stony-faced, he held out the knife until Raf hesitantly took it, and then moved through the crowd which opened up for him.

Somewhere in the distance a peacock called and was answered by another. The sounds passed unnoticed as the small crowd dispersed into the night.

"**N**othing, Foreman. No sign."

"You're sure, Orikon?"

The tall hunter nodded. "I followed his tracks all the way up past Emborough. He drove the animals hard and without break toward the Pass. He is gone."

Dr. Allid shook his head. "He won't be back. He has learned a lesson, I think. We foresters are not to be easy prey for city scum like him. Just as well we kept an eye on him." A few of the others grunted in agreement.

"Yet, I cannot help but wonder what that man will do when he returns to Miern," replied the Foreman, rubbing his eyes. "Traders talk, and when word gets around about what happened -"

"Nobody will listen," asserted Leiana. "People know better than to pay any attention to a revolting creature like that."

"Leiana, you don't know Miern. In a city that big, that dense, word gets around – even if it's from someone like Wesp. We can't afford to lose trade."

Tarvil nodded in agreement.

"Don't you worry about that. Resma and I will organize a Festival like the Aeril Forest has never witnessed, and people will arrive in droves. Good news will spread." Leiana stood up. "It's finally our turn to host it, and now that we have the coin, I will see Eirdale carved into Forest history."

Madame Ottery clapped enthusiastically.

"I'm sure you will, Leiana," answered the Foreman. "We need something positive now to focus on after last night's incident. In fact, I think I'll make an announcement after this meeting to let the villagers know our Festival is definitely happening and put pay to the rumors that were no doubt flying around."

Leiana rolled her eyes at this and gave a sour shake of her head.

The Foreman stopped on his way out. "How is Raf today? I didn't see him this morning and was hoping to have a word. He must be shaken after last night. It was foolhardy, but I for one am relieved he stepped in when he did. Word of the story has spread through the village, understandably, and he seems popular all of a sudden. People like an exciting story, I suppose. Perhaps...he'd like a place on the final bill to perform at the Festival?"

Tarvil laughed and then covered it up quickly with a hand to his mouth, pretending to cough. The Foreman looked at him suspiciously.

"I...er...I am not completely sure that that...would be such a welcome gesture, Foreman," said Tarvil carefully. "Raf doesn't much like performing. He gets stage fright and would pro-"

"- what my husband *means* is that Raf would be delighted to perform in the Festival for Eirdale," interrupted Leiana. "He could even play that instrument that he made. Orfea, was it?"

The Foreman looked at her and then at Tarvil who stood there pursing his lips as he looked at his wife out of the corner of his eyes. "Well, I'll leave it in your capable hands, Leiana. I'll go and let the village know our news now."

He started chanting the *farwelayre* and the others joined in. For a moment, the chamber resonated with vibrant harmonies, and then the Council shuffled out into the darkening dusk. Leiana immediately set off at a brisk pace toward their home and Tarvil had to rush to catch up with her.

"I think you might have considered that better, dear," he said tentatively, matching her strides.

She stared ahead. "I've no idea what you mean. The performance will be good for Raf. And good for the village."

"Good for Raf? Dear, you know perfectly well that he won't want to. He's made it pretty clear he doesn't want to perform."

She stopped and turned toward him, hands moving to perch on her hips, mouth tightening furiously. "Doesn't *want* to? This Festival is the lifeblood of the Aeril Forest! It is the single most important event in the year. Without it, we would…we…" She hesitated. "Well, it would be disastrous. It *must* happen. It *must* be spectacular. And we simply must have a few representatives from Eirdale in it this year, especially if *we're* organizing it. I'm sick of watching those Hunton Daire folk and the Three Ways show-offs hogging the stage. Raf is a competent musician and, although I have my own opinion about last night's incident, if the Foreman has offered him this opportunity, then he's doing it. There are no two ways about it." She marched off.

Tarvil trudged back home, deep in thought. As he walked up to the boys' branch of their sycamore, he caught sight of Rio and one of his classmates up ahead in a small thicket of bamboo, playing with some toy bows and arrows they had made.

"Rio!"

The boy turned to see him and then ran up pretending to shoot an arrow at him. "Oohhhhh… you got me." Tarvil staggered around on the spot, holding his hands to his chest while Rio giggled.

"Do you like my new bow, Dad? I made it today. Me and Fechin both made one. We're gonna hunt wild boars!"

"Wow," said Tarvil. "Can you make me one, too?" They both nodded delightedly at him. Tarvil reached down to Rio's tangled blond locks and gave them a fond ruffle. "Are you looking forward to the Festival, boys? It's not far away now."

"Yeah!" burbled Fechin. "Madame Ottery is teaching us a new song and everything. It'll be brilliant!"

Rio nodded enthusiastically in agreement.

"I hope so," said Tarvil. "Tell me, do you know where your brother is? I didn't see him at breakfast or lunch today."

"No, he was gone this morning when I got up," said Rio.

"Well, if you see him, can you send him to me? I'll be over eastside at the new buildings with the Foreman."

Rio nodded, and Tarvil got to his feet. He wandered down toward the building sites where he could hear instructions being shouted out by Foreman Manyara. There was precious little time now to get ready and the Foreman was pushing hard to make sure everything was perfect. Not that he liked to bully people; he was one of the calmest people Tarvil knew. In fact, he'd only ever broken his cool composure once that Tarvil had seen, and that was some ten years ago when he had caught his own cousin, Bhothy, trying to light a fire in the middle of one of the plantations.

Bhothy was a sad case. His birthright was to hold the official village Bard role, something which didn't really exist anymore – which was probably the reason he had turned out so irresponsible and reckless. The man had been so drunk that he had dropped a cask of gin over the fire which had then set ablaze the trunk of a beech *Ancient*. If the Foreman hadn't caught it in time, the consequences would have been too dreadful to imagine. Living up on their Forest platform held a few obvious, inherent dangers, after all.

. . . .

Raf woke up and looked around, rubbing his neck which ached from the odd angle he'd been slouched in. He hadn't been able to get to sleep after the incident with Wesp, so he'd crept out of their sycamore home just before dawn, walking around aimlessly and thinking about what had happened. He'd finally succumbed to fatigue when the sun was well up and had made himself comfortable against the soft moss on some oak roots before falling soundly asleep.

He wasn't completely sure where he even was; he'd taken no notice of where he was going other than heading in a generally south-west direction. His head had been spinning after the confrontation and he couldn't stop playing the scene over and over again in his mind.

Stretching and yawning, he rolled onto his knees and stood up, squinting in the mottled sunlight. He'd found his way into a thick banyan grove, it seemed. It was much darker here, with the banyans growing in a tangled mess that cut out much of the light. Every surface around him seemed to be caked in shades of green, from the dark green that carpeted the ground, to the streaks of bright moss and lichen that decorated the banyan branches and *Ancient* trunks.

Areas like this apparently used to be thick with olive and birch trees many years ago, but then these strangler figs - or banyans - that flourished in the Forest set upon them. One of his teachers, Vince, talked about it as if it was quite gruesome and, in a way, Raf supposed it was. The strangler figs basically colonized the other trees, growing all over them and around them, destroying them. But because of the way these vines grew, climbing upward and outward while at the same time sending loads of roots down to the ground to form weird trunk things, the whole process left behind dense, ropy webs.

Taking a deep breath of the fragrant air, he climbed over a mossy mound and moved deeper into the grove. For a while he walked on, stopping occasionally to break a watervine open for a quick drink, or to pick a few mulberries to eat. It was quite soothing, and he found himself relaxing a bit. Until he heard a strange laughing sound from up ahead.

He peered forward. It was definitely a human voice. He couldn't quite make out where it was exactly, but it seemed to emanate from the dark gap between two hanging curtains of banyan roots. Walking quietly, one foot in front of the other, he moved up to the gap and saw that the banyan roots had grown so thick that they formed two solid, gnarled walls. It was from somewhere down this natural passageway that the sound was coming. He walked forward into the gap, opening his eyes wide to adjust to the darkness, and after a few seconds he found himself standing in what seemed to be, for all intents and purposes, a covered porch to someone's home. This was rather bizarre! He moved further forward and saw a doorway leading inside, so he crept through it. There was an odd smell he had never encountered before; an acrid smell, vaguely floral, but sharp. Intrigued, he edged his head around the corner to peek inside.

It was a room. And it was a complete mess. There was a small candle set in the corner which gave off enough light to illuminate the shambles inside. Containers were strewn everywhere and clothes were lying all over the damp mossy floor. And there, slumped over on a leather bag, was an obese forester with a bushy, orange beard that curled out from his cheeks in great knotted tangles. As Raf watched, he held a small pipe to his mouth, sucked the end and then coughed in a burst of smoke.

That explains the strange smell, at least.

It *had* to be Bhothy, of course. Everyone knew about the Foreman's banished cousin, but no one ever saw him or had anything to do with him; it was strictly forbidden. And he'd been living here just a few miles south of the village all this time? Apparently all he'd been doing was eating; Raf had never seen a stomach like that on a forester! He shuffled sideways to get a better view but felt his foot slide on the slick, mossy floor, bumping a small table.

"What?" shouted the man spinning around. "Wh'sat? Who's there?"

Raf twisted desperately to back out of the doorway, but as he moved, both feet slipped on the damp moss again and he lost his balance, stumbling over to crash headfirst against the wall. There was a sharp wave of pain through his head before everything went black.

"**W**hat to do, what to do…" *Cough.* "Stupid kid."

Raf slowly came to. He lifted his head and saw the bearded man sitting on the same bag as before, puffing away at the pipe. He was rocking backward and forward, staring at the floor.

"Um," he mumbled, "excuse me, but…aren't you Bhothy?"

"Who's asking?"

"Raf. Raf Gency."

"Tarvil's boy?" The man snorted. "Just what I need. A Council cub sniffing around, trying to kill himself." He shook his head from side to side and then took another long drag on the pungent pipe. "I am Bhothy."

He exhaled thick smoke up into the air. The smell made Raf feel a bit nauseous, and his head wobbled a bit. The man looked at him, eyes bloodshot, and held out the smoldering pipe. "Want some?" He suddenly giggled. "Course not. Wouldn't be *prudent* for a Council boy."

He stared at Raf, eyebrows lifted high on his head, and then made a squeaking noise as he tried to hold in another bout of giggling but failed. He ended up wheezing violently and coughing into his arm sleeve. Then he turned back to Raf and, wrinkling his nose up, said in a husky voice, "You take it down wrong, you cough your lungs up."

Raf stared at him. The man was mad! "Are you all right?"

"All right?" snapped the man, "Am I all right?" He put his fingers to his chin in a thoughtful pose. "Now that you mention it, I'm just wonderful, thank you. The only human I've spoken to in over ten years is the Foreman, my marvelous cousin Eliath; a bit of a serious fellow, if you get my drift. And now you, who comes stumbling in here and almost gives me a blimmin' heart attack."

"I'm sorry. I didn't mean to -"

"Didn't *mean* to?" Bhothy scoffed. "How can you not mean to come poking your nose around this forbidden area? It *is* still forbidden, right?"

"I didn't know I was near here. Yesterday, there was... well, something happened and I went for a walk."

"Oooh, a walk," mocked Bhothy.

"Yes, a walk," replied Raf in irritation. "I thought I heard talking so I came to see who it was. Only, because you obviously don't ever clean the floor, the moss is quite slipp-"

"You mind your tongue," said the man sullenly. He glanced around the room and scratched his tangled beard. Crumbs fell out of it onto his chest. "I didn't know I'd have guests. Besides, that's hardly the way to speak to someone who's just healed you."

"What?"

"Of course, you wouldn't know; you were knocked out. Silly me."

Raf touched his forehead, remembering what had happened. He realized it didn't actually hurt that much - not nearly as much as he expected it to. He looked at Bhothy in confusion. "Are you a healer? Like Dr. Ferrows?"

"No, no."

"Well then wh-"

"Shhh!" Bhothy suddenly opened his eyes widely and moved his eyeballs from side to side, bringing a finger up to his mouth. "Too many questions."

"But...if you healed me, then I owe you my thanks."

"Rubbish. Anyone would have done it. You would've done it to me."

"Healed you? Not likely. I'm not even an apprentice healer.

I've no idea which herbs to use or anything."

"Herbs?" Bhothy hooted with delight. "Brilliant! A thousand years of music and we're reduced to using *parsley* to cure our problems." He laughed loudly, only stopping when he was taken by a fit of coughing.

"What would *you* use, then?" asked Raf, feeling a little peeved. "Sing a song to cure someone? Yeah, I can see how that would work. 'La-dee-dah' and your fever's gone."

"Worked well enough on you, Council boy," muttered Bhothy, turning away.

He put the small pipe clumsily into his mouth at an angle and then stumbled over to the table in the middle of the floor. There was a pot sitting on top, with a small bush poking out. It had no greenery on the spindly branches and seemed to be dead.

"Blast," mumbled Bhothy. "Running out."

He carefully picked up a small yellow, dried leaf lying on the table between his fumbling fingers, scrunched it up and inserted it into the hollow end of the pipe. Then he drew a thin pine splinter from a box next to the bush and struck it against the rough side. It sparked and flared up into a solid yellow flame that he held to the crushed leaf, drawing in a deep breath so that the end glowed brightly. He immediately broke into a bout of dry hacking and then, with a painful grimace on his face, offered a strained smile at Raf and flopped down onto the bag again, almost falling off in the process.

"Is that the end of your supply of leaves, then?" Raf asked. "What a pity it's all finished now."

Bhothy gave him a faint smile. "I think you'll find that if you look closely, it isn't all gone. Not at all..." He giggled and tucked his chin to his chest, closing his eyes.

Raf sadly shook his head as he took in the small plant. It had definitely seen better days and if it wasn't dead, it was certainly on its last legs. He thought he could hear Bhothy singing - of all things! - and lifted a hand up to cover his eyes in frustration. A tendril of violet suddenly flared up in the darkness behind his eyelids.

What! He opened his eyes and blinked them furiously to clear them. *Not again...*

He stood up and turned to say something to Bhothy - when he saw the bush move. It was vibrating. Every tiny branch on it was writhing in tiny motions. Then without warning, new buds appeared. They just suddenly emerged along the branches like tiny, green dewdrops, and as he stood watching in disbelief, they elongated smoothly and started unfolding.

Bhothy stopped singing and a soft snore gurgled from his throat, his head sliding sideways to rest against the side of the bag. Raf gazed silently at the bush which had now stopped moving. It was completely covered in a mass of fresh new leaves.

. . . .

"See if you can drape some over there, Farley. But not quite as close together as the other ones," called up Leiana. "No wait! Leave that one, just move over to the next one and try to make them more symmetrical." She rolled her eyes at the wiry little man clambering around in the foliage above.

Turning to the woman next to her she murmured, "Be a darling and make sure that he doesn't kill himself. Or worse - get the drapes wrong."

She marched off toward the north end of the patch where, a little to her left, a group of men was digging in the fields, chanting a two-part harmony.

"Yentl!" she called. A tiny woman turned from inspecting a scaffold that was being constructed and walked to meet her. "Any more since this morning's announcement?"

The woman pursed her lips. "You wouldn't believe it, Councilwoman, but eleven signed up right afterward and we've had another *seven* since then, which brings us to eighteen in total. The Foreman's address this morning has put some spark into Eirdale it seems."

"Yes…but, eighteen?" repeated Leiana. "Do we even have room for that many stalls here?"

"We can fit about fourteen here along the eastern edge of the patch, but I was thinking we might as well squeeze a few up around the small commons the boys are clearing out. I can't imagine that some of them are going to be too popular. I mean, old Selene Jaron has even requested a space to sell roasted cashews, of all things! I can't very well deny her, though. She may not be around for our next turn to host."

"Well, put her stall next to Jover's mead stand. Anyone who eats her cashews and the mounds of salt she smothers them with will be thirsty."

Yentl smiled. "Perfect," she said, and made a note on her list she was carrying.

They continued walking up the middle of the clearing, inspecting the various barriers and railings being erected on either side around the allocated plots for stands. Hundreds of flowers had been planted in patterns over every free inch of space, and while most were only just budding, they should blossom just in time for the arrival of the Festival visitors. Leiana suspected it would be spectacular when in full bloom. It was all definitely coming together.

Wandering up toward the school, she snuck inside to listen to the choir practicing. Leiana caught Resma's eye and nodded at her over the small crowd of enthusiastic youngsters who were running through the refrain of one of the Festival *ayres*. There were a few tuning issues, but the sheer enthusiasm of the kids made up for it and the overall sound was quite pleasant.

They came to the end and Resma signaled with her baton for them to stop. A few elderly bystanders gave a smattering of applause.

Clapping along, Leiana nodded to Resma as she joined her. "Wonderful." She gazed back at the milling crowd of children chatting amongst themselves. "Any genuine talent? Soloists?"

"Probably only three or four really," said Resma. "Your Rio is coming along nicely, but he's yet to find any volume and might struggle on the stage a bit."

"Pfff," muttered Leiana dismissively. "I'll have a word with him. We'll have both him and Raf ready for it." Resma nodded vaguely and turned to look back at the kids as Leiana asked, "Who else then?"

"Well, little Darren Tonder has a lovely voice. Tarryn Almary is turning into a superb little soprano, and there's one more – a bit of a surprise, really." She looked over to the crowd and beckoned to the young boy standing by himself. He quickly trotted up and greeted them politely. When he saw it was Leiana, his face opened into a broad smile.

"Hello there, Fergus," said Leiana. "I hope you're settling down well living with Jover."

"Oh yes, Mrs. Gency! Mr. Jover is letting me work for him up in the canopy farms. I climb to the ones right up near the top. He says I climb better than a marmoset! And he has a huge room in his tree-house that I live in. Just me by myself!"

Leiana smiled at him.

"You might be surprised to learn that this little city urchin has one of the loveliest little voices I've heard in a while. I'm teaching him one of the traditional *ayres* for the second night. I think it would be fantastic to have him sing during the feast. He only needs to hear something once and he knows it. Not to mention the fact that he's a natural when he's up on stage w-"

"- I used to juggle by the lake Docks," interrupted Fergus excitedly. "Sometimes the fishermen would even give me coins!" Both women laughed and Leiana reached down to tussle his messy sandy hair, ushering him back to the choir.

"Such a little darling," sighed Resma. "Have you given any thought to the main performances, Leiana?"

"Actually, and I hope you don't mind, I've taken the liberty of organizing something."

"Oh?"

"I asked Nathyn to speak to the Cedrusdale Foreman and invite their lutists to play. You know how good they are. My father has also mentioned a young ukulele player who's in Yaelstead for his sojourn; he's supposed to be superb. And," she lowered her voice, "- don't tell anyone, but I've found some iMahli hand-drummers."

Resma's eyes opened wide. "*Dholaki?* They don't normally play outside of their iMahli gatherings. How did you manage that?"

"I had a pigeon from Luanchester saying there were some around. A handful of bronze coins and they were interested," she replied. "Just think, Resma, the first ever performance by *dholaki* in the Forest, here in Eirdale - at *our* Festival!"

"But Leiana, we don't have the coin for it, surely?"

"Between you and me," said Leiana, "I've borrowed some from our family savings."

"Does Tarvil know?"

"No! With what we've planned and now the added treat of *dholaki* on the bill, this Festival will bring in more money than we know what to do with and I can have it back in the chest before he even realizes it's missing." Resma looked uneasy at this, but Leiana winked at her. "Stop worrying so much, old hen. This Festival will see all our fortunes change, mark my words."

. . . .

Raf sat poring over the manuscript on his lap, squinting at the strange writing on it in the murky light of the single candle. He'd been nosing around the room and found it curled up under a layer of dust on a shelf. It was made of some very old material that was much more fragile than the birch-paper they used in school. In between the foreign writing that was neatly traced, it had all sorts of odd wavy patterns decorating it.

Bhothy's head slid backward and stretched his throat so that he choked and jerked his head back up.

"Ehh? What?" he muttered groggily. His eyes slowly swam into focus to see Raf standing looking directly at him. "Who... wait, you... you're the Council boy, right?"

"Raf. We met earlier on. You feeling any better? You've been asleep for ages."

"Really?" Bhothy grunted a half laugh and then got to his feet. He stood there swaying dizzily, scratching his beard. "Why are you here, again?" he asked. Then he spotted the manuscript on Raf's lap. "Oy, what do you think you're doing with that!"

"I was bored waiting for you to wake up. You passed out, or maybe you don't remember that. You were busy telling me about singing or something, and you said you healed me."

"Nice of me."

"Listen, how did that plant grow so quickly?" Raf pointed behind him at the plant. "I've never seen anything like it!"

"Nothing to do with me." Bhothy yawned widely. "You're just seeing things. It's not very good light in here."

"You made that plant grow, I'm sure of it!"

"What plant?" said Bhothy.

Raf clenched his jaws. "The one right there! It was almost dead and then it just suddenly grew all those leaves. In seconds!"

"I don't have a clue what you're talking about, Council boy," said Bhothy blankly. He scratched his unkempt hair. "I don't suppose you'd like to leave me alone?"

"But how did you d-"

Bhothy deliberately turned his back on Raf and relit the pipe. Then he settled down onto his bag on the floor and puffed away, staring resolutely at the wall opposite.

Raf watched him for a few seconds and then turned and left the room with a resigned sigh, treading carefully on the slippery floor. He walked out through the passageway and found himself standing in the half-light of dusk. Dinner would be ready at home by now and they'd be wondering where he was. He scrambled his way out of the banyan walls and set off briskly through the trees back to Eirdale.

It was almost completely dark by the time he reached the commons. New decorations and floral arrangements covered the village – his mother's handiwork no doubt - but what might have been a vibrant rainbow of colors in daylight was now only a smoky orange in the glow of the lamps on the paths. From all around the village drifted sounds of families singing *metanayres* before their dinners, and from somewhere to the south-east came faint sounds of what must have been some farmers having a bit of a get-together.

He gave a wave to a family nearby who were using one of the fire-basins to roast a small boar on a spit, and then strolled up to the forked sycamore *Ancient* that was his family's home. He walked in and kicked off his sandals, looking down the hall to where the family were all seated at the kitchen table.

"Evening," he said casually. "Sorry I'm late. Lost track of time." He slid onto the bench next to Rio, grabbing a roasted sweet potato from a bowl.

"Nice to see you finally decided to join us," said his mother.

"Yeah, where've you been, Raf?" chirped Rio. "You've been gone for ages. Nedrick came round to see you before dinner."

"What did he want?"

"He said Orikon was going out hunting tonight and wanted to know if you were going."

"Tonight? Did he say when? Man, Orikon's been promising he'd take us for ages and -"

"Not a chance," said Leiana. "We have to discuss a few things to do with the Festival tonight."

"Aw, mom, Orikon's usually too busy to take us out. I can't miss it. The other guys will all be there. We can talk about the Festival some other time, can't we? It's still a whole week away."

"A week away?" Her eyebrows arched up dangerously. "This Festival must be extraordinary; I'll accept nothing less. And bearing in mind that we're expecting over a thousand people to be coming *on top of* the local villagers, a week is far less than we need! There is a huge amount left to do still."

"But it's nothing to do with me, is it? I already know the piece Ottery's teaching us for our year's performance, -"

"*Madame* Ottery," interrupted Tarvil.

"- so I don't get why you need me involved in it all." Raf looked questioningly at her and she stared back at him, pursing her lips. She seemed oddly hesitant.

"Um," mumbled his father, "I believe what your mother is trying to tell you is that you've been requested to perform at the Festival -"

"I know that," Raf said impatiently. "Our year is doing -"

"Solo." Tarvil looked down to carefully examine a potato on his plate.

"What?" said Raf. "By myself? Not a chance. You *know* I can't do that sort of thing, mom!"

"Oh of course you can, Raf!" snapped Leiana. "You're a very good musician, and after that foolishness last night – which we still need to speak about - the Foreman wants you in the final performance. It's a huge honor and as a member of our family, it w-"

Raf almost choked. "The *final* performance? Not only do you want me to get up there by myself and look like an idiot, but you want me to do it on the last day, in front of the *thousands* of people you are expecting? What world do you live in, mom, honestly?"

"Actually, Raf," said Tarvil quietly, "it's not so much a request, as, well…you're on the bill already."

Raf's mouth fell open.

"Think of it as an opportunity, Raf," said Leiana. "You're the only student performing on the final day. Apparently you managed to impress some of our misguided villagers last night. So now you have a chance to impress them with your musical talent."

"More like prove how much of a prat I can be!"

"Language..." said Tarvil.

"But it's so unfair! Why do I have to do it? I don't care about impressing a crowd of random drunk people! It'd be nice if I could maybe make my own decisions!"

Leiana turned away to stare at the wall, her fingers tapping furiously on the table-top.

Tarvil wiped his mouth with a napkin. "And on that note, I don't know if you know yet, dear, but it seems that our intrepid son has decided on his sojourn."

Raf stared at him. He was bringing this up *now*?!

Leiana turned back to face him. "Oh really?" she said, her voice oozing scorn. "And where would he be thinking of going? Some deserted hole in the ocean where he won't have to *perform* in front of people? Or perhaps he wants to travel up north and grow cabbages for a living? No pressure on you to succeed there, is there. Nobody watching y-"

"Miern."

The room went quiet. Leiana's eyes widened. She threw a look at Tarvil who found another interesting potato on his plate, and then turned to Raf. "Absolutely not! I forbid it."

"What? You can't forbid it! You can't tell me where to go on my sojourn. It's my choice!"

"That's just ridiculous, Raf! You can go up north to the sequoias. You can spend some time in the western ocean-villages. You can even go mulberry picking in Turner's Grove. Any one of the normal sojourns." She shook her head furiously. "But not Miern! I will *not* have you traveling to that revolting place. It's crawling with thieves and murderers and goodness knows what else - you saw what that disgusting trader was like!" Face red, she slammed her plate down on the counter and stormed out of the room.

An uncomfortable silence settled over the room. Tarvil lifted a piece of meat to his mouth. "Well, I think that went pretty well."

. . . .

The next morning, the sun was streaming down through the canopy, lighting up the Forest in a shower of beams. Raf grunted angrily as he whipped out another arrow, notched it and let it fly into the painted board fifty feet away.

"She didn't even ask me!"

"Could be worse," said Nedrick peering forward to see where the arrow had stuck. "Could be me up there."

Cisco laughed and patted Nedrick on his back sympathetically. "Would've been a great story, though." He lifted his hands in a dramatic pose. "Pay a fortune to travel through the deadly elements, avoid ruthless iMahli warriors and black mambas, to finally get to the wondrous Aeril Forest -only to be assaulted by Nedrick and his atrocious warble."

They all laughed at this. Nedrick was the tallest boy in their year and could grow what passed for a decent beard, much to the envy of the others, but his voice had only started breaking recently. He could barely sing three notes before his nasal tenor sprung up with a squeak into the voice of a six year old - a source of great amusement in classes with Madame Ottery.

"Nice shot. Dead center," said Nedrick, as Raf let loose another arrow. "I don't think you should worry so much. And it isn't such a bad thing to be on stage. D'you hear about Baruna?" The other two shook their heads. "Her father's making her stand up at the Prestonderry Road entrance and sing the *gretanayre* to all the travelers who come down."

"Poor girl," said Cisco, grimacing. "All I can say is that I'm glad my family doesn't have any Council aspirations for me. To be honest, I think they'd be glad if I just managed to finish school and get an apprenticeship like my brother did. Preferably somewhere far away, I imagine. Us Brunnows take life a little less seriously than you Council types."

Raf scowled. "Consider yourself lucky, Cisc. I reckon my mother's got her beady eyes on nothing short of Foreman for me. Probably Gerent as well!"

"It's really not so bad, Raf," said Nedrick. "You never know, maybe the sweet Rhani will see you sing and decide you're not such a geek."

Raf blushed and Cisco whistled at him, punching him on his shoulder.

Nedrick shook his head, adding, "Mind you, how she's keeping her hands off you now since you banished the trader with your famous flying dagger is a mystery to me."

Cisco shook his head. "I can't *believe* I missed it! The first time Gency actually did something even vaguely cool and I was asleep. What lousy timing!"

"That's not exactly how my mother sees the whole thing," muttered Raf. "Going back to the Council stuff, how did *you* get out of it all, Ned? The Festival, I mean."

"Get out of it? You must be kidding me," replied Nedrick. "I knew I'd be in it whatever – same as you - so I just waited to find out what. As it turns out, I'll be in a trio of sorts on the second day with Shaphi and Aaryl on the marimbas. Should be fun actually; they're both good."

"Shaphi Badroas? The foreign girl? I didn't know she played."

"She's fantastic on the marimbas! Can't sing to save her life, but give her a few mallets and you can hardly see her hands move. Crazy talented. And really nice, too."

Cisco and Raf glanced at each other and then burst out laughing.

"What?" asked Nedrick, turning bright red. "She's really

good!" His voice jumped up on the last word and he went even more beetroot-colored. He turned around to launch an arrow at the target, hiding his burning face.

The other two notched up their own arrows. Cisco, still sniggering, let loose an arrow that flew awkwardly and glanced off the side of the target to hit a tree behind.

"Oops. See? Can't even hunt. What good am I to Eirdale? Might as well give up and go and live with ol' Bhothy."

Raf darted a look at him. He couldn't possibly know about his visit yesterday! Nobody had seen him go there. If he told these two about it, they'd just want to go as well, and in a strange and rather selfish way, Raf didn't want to share Bhothy with them.

"We should probably get back, boys," said Nedrick. "I don't know about you two, but my parents are on edge right now and if I missed one of Dr. Allid's *fascinating* lectures on crop-rotation, they might actually kill me."

Raf and Cisco rolled their eyes and nodded. They quickly gathered up the scattered arrows and made their way back down to the commons.

. . . .

Raf was finishing up a delicious salad of pawpaws and figs, when his mother walked into the room.

"We're running behind with the preparations and I need you and your classmates to help, please. Dr. Allid informs me that you have already covered most of what he was going to teach you today, so he's given his permission for all of you to give Mitch a hand this afternoon."

Raf nodded slightly and then looked down at his food as he carried on chewing. This was the first thing she'd said to him since the argument the night before.

"Meet Mitch up at the chimes when you've finished. Once you've done that, I'll expect you back for dinner. The Perenesons are coming around."

Raf shook his head. "Can't do it. Already told Ned I'd go hunting with him."

"I think you'd find it quite useful to chat to Dalton."

"Why?"

"Well, when he was younger, he spent a few years captaining a fishing trawler in one of the southern coastal villages near Sayenham. I think if you chatted to him he m-"

"I'm going to Miern, Mom," snapped Raf. "It's my choice and I've decided. Stop interfering."

"But you'd love to work on the ocean, wouldn't you? On a fishing boat? You always said so before. Why have you suddenly got this horrible idea stuck in your head?"

"Way I see it, it's the only way I'll escape from people telling me what I should be doing all the time."

He pushed his chair back and marched outside, fuming. Behind him, he heard a whimper, and looking back through the front door to the kitchen, he saw that his mother had her face in her hands, her shoulders shaking.

He swore under his breath.

. . . .

"Raf!" yelled a voice.

Cisco came trotting up from the Brunnow residence on the west village border.

"You coming? Guess we're finished with Allid today."

Raf took a deep breath and then forced a smile on to his face. "Yup. Scooping out bird droppings, snake skins and spider webs instead. Sounds just wonderful."

They ran up to join the others who were all congregating on the commons by the village chimes.

"Right you lot," rasped Mitch. "You're in groups of three. Each of you 'ave six places to clean out so's my carpentry boys can get going an' prepare 'em for this Festival. I expect 'em to be shining when you're done." He held up a list and called out names for the groups. "Rhani Pereneson, Brody Ficus, Raf Gency. You three get going on this lot."

He handed them a map with a marked set of old abandoned homes. Raf groaned inwardly at his group. Brody was possibly the most boring person in the world, and as for Rhani – how typical was that? He looked around to see Cisco give a quick thumbs-up and whistle cheekily, before trying - and failing - to keep a straight face. Nedrick punched him in the shoulder to stop, but Cisco puckered up his mouth and stared nonchalantly at the canopy above making kissing noises. Raf scowled.

From behind him came a small sigh and Rhani, tossing her braided hair over her shoulder, gave Raf an exasperated look with her dark green eyes. Then she flounced forward past him to take the paper from Mitch and left without a word. It was going to be a fun afternoon...

Although it was occasionally interesting poking through the deserted *Ancients*, Rhani ignored him completely, even when he tried to make conversation. It didn't do much for Raf's mood either that, because she was uninterested in working particularly hard, they took ages getting it done. When they were only on the fourth *Ancient*, Cisco and then Nedrick both came to pull faces at him through one of the windows before heading home. Raf could hear them singing a love-duet as they walked back that was obviously meant for him to hear. He dusted noisily, hoping that Rhani hadn't heard anything.

When they finally finished the last tree and the very last cobweb had been carefully brushed off, the three of them walked back to return the map to Mitch.

. . . .

Raf waited until everyone had disappeared and then made his way to the edge of the commons where he ducked into one of the mulberry orchards and started walking down toward the banyan groves. He felt bad lying to his mother, but there was simply no way he was spending an evening with the Perenesons. Especially not after having spent the last three hours with their stupid daughter. Even if she *had* looked stunning in her silk top...

There were many farming patches down on this side of the village and Raf found himself walking through a quilted landscape; mulberries, oranges, banana plantations, a few scattered coffee fields, some groves of olive trees, and then finally the soft, mossy realm he was aiming for. He spotted the banyan walls that led into Bhothy's home and, waiting for his eyes to adjust to the dark, he stepped inside.

Sitting slouched on the dirty leather bag as if he hadn't moved, was Bhothy. In an arm that was flung out sideways, he held a small jug that was tilted precariously so that some of the liquid was dripping out. A different smell occupied the room this time, an overpowering aniseed tang that reminded Raf of the small brewery that Cisco's dad ran.

"Hi, Bhothy."

The reaction from the grizzly man wasn't quite as extravagant as the first time, and with only a small jump, he grunted and swung his head around in a wobbly arc to face Raf. He was very definitely drunk, his eyes drifting in and out of focus.

"Ah," he said in disappointment. "I didn't think you would come back...*hic*. I hoped, at least." He rolled his massive stomach over to the side and tried to stand up, managing only with the help of the chair next to him which was laden with clothes. The chair squeaked and groaned as he levered himself up and the clothes slid off onto the floor.

"Oh, bugg'rit," he stated solemnly, and then jerked his arm out to hold the jug in front of Raf. "Want s...*hic*...some gin? Made it myshelf. This one's two years old, *hic*. Cinnamon, fennel and h-*hic*-honeyshuckle. Fantashtic." Raf shook his head and Bhothy tutted. "I might get too drunk if...*hic*...if I finish it all."

"Yes, we wouldn't want that to happen," said Raf carefully. "Listen, I wanted to know if you remembered anything about yesterday."

"Nope," came the reply. Bhothy shook his head groggily. "Not telling anyshing about melforging." He swung his head clumsily back to look at the small bush that was already half bare. Raf watched him pluck some leaves from it.

That's what it's called! Melforging? So he was *doing something to the plant. I knew it!*

"Bhothy, how did you do it? How did you 'melforge' the plant?"

Bhothy snickered. "'Melforge the plant', he says! Pffff..." He eased himself down onto the bag and took a sip from the jug. "That was hardly mel-*hic*-forging, Counshil boy. But then, I'm not even a proper one. There hasn't been...*hic*...one for many generations. Not even my cousin the marveloush Eliath has any id-*hic*...idea about it."

He tilted the jug right back and then shook it upside down, staring forlornly as it turned out to be empty. "What'd they teach you 'n school, then?"

"We don't learn anything interesting like this at school," said Raf. "But it's all right. I mean, if you don't know much about it either..."

"Of course I know, Counshil boy," muttered Bhothy. "Wouldn't be...*hic*..a Bard if I didn't. It'sh about music. *Using* it. We know how to play music, but...*hic*...we used to be able t'do much more with it, somet-"

"Like what?"

Bhothy lifted a finger in irritation. "Don't interrupt." Then he whispered, "If you want to know what I think, well I think...*hic*...that music is..."

"Yes?"

"It's like food for...*hic*...for plants." He grinned slyly, showing off a ragged set of yellow teeth.

Raf stared blankly at him. Food? Music wasn't a substance.

You couldn't measure it in a cup.

"I don't think that that's *quite* what it is, Bhothy," he mumbled.

"I *knew* you wouldn't get it," said Bhothy, shaking his head solemnly and lowering himself onto the floor. "So, hic...why don't you, explain *this*, Mr. smart Counshil boy."

He took a breath and, closing his eyes, started to sing a common nursery rhyme. Bemused, Raf watched as the man swayed on the spot, and then turned to the bush – drawing a stunned breath. Yet again, there were tiny green buds appearing along the branches! The leaves already on it were growing larger by the second as well. Then the singing stopped and Bhothy slumped backward to lie on the ground, eyes fluttering. He hiccoughed a few more times and then, after a few moments, started snoring.

Raf stared at the bush. He could still feel goose-bumps that had risen on his arms the second Bhothy had started singing. But not because the singing was particularly good; there was something else to it that he couldn't quite grasp, something deeper than what he was hearing.

Why hasn't this ever happened before with that nursery rhyme? I've sung it a thousand times and nothing of this sort's ever happened.

Frustrated, he flung himself down onto the leather seat and lay back, staring at the ceiling. The crazy events over the last few days immediately sprang up in his thoughts. He really needed to figure out how he was going to get to Miern. *And* how to do it without his mother disowning him – or disowning his father for helping him! So much had happened in such a short time! And now Bhothy and this crazy plant nonsense, too?

The funny little nursery rhyme came to mind and he started humming it to himself as he lay there. His thoughts continued jumping between problems: from his mother, to his father, to Wesp, then Fergus, Rhani, Bhothy, Miern and the

Festival - all churning round and round in his head. And added to it all were the constant questions about how Bhothy had done that to the little bush. What did he mean 'food' for them? That couldn't be right, could it? And yet Raf had watched it happen with his own eyes. Twice now!

He was so deep in thought while he lay there that when his eyes grew heavy and closed, he didn't even notice the swell of purple that rose in the darkness.

How did he do it? He says it's the music, but I've never seen anything like that or even heard about it - and I've been around music my whole life! We all have. Anyway, he's too drunk to be making any sense. There must be a simple explanation, surely...

Questions burned in Raf's mind as he lay humming to himself quietly. He played the memory again and again, trying to spot any detail that might give it away. Something tickled his ear and he stopped humming. Instantly everything went black behind his closed eyes. At the very edges of his vision, he saw faint ripples of purple subside and only then realized that they'd been there all this time. Groaning, he brought his hand up to his head and then flinched as it came into contact with something soft near his face. Instinctively, he swatted at it. You got some pretty nasty bugs in the Forest. Opening his eyes, the murky room came into focus. And then he gasped and jerked backward, almost rolling back off the seat. He was staring at an enormous bush that filled up half the room and crushed up against the ceiling ten feet above. A long, leafy branch extended toward him and it was this that he had touched.

"Mmmmm," came an urgent grunt from somewhere in front of him.

Staring down, he saw that one of Bhothy's legs was sticking out from under the bush. Raf crouched down and grabbed hold of the foot, heaving backward. There was a wet snapping noise from the branches and the lower half of Bhothy's body slid out on the moss, followed by his enormous torso.

Groaning, Bhothy sat up and tried to rake his face and

beard free of debris with clumsy hands. Peering unsteadily around, his eyebrows bunched together in confusion.

"What...*hic* - where am I?" He squinted at the bush and then back at Raf. "How did I get outside? Why'd you take me...*hic*...outside, Counshil boy?"

"You're not outside, we're still in your home."

"But there's a bush..."

"Look," said Raf. His voice suddenly sounded very high, so he coughed and tried to add, more calmly, "There's your study area over there."

"What? How...did this bush get here?"

"I don't really know," replied Raf quickly. "I was...asleep."

"Did somebody...*hic*...bring it inside? Wait..." He stopped and carefully bent a branch toward him and stared at the leaves. "That's incredible!"

"What?"

"This is *my* plant! Look!" Bhothy pointed a pudgy finger at the broken remnants of the brown pot buried in the middle. "I've never...*hic*...grown it thish much before, though. I didn't think I had the ab-" He tilted his head at Raf. "Counshil boy... Is there shomething you're not telling me?"

"Me? Nothing! I don't know what you're talking about! I was over here!" Raf saw that his hand was shaking and quickly hid it behind his back.

Bhothy brushed off dirt from his tunic and heaved himself up onto the old leather bag. "*Hic.* I think you and I both know that's not...*hic*...true." He reached over and grabbed the pipe, putting it to his mouth and lighting it. Raf backed toward the doorway behind him, wiping an arm across his forehead.

"You're going?" said Bhothy. "But we need to talk about what...*hic*...happened and how you d-"

"I told you! It was nothing to do with me!"

Raf tore down the passageway, and as he reached the doorway he could just hear Bhothy shouting out, "Thanksh for the supply of leaves, Counshil boy!"

The wagon bounced along over the knotted path and Nathyn grimaced as he slammed back down onto the hard bench again. He'd been on the go since dawn, and had traveled a good eight hours yesterday after the Council meeting had ended. He'd stopped briefly in Hunton Daire to let the Foreman, Samuel Rosner, know that Eirdale had managed to source the funding and the Festival was back on track. It had been a short meeting but Samuel had been enthusiastically ringing the Hunton Daire chimes himself for a village meeting even as Nathyn left. After a short night's sleep in a small, fern-covered grove, he had made one last brief stop at Borilcester to rest and feed the goats before entering the huge crossroads that led into the outskirts of Three Ways.

He smiled as he mulled over the events of the last week. Only a few days ago, they were seriously considering cancelling the whole Festival as they couldn't afford it. It would have been unprecedented. No one had ever been *unable* to host it before. But the license fee always seemed to be increasing, and when you were situated so far south of the Pass, coin was hard to come by. He flicked the reins and urged the goats to speed up.

. . . .

Councilman Brinchley left his guest next door and returned to his office, the silver chains around his neck clinking with a pleasant metallic sound. He touched his chin thoughtfully, playing with the delicate waxed goatee as his eyes flickered over his office. It was tastefully adorned with some Miernan paintings and ornaments, and a stuffed boar head on each wall. The bookshelf was almost buckling under the weight of the collection of iMahli ostrich egg carvings he'd collected during his many years as a Three Ways Councilman.

There were approaching footsteps and a young boy came racing in through the door to stand breathlessly in front of him. "There's a man come to see you, Councilman Brinchley. From Eirdale!"

Brinchley adjusted the sleeves of his coat. "Ah, good. I was expecting him. Send him in." He moved around to the chair on the far side of the table and took a seat, careful to let the billowing sleeves of his embroidered coat settle neatly as he rested his hands on the carved arm-rests.

Councilman Tovier of Eirdale marched in and nodded formally to his Three Ways counterpart before launching into the *gretanayre* which Brinchley accompanied.

When they had finished, he sat down and started to speak, but Brinchley lifted his hand to stop him. "Before you go any further, I'm afraid I have some bad news, Councilman."

"Bad news?"

"Yes," said Brinchley. He paused and cast a thoughtful look at the shelves on the wall. "The world is moving quickly, Nathyn. We must make sure we don't fall behind."

Nathyn smiled. "And *that*, Councilman, is one of the greatest benefits of the Festival: to connect us with the world."

"Agreed. But it moves quicker and quicker, and there will be times when we must sacrifice and adapt just as quickly to survive."

"Is this about the fee, Councilman? Because, I -"

"It is well you came as quickly as you did,' interrupted Brinchley, standing up. "I was in the process of sending a message to you." He put his hands on the table and exhaled through his nose. "The Festival won't happen in Eirdale this year. It has been cancelled."

Nathyn's face fell. "What?"

"I take it you have come to pay the two hundred silvers for the fee?" He waited for Nathyn to nod. "The Miernan agent arrived here this morning to deliver the news in person to myself and Foreman Allium. He tells me that prices are increasing in Miern, as have the costs of travel – particularly the great distance from Miern to here. Keeping the trade routes safe and open is apparently becoming more and more difficult. He informed me that our fee has been duly increased."

"Well, we will just find a way to come up with more, obviously," replied Nathyn earnestly. "Even if we have to borrow money or sell our stockrooms of supplies, we will do it! We can all contribute from our personal savings, we c-"

Brinchley lifted his hand. "I think not, Nathyn. It's rather more than you can afford."

"You underestimate the value of Eirdale, Councilman," said Nathyn. "I'm sure that with some help from our neighbors we could raise as much as fifty, maybe even a hundred more."

Brinchley smiled sadly. "I'm afraid the fee has been increased to -" he crinkled his mouth up in disgust, "- five hundred silvers."

Nathyn took a step back. "That... That's ridiculous! *Five hundred?*"

"I was as shocked as you."

"But what will we do? We rely on the Festival for so much – the whole Forest does! It has been an unbroken tradition for hundreds of years!"

"I understand what you are saying, Nathyn, and I obviously voiced my concerns to the agent. But he was uninterested in negotiating."

"This is terrible..." Nathyn ran a shaking hand through his hair.

Brinchley straightened up. "I was not going to be beaten that easily, though, Councilman. I also believe, as you do, that our Forest needs the Festival - *must* have it. I spoke with Foreman Allium and we intercepted the agent before he made it to the Pass."

"And?"

"We offered for Three Ways to take over the hosting and

emptied our own coffers to pay the fee. We only just came up with the required amount ourselves - at the expense of much of next year's trading, I'll have you know." Brinchley smiled. "So you see, all is not lost. The Festival is rescued!" He walked up to Nathyn and grasped one of his shoulders in a bejeweled hand. "Of course, Eirdale will be offered stalls and performance slots – don't worry about that, my friend. We know all too well the valuable contribution that our southern neighbor can make."

"But, but, we're preparing for it - even at this moment. It's our turn, after all."

"Councilman Tovier!" Brinchley's face tightened. "I was hoping to avoid this, but…this irrational attitude forces me to bring it up. You have jeopardized trade for the whole Forest after the recent incident. Do you have any idea how hard it is to persuade people to leave Miern to travel through the brutal Pass to come here? We're only the tiniest sliver away from losing touch and fading into nothing, Nathyn. *Nothing!* We spend every day trying to strengthen ties with Miern, only to find out that all our efforts have been in vain because our southern neighbor doesn't know how to treat its guests!"

Nathyn suddenly registered what he was talking about. "The trader…?"

"That's right, Councilman. The whole appalling incident had already reached the ears of the agent when he came to me. It was almost a catastrophe! You gave me no choice. As we both agree, we *must* have a Festival. And it will now be here in Three Ways." Brinchley shook his head and sat back down at his desk. "Now, I'm very busy, Councilman. I will send word of what Eirdale's contribution will be."

Nathyn numbly turned and walked out the door, holding the bag of silver coins in his hand.

. . . .

The lavishly dressed Miernan snorted as he entered Brinchley's office from the adjoining room. He slid his rotund body onto a divan and took a sip from a cup of steaming spiced coffee as Brinchley sat down opposite him.

"I overheard the end of your conversation, I'm afraid. Tell me more about this trader. It sounds a promising tale."

Brinchley waved a hand dismissively. "It's nothing, Nabolek. A Miernan visited a southern village and after some misunderstanding there was incident in which he was assaulted, apparently. He's since returned to Miern."

Nabolek raised an eyebrow over his coffee. "Assaulted, you say?"

"Just a minor altercation, really. Nothing to worry about," said Brinchley. "And all the more reason to have the Aeril Festival here in Three Ways so that we can ensure the safety and enjoyment of our guests."

"You led me to believe that this was always the case."

"Yes," replied Brinchley quickly. "Some villages resent it though – even though they struggle to deal with just one trader in a civilized way."

Nabolek nodded slowly. "Obviously these criminals who attacked the Miernan citizen will be punished?"

"Punished? I suppose we...that is, yes, I suspect they will be," said Brinchley falteringly.

"And their presence at this Festival would be counterproductive, wouldn't you say?"

"Well, they may feel they have a certain claim to...er.... being here what with..." Nabolek's eyes narrowed the tiniest amount as he slowly lowered his cup from his mouth. "I mean, you're right, of course, Nabolek. They won't be invited. Obviously. Foolish of me to even consider it."

"Excellent," said Nabolek, bringing the cup back up to his mouth again to take a sip. "Now, about my fee."

"Ah, yes." Brinchley stood up and walked to the shelf behind him, retrieving a velvet red box sitting among several others. He turned and placed it on the table for Nabolek to open and inspect. "Two hundred silvers, as agreed."

"Councilman, I can't help but wonder why a man like yourself is living out here in this remote forest when you could do very well in Miern."

Brinchley carefully picked up the other steaming cup of coffee and lifted it to his nose. "Miern, you say?"

"Yes, my cousin is developing the city into quite an extraordinary place."

"You are cousin to the Gerent?"

"You did not know this? Why else would I have been chosen to oversee your Festival?" He sighed and looked out the window. "You would be overwhelmed by Miern. There is nothing to compare."

"I had not thought it would be possible to move there, and still afford the comforts I have here."

"Comforts?" Nabolek laughed. "In Miern, you would have a mansion with servants catering for your every need."

"And how exactly…?"

"I tell you what, my friend. If this Festival is a success," Nabolek paused, "- and if I can count on your assistance while I am here, I will personally smooth the way for you."

"It's that important to you?"

"The senators from Miern are friends of mine. Powerful friends who can make things happen. They here to provide feedback to the Gerent on whether to make the Aeril forest a barony under Allium. If they are impressed, I will do well. And if I do well…" He tilted his head at Brinchley.

"Then we must make sure they are impressed."

"I knew I could count on you." Nabolek smiled and, picking a few grapes from the bowl on the table-top, patted Brinchley on his shoulder and left the room.

Jan inserted the last of the watervines and then stepped back to inspect his work. He nodded approvingly and stroked one of the dense brown sideburns that grew down to the jaw line of his chiseled, beardless face. The two young assistants were grinning as they packed up the tools into a bag and cleared away the left-over bits of wood. After two days of working solidly on it, the project was finally completed. With the last intricate piece in place, Three Ways now had its very own pool. Jan had found a half-buried stump from a large oak that had died years ago and carved out the inside until it was about ten feet deep. Then he'd filled it with a layer of ironwood sap and left it to dry. After a full day baking in the mottled sun, it had hardened and become perfectly watertight.

Jan had thought everything out though, and with a flair of genius which justified the silver he was being paid, he had built a few holes into the pool into which watervines were slotted, and then crafted an outlet tube of sorts that let the overflow channel down the back of the guest quarters toward the farm fields behind. Fresh water was continually flowing into the pool keeping it clean and cool, and at the same time, it would benefit some lucky farmers.

Even as they stood there, the flow from the watervines slowly increased and the water level rose at the bottom of the pool, bubbling its way toward the top.

"That's brilliant," burbled the youngest assistant, but he was shushed by the other.

"That's all right, Tunit," replied Jan as he peered down into the pool and cast a critical eye on everything. "He's right. We've done a pretty good job with this."

It was pointless in his view, an unnecessary waste of water and effort; but he was a craftsman and had found the task challenging. It was also the most interesting thing he'd been asked to do over the last few weeks. Mostly, Brinchley had him involved in arbitrary building and fixing chores, the same as he'd have done in Eirdale if he was still living there, although being paid much more here. He was building up quite a nice sum of savings and was thinking about what he'd do with it when he was bored of working here. Perhaps move back to Eirdale and buy a decent plot of land or something. He wasn't sure yet. Fortunately, it looked as though there were only a few things left to do and he should be able to finish in time to get down to Eirdale for the Festival with a few days to spare.

With one last appraising look, he heaved the tool bag over his shoulder. It should have taken two men to even lift, but a lifetime of manual labor had endowed Jan with enormous strength. His swollen arms seemed to be carved from ironwood and his hands were broad and heavily callused.

"Come on, you two." He jerked his head at the two boys who were still admiring the pool. They set off toward the Three Ways commons and were met by sweeping pine arches adorned with jasmine. Scattered sculptures littered the commons, reminiscent of Brinchley's office, for which Jan had a thorough distaste. He looked up ahead and saw Brinchley himself, dressed in an absurd silk coat, engaged in a heated discussion with one of the other carpenters.

"- supposed to be finished! What have you been doing, Nerad? I specifically said the kitchens needed to be done by yesterday evening!"

"We hit some hurdles, Counc-"

"No excuses! If they're not done by lunchtime, you can pack your bags. There's no time for slip-ups right now, not with -" He stopped when he saw Jan standing off to one side.

"Ferthen? What are you doing here? Why aren't you working on the pool?"

"It's done."

"Complete? And it works?" Brinchley's face lit up. "Excellent. The Foreman will be most pleased." He rubbed his hands together in a way that made Jan's hackles rise.

"What I'd say is to give it a week or so to harden completely so that we can be sure there aren't any leaks, th-"

"A week?" said Brinchley. "I thought you said it works?"

"Well, it runs, but I h-"

"Then, I'm sure it'll be just fine. No need to dally here, Ferthen. Why don't you head straight on to the new blocks and get started on those new showers."

"Right now?" Jan glanced back at the boys who were standing at a distance.

"It must be finished by lunchtime tomorrow," urged Brinchley. "Think of the coin I'm throwing at you."

"If it's all the same with you, Councilman, we've been working solid and are overdue a break and some food."

Brinchley stared back at him, twiddling his goatee feverishly. "Fine, fine. But don't be long. There's plenty of time tonight and tomorrow morning to finish." He turned to walk away and then glanced at Nerad who was standing idly, leaning on his long axe. "You have things to get on with, don't you?" Nerad dipped his head as Brinchley lifted his coat up off the dirt and sauntered off.

Jan snorted in contempt. "Can you believe that man?"

"He's the one with the coin, woodsmith. Just do what he says," said the other man.

"True," replied Jan. "I suppose we better have a bite to eat and then get those showers done. Nothing wrong with the old ones, but they want new, fancy ones – and immediately, always immediately. You'd think the world was about to end."

Nerad smiled briefly and made as if to move away.

Jan added, "At least there are only a few days of work left

before we head down to the Festival. When you are leaving for Eirdale?"

Nerad looked down at the floor. "I think I'll pass on Eirdale this year."

"Pass on it?" Jan's thick eyebrows knitted together in confusion. "The Festival?"

"A bit too far to go. I'd rather relax here, maybe spend some coin, gamble a bit. Who knows." Nerad swung his axe onto his shoulder and walked off.

Jan glanced at Tunit who shrugged and tapped his forehead to indicate what *he* thought of Nerad.

....

Brinchley walked quickly along the edge of one of the new neighborhoods, eyeing the refurbished quarters. He had a good mind to move out of his family's age-old cedar home when the Festival was over, and take up residence in one of these new, luxurious ones. He reached the entrance to Foreman Allium's residence, a three-pronged cedar of enormous proportions, and knocked.

"Come in."

Brinchley straightened his cloak around him and stepped inside.

Allium was an uncommonly tall, wiry man with a high, nasal voice. Unlike most foresters, the Three Ways' Foreman had close-cropped hair and was clean-shaven, which served only to emphasize the large, hooked nose that dominated his face - and down which he tended to look at people. He was seated at a large table, poring over some parchment maps laid out in front of him.

He didn't look up. "You have news."

"Yes, Foreman," said Brinchley, bowing slightly. "The pool is finished. The new market area is even now having the last few finishing touches made to it. The main performance arenas will be erected ahead of time, and the musicians and performers themselves are g-"

"Don't talk to me about musicians, Brinchley. Just stick to the important matters." Allium paused and glanced at a section of the map. "The new showers?"

"Ferthen was going to work on them this morning."

"Going to?" The Foreman looked up slowly at Brinchley. "They are not finished?"

"Ah, no. Not as yet. The pool took more time than exp-"

"Excuses, Brinchley? Is this too big a job for you? If you feel you are not able to handle the pressure of managing this Festival..."

"Of course not, Foreman. It will all be finished in time."

"It better be. This Festival must stamp our mark on the Forest - and tie us firmly to Miern in the process, Brinchley." Allium started unrolling another map and paused. "I take it you have dealt with the Eirdalers?"

"I just spoke to Nathyn Tovier this morning."

"Problems?"

"He left with his tail between his legs. The trader incident couldn't have come at a better time. It played perfectly into our hands, Foreman. If we play this right, by the time they work out what's happened, the Festival will be over and you can proceed with your plan."

"And what about our Miernan guest, Nabolek? Is he aware of the circumstances?"

"I've only filled him in on what he needs to know, Foreman. His interests lie in a successful Festival, and he understands this can only happen if it is held in Three Ways. He seems very reliable."

The Foreman nodded. "Good. He has important links to Miern - to the Gerent himself, I understand - so keep him happy. This Festival will be the key to establishing Three Ways as the capital of the Forest and impressing the senators. When they deliver their advice to the Gerent – and it had better be glowing, Brinchley – I see no reason why I won't be granted the title of Baron. When that happens, I will need a good right-hand man to help bring the rest of the Aeril Forest under the new order."

Brinchley opened his mouth to reply, but the Foreman had already lowered his head to the map and lifted one hand, loosely flicking it. "That will be all."

....

"Um, good day. Could you possibly tell us where to find a Mr. Brinkley?"

Jan wiped his eyes and, holding the shower fitting in place, turned to see who it was. Standing at the doorway was a short middle-aged man with a small group of well-dressed people visible behind him on a wagon. Definitely not foresters.

"It's 'Brinchley', and I imagine you'll find him on the commons," he replied.

"Oh. Of course. The commons." The man nodded, looking around blankly.

Behind him, an elderly lady with a massive pearl necklace bobbing underneath her double chin said, "And where exactly is this commons, forester?"

Jan looked back up and rolled his eyes. He checked that the fitting wasn't moving and then climbed down the ladder which Tunit was holding steady.

"Right, if you look over there," he said, pointing westward toward the village chimes, "you'll see some offices in the cedar *Ancients*. If you walk past those in a straight line from here, you'll see the arches of the commons."

"Lovely. Thank you ever so much," said the lady. "We've traveled an awfully long way and are most looking forward to relaxing."

"Well, these showers I've fitted in will freshen you up. Tunit here can show you to one of the working ones we've done already if you'd like. I can't see anybody minding if you use one before heading off."

"Lov- oh, I'm sorry…heading off?"

"Apologies, I thought you had come for the Festival. I misunderstood."

"But we are! And we are most excited about it as it will be our first visit from Miern."

"Well, although you're early, you might as well head to Eirdale this evening or first thing tomorrow morning and enjoy a peaceful trip there. The path will get pretty busy in a few days' time, I'm guessing."

"Um…Airdale?" the man repeated vaguely.

Jan ground his teeth again and swapped a look with Tunit who was trying not to smile. "That's where the Festival is. It's the name of the village. Seems a bit odd they didn't tell you all this before you came."

"Well…yes, of course they did. They said it would be in 'Three Ways', the capital of the Aeril Forest." She looked frustrated. "Are you telling me that there will be *more* traveling still? It distinctly says that this is Three Ways on the map they gave us. No mention of this *Airdale* at all."

Jan looked askance at her. "The capital? Do you have a copy of this map by any chance?"

"Yes, here it is," she replied, offering him a rolled parchment from under a bench.

He took it and opened it out, admiring the quality of the paper and the craftsmanship of the illustrations and writing. However, his lips tightened when he started to read it. The Aeril Forest map had been left almost completely blank with no reference to any of the villages and homesteads that lay to the south and west of Three Ways. The only detailed part was Three Ways itself and the surrounding cedar-dense areas. He scrutinized it for a minute and then, spotting the author and date, cursed loudly and scrunched it up.

"Excuse me, but that's my map!" accused the woman.

"There's been a mistake," snapped Jan gruffly. "Tunit, stay here and finish off the fittings. I may not be back."

He stormed out of the room into the dappled afternoon sun and marched off at a swift pace toward the village chimes, leaving behind the puzzled visitors. Up ahead, he recognized one of the carpenters.

"Nerad!"

The other man remained seated on the bench and watched him approach.

"Nerad," he called again, "what's going on?" The stocky carpenter stared at him blankly and then picked his drink up, taking a sip from it. "What's this rubbish about the Festival being held in Three Ways? How can anyone make such a huge mistake?"

Nerad cleared his throat and then, staring into his drink, said, "Perhaps take it up with Councilman Brinchley."

Jan stared at him. There was something odd in the expressions of the others standing around, and he had a growing suspicion that there was something he was missing. He turned and almost walked straight into the travelers who had caught up with him. Growling impatiently at them, he pushed past and left them behind as he marched up toward the Council offices. He approached the large oval door of Brinchley's office and, hearing indistinct talking inside, he rapped hard on the door. The talking stopped.

A moment of silence and then, "Who is it?"

Jan yanked the door open and entered. He came face to face with Brinchley who had half-risen from his desk, an expression of indignation on his face. Next to him was an expensively dressed stranger who remained quite calm in the face of the interruption; he sat in a relaxed pose at the table, one fist held to his chin, the other resting on his massive stomach which was protruding over his belt.

"Ferthen? Who do you think you are, barging in like this?" spluttered Brinchley. "I am with an important guest. It is a

100

complete outrage! I *insist* you remain outside until I am ready to speak to you."

"I have an issue I need to raise with you. Regarding the Festival." Jan thrust out the crumpled map. "Somehow, I don't think it's a mistake that it says Three Ways on these."

Brinchley slowly straightened up, smoothing the folds of his stole. "Unfortunately, there have been complications very recently. We have had to accept the responsibility ourselves here in Three Ways to maintain the tradition of hosting a Festival on behalf of the Aeril Forest."

"Very recently, you say?"

"It was only yesterday that I spoke with your own Councilman Tovier and resolved the issue." Brinchley walked to the door and held it open. "That is all I have to say on the matter. Now leave."

"It is interesting then that on this map, it shows Three Ways as the venue -"

"As I said, I spoke t-"

"This map was made over a *month* ago! Plenty of time to distribute them in Miern," snapped Jan. "You had this planned all along!"

The foreigner did not move, but looked at Brinchley with a strange calculating look. Jan watched as Brinchley brought his hand up to fiddle with his goatee, a small bead of sweat rolling down his forehead.

"Well?"

Brinchley smiled nervously at the stranger sitting to his left and then sat down at his table. "You are correct."

"What? How can you do this!"

"Think about it, Ferthen. Your village could not possibly have hosted the Festival. It's far too big an event. Three Ways will be the host this year, and for every year following. Eirdale and all the others need to accept it. And be grateful that Three Ways, at least, is able to handle such an important event for the Forest."

A wave of fury erupted inside Jan and he lunged toward Brinchley. "You fickle excuse for a Councilman! You're lucky I don't drag you to Eirdale right n-"

There was a snap of movement in the room. Jan paused. A pale gleam of sunlight glinted off the thin, steel saber pointed at his throat.

"Easy," said the stranger.

He had moved surprisingly quickly to draw his sword, at odds with his obese frame. Jan turned to look at the man. He had a thick, greased beard that was long enough to almost touch the bright red, embroidered lapels of the coat he was wrapped in.

As quick as an adder, Jan whipped his right hand up to seize the blade and, with a powerful jerk of his arm, he yanked the saber clean out of the man's hand. It flew through the air and clattered against the wall.

Brinchley cowered against the back wall stammering in panic. "Nabolek, call your soldiers!" He moved sideways along the wall toward the nearest window.

Jan squared up to the stranger who was eyeing him warily, a hand placed on the hilt of a small jeweled knife tucked into his belt.

"No need. I'm leaving. I quit!"

"You won't be paid, I promise you that! You won't see so much as a bronze piece from me! And I'll see to it that you never set foot in Three Ways again, you hear!"

"I don't want your money. When the other villages hear of this they will have something to say about it. The Overcouncil will restore the Festival to Eirdale, and you most *certainly* will be banished. You and Allium, and -" Jan pointed at the stranger, "- whoever this is." He left the room.

. . . .

Nabolek stooped down to pick up his saber, taking a quick glance down the blade. Brinchley coughed and straightened his coat. "Apologies, Nabolek, that man is a menace and sh-"

"Quiet!" interrupted Nabolek. "Do you think I've traveled all this way to be humiliated like that?"

"Foreman All-"

"I said quiet!" snapped Nabolek. "And by a *carpenter*...!"

"Yes, yes," replied Brinchley desperately. "He's from the same village that the trader was attacked in. They're an unruly bunch down there – criminals, many of them. But none of them will be invited to the Festival, I can guarantee it."

"How blind you are to the consequences of the man reaching his village."

"I don't see what you m-"

"I thought I could trust you, Councilman, and yet now I discover you haven't been completely honest with me about your Festival." He slid the saber back into its sheath. "But I suppose I am heartened to see that you are ambitious and want the best for your forest, at least. You almost managed to pull off this cunning little Festival switch. A pity you were so clumsy with that carpenter or it might have even worked. But now..." His hooded eyes flickered around the room thoughtfully. "That man could ruin everything, all of your plans. And all of mine. We can't have that, Councilman; there's far too much at stake here." He reached up to a shelf and took down a small map of the forest, peering at it. "I hate loose ends, and I certainly don't intend for this one to stay loose for very long."

Brinchley swallowed. "Of course, Nabolek, you have permission to do whatev-"

"*Permission?*" said Nabolek. "We really aren't getting off to a very good start here, Councilman. The Gerent will not take kindly to his relatives being threatened." He poked his finger into Brinchley's chest, pushing him against the wall behind. "I do not need your permission. And if I am embarrassed in any way again..."

Brinchley swallowed and sent his many chins wobbling as he nodded fervently.

"Good. I like you, forester. I would hate to see our friendship break down over this. But business is business. Everything rides on this Festival going forward smoothly." Nabolek walked toward the door, the hem of his red coat rustling as it slid over the polished floor.

Brinchley glanced out the window. "And the carpenter?"

Nabolek halted in the doorway. "As a favor to you, I will clean up your mess, Councilman."

Raf yawned and rested his chin on his folded arms on the table top. At the front of the class, Yurgin Klee was droning on about something to do with crops. It was probably worth listening to him as he was easily the most knowledgeable farmer and ran some of the largest farms in Eirdale, but it was a beautiful morning outside - and he was so boring!

He quickly reached over and nudged Cisco whose head had flopped back for the fourth time, emitting a strangled snoring noise. He jerked his head back upright and then looked at Raf through half closed eyes. "How much longer is this going to go *on* for?" he said under his breath.

"Yes? Young Brunnow I believe it is? Do you have the answer?" came Yurgin's voice from the front.

Cisco panicked and looked around desperately for help, so Raf held his hand up to hide his face and mouthed '*potatoes*' at him.

"Er...potatoes, sir?"

The class burst into laughter and Yurgin himself chuckled so that his bony shoulders bounced up and down. "Four years of studying farming and you think that the plants that grow best in the upper canopies are potatoes?"

Cisco glared at Raf who was in muffled hysterics, leaning on Nedrick's shoulder.

Yurgin cleared his throat to quieten the class but there was a knock at the door. A message was delivered calling him away, so he ended the class early.

"Let's get out of here," said Nedrick, and the three boys

sidled out through the door and then raced down the path.

"Fancy a bit of a climb?" challenged Cisco.

"You're on!" said Nedrick. "Where?"

"*Nviro?*"

The boys looked at each other and then nodded. They sprinted down toward old Jover's farms, tussling with each other as they scrambled between the trunks and bushes on the way. Around the side of a white beech *Ancient*, they suddenly found themselves in the midst of a large herd of *saanen*, and amused themselves for a while trying to catch one of the woolly goats before continuing. Finally, they came to the border of Jover's lands and saw their target standing at the crossroads of some farming patches ahead. *Nviro*, an elm *Ancient*, had a network of strangler vines that ran crisscrossing up its entire trunk which made for a usable ladder. It was the most used access point to get to the canopy farms on this side of the village.

They walked up to the bottom of *Nviro* and each moved a few feet apart to start climbing. Like most foresters, the boys were competent climbers and after only a short while they found themselves hundreds of feet up the trunk. Higher and higher they went, until the ground below them grew distant and murky. It was much lighter up here, and sensing the tree crown nearing, they sped up, laughing and singing as they clambered upward. Before long, they found themselves crawling out onto a wooden platform where they finally stopped. They took a few moments to catch their breath and absorb the view that had now opened up to them. Although they'd been up here many times before, it was still astonishing, and all three of them wore open grins at the sheer beauty of the multicolored panorama. When you were used to living in constant close quarters with the trees down below, the openness of the sky above the Forest, its unending vastness, was dizzying.

"I am *so* going to speak to my parents about getting an

apprenticeship up here," said Cisco quietly. "I could do this every day."

His voice sounded tiny. Every word seemed to be sucked away by the breeze and scattered into the shimmering tree-tops that stood swaying like rolling fields of barley. Every few hundred feet or so, an *Ancient* would punch out of the lush green foliage to continue upward, ending in a bushy crown high in the azure sky.

"How sweet does it smell here..." whispered Nedrick. "Not that I'm surprised. Have you two seen those?"

They looked to where he was pointing and saw a spindly walkway leading up to a sprawling field of jasmine, thousands upon thousands of the delicate flowers hanging from every branch in sight. Then there was a shout and a small figure came running down the rope path toward them. It was Fergus.

"Raf!" he called excitedly, and rushed up to give him a hug.

"Hey, Fergus," replied Raf. "What are you doing up here? You sh-" He broke off as he got a proper look at the boy's face. "How *brown* are you!"

"I know! Mr. Jover's teaching me to be a farmer and I've been spending every day up here. I'm in charge of loads of things already. Just me! It's great!"

Nedrick and Cisco were standing to the side, watching the two. Glancing back at them, Raf stepped aside for introductions. "Fergus, these are my two friends, Cisco and Ned." He pursed his lips a little and then added, "I think you guys know who this is, right?"

"We sure do. The latest addition to Eirdale," said Nedrick, and he walked up to enthusiastically shake Fergus' hand. "How are you finding our little village in the trees compared to the city?"

"Yeah, tell us about Miern!" urged Cisco.

"Oh, it's all right," said Fergus. "I like the canals and the boats and things I suppose. But it's much better here in the Forest!"

"Wh-" started Cisco, but was interrupted by Fergus who was in full flow now.

"And Mr. Jover says he wants me to look after his cashew grove as well as the coffee because his leg hurts. He says I'm a really good climber for a city boy. And he's let me have my own room in his tree-house!"

Raf couldn't help but chuckle at the boy's enthusiasm. "I'm glad you're enjoying being here, Fergus."

"Yeah, I bet you're really happy that you met this guy, huh?" said Cisco, winking at him and playfully punching Raf's shoulder.

Fergus nodded eagerly. "Oh, yes. I would never have been able to stay if he hadn't helped me." He beamed up at them and then added in a conspiratorial way, "And he let me look after Orfea! Isn't that brilliant?"

Cisco looked at Raf. "Orfea?"

"The trader tried to sell it to the Foreman, remember? The flarehorn he made?" said Nedrick.

"Oh yeah..." Cisco said. "And where *is* this marvelous thing you made? I've got to see it. Who'd have thought ol' Gency could actually make something valuable!"

"I always keep it in my room. Want me get it?"

"Oh, don't worry if it's all the way back down there, Fergus. We can always see it another time."

"I can get it for you. It won't take long I promise! I'm a really good climber – even Mr. Jover thinks so."

Without waiting for a reply from the boys, he ran toward the other side of the tree trunk that they were on where a branch extended out into the air. Before they could say anything, he leaped off, somehow catching hold of another thinner branch in the thick foliage of an elm tree. The three boys stood watching, their mouths open wide in horror.

"I think I'm gonna be sick..." moaned Cisco, staring at the patch of leaves below them where the boy had disappeared. There was a flash of color and he reappeared running down another path.

"What a brilliant little fellow," mused Nedrick. "While he's gone, are you lads hungry?" They turned to see him staring upward at a heavily laden grapevine in one of the twisting upper branches of the tree.

They climbed up and edged out along the branch where the grapes hung in swollen green bunches. Before long, they were stuffing their mouths with the delicious morsels, grinning at each other as they gorged. They had barely finished eating a bunch each when they heard some rustling down below and, leaning over the edge of the branch, they saw Fergus emerge. He was jumping nimbly from branch to branch, until he reached the tall trunk of a tree opposite theirs and, despite no evidence of handholds or small branches of any sort, he scaled it easily. When he reached level with the main platform on which they had first disembarked, he looked around curiously.

'Up here, monkey-boy," laughed Cisco.

Fergus grinned at them and, without a thought, launched himself across the divide between the two trunks to latch on to the vine ladder. Within seconds, he was up the trunk and standing next to them, panting as he unstrapped the instrument from his back.

Cisco shook his head. "Look, kid, you *got* to warn me when you're going to do something like that."

"Don't worry, Mr. Cisco. I've never fallen in my life!"

Raf and Nedrick were both still staring at him, white-faced.

"See what you've done to them?" said Cisco.

Fergus smiled shyly and then unwrapped Orfea to hand it to Cisco who took it gently. The smile on his face dried up and after turning the instrument around in his hands, he looked up at Raf and said, "Are you being serious? You made this?"

Raf shrugged. "It's nothing special."

"It's pretty good," muttered Cisco. "I've never seen an instrument like this. How did you get it so smooth? This wasn't done with a knife. There isn't a single scratch or edge on this.

The whole thing looks polished or…more like…well, it looks natural. It's amazing."

'I know!" chirped Fergus.

Raf turned to look away; he felt troubled and had lost his buzz of excitement. Orfea and Fergus had brought back disturbing memories and unanswered questions.

"I think I'm going to head home, boys."

"You're kidding me, right?" replied Cisco. "You want to leave already? We still need to see what else this little monkey is up to. And find out how I can get his dream-job as well." He winked at Fergus who laughed and tried to wink back at him.

"You guys go ahead. I'm not feeling so good suddenly. Think I had too many grapes."

"Suit yourself," said Cisco, shaking his head.

"We'll catch up with you in few hours?" said Nedrick.

"Yeah, yeah," said Raf. "I'll probably see you guys at the commons later."

"Bye, Raf," said Fergus, a disappointed expression on his face as he walked off with the other two.

Raf silently watched them strolling along the walkway toward the distant canopy farm, and then started the long descent back down *Nviro*.

Night was falling quickly and Nabolek had just finished his dinner when he saw the two soldiers walking toward his quarters. He stood and walked to meet them.

"Jugak."

The short, stocky man gave a small bow by way of response and indicated the soldier next to him. "This is Nadherna."

The other man gave a curt salute.

"And Henja?"

"On his way." Jugak turned around and glanced back to a man who walked slowly toward them in thick leather sandals and a dark cloak. There was something awkward about his gait. He didn't seem to walk so much as wade forward, his thin body moving in uncomfortable jerks.

Nabolek watched him approach. "Henja."

The newcomer didn't reply, but merely stood slightly apart from the other two, long unkempt hair hanging loosely over his face, breathing slightly ragged breaths. Nadherna eyed him with distaste and moved away slightly.

Nabolek gave Henja an annoyed look. "I've no idea why you were sent here with me, but I have a problem that needs fixing." He pointed over their shoulders. "Go with these two. Take the path south. A woodsmith called Ferthen left earlier to return to a village called Eirdale. He cannot get there." He leaned closer to them. "This is a sensitive matter. Should anyone else learn of it, they will become...an inconvenience."

Jugak bowed his head. Nabolek nodded and then retreated to his quarters.

111

Tunit chewed his lip as the three soldiers walked away, careful to remain hidden behind the window of the room he was tidying up. Mind buzzing, he moved backwards and bumped into a chair. The noise wasn't loud, but the third soldier – the strange one called Henja – snapped his head around to stare at the house. Tunit dropped to the floor. He frantically crawled to the back of the room and cowered behind a bench, peeking out through a crack in the wood. How had the guy heard that?!

Henja came into view outside the entrance, sniffing the air. And then he suddenly flowed forward with his weird way of walking and stepped into the doorway of the room. Tunit held his breath, but kept an anxious eye on the man.

Stretching one hand up to hold on to the frame of the doorway, Henja leaned inside and tilted his head back to breathe in deeply. Looking from side to side, he scanned the room. It was a mess, full of construction materials and carpentry tools all over the floor and on the table. If the man was somehow smelling him – and that's what he seemed to be doing! – then Tunit was relieved he hadn't packed away the pungent varnishes and paints yet. And indeed, with an angry grimace at the open containers, Henja let go of the frame and disappeared outside.

Tunit breathed out slowly and eased himself back up from behind the bench. His heart was beating furiously and he could feel sweat on his back. He sidled up to the window and moved his head a tiny bit past the window frame, just in time to spot Henja disappearing around an *Ancient* with the other two soldiers.

His hands were shaking and he leaned back against the wall, clenching his fists to try to calm himself. What was going on? Why had those men been sent by the Foreman's Miernan guest to stop Jan getting home? And *who* was Henja? The man had a creepiness to him that made Tunit's skin crawl. Jan was stronger than anyone Tunit knew, but there was something about Henja that made him nervous for the woodsmith. He had to get help - and quickly. He wiped his forehead with the back of his arm and then crept up to the doorway, stepping lightly over the equipment and pieces of wood from the new shower fitting. Standing there, he paused. There was a strange smell, something quite unpleasant that overpowered even the varnish odor. He looked around for the source and stopped when his eyes passed over the frame of the door. There was a small dark mark where Henja had gripped it. Almost a hand-shaped mark...

He reached up to touch it, but as his fingers made contact, the wood broke off, crumbling to pieces. Tunit jerked his hand back with a sharp intake of breath and covered his nose with a sleeve. It was completely rotten.

. . . .

Raf jumped the last few feet to the ground and then dusted himself off. He made his way through the farms toward the residential area and finally arrived at his own home, sweating in the humid afternoon air. He entered the kitchen to find their farm manager, Moraes, sorting through some baskets of food.

"Hi, Moraes."

"Why, good day, Master Gency," replied the old man, smiling affably. "I see your classes are as irresistible as ever."

Raf grinned back at him. "Actually, we got the afternoon off. Not that anyone was listening." Moraes chuckled and carried on rummaging through the baskets. "D'you know where Dad is?"

"I believe your father is taking care of Festival business on the Eastside. From what I can gather, they're running late and your mother has been...shall we say 'relentless' in her directing of the whole affair."

"Yeah, I bet she has," replied Raf, eyeing the fruit Moraes was sorting through. "You doing anything at the Festival?"

"I have the honor of running both your father's fruit stall as well as singing in my small choir group on the second night."

"Nice. You nervous?"

"Not overly, Master Gency. Not as much as if I were performing in such an anticipated manner as yourself, anyway."

Raf rolled his eyes comically at Moraes. "Yeah, I'm still trying to figure out how to get out of that."

"Get out of it? I would have thought it would be a great privilege to sing in the Festival. And you've always so enjoyed your music."

"Yes, so everyone keeps reminding me. And everybody still seems to think that I'm eight years old, too." He shook his head. "I love music, I do. Just…not standing there in front of people who are watching me do it. I'll fall to pieces."

"Can't you simply close your eyes? I find I can appreciate it more like that, connect with it." Moraes smiled faintly and turned back to the fruit. "But, you must do what is right for you. I, myself, chose to leave West Peaks because my father was threatening to send me to work on the boats out of Toviton. I wandered for many years up and down through the Forest trying out different things. I was very lucky to gain employment with your father when I passed through Eirdale. And here I've been since, far from boats, and rather enjoying my life."

"I'd *love* to work on the boats."

"Ah, but Master Gency, you do not have an inhuman fear of being on the water," he chuckled. "Anyway, listen to me going on like an old fool. I'm sure you have more important things to do."

Raf patted the old man's shoulder affectionately and looked down into the basket; it was a veritable rainbow of fruit, and the grapes he had eaten seemed a distant memory. With a lightning-quick move, he snatched a golden mango from the basket and quickly skipped out of the room, just ahead of Moraes' lunge to catch him. The old man waved a gnarled fist at the boy and then went back to the table chortling softly to himself.

Raf climbed up the winding passage to his room and straddled the thick window ledge, biting into the mango. It was delicious. He felt the juice running down his chin and wiped it with his arm, leaning his head back and letting his thoughts catch up with him.

Just close your eyes. That's what Moraes had said about listening to music. Which was weird because that was the only time Raf saw those stupid colors. There was some sort of link between them and what Bhothy had done. But what, exactly?

The sound of voices in the kitchen indicated that his mother was home. Raf groaned and swung his other leg over the side of the window, using the vines to climb down to the ground.

I'm not in the mood to deal with her right now.

He jumped down the last bit, landing softly on the ground and paused, making a decision.

I've got to find out more. If I don't get answers soon, I'm going to lose my mind. But there's only one place I'll be able to find them...

Panting, Raf reached the hanging banyan walls and marched through into Bhothy's lair without knocking.

"Bhothy?" he wheezed, craning his head around the room. The huge bush had been trimmed a bit, and along one side, Bhothy had hacked it away completely to unblock a doorway. "Hello?"

There was no response so he slumped down on a leather bag and pursed his lips disappointedly. Where was the drunken old fool?

Probably hiding from me. Me and my questions.

He glanced over at the bush again.

He seemed interested enough to talk when that stupid thing grew yesterday. He genuinely didn't think he'd done it himself.

"But it can't have been me," he whispered.

However, he *had* been singing at the time, and those weird colors had appeared again.

I wonder if Bhothy sees colors, too. Maybe that's the secret?

Intrigued, he summoned the nursery rhyme to his mind. The familiar tune came to him easily and he started singing. Closing his eyes, he stared into the blackness and waited for the colors, barely taking any notice what his singing sounded like. Probably rubbish. It didn't matter though. It was the colors he was interested in. He strained forward in the darkness, seeking them out. But there was nothing.

He stopped and cursed. When he didn't want to see colors in his head, they popped up and almost blinded him, but now, when he actually wanted them, he couldn't find them! What was going on? Was he looking hard enough, or in the wrong way, somehow?

Maybe that's it, though; I'm looking for it. I've never done that before. Normally I just kind of.. happened to notice it.

Suddenly he chuckled as he realized what he was thinking.

It's music! That's what Bhothy said. And you don't look for music, you idiot, you listen for it...

Shaking his head at himself, he closed his eyes again. This time, he tried to ignore his eyes and instead focus on listening to the song as he sang it.

A flush of excitement enveloped him as he instantly became aware of a glimmering wisp of color flickering in front of him. And he had some serious goose-bumps! From the top of his neck, down his back and out along his arms and legs, a million tiny hairs rose up in a prickly wave. It was weird, but kind of exhilarating, and he let himself relax, welcoming the sensation.

Okay, so how do I make the plant grow?

At the thought of the plant growing, there was a strange turbulence in front of him and a ripple of purple seemed to bubble and condense out of the other colors. Raf watched in fascination as it ducked and weaved invitingly.

And now? What do I do?

He tried pointing at the bush and moving his hands in a sweeping gesture toward it, but when he cracked open an eye to look, still singing, he saw no noticeable change in the bush.

Grow, he urged.

The purple colors thickened even more; they filled his mind and raced around in front of him. But still nothing happened.

Frustrated, he stopped singing and shouted, "Grow!"

There was a crash behind him and Raf snapped out of his hazy state to spin around. The door to the room had been thrown open, and standing in the entrance was Bhothy, swaying drunkenly.

"What'sh going on?" he stammered, holding on to the frame for support.

Raf was about to greet him when Bhothy staggered clumsily off the step and slid on the mossy floor, bumping the side of a shelf on the wall. It tipped up wildly to slam into the shelf above which jettisoned its cargo: a heavy wooden chest. It plummeted, smashing straight into Bhothy's head with a horrible crunch. He collapsed to the floor like a felled tree and lay motionless.

Raf stared in shock and then flung himself down to the side of the unconscious man. "Bhothy!"

Already, there was an egg-sized bump on his head. He held his head down onto Bhothy's chest. There was only the faintest pulse of a heartbeat. "Oh, no…"

He shook the flabby shoulders desperately, trying to jolt him awake. "Bhothy, are you okay? Wake up, please!" He stared at the man's face and felt a wave of nausea swamp him as Bhothy's face started turning a waxy grey.

He's dying!

Raf wrung his hands. His father would know what to do, but he was too far away to help. Everyone was. It was up to Raf to do something – and right now. He seized on a desperate impulse and closed his eyes, throwing his arms forward to grab Bhothy by his shoulders. Then he burst into song. The first thing that came into his head was the *gretanayre* and he sang it loudly. No colors came. He stopped and forced himself to calm down, ignoring his frantic, racing heart. He started singing again, but this time softly. He closed his eyes and concentrated on hearing the music…and felt a shiver of relief as the colors reappeared.

Heal him! he yelled in his mind.

This time it was molten blue that burst into sight and filled his vision, its frenzied motions echoing his own panic.

Go!

Something odd happened. He tried to mentally push the

color, and felt himself move forward in his head - *into* the color somehow, until they merged. With startling awareness, he realized suddenly that it was now a part of him - or he was a part of it; they were extensions of each other. He could *feel* it. And control it! Without hesitation he concentrated on Bhothy in his mind and flowed straight into the man's body, surrounded by a billowing cloak of the rich blue color. He focused on the man and impelled the color to cover him, imagining his heart pounding, desperately willing it to beat faster and for his injured head to repair. He concentrated his mind and energy at the same thought, again and again, directing the color with one clear command in his mind: *Heal!*

"Aaargh..."

The noise made Raf jump backward in fright and his eyes flew open. Bhothy was rolling from side to side, holding his head in both hands, groaning loudly.

Raf scrambled to his feet, feeling his hands shaking with adrenalin as he watched the huge man writhe on the floor.

He's alive!

Bhothy squinted up into the dim light and groaned, "What happened? What did y-"

Raf was out the door and gone before he heard the end of the sentence.

. . . .

In the distance, the village chimes started ringing and Leiana lifted her head from scrutinizing the schedule in front of her. Eirdale had guests, it seemed. She quickly tidied up her papers and then donned her bright green Council stole before heading out the door. The Foreman and most of the Council were over on the west side so she would have to greet the visitors herself.

More and more people were flooding toward the commons and she could already hear a swelling chorus of the *gretanayre* echoing through the trees. Leiana smiled approvingly. It was a pleasure to hear the Eirdale folk enthusiastically getting into the spirit of everything. After all, the Festival was only a few days away.

She made her way through the crowd, people moving to let her pass when they saw who it was, and she was greeted with the sight of a familiar figure leading the welcome. Abuniah hopped around energetically, banging on some little wooden kettle drums for the visitors who had arrived. Leiana couldn't help grinning with delight at the sight of them: four *dholaki* standing right there in front of her! In her village! The iMahli hand-drummers were legendary, and nobody knew that they were actually here to perform at the Festival. It was too exciting.

Two of them were seated on the back of their small wagon and two stood in front holding the goats' harnesses. All of them silently watched the proceedings. That they didn't join in or seem to appreciate the welcome was a bit disappointing, but Leiana suspected it was probably all a bit overwhelming seeing a forester greeting for the first time like this.

The crowd gradually calmed down at Abuniah's bidding and then Leiana stepped forward. She dipped her head to the iMahlis. "Who is Edokko?"

"I am Edokko." The shortest one, wearing an ornate ivory necklace, padded barefoot up to stand in front of her.

"I am Leiana, Councilwoman for Eirdale. Welcome! You've already met Abuniah, I take it."

The little man nodded. "He would make good *dholaki*."

Abuniah bowed theatrically and was applauded by some of the crowd in front.

"He would make a good clown as well, Edokko," she replied laughing. "But you can't have him, I'm afraid."

Edokko didn't smile, but turned to say something to the other iMahlis and one jumped lightly down from the wagon to the ground. The fourth iMahli, muscular and much darker than the other three, remained sitting in the back. He was dressed in a simple leather skirt and sat staring idly at the side of the wagon.

"Where are shelters?" asked Edokko. "Water and food, also."

Leiana, slightly taken aback by his abruptness, beckoned to one of the youngsters standing behind her. "Aden here will show to you to your quarters. If you need anything else, please don't hesit-"

"Coins," said Edokko. "You must pay."

Leiana quickly stepped closer to him, lowering her voice. "Of course, of course. I will bring it myself as soon as you are unpacked."

Edokko nodded and then turned to issue instructions to the other iMahlis before climbing up onto the driver's bench. The others settled down in the back next to the dark iMahli who scowled and muttered something in iMahli which didn't sound particularly polite.

"So." Leiana sidled up to Abuniah smiling. "Real *dholaki* here in Eirdale! Not too bad for a little sparkle in our Festival, yes?"

Abuniah didn't answer, an odd, uneasy look on his face as he watched the wagon move slowly away led by Aden.

Her grin faded a little and she peered at the wagon. "Don't seem very friendly though, especially the one in the back. Perhaps he's some sort of chief or warrior type? He's certainly big enough."

She shrugged as Abuniah offered no comment and added, "I think a pre-Festival warm up feast is called for tonight to welcome our guests, don't you?"

"It...would be..." Abuniah followed the wagon's progress with a dark look until it disappeared around a tree. Then, noticing Leiana watching him, he nodded. "I... Yes, of course. It would be poor of us not to." He turned around to the small crowd. "Master Hetton, if you would do the honors?"

One of the older boys ran out of the crowd toward the village chimes.

Leiana started walking away. "I'll speak with Orikon and see what he can catch us for dinner."

"He actually left a while ago. I'm not sure where. You'll have to speak to one of the other hunters, Councilwoman."

"No matter. The Festival is finally firing up, and having these *dholaki* here will surely stoke everyone's excitement! We need to let everybody know the good news." She patted Abuniah enthusiastically on the shoulder. "It all starts!"

"Did that chief mentioned something about paym-"

"Don't you worry about that, Abuniah," she interrupted.

He eyed her suspiciously, but she raised her eyebrow at the unspoken question and, to her relief, he left it alone. Before anyone else could approach her, she marched off through the crowd to tackle her long list of things to do.

17. <u>**CHERRYBLOSSOMS**</u>

*S*plutter.

Jan woke up choking on what turned out to be a collection of soggy petals that had fallen onto his face. Coughing and spitting on the ground, he brushed them off his head and face and then retrieved his backpack which was almost buried under the carpet of cherry blossoms. They were falling in great thick sweeps, buoyed on the wind, and all around him he could hear the whispering of millions of petals floating down from the canopy. There were other areas in the Forest where certain types of tree grew in abundance like this dense grove of cherry-blossom *Ancients*; they were all beautiful in their own way, but nothing was quite as queer, or charming, as this deluge of soft pinkness.

He lifted his head and breathed in the fresh air. It had a distinct fruity fragrance to it. Jan sniffed again. Actually, there was something else in the air, something underneath that wasn't quite so pleasant; something moldy or rotten. He looked around, breathing in and found that it was coming from his right somewhere, so he searched the area where it seemed strongest. He walked past a thick banyan vine snaking its way up a cherry blossom *Ancient* and realized he'd found the culprit. The banyan seemed healthy enough at first glance but it absolutely reeked up close. He reached up to a crack in the bark and ripped a piece off. The smell immediately intensified and he stepped back. The inner wood was a light brown color, but a thick, green liquid immediately started oozing out of it.

"Bit of a stink coming from that, eh?" said a voice.

Jan turned to see a short, rough-looking man standing not ten feet from him with his thumbs tucked behind his belt. He was dressed in a military uniform.

"And who are you?"

"Name's Jugak. Traveling to a village south of here," the man replied.

Jan felt he had handled the meeting rather clumsily. "Apologies for my abruptness, Jugak. I myself am heading down to Eirdale. Is that the same village you're making for?"

The man casually chewed one of his nails. "Would you be the woodsmith Ferthen?"

Jan nodded, perplexed, and was about to ask how he knew when he noticed Jugak's eyes flicker for a fraction of a second to something behind his left shoulder. Everything happened at once. Jan saw a flash of movement out of the corner of his eye and spun his body around just in time to find another man charging at him with a short-sword. Jan jerked out of the way, feeling the blade slice through the front of his tunic, just missing his stomach. The attacker, expecting to meet resistance, stumbled past him and tripped over to land sprawled on the ground.

"Get up you fool!" hissed Jugak who had now drawn his own sword, a curved saber, and was slowly circling Jan. The fallen man scrambled to his feet and moved around the other way.

Jan stared back at them, trying to keep both men in his line of sight. "What do you want with me?"

Jugak feigned a lunging stab, and Jan jerked backward from him but realized that he'd lost sight of the other man. He spun on one heel and just managed to twist out of the way of another attack, except this time, as the man stumbled past him, he swung a heavy fist as hard as he could onto the man's arm, feeling a wet snap.

The man dropped the sword and fell to the ground, screaming in pain and holding his arm which was bent backward at an unnatural angle. "He broke my arm! The dog broke my arm!"

"Get up!" barked Jugak keeping a wary eye on Jan.

Another hissing sound suddenly became audible over the noise of petals and Jan glanced over as a new figure moved into view. It was a third man, but not dressed in uniform as these two were. He wore a dark brown outfit, and had long, greasy hair that hung loosely around his face. He walked with a sort of strange wading motion and was making the odd hissing noise himself. He wasn't armed though, and Jan was unimpressed with this attempt to intimidate him.

Jugak beckoned with his saber. "Help us, Henja! He broke Nadherna's arm!"

The pink petals from the wind-shaken cherry blossoms were still falling thickly all around them, but it was the ones that landed on this new man that caught Jan's attention. As he came closer, he saw that it wasn't this Henja making the hissing noise himself; it was made by the petals which fell on his arms and face. As they touched his bare skin, they curled up and shriveled into dust.

Jugak pointed his saber at Jan. "Get him!"

Henja, still wading forward slowly, tilted his head and peered down as he reached the moaning form of Nadherna. He crouched and stretched out a delicate, pale hand to touch the broken arm. Nadherna shrieked. It was a piercing noise, like a boar being slaughtered. His legs sprung out and his back was wracked by a violent spasm so that his head wrenched backward.

"What are you doing to him? Leave him!" Jugak's face turned white and the saber he was holding out in front of him started shaking erratically.

Nadherna vented a last chilling wheeze and then didn't breathe again. Every cord in his neck stood out as he convulsed, his face turning purple and then slowly grey as his eyes glossed over.

Jan felt bile rise in his throat and fought to control it, stumbling backward and knocking against the tree behind him. He edged sideways as quickly as he could along the trunk; he needed to get away from whatever was happening here. Henja calmly stepped over Nadherna's body and edged toward Jugak who, with a shrieked obscenity, turned to flee. Jan lunged forward and seized him by the shoulders before he could get away.

"What did he do to that man?" he shouted.

Jugak gibbered in panic, trying to turn his head back to see Henja, so Jan swung his arm back and slapped his face with such force that the man spun in a half circle and landed on the ground, face-first.

He reached down to yank the man up again. "Who *are* you people?" he yelled. "What do you want with me? Tell me!"

Jugak swallowed. "We were sent! By Na-"

He stopped. His head arched back and he screamed. It turned into a wet gurgle and then quickly tapered into a thin rasping sound. Jan stared at his reddening face and then became aware of the hissing noise again. It was much closer. He saw a slender hand appear and slide softly around Jugak's neck from behind, the fingers moving gently along the taut skin which instantly swelled up underneath them and turned blotchy and grey. With a soft creak, the body of Jugak crumpled to the ground. And as it did, Jan was left staring into Henja's eyes. His thin, dry lips were open and he looked at Jan with an almost tender look on his face.

Jan couldn't move. His eyes followed Henja's hand as it lifted slowly. The thin fingers reached up toward him. He could see each individual cherry blossom land on the skin of the hand and die. It was close enough for him to even see the tiny movements in the network of blue veins in his hand as blood coursed through it. A fingertip brushed against the skin of Jan's cheek and everything burst into pain. He tried to scream, but couldn't as every muscle in his body contracted, crushing his lungs, crushing his throat. He could feel a building pressure in his head, threatening to rip it open. The pain was unbearable, a wall of agony closing in on him, shutting down his senses. A wet thud right in front of him brought a small wave of release and he collapsed to his knees. Letting out a ragged gasp, he squinted through stinging eyes and saw Henja struggling with something. Something in his chest. An arrow! The man was growling as he tore at the arrow and Jan could hear a wet sizzling noise as his fingers grasped the wooden shaft. He watched as it wilted and then crumbled in his hand. He knew he should have been terrified, but was only able to observe it with a dull, detached interest.

Henja covered the wound with one hand as he peered into the bushes behind Jan, still growling softly at the back of his throat. There was a thick trickle of dark blood leaking down between his fingers. In a tiny, dwindling part of his consciousness, Jan was aware of another slim arrow that suddenly punctured Henja's chest, followed by yet another in quick succession, and the man stumbled backward out of his vision.

The numb feeling inside him grew and Jan crumpled forward onto the pink carpet. A shadow moved over him. Someone spoke in a muffled voice, but Jan's mouth wouldn't move. He slipped out of consciousness.

. . . .

Raf woke up late the following morning having spent the night in the mossy grove again. He'd gone on another stroll in the middle of the night having been unable to get to sleep after what had happened with Bhothy; he still had questions circling round and round in his head. How had he done it? How had he…*cured* him? The man had been dying!

He strolled back toward the village, dreading the inevitable encounter with his parents and their questions about where he'd been. He dragged his feet as he found his way onto the path leading up to his home and then saw Nedrick hailing him from further down toward the commons.

He jogged up to Raf and looked at him curiously. "There you are. You completely disappeared yesterday. Where'd you go?"

"Oh, just for a long walk. I needed to get some stuff off my chest."

"Mm-hmm," replied Nedrick, nodding carefully. "You sure everything's all right? You look exhausted."

Raf nodded. "Fine. Didn't sleep well, that's all. What are you up to?"

"You don't know?" asked Nedrick.

"Know what? What's happened?"

"You've missed everything! First, we had some visitors yesterday. *Dholaki,* Raf! Real, live iMahli drummers here in Eirdale!"

"No...!"

"It's true! I wanted to hang around and see them play this morning, but then everything went crazy because Dad arrived back from Three Ways this morning and the Council went straight into an emergency meeting. I didn't even know he was back until I saw his cart at home; he must have driven through the night. Something bad's probably happened, but you know they won't tell us anything till the meeting's finished. They were going to put on a huge feast for the *dholaki* later this evening, but there's probably going to be a village meeting before that about whatever's happened. That's why I came to find you."

"Where's Cisc?"

"Oh yeah, I forgot about Brunnow. He's taking a junior group out tracking."

"The lucky git!"

"No kidding. Orikon went off somewhere yesterday, so Cisc is covering for him. It's been a crazy morning."

"Sounds it," muttered Raf. "Well, we better head up there then, and see what the story is." As they started off, the village chimes suddenly jolted into action again.

"Guess we're right on time," said Raf. "I hope there's something to eat, I'm starving."

"I'm not so sure," said Nedrick, looking worried.

"Why not? What's wrong? I'm sure w-"

"Just listen, you idiot! Don't you know your own village chimes yet? That's the emergency announcement."

Raf blushed and covered it up by peering at some groups of villagers ahead of them who had quietened at the chimes. As one, they all turned and made their way toward the Council offices.

When the boys arrived, a big crowd had already built up and there was a rumbling of anxious voices everywhere. They pushed their way toward the front until they reached an area in front of the Council chambers. The Foreman walked out, followed by the Council members and they stood in a group on the dais above the crowd. Raf saw his mother standing next to a very pale Councilman Tovier, a furious look on her face.

The Foreman rested a hand on the ledge in front of him. He looked down briefly, and then said in a loud voice, "News has reached us this afternoon from Three Ways. It is with a heavy heart that I tell you…the Festival has been cancelled."

Raf would have expected an explosion of outrage from the crowd, but instead, there was silence as hundreds of people drew their breaths in shock and simply stared up at the Foreman.

"Believe me when I say that no-one is more distraught about this than me and the other Council members, and we plan to register our strongest disapproval of what has happened and learn how this all came about. Nonetheless, the die is cast. We will not be hosting the Aeril Festival this year."

He looked bleakly at the crowd and then turned to lead the Council back into the chambers. Raf and Nedrick stared at each other.

"Man, I wish I could hear what they were talking about."

"Hmm."

Raf turned to him. "What are you thinking, Ned?"

"I don't plan to miss out on this and I think I know a way for us to...well, -"

"Don't even tell me; just go and I'll follow."

Nedrick nodded and walked nonchalantly away from the stunned crowd toward a bamboo thicket that grew alongside an olive tree. He looked around as they approached and then, seeing that no one had noticed them, quickly scrambled through the dense bamboo poles to the side of the olive tree, closely followed by Raf.

"All right, Gency. Feeling agile?"

"Right behind you."

They easily scaled the wrinkled olive trunk to where it branched and spread out, following a thick branch that grew back toward the Council sequoia. With the dense wiry leaves to hide them, the boys crawled along until they reached where the branch ran closest to the sequoia trunk.

"What now?" whispered Raf. "We still can't get in from here."

"We don't need to, idiot," replied Nedrick. "Just shut up and listen through one of these room vents." He straddled the branch and lent down low to hold his ear against a small round opening in the tree bark.

Raf punched him on his shoulder and then looked to find another one of the vents which served as the airing holes for the windowless Council rooms. He eased himself up a few feet along a ridge in the bark and found another one. As soon as he put his ear to it, the sound of voices drifted up. He smiled slyly at Nedrick who tapped his head and winked.

"*- doesn't matter though! It's still unacceptable, Tarvil."

"I know, dear, I know. I'm merely pointing out that Brinchley obviously feels he has a duty to the Forest as a whole and has taken this decision t-"

"Rubbish," came the voice of Dr. Allid. "He's done this to further his own ends, nothing less. That man would sell his own family to make a few coins."

"He's always been greedy," snapped Leiana, "and now he's blatantly gone behind our backs to steal the Festival from us. What did he think? That he wouldn't be caught?"

Nedrick looked up at Raf and grimaced uneasily.

"Which is why, Leiana," came the calming voice of the Foreman, "we must approach him and get to the bottom of all this. It doesn't make sense at all. Even bearing in mind that whole unfortunate incident with the trader. I've met Councilman Brinchley many times, and although I don't care for him personally, I think this is beyond him."

"How can you be so blind, Eliath?" replied Leiana again. "It's not just him, it's that scheming Allium who'll be behind this. You know he's always had an appetite for power."

"Leiana, dear, calm down. What we need to do now is make sure we look after our people here, and send up a party to see what exactly has happened. Until then, there's no point ranting uselessly."

"I hate t'change the topic," came the frail voice of Jover, "but I'm rather worried about the strange reports around some of our out-lying farms. I've sp-"

"Do you really think it's the time to be bringing up *farming* issues, Jover? Now, when so many other more urgent things are snapping at our heels?"

Raf rolled his eyes at his mother's acid tone, and Nedrick smothered a chuckle with his hand.

"Beg your pardon, Leiana, but I 'spect you wouldn't 'ave that same sentiment when this time next year we suddenly 'ave a food shortage an' widespread disease."

Leiana made a scoffing noise, but it was Vince who interrupted. "Disease? What are you saying, Jover? What's this?"

"Well, I've been speakin' to some of the farmers who live far out on the eastside o' the village and a few on the nor'west side and...well, there've been complaints of rotten smells. Loads of 'em. I spoke to Manny about it and he said he found a few rank trees but nothing else. It ain't goin' to be dead animals as they'd be finished off quickly by scavengers, and we ain't found none, anyway. I wouldn't have bothered you with it but it seems odd t'have it on two opposite sides of the village, y'see."

"Hmm, right," responded the Foreman. "Sounds... ominous. I really could do without any other challenges at the moment. What do you think, Vince? You know more about trees than anyone else in the Forest."

"I'm not sure. I'd need to see more."

"Well," interjected Tarvil calmly, "unless you disagree, Foreman, why not have Vince head out with Jover and Manny tomorrow morning and see what they can find? I hate to point it out, but they don't have anything to do now really what with... well..."

"Yes, I see what you mean," replied the Foreman. "What do you think, Jover?"

"Absolu'ely, Foreman. I think we need t'get to the bottom of it, whatever the case."

"Good. Well let's sort that out. Leiana, can I ask y-"

Whatever the Foreman was going to say was cut off by the sudden ringing of the chimes for the second time. It wasn't a structured chime pattern - nothing musical or traditional - just a frantic beating of the gongs. On the branch, the boys looked back over their shoulders and, before they even saw the crowd, they heard it: a throng streaming in from the direction of the Hunton Daire passage.

The two scrambled back along the olive branch and crawled across as fast as they could to the trunk and then down to the ground. Running toward the noise, they rounded the corner and came face to face with the crowd. Orikon was staggering along the path carrying someone on his back. Raf stared at him. Sweat poured off his head, his clothes were drenched, and a terrified expression tightened his usually somber face as he struggled with the weight of the body.

Questions were flying through the air from everyone and Raf turned to Nedrick to say something when his friend elbowed him in his ribs and, in a shocked voice said, "Look! On his back! It looks like... It's Jan Ferthen!"

It was indeed Jan. Except that something was very wrong. His head and body were flopping around uselessly as Orikon staggered toward the Council chambers. For a brief moment, his head tilted sideways and Raf saw his face and gasped in shock. The woodsmith's eyes were half open and a ghastly yellow color, his cheeks sunken and sallow. His whole body seemed to have shriveled up.

"Gency!" Raf saw Orikon beckoning him frantically. "Where's your father? Where's the Council?"

Both boys pointed to the sequoia. "Inside!"

"Get Briana Ferrows. Now! Quick, bring her here!" he yelled, and then stumbled up to the chamber door.

Raf bolted away toward the nursing rooms to find the village's healer. It barely took him half a minute to get there at a full sprint, and soon he found her in one of the medical rooms.

"Dr. Ferrows! Dr. Ferrows! They need you at -" Raf broke off panting, "- at the Council quarters. Something's happened to Jan Ferthen! Orikon's brought him; he carried him on his back!"

Eirdale's doctor looked up, her long braided hair swishing behind her petite frame. "The woodsmith?"

Raf nodded. "He looks really, really ill. You must hurry, please!"

She put the watering flask down and then, seizing a small medicine case from the table, started jogging quickly after him. By the time they reached the commons, a massive crowd had built up. Raf saw Nedrick doing his best to get people to move out the way to let Dr. Ferrows move through. She passed through the crowd without a word and walked up to the door which was immediately opened by Dalton Pereneson. The second she stepped in, Dalton closed the door behind her and the crowd waited, whispering uneasily.

Hardly any time had passed before she opened the door again and called to one of the farmers nearby to bring a wagon to the door. Raf noticed that her face had gone very white. When the wagon had been brought to the entrance, the door opened a bit wider and Orikon and Tarvil made their way out carrying the limp form of Jan. They lay him gently down on the cart and walked beside it as the two goats were ushered along toward the medical rooms. It was a grim wake that followed the wagon and its cargo; the sight of Jan's ghastly, gaunt face and wrinkled skin silenced one and all.

. . . .

Dr. Ferrows looked up from the bedside to glance at the oval window through which the nervous chatter of the villagers filtered.

"Should I send them away?" asked the Foreman.

She shook her head. "No. I can sympathize with them. The

cancellation of the Festival hasn't even really sunk in yet, and now this attack on Jan." She dabbed a damp cloth on the woodsmith's face. "Tell me again, Orikon. When you came across the attack on him, did you see a weapon? Anything that might have carried poison?"

Orikon, who had been standing stock-still in the corner of the room, shook his head and whispered, "Nothing."

She looked up at him questioningly. "And the attackers?"

"Just one. A thin, pale man. When I shot him with the first arrow he...pulled it out. Then he tried to attack Jan again."

She watched his face. "You killed him with the other arrows you shot?"

Orikon shook his head. "He ran away. But..."

"Yes?"

The brawny hunter looked down at the floor, his jaws clenching. Finally, he looked back at her. "I cannot understand it."

"What, Orikon?" urged Dr. Ferrows. "I've never known you to quail at anything."

He looked at each of the Council members standing around him. "Three times in the chest with arrows – three times, I hit him! It isn't possible to be able to run away. The man was not normal. He -"

"Orikon," Leiana said, striding in front of him, "this is the very last thing we need to have spreading around Eirdale. A killer who can't be killed?" She made a dismissive noise. "If you say you hit him directly, I believe you; but I also know in the heat of the moment, things can get confused." She ignored the steely look that flared up on Orikon's face and carried on. "You say you hit him? Well, if he's injured badly – and he must be - he can't have got very far. Could you track him?"

There was a wet cough behind them. They spun around and stared at Jan who had opened his eyes and was staring groggily at them.

"Ferthen!" hissed Orikon.

The woodsmith tried to open his mouth but his face contorted in pain.

"Easy, Jan," urged Dr. Ferrows. "You need to conserve your strength."

The woodsmith nodded almost imperceptibly and then whispered, "What happened?"

"You were attacked, but Orikon scared him off."

The Foreman sat down on the edge of the bed. "A young carpenter in Three Ways overheard a conversation and sent a pigeon to Orikon. He was able to get there just in time."

"A carpenter?" Jan's eyes started closing again.

"Tunit. You may owe him your life for his quickness in alerting Orikon."

"Yes," Jan whispered. "It must have been that M-" He arched as a seizure crushed the wind out of his lungs.

"Easy, Jan, try not to talk too much," said Dr. Ferrows. "Where does it hurt the most?"

"Everywhere," came his feeble response. "I will soon be like…the other two."

"Which other two?" said Leiana and the Foreman at the same time.

But Jan's eyes had closed again, his breathing shallower. A line of sweat moved slowly down his sunken cheek.

Orikon spoke up from the back of the room. "Two men – mercenaries, maybe - were killed before by the same man. But," he glanced at Leiana, "I don't understand how. When I found their bodies, it was if they'd been lying dead for months." He stopped speaking and stared at the wall, horror written all over his face.

"We're not discussing this further," stated Leiana firmly. "There's enough emotion running wild as it is. It sounds like it can only have been poison."

The Foreman nodded. "I'm sorry to have to ask you to do this after running as much as you already have today, Orikon…" The hunter gestured for him to carry on. "I need you to take a party of men, arm yourselves, and track this man down. And quickly. He can't have gone far. Don't enter Three Ways, though. Not until we find out more about why there are mercenaries running around our Forest." Orikon nodded and immediately left.

The Foreman beckoned to the others to join him on the other side of the room. He glanced back at Jan and then up at Dr. Ferrows. "What do you think, Briana?" he whispered.

"Poison, in my opinion. His body's in a bad way, Eliath. If we don't find a way to heal him, I fear the worst. When he wakes – *if* he wakes – hopefully he can shed some light on what's going on. Because, I've never seen anything like this before." She shook her head. "But of one thing there's no doubt. He's dying."

"You can't help at all?" asked Tarvil.

"It is beyond my skills. All we can do for now is look after him as best we can and let his body fight it."

Later on, Raf and Cisco sat idly at an empty bench in the village commons. The chimes had been rung a while ago to invite people to the feast, but only a handful of people had arrived. The *dholaki* were talking amongst themselves as they ate at one of the tables. Some movement drew his attention and Raf looked across to the iMahlis' wagon which was parked fairly close to where they were sitting. In the back, the fourth iMahli had changed position and was now facing away. In the flickering light of the lamps, Raf caught sight of a pretty vicious-looking wound across his right shoulder.

"Not much of an audience for these guys," said Cisco. "I know things have flopped with the Festival but, still, what a waste! Your mom must be furious."

"My mom?"

"She's the one who invited them."

Raf frowned. "We haven't spoken much recently, to be honest. But, I don't think she'll worry too much really, not with Jan sick and the Festival cancelled now."

"I suppose. But it's still a lot of money to throw away."

Raf looked blankly at him. Cisco suddenly laughed and shook his head. "You really don't know, do you? My aunt was there when they arrived and apparently they wanted payment from your mom. She's paid them a lot of coin to be here." Cisco grimaced. "I don't think the Foreman will be too happy with her paying them in advance now that it's all for nothing."

Raf mulled over this news. The school chimes went off for evening choir practice and they looked at each other, and then simultaneously shook their heads, settling down more comfortably on the ground.

"If Ottery thinks we're missing out on a chance to see these guys play..."

They looked up as one of the *dholaki* started drumming out a rhythm on a small jembe to the delight of the tiny audience.

The soft breeze picked up and made the lamp near them flicker. It was getting dark now, and not just because it was late. There was a huge storm brewing somewhere and the clouds were speeding toward them in dark, bulbous mounds, with muffled booms of thunder echoing through the trees. It was going to get very wet, and soon.

"Typical," said Cisco. "*Just* as they pull out their drums."

. . . .

The next morning, on the very western border of Eirdale, a small group of villagers clambered awkwardly through the dense brush in the steady drizzle. They made their way underneath a natural bridge that had been formed by the collapse of a tree trunk and found themselves entering a small but deep basin that was sprawling with banyans.

"Over here," called Farley.

Vince strolled over to where the wiry man was standing. He sniffed the air. "I think you're right, that's got to be it. It's pretty revolting."

"Is it an animal carcass?" ventured one of the others.

"Possibly," admitted Vince. "It's far too strong to be from a plant. But it'd still need to be something big to give off such a smell. Or maybe more than one." He looked around, scanning the Forest. "I wonder what sort of pack animals are living in these banyan patches."

"Banyans? I thought these were elm trees?" asked a young apprentice hunter.

Vince looked in his direction with a slightly disapproving

look. "They used to be elms but they've been taken over by banyans so that almost all of the elms here are dead now. Disappeared." He pointed to a tree on their left. "You can see here that the banyan is growing around a live elm; but it won't be long, a few years or so, before the elm is choked to death and all that's left is the banyan. Understand?" He frowned at the blank expression on the lad's face, and walking up to the tree, he tapped on a thin pole that linked the branch above with the ground. "You see this? Do you know what it is?"

"An elm trunk?"

Vince hissed with impatience. "Pah! Where are the branches and leaves, then?"

The youngster stared up at where it seemed to connect with an overhanging elm branch and shrugged.

"It's a root. A banyan root. The seed was probably deposited up there by a bird, and then it grew down here until it reached the ground. It slowly became thicker and thicker until now, it looks like this. See?"

The boy made an 'o' shape with his mouth. "So, are there lots of these banyans in the Forest?"

"Banyans are all over the Forest. You'd probably find that half the trees that grew here have been replaced by banyans. Very clever trees. Parasitic, killing off whatever they grow on. They're opportunists and -" He pushed past the boy as a shout came from ahead. "Jover?"

"The stench!" Jover was stumbling back. "Comin' from there where the ground dips!"

"Are you sure?"

"It's the same smell as I smelt over on the sou'east patch. Exact same. It's 'orrible..." Jover took his flat cap off and held it over his mouth.

Vince walked cautiously forward, peering around the ground, looking for any signs of a carcass or something dead. The rain was heavier now and it drummed down through the canopy, splashing on the tangled path and running along the sloping ground in front of him. He walked forward a bit more and then stopped where the smell was strongest. It was exactly where he was: the lowest section of the depression, but he still couldn't see anything.

He beckoned to Farley, rubbing the rain out of his eyes. "Well, we know it's here. My guess is it's buried." He crouched down and examined the ground nearest him. "Jover, get one of the boys to bring me a spade, would you? I want to find out what it is before this rain washes it all away."

. . . .

By the afternoon, the rain had finally eased up somewhat and could be heard as a continual hissing sound on the canopy. Water streamed in rivulets down trees, and between the trunks there was a thick, drenching mist. The two boys sleepily watched as occasional heavy drops made little ring-shaped impressions in the dirt. Behind them, inside the hollow snag they were leaning against, the swishing echo of running water could be heard.

"Hello, boys."

They both craned their heads up to see Tarvil approaching and Cisco scrambled to his feet, uttering a quick, "Afternoon, Councilman Gency."

Tarvil smiled back briefly in response and sat down next to them. "Challenging day, yesterday."

"No kidding," replied Raf. "How's Jan this afternoon? Any better?"

"He's holding on. Just. Problem is we've no idea what's wrong with him. And until we do, we can't figure out how to help."

The boys looked forward glumly at this news.

Tarvil looked over at Cisco. "And how are you, Master Brunnow? Planning to travel soon?"

"For my sojourn? Absolutely!" responded Cisco. "I've

already got it planned and everything."

"Where's your choice?"

"The idiot's picked the most dull place he could find: Jaysonbury," said Raf with a shake of his head.

Tarvil held a finger to his mouth thoughtfully. "I seem to remember a friend of mine sojourned there when we were your age. I can't recall much about the place other than their reputation for strong rum, bear-wrestling and, if I remember correctly, the unusual occurrence of green-eyes – especially among the women."

"Really?" asked Raf, grinning. He slowly turned to his friend and nudged him in his ribs. "Funny how you didn't mention that bit to me."

Cisco shrugged. "Only room for one, you see. Don't need any competition." He grinned mischievously at Raf. "You should be concentrating on things here, anyway."

"What's this?" asked Tarvil curiously.

"Nothing," snapped Raf, giving Cisco a dark look. "He's just ta-"

"Your son, Councilman, has his greedy eyes on none other than Councilman Pereneson's lovely daughter."

"Rhani?"

Raf blushed bright red and picked up a piece of wood lying next to him, toying with it.

Tarvil smiled and then looked up on hearing a noise. "Aah," he said quietly. "Prepare yourself, Raf."

Raf's head jerked up. "Rhani?"

"No. Your mother."

Leiana came walking around an oak *Ancient's* trunk side by side with the Foreman, and when she caught sight of Tarvil and the boys, she made a bee-line for them.

"Good evening Councilwoman Gency, evening Foreman," said Cisco, suddenly uncomfortable amidst all the authority.

"Tarvil, we've decided to send a party off when Orikon gets back." She lifted a finger fiercely as she spoke, waving it around like a baton. "We must confront Brinchley directly and get to the bottom of this Festival nonsense."

"Ma'am, will we get the Festival next year, at least?" asked Cisco.

"Of course."

Tarvil added, "Assuming no permanent damage has been done to our relationship with Miern. A pity Jan hasn't able to tell us more about what's been happening in Three Ways before now."

"Yes, that would certainly be useful information, but we can't wait. It may be that he doesn't recover," said Leiana.

The Foreman, in a bid to change the topic, looked down at Cisco and said, "I understand from your father that you've chosen Jaysonbury for your sojourn?"

"News travels fast, sir," replied Cisco with a quick smile. "I have a cousin who lives in North Hordham and they're going to help me out."

Leiana nodded approvingly. "That sounds very good, Cisco. An interesting area with some lovely music. Their lutists, in particular, are known to be superb."

"Yeah, that's exactly why he's going Mom, for the lutists," mumbled Raf sarcastically.

"At least he is using his sojourn as a learning opportunity and not as a way to annoy people."

"Mom, just leav-"

"- *and,* he has a decent chance of actually making it back alive," she snapped.

"Leiana, dear, perh-"

"Don't tell me to calm down, Tarvil! I'll not have my son stroll off into danger. He will find no music there. He will find no culture there. He -" She spun around to stare as one of the *dholaki* suddenly began drumming a loud, energetic rhythm. "I do wish they'd be a little quieter," she said through clenched teeth.

"Well, at least you're getting some value for the money," Raf muttered.

Her face tightened and a livid red bloomed on her cheeks. "How dare you, Raf!"

Tarvil, eyebrows furrowed. "What's this?"

"In case you didn't know, mom paid those drummers already for the Festival. Seems a bit odd not to enjoy them," said Raf.

"Paid?" said Tarvil.

The Foreman frowned. "I didn't authorize that, Leiana. Whatever possessed you to use the village coffers for this? I'm sure we could have attracted many good musicians without having to pay."

Leiana straightened her stole. "I didn't use the village coffers, Foreman. I used our own." Tarvil tilted his head at her questioningly. "I had to. Real iMahli *dholaki* for the first time in the Aeril Forest? Ever! People would've come from everywhere to see it!"

"Leiana, I really wouldn't have allowed you t-"

"It wasn't your call to make, Foreman, it was mine. You put me in charge of organizing the Festival, and this is what I saw fit to do. I would have covered my costs on the first day – in the first hour - if Brinchley and Allium hadn't played foul!"

Raf looked down at the ground sullenly, a wave of guilt stealing over him. He hadn't really meant to do it. It had just slipped out. A shadow cut across his feet and he saw a group of figures walk up to stand behind Leiana.

"Excuse me, Foreman?"

Leiana turned around, saw that it was Jover, and snapped, "No! Not now, Jover! We don't have time to be talking about smells in the woods. The Foreman has a million more important things to sort out right now. Honestly!"

The old farmer stammered under her furious gaze, folding and unfolding the flat cap he held at his chest. Leiana turned her back on him again but Jover urged, "But, Cou-"

"What do you want?" Her voice rose as she put her hands

on her hips. "Has the broccoli turned *orange*? Have the bees stopped buzzing? Can you not just speak to Vince about whatever it is this time? *Well?*"

"Ma'am, Vince is dead."

"**D**ead?"

Jover nodded and the Foreman stepped forward to take hold of his shoulders as the old man's eyes welled with tears.

"Foreman," said Farley from behind, "we were searching for the rotten smell, and we found a place where it was very strong. Councilman Ghitral was trying to find what it was, but the ground broke under him. It just…opened up and he fell through."

"Broke under him?" Leiana's voice was muffled as she clamped her hands tightly over her mouth.

"Yes, Councilwoman."

"What could've happened?"

"That rotten smell, ma'am, is the trees. The branches underneath were all rotten, that's what the smell was."

"*Underneath* us?" hissed Nathyn.

"Raf," said the Foreman quietly. "The chimes. Now."

. . . .

Raf didn't let up thumping the beater against the huge wooden gong until he heard a faint shout over the booming peals.

"Oy!" yelled Cisco. "Quit! Everybody's here now."

Raf climbed down off the platform, removing the thick woolen ear muffs from his head. "The farmers as well?"

"Raf, I think there are people here from North Hordham! Trust me, you got everyone's attention. Let's just go, I want to find out what's going on."

146

They jogged over to the commons which was absolutely heaving with anxious villagers shivering in the drizzle. The Foreman was standing silently next to a pale-faced Leiana while the rest of the Council spoke quietly amongst themselves to one side. Cisco and Raf made their way up through the crowd as the Foreman stood up and stared out at the faces.

"There has been a terrible incident. Vince Ghitral tragically died this morning." There were gasps from the crowd – not as many as Raf would've expected, but then news always spread quickly in the village – and the Foreman held up his hands. "We are still trying to find out how it happened, but it seems there may be a strange disease affecting some of the trees. It's very important that we work quickly to find out what the cause is and find a solution. Our homes – indeed, our very lives – may depend on it." His booming voice echoed around the commons and every face tilted to hear what he was saying. "There have been some reports recently of a strong rotten smell around Eirdale. I need to know if anyone else here has come across it."

He watched the crowd as there was a quiet humming of people talking amongst themselves. A hand was raised in the middle and the Foreman nodded at him questioningly.

"I live up on the north-west side, Foreman, and I've noticed something foul recently when I've been hunting. Maybe a mile or so out?"

"The north-west side you say?" asked the Foreman. "That's where Vince died. Anyone else?" Another hand tentatively went up. "Damen? You're over on the north-west side as well, aren't you?"

"Yes, sir, but I didn't smell it there, I smelt it on my way to my cousin's home south-west of here in Turner's Grove. Something really nasty. Could never find what it was, though."

The Foreman looked at him and exhaled through pursed lips.

Then another elderly farmer, Sikinos, added, "Now that you mention it, Foreman, if we're talking about something that really reeks, a few of my boys were talking to me about an odd smell on the east farms the other day. We just thought it was some dead animal."

The Foreman lifted his arms once more. "Let's do this, then. How many of you have smelt something rotten in the Forest recently, put up your hands." A scattering of hands lifted in the crowd. "Right," he said, "you lot come here. The rest of you go home. I would seriously suggest that nobody moves far from the village until further notice."

With that he jumped down to the ground. "Raf, go to the Council rooms and bring me the map on the table and a piece of chalk," ordered the Foreman.

Raf came back shortly with a large, detailed map of Eirdale. The Foreman laid it out carefully on a sheltered table and asked the remaining people to plot out where they had smelt the decay with chalk. After the last person had marked it, the Foreman straightened out the map with four mugs and stood back. Eirdale village was in the middle: a rough, circular patch of dots, and the chalk markings were in small clusters that surrounded the village.

"This is incredibly bad," muttered Dr. Allid.

"But, thankfully, no mention of it within the village borders," commented Dalton. "Or on the main paths out of the village."

"Well, what can we do?" demanded Leiana angrily. "There must be a remedy, surely?"

She looked at Dr. Allid who shook his head gravely. "I'm no tree specialist, Leiana; this is beyond me. Vince was the expert. Nobody knew more than him about the Forest."

"So that leaves us standing here on ground that might break open at any moment?"

"But there are no signs of the rot inside the village, Leiana. What we need to do is speak to an expert. *Someone* in the Forest must have some knowledge about this sort of thing. We need to send messengers out to all the other villages."

"When the ground's rotting underneath us?" spluttered Nathyn.

Tarvil felt a tap on his hand and stepped aside to let the scrawny form of Fergus move shyly to stand in front of them.

"Fergus? We're having an important conversation here right now," said Leiana.

"Um, I thought I should tell you that…that…I -"

"What, boy? Out with it," snapped Nathyn.

Resma knelt down facing the boy. "What's wrong Fergus? Don't be afraid to tell us."

Fergus swallowed, keeping his face turned down toward the ground. "When I was traveling here with Mr. Wesp, he made a big fire off the path -"

"In the Forest? You made a *fire* outside one of the fire-pits?" interrupted Leiana furiously. "Surely you must know that's dangerous, Fergus!"

Resma hushed her and turned back to Fergus. "Then what happened?"

"Well, Mrs. Ottery, the fire was going and then the ground broke. There was a really big hole."

"It was probably the fire," said Nathyn. "There's a reason we have these laws! If only these travelers w-"

"No sir, it was *definitely* something in the wood, sir. Mr. Wesp made me climb down to get his bag and I could see the ground where it broke. It smelled really, really horrible like the Foreman said. And it was green like…like old bread."

"He made you climb down into the hole in the ground to get his bag?" asked Tarvil softly.

"Yes, sir; but, don't worry Mr. Gency, I'm a good climber. I've never fallen, except…I did kind of fall down the hole a bit…" He looked uncomfortably at the ground front of him.

"Fergus," said the Foreman, "where did this happen?"

"Well, you know where all the roads turn into one big one to go to Three Ways?"

149

"That's all the way north near *Borilcester!*" came the strained voice of Nathyn. "I just traveled past there!"

"Foreman, you need to make a call now," said Tarvil. "We have to warn the other villages if they don't already know. We must assume the entire Forest is affected and although it's a risk traveling, we need to work together to find a solution urgently. Someone must know something that can help."

"I agree," the Foreman responded. "I'll summon an Overcouncil. We should send pigeons at once."

"We don't have nearly enough, and it's too slow, too many villages. We need people to get here now, immediately, before things get any worse. It'll take some people days to get here as it is, and every hour is precious. We must resort to…desperate measures."

"Then what? What other options?" The Foreman suddenly threw a sharp look at Tarvil. "Do…do you mean what I think you do?" Tarvil nodded firmly.

"What's this? What are you talking about?" asked Leiana.

"The *Ash-knell*."

. . . .

"When our ancestors were chased here by the iMahlis centuries ago, they lived in communities far apart in the Forest and needed to work out a way to call meetings in times of emergency. It had to be something that was quick and effective, so they crafted these Ash trees – four of them – in specific locations through the Aeril Forest."

"Crafted?" asked Dalton.

The Foreman shrugged. "Something like that. Whatever they did, the *Ash-knells* were built to have one main quality."

"And what is that?"

"They're perfect resonating chambers. Basically, huge bells."

"How do they work?" asked Resma.

"No idea," replied the Foreman. He looked at Tarvil who shook his head. "Nobody's used one in generations. But they're supposed to emit a sound that can be heard throughout the entire Forest."

"'Supposed to'? Can you be sure they work? Or that they even exist?" asked Leiana.

"I have to trust that they work. And as for whether they exist, ours is in Jacaranda Dale. My father showed it to me many years ago. Every Foreman knows where their nearest one is."

"What, south-east? Through this huge patch of decay?" stammered Leiana, tapping a heavily chalked area on the map. "That area is one of the worst!"

The Foreman rubbed his head. "It's not *too* far, and there must be some way to get to it safely." He looked upward. "The canopy walkways?"

"They don't go far enough, Foreman. Half way at best."

"Actually, Foreman," came the hesitant voice of Jover, "I've been expandin' my canopy farms a little, and with a new technique I've come up with, it should be possible t'get pretty close, I reckon."

"New techniques, Jover?"

"Well, some rope 'arnesses and pulleys, mostly."

"Aren't you a bit long-in-the-tooth to be swinging around tree-tops these days?" asked Nathyn incredulously.

"You'll 'ave to forgive me, Councilman, when I say 'me', I'm actually referrin' to my apprentice. He's got it down perfectly."

"Who's this?" asked the Foreman. "Can we get him in here right now?"

"He's standin' behind you, Foreman."

They all turned around to look back at Fergus who had a nervous, lopsided grin on his face. He raised a hand and waved it in embarrassment.

"Is that right, Fergus?" said Tarvil. "I've been hearing

stories about your antics up there. Do you think it's possible for us to get to Jacaranda Dale from here? Using the upper canopy?"

"I don't know where that is, sir, but I've been almost all the way to Hunton Daire up there before." Jover patted his shoulder as the young boy beamed a grin back at him.

"Well," said the Foreman reluctantly, "if this young one can do it, then it's worth trying. I wonder if it might be safer to go with someone other than me, in c-"

"I'm sure Raf would be willing to go," said Leiana.

Raf clenched his teeth and started to say something in reply when Cisco added, "If he's going then I'm going as well, Mrs. Gency!" He wrapped an arm around Raf's shoulder and grinned at Leiana.

The Foreman looked at them both dryly. "I suppose that'll do. But no more. And I think we should leave immediately seeing as the rain's letting up. It'll take us a good while to get there and speed is of the essence."

He looked at Fergus. "What do we need to take with us, lad?"

"Nothing, Foreman. All the stuff's at the top of *Nviro*. I'll get it when we're up there."

The Foreman nodded and strode off past the Council.

"Good luck," muttered Dr. Allid.

The Foreman turned back to face them as the three boys walked past. "If this works, we will have guests from every corner of the Aeril Forest here, hopefully within days, in some cases, hours. Get yourselves prepared for an Overcouncil. Leiana, you know what to do."

"And the funeral?" asked Tarvil.

"Do it today."

Raf and the other two waited for the Foreman to catch up and then set off toward *Nviro*, the sound of the Council singing the *farwelayre* fading into the distance behind them.

"**H**e's quicker than I thought he'd be," said Raf under his breath. The two boys were standing on a small platform, staring up at the muscular frame of the Foreman who was scaling *Nviro* above them.

"Yeah," agreed Cisco. "He'd probably look even more impressive if he wasn't next to monkey-boy, though. Look at the little guy go!"

Above the Foreman, Fergus was using hanging vines to help haul himself up the trunk, swinging and jumping acrobatically toward the canopy.

"You just wait till he grows up and weighs what we do," said Cisco. "Come on, let's get after them." He took hold of the ladder and hoisted himself up.

They climbed for another few hundred feet until they were on the exact wooden decking that the boys had been on only a few days before.

"All right, Fergus," said the Foreman. "I'd say we have maybe three hours before it gets too dark to climb so we'd better get going." He stood up and peered toward the southeast Forest. "What do we need for our little expedition?"

Fergus disappeared up the trunk into a dense clump of leaves. There was some rustling, and a few minutes later, a warning: "Watch out!"

A huge coil of vine-rope flopped down, followed by a bulging, rattling sack. Fergus sprang down lightly after it and dusted his hands off.

"That's it?" asked Raf.

Fergus nodded enthusiastically and opened up the sack to show them some dark brown ironwood harnesses. Each one was connected firmly by a curved rod to a chunky wooden wheel.

"Mr. Jover made the wheels. I don't really need this, but I don't think you'll be able to cross some of the bits."

"I suppose I should really watch my weight a bit more," said the Foreman blithely. He winked at the boy who grinned back and then took hold of the rope to loop it around his shoulders. "Let's go."

Fergus lead them to a stout walkway which they mounted in single file and followed for a few hundred feet toward some oak *Ancients*. The wooden slats creaked under their weight and although the thick new ropes they held on to seemed solid, Raf found the swaying of the bridge a little disconcerting - especially walking so high above the canopy in the open air. Looking through the cracks between the wood, he could see a crown layer some two hundred feet below him, a rough quilt-work of dark, leafy tree-tops that was punctuated here and there with a splash of floral colors. Scattered around were flat patches on the *Ancients'* branches identifying canopy farms, and connecting them all, a sprawling network of walkways like the one they were on, giving the appearance of a gigantic spider's web.

When they reached the end of the bridge, they arrived at a large wooden platform that connected two adjacent oak *Ancient* trunks.

"Here we are," said Fergus.

"I'm bushed," said Cisco, flopping down to rest on his back against the heavy side-netting. "Ahh... This is so comfortable! A nap would be perfect."

The Foreman slipped the ropes off his shoulder. "No time for that Master Brunnow. Still a fair ways to go."

"It's going to be much harder from here, Cisco," said Fergus.

"I'm almost scared to ask this, monkey-boy, but, what's your plan?"

Fergus smiled shyly and turned toward the opposite end. "We've got to get over there." He pointed and they gazed out along the solid floor of green crowns to where, sprouting out of the foliage, was a twisted olive *Ancient*. It looked strangely like an old woman's hand. Between the nearest branch and where they stood was a deep gully, perhaps eighty yards wide.

"So, how do we get there?" asked Cisco.

"We have to use the harnesses. But wait for me to get it all ready, okay? Can you hold this?" said Fergus, handing him the end of the rope, which was on the floor in a neat coil. "And don't let go!"

Cisco stared in shock as the young boy sprinted to the end of the deck and launched himself into the air. He somehow latched onto the supple ends of a spray of thin branches he flew past, which sent him spinning through the air toward a heavy vine. As soon as he reached it, he grabbed hold of it, sending it swinging wildly up into the air. He waited for a few moments until it steadied and then crawled up quickly, wedging the rope between his feet as he reached up for more purchase.

The rope whipped and rustled as it played out, and Cisco wrapped the end around his hand, steadying himself. He felt a tug on his belt from behind and looked around to see the Foreman grabbing it.

"Just in case." The Foreman grinned at him.

Cisco gulped and turned back to stare at Fergus who was now running, stooped low, along another thick branch. He leaped off and caught hold of another hanging vine which swung him toward the olive *Ancient's* main trunk. Catching hold of the edges of a crevice in the bark, he immediately clambered his way up, taking no time at all to get to the branch he'd first pointed out opposite them. Looping the rope around a waist-thick stump of bark, he fastened it securely.

"Our turn, I think," said the Foreman. His face had gone a

slightly green color as he peeled his hand off Cisco's belt and brushed the hair back out of his eyes.

"I'll go first," said Raf. He found himself slipping into one of the harnesses, wondering why he'd volunteered. "No idea what I'm doing, though."

Behind him, the Foreman heaved on the rope until it lifted in the air, forming a taut line down to the other tree, and then tied it firmly around a thick branch behind them. Then he joined Cisco and they peered at the wheel contraption that Raf was fiddling with.

"Any idea how you attach yourself to this thing? Does it just clip on or what?"

"It's a bit daft of him, actually," said Cisco, "leaving us here clueless. And what are we supposed to do with the rope when we're all across? It doesn't untie itself, you know."

The Foreman scratched his head irritably as the three of them stood examining the harness.

"Back!" came the voice of Fergus from behind them.

"What the… How…?" stuttered Cisco, jerking in fright.

"No good you all coming across and leaving the rope here. We'll need it a few more times still," said Fergus brightly.

"Of course. Er…that's what we were just saying," said Cisco. The Foreman barked out a laugh and patted Cisco's shoulder.

Fergus took the rope from Raf, twisting it into a loop, and then slotted it through the buckle so that it held securely. Then he reached up to slip it onto the rope above them in one easy motion.

"There we go, Raf. Now just hold on to the sides of the harness and make sure you use your feet to land against the tree. The first time I did it, I missed it and almost fell off!" He stood back watching Raf excitedly.

"Right. I can do this," said Raf, taking a deep breath. Before he had time to even think about it, he made himself step up to the edge. He grabbed the harness tightly with his hands and, squeezing his eyes shut, he pulled his feet up off the ground.

Nothing happened. He hung there, swaying slightly in the wind.

Fergus sidled up to him and whispered, "You need to run at it a bit, Raf. It's quite flat."

Behind him, there was a snorting noise. Raf swung around to see Cisco covering his mouth, his shoulders bobbing up and down. The Foreman hid a smile with the back of his hand.

He cursed under his breath and lowered his feet to the ground again before stepping a few feet back from the edge. "You're sure this is safe?" he asked, nervously poking the buckle.

Fergus nodded. "Go fast, though, Raf. You don't want to get stuck in the middle."

Raf peered down the long rope and then nodded firmly. He rocked backward and then sprinted awkwardly up to the edge before launching himself into the air. There was a moment of weightlessness where he felt his stomach fly into his throat, but then the wheel caught on the vine-rope. Raf's weight was held and he found himself speeding smoothly down the slide. He was flying! He couldn't make out any details below him, only blurs of color as he sped over patches of jasmine and cherry blossom and honeysuckle. There was even a flash of a flying lourie at one stage, its gorgeous red and green plumage flaring up in the sun briefly as it passed below Raf.

He was so mesmerized by the flight that he only remembered about the warning from Fergus a few seconds from landing. Frantically raising his legs, he crashed through a thick bush of leaves and then saw the massive tree trunk racing toward him. Even with his legs taking the majority of the collision, he smacked against his side heavily, knocking the wind out of himself. He reached up in pain to unhook the rope from the buckle and then flopped onto his back on the thick branch.

"Raf!" came a shout across the gully. "Are you all right?"

He lifted his arm and gave a feeble thumbs-up.

The Foreman came hurtling down the rope a while later, although he had more luck with his landing and managed to run in comfortably, stopping well before the trunk.

Cisco took a massive leap and came flying down the rope, but to his dismay, he somehow managed to spin himself around so that he was speeding down backward. Screaming in a high pitched voice, he slid toward them, legs kicking violently. Raf and the Foreman watched as he approached the branch they were on, and just before he crashed into the tree, the Foreman jumped in front of him and caught the struggling boy, taking the brunt of the force with his chest. Cisco's scream was cut off by the jarring impact while the Foreman merely grunted and let the boy down so he could stand on his own.

"I almost died!" he stammered.

Raf held his stomach and laughed until he couldn't breathe anymore. "You clown!" he wept, pointing at Cisco's bright red face.

"Shut up, you!" snapped Cisco. "You're hardly one to talk with blood all over your face."

Raf reached up and felt a bruise where he had collided with the tree; he had a bloody nose. "Great," he muttered. "But at least I didn't do a peacock impression sliding down the wrong way..." He laughed again, wiping his nose on his sleeve.

The Foreman dryly shook his head. "All right, you two, we've got a long way to go. Come on."

"What about Fergus?" asked Cisco.

"If you'd been paying attention instead of bleating at each other like two goats, you'd notice that he's untied the other end and is almost back now."

They both turned to watch as the boy leaped off a vine and scrambled up to the branch they were on. The Foreman nodded approvingly to him and then hauled in the rope, coiling it neatly on the floor until the end came slithering up through the branches below.

"Err...how many more of those do we have to do, Fergus?" asked Raf, getting to his feet.

"Not many. Maybe four?"

Raf groaned and cast a pained look at Cisco, who said, "At least the rain's eased up a bit now."

. . . .

There was a knock at the Council chamber door and Leiana broke off mid-sentence. "Come in."

The oak door swung open and a familiar chiseled face appeared. "Orikon!" said Resma in surprise.

"You found him?" asked Nathyn.

The tanned hunter shook his head. "No sign of him. I tracked him all the way back up to the crossroads at Borilcester." Nathyn cursed and slammed his fist down on the table.

"Anything else?" asked Tarvil.

"Nothing," replied Orikon. "All I found were the bodies, a map and Jan's bag."

"A map?" butted in Leiana. "Jan had a map? Of what? He wouldn't need a map."

"It's... Well, you should probably see for yourself, Councilwoman," said Orikon.

He laid open a rolled parchment on the table and moved back to let them all see. After only a few seconds, an eruption of exclamations and curses filled the room. Tarvil took a measured glance at the map and then retreated to one side to stare out the window thoughtfully.

"This is unacceptable!" ranted Leiana, waving her finger in the air.

"These were given out in Miern?" said Nathyn. "Brinchley lied right to my face!"

Leiana's voice rose another notch. "And the *Capital* of the Aeril Forest? The pompous swine!"

"There must be more to this," said Dalton.

Tarvil nodded. "We can't jump to conclusions here; we have no idea who else is involved and it m-"

"Oh, this is Allium's doing all right," said Leiana. "It reeks of him and that Brinchley!"

"What's interesting, though," said Tarvil, "is that these were made quite a while ago, which would explain the scarceness of traders this season; a mere handful compared to last year. I imagine that most traders and travelers – especially new ones - remained at Three Ways. Why wouldn't they when we don't even appear to exist on this map?" He grimaced. "Which obviously doesn't bode well in the future for us – or anyone other than Three Ways." He shook his head, sighing, and looked up at the hunter. "There's been an incident, Orikon. Something's happened since you left that presents us with an even greater challenge than all this." Orikon frowned as he took in their serious expressions. "You may be wondering why Vince isn't here."

"Last one," said Fergus. He took the rope and disappeared. The others stood wearily and gazed at the lush purple crowns splayed out in front of them, keeping an eye on the fleeting figure of the boy as he crawled his way along a thick branch a few hundred feet away.

"I love jacarandas," said Raf quietly. He wiped the sweat away from his forehead and stepped down to the tiny platform the other two were lounging on. The Foreman and Cisco grunted in agreement.

Off to their left there was a huge spruce crown which was overrun with chattering capuchins, unnerved by the presence of the foresters. From somewhere below them came the squawking of parrots, and in the slender elm that was next to them, Cisco spotted a small vine-snake that slowly unwound itself from one of the branches to slide away from them.

"Disgusting things," he muttered. "One of these days I'll be happy climbing, reach to grab a branch and you just know I'll end up holding a blimmin' snake's tail."

A faint whistle drifted across the gully and the Foreman looked to where Fergus was waving from a branch in the jacaranda *Ancient.* "Here we go."

Experienced as they were now, the three of them were across the gorge quickly, and a short while later they all gathered on a branch underneath the purple crowns.

"Now what?"

The Foreman turned to them. "I will show you where this tree is, but," he scratched his head, "I have no idea how this *Ash-knell* works. I hope it's simple."

The boys followed him along the branch into the midst of the purple grove, climbing down onto the lower, thicker branches. They eventually came to a strange section where the jacaranda trunks formed a closed circle of sorts, with foliage filling the gaps between them.

"Funny how gloomy it is as you get lower," commented Cisco. "You never realize how much darker it is under the canopy until you've been up here for a bit. Makes me wish I listened to Yurgin a bit better in class and m-"

"Cisco," said the Foreman. "Could you keep your thoughts to yourself for a bit?"

"Sorry, sir." Cisco grimaced at Raf who shrugged, and the group moved on silently.

The Foreman made his way up to the circle of giant trunks and then the four of them edged through the foliage on one of the branches that penetrated the dark enclosure. They pushed aside the dainty clusters of leaves and, as their eyes adjusted to the darkness inside, they realized they had reached their goal.

A huge, dark tower of a tree came into focus. It had no branches or leaves; it was simply a thick, cylindrical trunk that stretched down into the murky depths below, and grew up straight as an arrow to disappear into the thick crowns above.

"That doesn't look right," said Cisco. "How is it so perfectly smooth? Not even the Council's sequoia *Ancient* is that perfect!"

The Foreman stared thoughtfully at it.

"Are we supposed to beat it with a stick or something?" asked Cisco.

"That seems logical; it's called a knell after all. Maybe there's a beater somewhere?" replied the Foreman.

Cisco walked along the branch to the trunk and reached out to give it a hard rap with the back of his hand. There was a dead, muffled sound and he scowled, rubbing his bruised knuckles. "Nope. *Way* too hard. Feels like it's completely solid."

The four of them climbed their way around the trunk, hopping from branch to branch of the surrounding jacarandas. They tried beating it with sticks, kicking it and slapping it, but nothing worked. Eventually, they gave up and sat down.

"You know," said the Foreman, pointing at a section of the trunk near them, "if you look at it from this angle, it's almost like there's a round bit of lighter wood just there."

"Oh yeah..." said Cisco. "That's definitely not natural. It's almost a perfect circle." He walked up to it and peered closely at the trunk. The circle of lighter wood was about two feet in diameter, and exactly in the center was a small hole about the size of an acorn.

"What do you think that is?" asked Fergus.

"No idea. Maybe a woodpecker or something made it. It's weird though. Even the hole is very neat." He peered closer. "Too neat."

The Foreman walked up to join them and squinted at it, shaking his head in annoyance. "It should be easier than this! Why would they make something so complicated to work out how to use in an emergency?"

"What should we do?" asked Fergus.

The Foreman crouched down and smiled at him tiredly. "If we can't work it out, we must concede and make our way back quickly to do what we can with the pigeons." Fergus twisted his mouth in disappointment.

Raf sat back and stared at the tree. It stared back at him. How could it work? It must be a drum, surely? He started humming softly to himself as he looked blankly at the jacarandas and then leaned back against the trunk, closing his eyes for a moment.

It came to him immediately, a glimmer of understanding that flashed up in his consciousness. It was just suddenly there where there had been nothing before. His eyes sprang open and he jumped to his feet. The others turned around and looked at him curiously.

"Musicians…" he whispered.

"What about them, Raf?" asked the Foreman.

"Our ancestors, the people who grew these, were musicians, not drummers."

"Well, some would argue that drums are also instruments, but never mind that - what are you saying? That this isn't a drum? How else does it work?"

Raf ignored them and walked along the branch as the idea crystallized in his mind. After quite a bit of searching, he found a slender stalk of bamboo that extended up alongside a jacaranda trunk. A few quick slashes of his knife and he had a piece small enough to work with. Cutting carefully, he carved out two flat, tapering pieces.

"Are…are you making reeds, Raf?" asked Cisco.

Raf nodded vaguely and walked up to the tree trunk. He moved up to the circle of lighter wood and then held the reeds together to insert them into the tiny hole in the middle. They slotted in perfectly. He leaned forward to hold his weight with his arms against the trunk and then took the reeds between his lips. Drawing a deep breath, he blew into them. They stuck rigidly to start with as he hadn't wet them, but as he continued to blow steadily into them, they suddenly caught and vibrated. At first there was a feeble whine which echoed up the trunk; then it expanded into a richer hum. And then with no warning, like a roll of thunder, an enormous sound erupted: a deep rumbling that blasted out into the night air. He could feel it amplifying and expanding until, instead of a sound, it was an almost physical pressure, filling the air, squeezing him.

After a few seconds, he ran out of breath and pulled away to catch his breath. The sound didn't immediately stop, though. It faded reluctantly, leaving behind a creepy, pulsing bass note that throbbed as it grew weaker and weaker.

Raf stood in a daze, eyes still fixed on the trunk. He could hear the faint rumble below him, although it was already being replaced by a high-pitched, painful whistle in his ears. His little reverie was shattered by a squawking noise behind and he turned to see Cisco crouching on the floor, his arms clamped firmly around his head.

"Stop!" he screeched. "Too loud!"

The Foreman sat there with his face twisted in discomfort and his hands covering his ears.

"Sorry," said Raf, holding up a hand apologetically.

"Sorry?" shouted Cisco, opening one of his eyes to glare at him. "Sorry?! You have to give us some warning before you deafen us with your stupid tree-flute, you *idiot*! I almost fell off the branch!"

There was a choking noise from the Foreman and Raf looked around to see him suddenly roll back onto the ground and burst into laughter. After a bit, he pointed at Cisco as if to say something, but saw the boy's startled expression and collapsed again, doubled over. Raf bit his lip and held back a chuckle; he'd never seen the Foreman like this before.

Eventually, when he could breathe again, the Foreman sat up and dried his eyes. "How did you know how to do that?"

Raf shrugged uncomfortably. "A guess. How much more do we have to do it?"

The Foreman gave him a curious look. "You are full of surprises these days, mysterious Master Gency." He looked back at the tree thoughtfully. "That was surely so loud they'll have heard it all the way in Miern. Just a few more times to make sure, and then we should head back."

. . . .

Leiana looked up at the canopy to gather herself. The sun was successfully pushing back the remnants of the storm to send slivers of light streaking through the commons, seemingly at odds with the somber atmosphere of the congregation. She stood up on the dais and waited for the crowd to quieten before addressing them.

165

"As you know, Vince Ghitral has died. It is the manner of his death, though, that is most distressing. After exploring some of the patches you pointed out to us, we have discovered that they are not isolated incidents. Something is wrong with our beloved Forest. A disease of some sort that is affecting the trees. In a few areas, it has even rotted the *Ancients'* branches that run underneath us in the ground, which is what happened to Vince." She paused, letting her words sink in. "There are many areas around Eirdale - and the rest of our Forest - that are afflicted, so my advice is to stay within the village, which is still completely safe. In the meantime, the Foreman is calling an Overcouncil so that, together with our fellow Council members, we can solve this problem."

At this, silence fell over the commons. Tarvil stepped up behind Leiana and put a hand on her shoulder. Leiana smiled briefly at him and lifted her voice again. "We don't have Vince's body to take to a burial chute, but it has already found its way to the Forest floor, so all that remains is to bid farewell. Abuniah?"

Abuniah nodded and stood, but hesitated as the tall, slim figure of Arige Ghitral, Vince's sister, emerged from the crowd. She had a shock of red, wavy hair, and eyes that were raw from crying. Abuniah walked up to embrace her. "Do you want me to lead?" he asked softly.

She shook her head and smiled briefly. Abuniah nodded and moved away from her to sit down. The other villagers, one by one, followed suit until they were all seated, their heads either bowed or looking at Arige. She closed her eyes and started singing.

The dirge she sang was an ancient *ayre*, haunting but sweet at the same time. The rest of the crowd joined in after a bit and the sound echoed through the branches of the trees, drifting down amongst the villagers like a soft, soothing blanket.

A while later, spent and weary, people were gradually getting to their feet and offering condolences to Arige when a sudden deep boom rolled through the Forest. They all looked up at the Council, feeling the rumbling note vibrate up through the ground under their feet. Leiana gave Tarvil a relieved look and Abuniah, nodding resolutely, climbed up to the dais.

"All right, folks," he said. "We will soon have a group of guests arriving, the likes of which we've never hosted. Hunters and farmers over here with me. The rest of you head home, and please, please, be careful."

Foreman Allium jumped up from his desk as the faint booming note rang through the office, resounding off the walls. He rang a bell on his desk and immediately, a young boy entered.

"Sir?"

"Fetch Councilman Brinchley immediately."

A few minutes later, Brinchley hurried through the doors. "You called for me, Foreman?" he asked nervously.

"Have you made the announcement?"

"About the travel ban? Yes, Foreman. I spoke to the Council and addressed the villagers about the collapses down south. It should put off any interest in traveling to Eirdale. Or anywhere else, for that matter."

"And did the Council have any objections to the Festival being held here?"

"A few complainers. Dawsley in particular wanted to know how it was that we already seemed so well prepared for it."

"You dealt with it?"

"I gave him the usual nonsense about needing to develop quickly for the future." Brinchley stroked his goatee. "This news of the collapse was incredibly convenient, Foreman. How did you find out about it so quickly?"

"Even in Eirdale there are some high up who appreciate what I am trying to do," replied Allium. "But don't let that concern you. Now that we have set ourselves up perfectly here in Three Ways for the Festival, I'm more concerned with how you've failed me with the Eirdalers."

"Failed you, Foreman?" stammered Brinchley. "Is this something to do with the noise th–"

"You imbecile!" Allium snapped. "Of course it is! That noise was the sound of Eirdale showing its claws. I gave you one small task which was to convince that idiot Tovier that this was the only way forward. We even had the incident with the assault on the trader to help you!"

"But, Foreman, I did what you asked and he completely bought the story!"

"As they have taken it upon themselves to call an Overcouncil, I'm assuming that you did *not*, in fact, sell a very good story. Your small problem has just grown into a larger, and considerably more complicated, one."

"I... My problem?" Brinchley's chins wobbled underneath as he stuttered indignantly. "But Nabolek assured me he would handle it!"

"Oh he did, did he? Delegating your duties to the Miernan? Interesting." Brinchley stepped back at Allium's icy tone. "So, how are you going to fix this disaster, Councilman? This couldn't have come at a worse time with the Festival only three days away! I expect you to find a way to ensure that there are no problems until at least after the Festival finishes. By that stage, I will be ready to speak to them all about my plans and dissolve the Overcouncil, anyway." He flicked his hand toward the door. "Go. See to it. Inform me when you have mended your mistake. And do not disappoint me."

. . . .

Brinchley left the office in a fluster, and walked straight up to Nabolek's quarters. When he arrived, he couldn't find the man and searched until he spied him in the pool that the woodsmith Ferthen had built. He was lounging back against the side, eyes closed, a tankard of mead in one hand. As he approached, Nabolek's eyes flicked open.

"Ah, Councilman. What can I do for you? You seem anxious. Anything to do with that strange noise?"

Brinchley fiddled with his goatee. "I thought you said you would deal with our...loose end." He whispered the last bit, looking around nervously.

"And I did, dear Councilman. Losing two of my men in the process, I'll have you know. It seems you were right about these southern barbarians. And a good thing I was here to offer assistance."

"Well, it didn't work! Ferthen must have returned and lit a fire under them because they've called an Overcouncil – which is huge trouble for us."

Nabolek sat up, splashing water out of the pool as he put his drink down. "The carpenter made it back there? He wasn't supposed... Henja assured me he was as good as dead."

"Well, *somehow* they've found out something and they've called a meeting of all the Foremen. It's likely that we'll be contacted - or even visited - soon. If they were to come here, they would disrupt the whole Festival and almost certainly wreck our plans."

Nabolek lay his head back down, closing his eyes. Brinchley stood waiting, his fingers making their way up to stroke his goatee again, and then he jumped as the Miernan suddenly sat up and climbed out of the pool to grab hold of a towel. He looked over his shoulder and gave a sharp whistle. A soldier instantly appeared from the nearby barracks and trotted up to them.

"Fetch Lethar." Nabolek turned back to Brinchley as the soldier ran off. "I will take care of it from here."

"But how? I can't see them taking too kindly to any Miernan presence at the Overcouncil."

Nabolek walked away without acknowledging him, and disappeared into his quarters.

Cisco yawned deeply and stretched his arms up into the air, eyeing the distant masses of clouds that were lit up in dark pastels of the fading sunset. "Can we take a bit of rest before we go any further?"

"Actually, I think we should sleep here tonight, boys. It's getting very dark and I'm not going to risk an accident happening with the last few slides back to *Nviro*; it would ruin what's been a successful day. Speaking of which," he added, laying the rope down on the decking, "I must offer my thanks, Fergus for your assistance today. And to you Raf for your unexpected intuition. If that's what it was."

He smiled at them all and then moved to crouch down on the edge of the decking where the thick netting was wound tightly around a corner post. Fergus scrambled up into the dark branches above them and disappeared for a bit, so Raf and Cisco wandered over to the side and stared out at the star-sprinkled sky. A few minutes later, Fergus came back down with a handful of succulent monkey-ear mushrooms.

"I thought you might be hungry," he said, walking up to the Foreman and handing them to him.

The Foreman smiled at the boy and put them down beside him. "Thank you, Fergus. I'll eat in a while."

"Are you all right, sir? You've been quiet since we left the *Ash-knell*."

The Foreman sighed and looked fondly at the young boy. "I am sad, Fergus. I've lost a good friend and in all the panic of finding the *Ash-knell*, I haven't spared even a moment to think about him. Vince was a good man; one of the best. I've known him my whole life and we grew up together in Eirdale."

Raf heard the conversation from where they were standing and felt a twinge of regret. "I forgot all about that," he confessed to Cisco, who nodded back at him uncomfortably.

There was a deep humming and they turned to watch the Foreman who had started singing softly. He stood there, a melancholy silhouette against the pale light of the moon. It was an old song that Raf didn't know and the boys sat quietly, trying not to intrude. There came a point though, when the Foreman had been singing for a while, that Fergus softly joined in. When there was no reaction from the Foreman, Cisco and Raf looked at each other and then joined in softly themselves. Cisco wasn't particularly confident and merely hummed along, but Raf sang aloud, his alto voice complementing the Foreman's bass beautifully. Their voices bloomed in harmony, filling the damp Forest air. He faltered a little as it occurred to him that he'd never sung in a small group like this with the Foreman, but the gloomy dusk was a cloak and he shrugged off the bite of nervousness.

When his eyes inevitably closed, a surge of exhilaration took hold as wavering tongues of multicolored flame rushed toward him. Goose-bumps covered his skin as he felt himself drawn into the colors, embracing them, merging with them as he had done before with Bhothy. With the intense connection made, he grew aware of the colors in a deep, personal way, feeling himself buoyed by their energy and beauty, losing himself in the music.

The sound of talking behind him caught him by surprise, and with the awkward disorientated feeling of someone awoken from a deep sleep, he opened his eyes. Cisco and Fergus sat watching him, grinning, as Raf quickly tried to gather his wits about him.

"Well, Gency," said Cisco, "I hate to tell you this, but that was actually rather nice."

"Yeah!" gushed Fergus who was sitting on the decking, hugging his knees. "You sing really well, Raf."

"Oh...thanks," he muttered, feeling a burning spread across his face.

"You gave me goose-bumps there from the second you

started singing," said the Foreman from where he was standing. "I feel really quite moved by that. Strangely -" he looked up at the darkened sky, searching for the right word, "- happy." He smiled, but frowned a little at the same time.

Raf fidgeted nervously and then quickly walked over to the netting behind him. He lay down on his side facing away from the others. But not long after, footsteps approached.

"Nice job!" whispered Cisco mischievously. "I think you've just earned yourself quite a few public performances after that. No way the Foreman's not going to tell Ottery about it!"

Raf glowered at him. "Shut up, you idiot. The Festival's not *happening*, unless you've forgotten. And by the time there's another one, he won't remember anyway."

"Don't count on it," came the amused voice of the Foreman.

Cisco laughed silently into his hands and then sprang backward to avoid a punch from Raf, before settling down on the netting and making himself comfortable for the night.

. . . .

Ramsey glared irritably at the two boys on his left. "Shhh!"

They quietened and looked sullenly down the path. In the distance there came a soft clinking noise and as they watched, a wagon appeared around the bend of an *Ancient* with three passengers. Ramsey stepped in front of them with his hands raised and the cart jerked awkwardly over the uneven ground as it drew to a stop.

Two of the foresters were men dressed in tunics and breeches of tan-colored cloth. One had a bushy white beard underpinning a wrinkled face and light blue eyes, and the other was very similar - although a much younger version. Next to them sat a middle-aged woman with long tumbles of mahogany hair, dressed in a dark grey robe with a green stole around her neck.

Ramsey bowed to them and started singing the *gretanayre*. The new-comers scanned the area curiously, but then disembarked from the wagon and responded formally. When they had finished, the younger man stepped forward frowning. "Good morning, friend."

"I am Ramsey." He bowed. "Welcome to Eirdale."

"I am Trenz Wrighk, Foreman of Upper Radley. This is my uncle, Foreman Wrighk of Saanenbury."

The woman dipped her head elegantly. "I am Bilotusia Kess, Forewoman of West Peaks. Tell me, why has the *Ash-knell* been sounded? There had better be a good reason for us to have sped here recklessly through the night, Councilman."

"Oh, I'm not in the Council," replied Ramsey. "My role is to ensure you are escorted safely to the village."

"Safely, you say?" said the older man.

"Yes, Foreman Wrighk. I ask that you trust me; all will be clearer when the Overcouncil convenes."

The three looked at each other and the Forewoman Kess nodded. "Lead on."

Ramsey bowed again and then turned around and nodded at one of the boys. "Marc here will lead you. Do not stray from the route he takes, please."

. . . .

A short, lean soldier stood nervously in the shadows under a low-hanging olive branch as Nabolek sauntered up to him.

"Being in the right place at the right time, Lethar, is a useful talent to have in life. Jugak failed me and paid the price. I am promoting you to captain," said Nabolek. "I have word that criminals are on their way to cause havoc with my Festival." He looked at the soldier from underneath his thick, hooded eyes and lowered his voice. "Take a division of men and make sure that access to this village from the south is challenging. The more challenging, the better."

Lethar saluted. "Understood, sir."

"If any local villagers try to travel south defying the ban, you know what to do?" The captain nodded again. "Your promotion will be short lived should you fail in this task, Lethar. Don't disappoint me." The soldier saluted again and jogged off.

Nabolek watched him disappear toward the soldiers' quarters and then strolled back toward the three richly dressed Miernans. One of them saw him coming and beckoned to Nabolek to join him out of ear-shot of the others.

"Is everything all right, Nabolek?"

"Fine, Senator Hysik," replied Nabolek. "More than fine, even."

"How so?"

"As it turns out, our friend Allium employed some underhand measures to have the Festival here in his town. But he rather bungled it; there are now issues with disgruntled foresters south of us. Some are even getting rather violent."

"And how is this 'more than fine'?"

Nabolek smiled. "I now have an excellent excuse for the two hundred soldiers you've lent me. They will be official peace-keepers when they get here."

The senator nodded and sipped his drink. "I have every faith in you, Nabolek. I'll deal with these other two fools. When your work here has fed my funds sufficiently, our time will come." The corners of his mouth twitched upward. "And as for our...friend, early retirement beckons."

They turned at footsteps behind them and saw the other two senators approaching.

"What's this about an early retirement, Hysik?"

Nabolek laughed. "I was saying that I hoped you found this forest to your liking, Senator Boltos. It would be a perfect place to settle once you are tired of the relentless pace of Miern, yes?"

"It *is* really rather lovely out here, true. I wasn't sure what

I would make of this Aeril experience and will admit that I had misgivings about spending any time on this infamous forest platform, but I've actually found it to be thoroughly delightful. Which will make our trip back next week all the more unpleasant."

Nabolek dipped his head. "I won't be accompanying you, Senators. I think I'll remain here for a while to bring Allium up to scratch on his new role. That is, if you intend to endorse the barony request."

"We'll see," replied the other senator gruffly. "This Festival is yet to even start. Although, so far, I will say that this Allium appears to be competent. Let's hope you don't ruin this opportunity as you have so many back in Miern, Nabolek. Your cousin's patience is not bottomless."

Senator Hysik lifted his drink quickly as Nabolek's face tightened. "A toast. Let's enjoy the day and think about the long term profits that will flow into Miern's coffers, Senators. The Festival starts in a few days and Nabolek has brought us here to a forest that is surely ripe for the picking."

. . . .

The newly-appointed Captain Lethar sat on a large wagon moving down the southern pass out of Three Ways. The path had slowly widened over the last stretch, although it was still bordered by the walls of thick brambles it bisected. Next to him, a young forester walked along beside the wagon enthusiastically playing a wooden flute. Behind them, a line of marching soldiers stretched to the other, much larger wagon some fifty feet back which was covered with hide.

"How much longer, forester?"

The young man laughed and pointed his flute up toward one of the enormous trees ahead around which the path bent. "The crossroads are just beyond that *Ancient*. Are we in so much of a rush?"

Lethar ignored him. They probably didn't even need a guide as the path was easy to find – not to mention the only means of traveling through the thick vegetation. But he preferred to be safe rather than risk a mistake and have to deal with Nabolek.

The procession finally made its way to a large, open space where a few paths merged together in a worn, open junction. Lethar looked back to the other wagon and gestured for the soldiers to stop. He jumped to the ground and pulled out a rolled up map from a box on the side of the wagon, stretching it out in the air.

He tapped a spot south of Three Ways. "So this is where we are?" The forester walked up, squinted at the map and then nodded. "And all paths from the south join here to head up along the path we've just come along?" The forester nodded again. "No other way to get to Three Ways except on this path?"

"Well, not unless you're coming from west or north, obviously. But from down here, it's the only way. No way you're getting through these brambles." He waved his hand vaguely at the bushes next to them.

Lethar looked out at the junction. "Well, don't let us keep you from your Festival."

The forester tilted his head. "Are you setting up camp or something, Captain? And what's in that huge wagon? Is this something to do with the collapses in the south we've been told about? The travel ban and al that? Are you going to help?"

"Something like that, forester. It's Miernan business, though; nothing for you to worry about. Now, please go, we've got work to do."

The forester shrugged and made his way back down the path. As he passed by the back of the large wagon though, one of the soldiers unhitched the coverings and the side slipped down to reveal the contents. The forester gasped at what he saw: rows of bright silver axes, lined up on racks; great mounds of rope coiled in neat piles on the floor; and two enormous twelve foot saw-blades held in straps.

His face dropped as he took it in. "Wh-what are those for?" He started backing away from them, pointing at the blades. "You can't cut down trees! It's against the law, Miernan. Is that what you're doing?"

"Yes, they are for doing some pruning. That huge one over there is a perfect starting point." Lethar sighed. "You really didn't need to be so nosy. I told you, this was Miernan business." He reached behind the bench he was sitting on.

"The *Ancient?*" hissed the forester, staring past him. "How could you even *think* about cutting it down? The Council will never allow it!" He turned and sprinted back up the path.

A second later there was a sharp explosion and the forester was lifted a few feet into the air before crashing back down onto the ground. He let out a wet, gurgling breath and then was still.

Lethar lowered the pepperbox and returned it to its holster. The soldiers continued unloading the wagons, stepping around the mangled body.

The four of them walked back briskly through the farms, leaving the towering form of *Nviro* behind them. The sun had risen hours earlier and they had taken their time on the return trip, nursing stiff muscles and blisters from the activities of the day before. In the distance, the village chimes rang.

"Sounds like it's already getting busy down there," observed Cisco.

"Let's hope so," said the Foreman.

Cisco looked over at Raf and wiggled his eyebrows. "With all the blaring of the *Ash-knell* yesterday, I wouldn't be surprised if we were visited by an Elder or two..."

"An elder?" responded Fergus curiously. "You mean like Mr. Jover?"

Cisco laughed. "No, no, not like Jover; although I know he *looks* old and shriveled. No, I'm talking about other people in the Forest – *very* old people. People say they're as old as the *Ancients*."

"You been talking to your nan again?" said Raf, shaking his head. "Don't listen to him, Fergus. Cisco's nan is chock-full of excellent bedtime stories."

Cisco ignored him and continued. "They're very secretive, living deep in the Forest and nobody ever sees them. It didn't always use to be like that though, and my nan told me they used to be our leaders, like the Foreman, a long time ago."

Fergus' eyes lit up. "Did you know that, Raf?"

Cisco patted his friend's shoulder. "Knowing the Gency family, Raf's probably got an Elder for a cousin."

179

"Shut up, you idiot," muttered Raf, speeding to catch up with the Foreman.

Cisco laughed and beckoned Fergus to follow as he jogged after them.

....

They made their way directly to the Council quarters, walking straight in to a picture of delighted expressions.

"Foreman," greeted Leiana. "Good job! And welcome back."

"It worked marvelously well. Gave the Forest a good old rattling," added Dr. Allid. "I'd rather like to have seen this mysterious *Ash-knell*."

"Not an easy trip, but no problems with the rot and we all survived." The Foreman indicated the boys with a jerk of his head. "I may as well have not been there, to be honest. It's all down to this lot. Raf was the one who worked out how to sound the *Ash-knell*. We even - and you'll probably find this more newsworthy - managed to get him to sing for us. It was quite a show." Fergus and Cisco beamed at Raf who looked down at his feet.

The Foreman grew solemn again. "Now we just need to see if it was worth it."

"But we have proof already, Foreman," said Leiana. "Fifteen Foremen have beaten you here."

"Already?" The Foreman was taken aback. "What about the rotten ground? It's such a huge risk -" He paused and Raf looked over to see his mother standing with her hands on her hips and giving the Foreman a thoroughly frosty look.

A flicker of a smile danced across his mouth and he dipped his head apologetically. "And how have you organized everything, might I ask?"

"There's a reason you have a Council, you know." She raised her eyebrow at him and sat down at the table. "While you have been away we have sorted ourselves out and prepared everything in readiness. Even as we speak there are scouts manning all the paths leading into Eirdale. Each knows a safe route through the rotten patches."

"Are they being told what the situation is?"

"No. Of those I've spoken to, they've all come across the rot somewhere, but have had no casualties, which is a relief. You can broach the subject tonight at the Overcouncil."

The Foreman nodded slowly in approval. "Who's here already?"

"Most of the closer ones obviously, but also some who traveled through the night," replied Dalton. "Samuel, Shant, Terrell, the Wrighks and Jethem. Bilotusia's even here already from West Peaks."

"What about Jon Pentrige, Mvusi and Raol?"

"No, not yet. But bear in mind that it may have taken a while for some of them to realize what it was, and then travel all the way down here. I'm confident though that the majority will arrive in time for the meeting early this evening."

The Foreman vacantly scratched his cheek. "An Overcouncil, huh? In my time..." He looked at Leiana. "Perhaps we can make this slightly less daunting with some entertainment? This is a rare crowd to have in our village. Maybe get some use out of those *dholaki* and give Eirdale a little unexpected flair?"

A flush of red bloomed on her cheeks and she started to say something but Abuniah spoke first. "No luck there, I'm afraid, Foreman; the iMahlis left earlier today. Heading up to the Festival in Three Ways is my guess."

"What?" burst out Leiana, turning to him. "But...they were supposed to perform here. We had a deal!" She deliberately avoided eye-contact with Tarvil who knuckled his chin and stared off into the distance through the window.

"Don't fear, Leiana," said Abuniah soothingly. "We aren't completely untalented, the rest of us."

Raf crawled up through the tree trunk and sat in the small hollow, yawning as he brought his knees up to his chest. He looked up at his carving attempts on the shelf and smiled faintly as he thought of the delight that Orfea's new owner would have playing her. Fergus would be as careful – and enthusiastic - a keeper as anyone.

The idea of trying to make another one took hold of him, and he crept over to the window. Spotting a vine branch that was about the right size, he pulled out his knife, and with a few quick slices severed it from the main limb. Propping the stick carefully on the thick ledge of the window, he drew a breath and closed his eyes. The song the Foreman had been singing by the *Ash-knell* popped into his head, and he began to hum it softly.

The colors lit up the darkness behind his eyes in churning waves, and he focused his thoughts on making an instrument – on *growing* one. No sooner had the idea crystallized in his mind when, out of the glimmering hues, a vein of violet unfolded, expanding to cloak all the other colors. As he'd done before, Raf pushed himself into it, felt himself shift forward and become one with the color. He kept the goal of what he wanted to make in his thoughts – some sort of pipe instrument - and guided the rich violet color toward the stick. He couldn't see it with his eyes closed, obviously, but he held the idea of where it was in his head and made wave after wave wash towards it, imploring it to grow. After a few minutes, unable to stave off his curiosity anymore, he stopped singing and then nervously eased open his eyes.

He wasn't disappointed. Where the vine branch had been, there was now an odd, tangled wooden shape that in a strange instinctive way he knew was an instrument. Bends and loops and flares curved organically into and around each other in an intricate pattern, forming what was some kind of horn.

He reached down to pick it up but found that it was stuck. On further inspection, he realized that it wasn't stuck so much as…

"How's that possible?"

The stick he had sliced off and then laid on the window ledge was now firmly attached to one of the vines it had been leaning against. In fact, it seemed to be somehow growing *from* the vine again. They had joined! Seamlessly. As if part of the same plant again. Mouth hanging open, he gently bent the horn backward and forward until there was a soft snap. In trembling hands, he lifted it up and turned it over in his hands in sheer delight. He positioned his hands intuitively, feeling them fit into place over the complex arrangement of holes, took a breath and then blew gently into the flattened mouthpiece. The note that came out of the flared bell at the end was soft and haunting like a lark's call, and Raf felt an icy stream of goose-bumps immediately flood over his arms. He tried playing a simple tune, savoring the delicious texture of the notes, when there was a sudden bump from the hollow trunk below him.

"Hello?" he called.

There was a scuffling in the tree-trunk, so he put the horn carefully down on the floor and then moved on his hands and knees to the top of the make-do ladder, sticking his head over the edge. There was a glimmer of indistinct movement at the bottom and then the sound of snapping twigs outside, so he clambered as quickly as he could down the inside of the old snag, dropping recklessly to the floor and crawling out the narrow entrance.

He turned around, staring into the bushes and trees, but couldn't see anything. Then there was a noise further up the road toward the village center and he caught sight of a flash of dark brown through some thick brush. He sprinted up toward the patch, but when he got there, there was no sign of anyone. He scratched his head and stared up the path in frustration

183

until he caught another glimpse of dark brown along the other side of the path, quite a bit further ahead. He darted up and crashed wildly into the bushes, trying to startle whoever it was, but again, there was no one. Exasperated, he started running down the path, and only stopped when he almost flew headfirst into Cisco.

"Was it you?" he accused breathlessly, jabbing a finger into his friend's face.

"Um...?" Cisco gave him a dubious look.

"Where've you just been?" demanded Raf.

"I was just looking for you, you weirdo. The Overcouncil's going to start soon. Anyway, where've *you* been?"

"Wait, did you see anyone running past here? Dressed in brown?"

"Nope. Just you. So are we going now or what? I mean, it's nothing important - just the entire future of the Aeril Forest at stake."

"What?" Raf paused. "It's happening already? Now?"

"Yup," replied Cisco. "Abuniah's apparently leading the entertainment tonight along with Ottery's junior choir. It looks like your brother's got roped into it, so your mom will be half pacified at least."

Raf bit his lip, casting a half-hearted glance around the bushes again.

"Come on, let's go! I don't want to miss this, Gency."

"But we can't get in anyway, Cisc; it's closed to non-Council members."

"Well, obviously we can't just walk in and join the Overcouncil, you dopey git. I was thinking more of, well, Ned told me about a place you two went the other day..."

Raf broke into a grudging smile as Cisco's impish grin won him over.

. . . .

They were sprinting around the back of a large elm *Ancient* when a shout brought them to a halt. Turning, they saw Nathyn Tovier beckoning them. They quickly walked across to the smartly-dressed Council member and saw Nedrick standing beside him looking uncomfortable in a long, dark dress-robe.

"Good afternoon, Councilman Tovier," both the boys greeted.

"What are you doing haring around the village?" demanded the Councilman. "Don't you have things to help with?" The boys stammered about being on their way. "I don't want to hear excuses," he interrupted, holding a hand up. "We have important guests here, and you should be dressed properly and assisting with preparations. Go!"

"Yes, Councilman."

There was a quiet cough from behind them and they turned around to see two strangers watching them in amusement. One was short and completely bald, and the other was a monstrously large man with a foot-long, black beard. They both carried chains of office around their necks.

Nedrick's father gasped and immediately bowed. "Foreman Tannunder, Foreman Thraen! I beg your pardon, I did not know you were there."

The shorter of the two men chuckled and leaned lazily on the thick staff he was carrying. "That's quite all right, Councilman. Myself and Thraen here did not wish to intrude on your discussion, but now that you are finished chastising the lads, I wonder if you could be of assistance? I fear we're late for this Overcouncil."

"Of course, of course," gushed Councilman Tovier, dipping his head. "Actually, you're just in time. The meeting is about to commence. If you'll kindly follow me, I'll take you there immediately."

The three men walked off talking, with the Councilman bowing fawningly every second sentence.

Nedrick shook his head slightly and muttered under his breath, "Look at him. He's like some sort of rooster with all that head-bobbing."

"Is that really *the* Foreman Thraen?" asked Cisco in an awed tone. "The one who killed the bear?"

"The very one," said Nedrick.

"That's just a myth," said Raf. "Have you been spending time with Cisco's nan as well, Ned?"

"Oh no, it's definitely true," said Nedrick. "We went to visit a few years back and I remember seeing the bear's head mounted on the wall of his *Ancient*."

"Nonsense."

"Raf, look at the size of him. He's easily a foot taller than our Foreman - and probably twice as strong as Orikon."

As they watched, Foreman Thraen glanced back in their direction. Seeing them staring at him, he winked before turning back to listen to whatever drivel Ned's dad was spouting. The three boys grinned at each other and then turned to head down toward the commons.

"Nedrick!"

Nedrick cursed as his father beckoned impatiently. "Sorry, guys. Guess I'm also supposed to be a rooster. See you later." He jogged to catch up to his father.

The other two made their way quickly to the cluster of thick bamboo stalks, and in a few minutes were crawling along the branch sloping toward the sequoia trunk. Because there were so many visitors, the Overcouncil was being held in the largest meeting room which was actually adjacent to the room Raf and Ned had eavesdropped on before. There were long thin windows along the side of one of the walls of this room, so they climbed carefully around the trunk and positioned themselves comfortably in some deep clefts in the bark before peeking inside.

From their vantage point, they watched as the two Foremen they had met on the path were shown to seats at the massive head table with Eirdale's Foreman Manyara. Nathyn and some of the Eirdale Council offered up their spaces and then moved down to join the other visiting Foremen and Council members. In the end, the head table had Eirdale's Foreman and Leiana at one end, and then a double row of around thirty Foremen stretching down from them, with a few small tables of Council members around the periphery.

It was an intriguing gathering of authorities - most of whom had traveled through the night - which created quite a strained, bristly atmosphere, and Raf was relieved when Foreman Manyara finally stood up and began the *gretanayre*. The others responded in unison, and at the powerful sound that filled the room, Raf gave Cisco a delighted smile and nodded his approval.

The Foreman welcomed the guests formally, introducing them one by one. Then he explained the reasons for sounding the *Ash-knell*, starting with the Festival and the implications of Allium's map, to which there was an instant reaction.

Augin Rohloff, the young Foreman of Matusbury, stood up angrily. "We will make sure that no-one - not *one* forester in our villages - takes part in this false Festival, Eliath. You have our word on that. As soon as we return, we will send pigeons to everyone and make sure they know of Allium's treachery."

"How could the man think he'd get away with this?" mocked the bald-headed Foreman Tannunder. "Did he honestly think we might just...*fail to notice* that nobody was here for the Festival?" There were a few mirthless laughs from the others.

Foreman Manyara lifted a hand up to get their attention. "I hope no one here thinks I am so petty as to call an Overcouncil just to deal with this. Please listen, there is more." He squared his shoulders and waited till he had their full attention. "Sadly, this Festival nonsense is unimportant in light of what's happened recently and what we've learned. It affects us all."

He ran through their recent discoveries of all the rotten

smells and concluded with the news about Vince's death.

"I hope you will forgive me for calling this Overcouncil here in Eirdale, forcing you to travel through what has seemingly become quite an unstable Forest. It was brash and risky, but I believe it was necessary. This is something we must solve together and while we are fortunate that none of you was hurt traveling here, it is surely only a matter of time before tragedies occur. We *must* find a cure for this disease if we are to survive. And quickly. If we cannot..." The Foreman paused, looking around slowly. "If we cannot, I put it to you that we must leave the Forest. It would simply be too dangerous for anyone to remain here."

As dusk settled on the village, the roasted boars that had been cooking for hours on spits outside were brought in to the Overcouncil so that intense conversations could continue without pause. Raf's grandfather, Luka Pollath, was arguing fervently with a pair of Foremen from up north when a young forester entered and pulled him aside. The look on Luka's face darkened as the young man delivered his message and then, dismissing him with a grim nod, he approached Eirdale's Foreman and spoke quietly into his ear.

"*What!*"

The room froze at the roar from Eirdale's Foreman.

Rip Thraen called out from a table at the back, "What is it, Eliath?"

"Apparently, there -" Foreman Manyara paused and looked around at the worried faces. "Apologies, this really isn't important bearing in mind what we are discussing now."

"Go on," urged Luka. "They'll want to know."

"Well, Allium, it seems, is no longer even trying to hide his agenda. The crossroads near Borilcester have been destroyed. Miernan soldiers have cut down an *Ancient* there and collapsed the area."

"Allium has had an *Ancient*...cut down?" Raf watched as the elderly Foreman Feko'la got unsteadily to his feet and held a hand to his wizened face in dismay. "But, why?"

"He means to stop us reaching Three Ways," said Rip Thraen quietly. "He thinks that any visits from us to his Festival will bring trouble for him. I tend to agree with that suspicion."

There were shouts and curses as an uproar broke out from the rest of the room. Augin Rohloff announced he was heading up to Three Ways to confront Allium immediately and was supported loudly by some of the other northern Foremen.

Raf pulled himself back and exhaled slowly. Miernan soldiers cutting down *Ancients*? What was going *on*?

"Have I come at a bad time?" said a loud, dry voice suddenly.

Raf quickly pushed his face back up to the window. An old man had stepped into the room. As he turned in the candle-light, Raf realized that 'old' was actually a complete understatement. His face was as wrinkled as a prune and the stray wisps of white hair dangling from his chin did nothing to reduce his haggardly appearance. He was dressed in simple brown robes with a leather sash around his bony waist, and held a long bamboo pole in a knotted hand for support.

"Who's that d'you think?" whispered Cisco.

"Don't have a clue," mouthed Raf.

The stranger stepped slowly into the middle of the room and looked around at the frieze of surprise in front of him, before reaching out and taking a piece of dried meat from a nearby bowl. He popped it into his mouth and chewed it vigorously.

Foreman Manyara frowned. "Who are you, forester? This is an Overcouncil, a private meeting."

The stranger continued chewing. "I heard the *Ash-knell*."

"I don't recognize you, friend, and this Overcouncil is for Foremen and Council only. We have some pressing matters to deal with, so I would ask you to kindly leave. I will happily speak with you afterward."

He looked over at Nathyn who nodded and stood up to escort the old man out. As he did though, there was a shuffling in the ranks of onlookers and they made way for someone at the back. Raf watched as Foreman Feko'la shuffled forward on his bandy legs. He threw a sharp glance at Nathyn and flicked a hand at him dismissively.

"Foreman Feko'la? You know this man?"

Mvusi ignored Nathyn and bowed low to the stranger. Then he started singing a strange little ditty that Raf didn't recognize.

"What?" Cisco hissed. "He's the oldest Foreman in the Forest, isn't he? And he's *bowing* to this guy?"

Raf tried to get a clearer view as the newcomer dipped his head at Foreman Feko'la and then sang what was apparently the response. Mvusi then turned around slowly, straightening up with a somber expression. "Foreman Manyara, the rest of the Overcouncil, I would like to introduce you to Elder Bolyai."

"He's an *Elder?*" whispered Cisco. He looked over at Raf. "I *told* you!"

. . . .

Below them, the Elder looking around calmly as the room reacted in silent astonishment to his introduction. Eliath in particular seemed at a loss as to what to do and it was only when Foreman Feko'la indicated his chair with a quick dart of his eyes that he vacated it and offered it up to the guest.

The Elder sat on the proffered chair and then reached across the table to take the Foreman's mug of mead. He took a long draught and wiped the foam off his beard. "I haven't been to Eirdale in a while." The Overcouncil looked at each other awkwardly, unsure of how to react. "Seems very serious in here. And very quiet. When Barreth was Foreman, I wouldn't have been able to even hear the *Ash-knell* for music and festivities."

"Barreth Manyara?" said the Foreman. "You knew my grandfather?"

"Quite well." The Elder reached over to take another piece of dried meat from the bowl. "Tell me, why was the *Ash-knell* sounded? It has been an age since I last heard it."

"The trees have caught some sort of disease which is

191

rotting them and we recently had a collapse which killed one of our villagers, sadly. Have you not smelt it on your way here?"

"Like a rotten carcass?" responded the Elder. "I've smelt something like that a few times recently." He looked up at the roof thoughtfully. Raf and Cisco instantly ducked back out of sight. "And you say someone has died? Well, tomorrow morning you must show m-"

The Elder looked up as there was a knock on the doors of the chambers and one of Dr. Ferrows' young assistants entered.

Foreman Manyara pushed forward past the others. "Is it Jan?"

"Dr. Ferrows says to come quickly. He...won't last much longer, Foreman."

"What's this?" asked the Elder.

The Foreman started explaining about the attack and the strange disease eating away at Jan, but Bolyai waved him off. "Tell me on the way. Quick, take me to him!"

Raf looked at Cisco and the two scrambled their way back down to the ground to join the others heading toward the medical rooms.

. . . .

When they got there, the Elder spoke quickly with Dr. Ferrows and then asked them to bring Jan out and lay him on the ground. Three men complied immediately and the Foreman himself helped to lay the yellow, shriveled body of the once massive woodsmith on the mossy ground. Around them, people gasped with dismay at the sight of the Jan's emaciated figure.

Bolyai knelt down over him, touching his face and arms softly with his fingers, muttering to himself under his breath. The woodsmith's breathing was shallow and slow, and even in the fading evening light, the sickly yellow color of his skin stood out.

Bolyai spun around to face the Foreman. "A *haelanayre*. Any one, just sing now!"

The Foreman turned desperately to Abuniah and Ottery who were standing behind him. "Do you know what that is?"

"I've never heard of it," said Ottery, wringing her hands. Abuniah shook his head.

Bolyai cursed and then started singing a soft song himself, holding his hands above the body of Jan. From behind Raf came some whispering and he turned to see some of the much older villagers lifting their voices to join in. The Elder looked back at them with a nod and then closed his eyes to focus on Jan. Raf listened carefully and as soon as he felt comfortable with the melody, tried to join in. He was one of the first to do so, but soon more took it up and then the entire crowd was singing along softly.

Raf felt the swell of music fill the air around them. And then he closed his eyes. In the darkness, colors sprang to life and spiraled excitedly in the air around him. As he focused in front of him, however, he noticed that there was some unusual movement to them instead of the usual disorganized chaos. Trying to identify the cause, he floated in closer. A faint wisp of pale blue was slowly drifting down to the floor, and in the space where Jan's body lay, he saw an area of dark blotchiness. He could sense something unpleasant about it, so he pushed even closer and saw that the blotches weren't solid so much as a sort of twisted weaving of black threads which pulsed disturbingly throughout his entire body. The mist of blue curled in amongst the threads, forming pools of color around them, and as they did, the blotches seemed to lighten a tiny bit at the edges. But the blue faded as quickly as it arrived, almost as if it was being drained. Raf suddenly knew what was happening without fully understanding it.

It's trying to help him, but it's not strong enough. It's just getting absorbed by that black stuff.

He swam forward into the drifting currents, trying to urge them to flow thicker and move faster. As soon as the concept of healing entered his thoughts he felt a rushing sound as, from all around, the thin streams of blue mist thickened and swelled into a frothy flood of deep blue. It churned through the air in a powerful current that crashed over the dark threads, saturating them. They resisted for a few seconds and he could just make them out pulsing defiantly behind the swirling blue tide, but the sheer strength of the color was too much and they lightened and seemed to dissolve. Before long, they had disappeared altogether.

A noise pricked the back of his mind and it took him a moment to realize that there was shouting in front of him. He stopped singing and looked up just in time to see a glimpse of Jan's open eyes staring upward, before the crowd thronged forward, blocking him from view. In that moment, Raf saw what a massive change had come over the woodsmith. Instead of drawn, sallow cheeks, there was now a fierce redness to them, and the skin that had been dry and crinkled was softer and had a sheen of healthy moisture to it. All around him, people cried out excitedly, and Dr. Ferrows knelt with her mouth open as she held Jan's hand and felt warm blood pulsing through it. The Elder was on his haunches, staring around in a daze at the crowd.

Raf's mind spun. He almost fell backward as he lurched to his feet and stumbled numbly away from the scene. He reached the sycamore *Ancient*, climbed up to his room and then staggered to his bed where he collapsed on his back, his heart pounding and his thoughts spinning.

The brash calls of a peacock somewhere outside pierced the window and Raf came to, staring groggily at the knotted ceiling above him. He sat up, rubbing the sleep out of his eyes.

"Morning, Raf," came a chirpy voice.

"Hey, Rio. How you doing?" he responded, yawning widely.

"Did you know that the Elder healed Mr. Ferthen? Everybody's talking about it!"

"Mm-hmm. I heard last night." Raf nodded vaguely. "So he...better now?"

"Yeah! Dr. Ferrows said so," Rio replied, putting his sandals on. "You coming down for breakfast? Grandpa's still here."

Raf walked over to the corner of their room and undressed before stepping behind a thick fold in the wall that jutted out into the room. Behind was the thin cranny that served as their shower space. Reaching up to take hold of the watervine, he unclipped it and let the cool, clear water pour over him, washing away the dirt and fatigue from the day before.

When he'd dried himself off, he dressed and made his way down the main stairway to the kitchen, where he came face to face with a broad smile from the grey-bearded Luka Pollath.

"Morning, Grandpa," he said, and then looked up to the others at the table. "Morning."

"Did you sleep well?" asked his grandfather.

"Yes, thanks." He walked up to take a few pieces of fruit and sat down next to Rio. "I thought you left with all the other Foremen this morning?"

"The rest departed at first light. I thought I'd catch a leisurely breakfast before navigating my way back home to Marondale. Besides, it's not every day you come across an Elder."

"How's Jan?"

"Mr. Ferthen, you mean?" replied his father, pouring himself some coffee. "Whatever this Elder did, he seems to be completely on the mend. It's astounding."

Raf glanced up at his grandfather who smiled back affectionately and said, "So, I understand the Foreman thinks highly of your musical abilities?"

Raf shook his head with a roll of his eyes.

Luka laughed softly in his quiet husky voice. "I imagine your mother's very proud, Raf, what with our musical heritage. I'm sure you know that my great uncle was the Bard in Yaelstead many years ago. An excellent lutist, I've been told. Perhaps you should visit sometime and find out more. Speaking of which, it must be almost time for sojourns, surely? Maybe a trip up north?"

Raf looked down at his plate in front of him, but was spared having to answer by his father, who said, "It's been a matter of some debate, actually, Luka. Raf has some rather... adventurous ideas about his sojourn. There are some safety issues."

"You can't be too adventurous with your sojourn, Tarvil," responded Luka with a chuckle. "I, myself, traveled to the Marshlands and stayed in one of the floating villages there. It was quite an experience really, and -"

"Perhaps we could *not* talk about this?" said Leiana sharply from the end of the table. "It doesn't concern you, father."

"But, Lei, the whole tradition of sojourns is about experiencing new challenges and new cult-"

"Then he can go to Dimb's End or Sayenham! Just leave it alone," she snapped. The kitchen was silent apart from the sound of Leiana cutting up a watermelon. "And anyway, until we find a cure for this tree disease - assuming there even is one - nobody will be going anywhere."

Luka grunted something inaudible and got up from the table to shuffle out the kitchen. Leiana clenched her jaws, carving up the watermelon with long, violent slices as Tarvil stared out the window and sipped his coffee. Raf toyed with some blackberries on his plate, wishing he was anywhere else at that moment.

Fortunately, a welcome distraction came in the form of the chimes suddenly ringing for a Council meeting. Elder Bolyai, it seemed, had returned from his visit to the area where Vince had died.

. . . .

The Foreman stood with the Elder in deep conversation when the last few Council members arrived at the chambers. The chattering died down as the Foreman held a hand up.

"Elder Bolyai has returned from visiting the diseased area. Unfortunately, he doesn't know of any cure himself, but -" there was a groan from Nathyn as he continued loudly, "- but, he has heard of an expert in iMahliland who he will seek out immediately. Jover and Fester have already kindly offered a wagon with a team of *saanen*."

This quietened the Council somewhat and there were a few hopeful looks cast across the room.

"Elder Bolyai has also asked for an assistant," continued the Foreman. "While it would seem that sojourns are unlikely to happen for a long while, this would be an opportunity for one of our school leavers to travel with the Elder. A rare privilege."

"Who will go?" asked Dalton.

"I will choose," replied the Elder. "The journey will be long and I would prefer one with some musical ability."

"How will you decide, might I ask?" inquired Madame Ottery. "Many are musical."

"Just bring the students here as soon as possible. I want to leave before noon."

. . . .

"Good morning," said Bolyai, once the assembled students had finished their response to his *gretanayre*. There were sixteen of them and they looked around at each other in excitement. "I had not expected so many."

Madame Ottery shrugged. "These are the ones of sojourn age who I would consider musical."

Bolyai waved a wrinkled hand dismissively, waiting for her to leave the room, and then faced the students. "I am leaving for iMahliland in a few hours and need an assistant. It will be hot and dangerous, but is important for all who live in the Forest." He turned around to point at a table behind him. "You have only one task, play this for me."

He removed a cloth and underneath lay a wooden instrument that looked vaguely flute-like at one end, with a few unusual loops in the middle and holes down one side. There were some strange levers toward the top as well and the bottom split into two bells that flared out delicately.

He pointed at the boy nearest him. "Name?"

"Err...Lewis Frenk, sir."

"The Frenks of Abiesborough?"

"Yes, sir," replied the boy, impressed. He turned and smiled proudly to his classmates who, as one, rolled their eyes at him.

"You, first."

Lewis stepped up to the instrument, put it to his mouth and blew into it hard. Nothing happened. Not even the sound of air moving through it. Lewis blew until his cheeks turned bright red.

"I think it's stuck, sir," he said, shaking it curiously.

"Yes, that's fine, thank you, Master Frenk. You may go."

Lewis placed it on the table carefully before walking out the room, blushing furiously as a few of the others sniggered.

"You, next. Name?"

"Luke Parron, sir." The muscular blond boy walked up to the instrument and struggled to blow it for half a minute, pressing different combinations of levers and holes to no avail, before he, too, was dismissed by Bolyai.

And so it carried on. One by one, the students attempted to play it and failed, to be sent out the room unceremoniously by the Elder. By the time the last one – a nervous Cisco – tried and was sent away, the Elder's face had turned flinty. He snatched the instrument up and left the room. Outside, a few of the Council were seated around a bench and looked up in interest.

"Who is it to be, Elder?" asked Dalton.

"None of them. Not one single student in that miserable bunch could play a single note on this," he snapped, holding the instrument up for them.

Madame Ottery frowned. "Elder, I am a journeyman musician and well-traveled, but I must confess that I've never even seen one of those before."

Bolyai grunted and started packing the instrument away. "It's called a *paodrin*. It's fairly old, but I was sure that there was at least one who would have the gift."

"And Raf wasn't any good?" the Foreman asked. "With all his recent surprises, I'm a bit disappointed, really."

"Who's this?" asked Bolyai, his eyes narrowing. "I thought you brought me all the students who were musical?"

"My son," replied Leiana frowning. "Was he not there?" She turned to Madame Ottery. "Resma, I thought you had collected them all?"

Resma pursed her lips and turned to Abuniah who shook his head. "Apparently we must have missed him."

"Well, never mind," said Tarvil, "he's just over there."

They looked to where he was pointing and saw Raf talking with Cisco, walking away toward the schools.

"Raf! Could you come here for a minute?"

. . . .

Raf looked up, and then grimaced when he saw his parents and a bunch of others standing with the Elder. He trudged up toward them nervously and mumbled a greeting, avoiding eye contact with his mother.

"Do something for me, boy," said the Elder. "Play this *paodrin*."

Raf squinted at the weird wooden thing. "I...er...I don't think I've ever heard of one of those before, Elder. Sorry. Perhaps someone else w-"

"Just try playing it, Raf," muttered Leiana irritably. "It would be nice if, just for once, you did what you were asked instead of immediately finding any way possible to avoid doing it."

Raf felt his cheeks heat up and glared at her.

She tilted her head at him, exasperated. "Just try!"

"Fine!" he snapped.

He took the instrument from the Elder and looked down at it, turning it over in his hands. Then, without a moment's hesitation, he slotted his hands into position and put the mouth-piece to his lips. A reedy but powerful note warbled out of the flared end and Raf played a few more different notes before thrusting the instrument out to Bolyai. "There. Can I go now?"

They were all looking at him with baffled expressions and the Elder's expression was intense and penetrating, his white eyebrows arched up to deepen the creases in his forehead. "How did you do that?"

"What, play it? I don't know. It's just obvious, isn't it? You have to suck the air through it, otherwise it won't work. It's a bit squeaky, but I think that's just because I've never played one before."

Bolyai took the instrument gently and looked at it blankly for a few seconds before turning to the Foreman and nodding almost imperceptibly.

The Foreman turned to Leiana. "Are you all right with it?"

"Of course," she said in a frosty tone. "It's for the good of the Forest after all. But you'll have to see if he's interested; I've found him less than amenable recently."

Raf looked at them suspiciously. "What?"

"The Elder is requesting your company on his journey to iMahliland to find a cure for the tree disease," said the Foreman. "Will you go, Raf?"

Raf looked at the crowd of Council members standing in front of him.

It's an important trip, I know, but it sounds so boring! I mean, iMahliland? It's just sand and stuff. Nobody even sojourns there.

He looked up at all of them. His mother tilted her head impatiently and raised an eyebrow.

Still, anything's better than staying here, surely...

Half an hour later, Raf walked with his father up to the East Ulnus path carrying a sack over his shoulder. In front of them, the sturdy wagon crawled along with the Elder and Orikon sitting on the driver's bench. It slowed and pulled up to a creaky halt as they reached the small crowd waiting to see them off.

"Ready?" asked the Foreman. "I'm sending Fergus with you to Luanchester, Tarvil. He's the most able of all of us to navigate around the rot. If you smell anything unusual – anything even slightly wrong - take no chances. Between Fergus and Orikon, you should find safe passage."

Tarvil nodded. "We'll reach Luanchester tomorrow morning if we travel hard; Orikon and I will try to get back straight away." He walked over to where Leiana was standing and embraced her.

Raf walked up behind him and stood awkwardly. "Bye, mom."

Leiana moved to hug him fiercely and then pulled away. "Look after him, Elder." She wrapped her shawl around herself tightly and walked away with Resma.

The Foreman started singing the *farwelayre* and the others joined in. Bolyai nodded to Orikon who flicked the reins and the wagon creaked back into motion. A few hundred feet down the path, they rounded a bend and the village disappeared from sight.

Raf scratched his head anxiously. It had all happened so quickly. He hadn't even had a chance to say goodbye to Cisco or Nedrick; he'd literally shoved some clothes into his bag and then left. He was actually leaving the Aeril Forest. And if that didn't feel bizarre enough, he was on his way to iMahliland!

Pulled by the four wiry *saanen*, the wagon moved along at a steady pace on its way down along the path. Tarvil and Orikon walked in quiet conversation in front of the wagon while Fergus skipped along the path singing to himself, staying far ahead of them.

"Play the *paodrin* for me again," said Bolyai suddenly. "We have a ways to go yet."

Raf took the odd instrument from the Elder's out-stretched hand. He turned it over in his hands, examining it a bit closer than he had earlier on. It really was an odd shape; the loops in the middle winding around each other with the strange levers on top. It reminded him a bit of the instrument he had made in his hidey-hole yesterday. He hadn't even had time to collect *that*, he realized. What a waste.

He held the *paodrin* up to his mouth, positioned his fingers where they felt most correct, and then inhaled softly through the mouthpiece. A simple tune came to mind and, although it took him a few goes to work out how to use the two levers perfectly and get the breathing right, he managed to run through the song a few times with increasing skill.

"That was nice!" said Fergus from the path ahead.

Bolyai stared at him silently.

Raf held out the instrument. "It's got a funny sound though, Elder. Am I doing it right?"

Bolyai shrugged. "No idea. I've never heard it played before."

Raf looked up at him. "Never? Cisco said you asked everyone to play it."

"And?"

"I....er..." he replied falteringly. "Surely it's not that complicated, Elder? Anyone can play it, you just have to breathe *in* through it."

"I'm sure they could if they knew it worked like that. But perhaps still not as well as you just played it. You have some small amount of natural talent, boy, I'll give you that."

"So, what does that mean? Did you ask for me to come along simply so I could play this silly thing for you?"

Bolyai turned slowly to peer coolly at Raf out of the corner of his eye.

"Er...I'm sorry, Elder, I don't mean to be rude. I just don't understand why you asked *me*. There are other students who're loads better."

Bolyai let out a loud scathing laugh which caught the attention of the two men in front who looked back curiously. "True musical talent is less common than you think."

"But why's that important, though? It's just music, right?"

"That," said Bolyai softly, poking Raf in his chest, "is exactly where you are as ignorant as the other foolish villagers. Music is fundamental."

"But, how?" replied Raf, shaking his head. "That's just the same sort of thing that Bhothy kept going on about, but -"

"Bhothy?" said Tarvil sharply from in front of them. "Don't tell me you went to the banyans, Raf! You *know* that's forbidden!"

Raf clamped his mouth shut and looked down quickly, furious with himself.

"Well?" Tarvil asked again, walking back toward him with a stern expression. Raf nodded glumly, refusing to meet his eyes. "Raf! If your mother knew you'd been there, your life wouldn't be worth living!"

"Wait, Bhothy Manyara? Eliath's cousin?" asked Bolyai. Tarvil nodded. "I seem to remember he was the village Bard. Not a particularly good one, but the Bard nonetheless, yes?"

"It's complicated," replied Tarvil, still frowning at Raf. "He did something very foolish years ago and the Foreman banished him."

"You banished your Bard?" replied Bolyai incredulously.

He threw his arms up in the air.

"It was for the good of the village, Elder."

"No wonder we've got problems! He is the caretaker of our musical heritage, the -"

"More like the caretaker of alcohol..." muttered Raf.

"And I don't blame him!" retorted Bolyai. "If -"

He paused as a shout came from up the path. "It's here! The smell!" yelled Fergus.

Raf breathed in deeply through his nose and caught, amidst the floral aromas, a whiff of moldy decay.

"Where's it coming from?" Tarvil scanned the terrain in front of them nervously.

"The path goes into two here, sir, and...I can smell it really bad down the left one. Do you want me to go closer and s-"

"No!" called all of them at once.

Tarvil pointed down the right branch of the path. "We have to hope that it doesn't extend down there as well. I don't much fancy slogging our way through the thick brambles around here."

"There isn't any smell from there, Mr. Gency. I think it's safe."

A rustling to their left drew their attention and suddenly, with a crash, a man burst out from between two bushes, sprinting across the path directly in front of them. It was the dark iMahli – the fourth *dholaki*. He turned toward them, jumped in fright, and then tripped over a root. He had barely landed on his chest in the dirt before he leaped to his feet again and took off down the path, but it was too late. From behind them, there was a whistling noise overhead and something shiny flew spinning through the air. The group watched in shock as a weighted rope whipped around the iMahli's legs and he fell to the ground again. Three other iMahlis crept into view from the thick brush, ululating loudly.

It's those dholaki *that mom hired!* thought Raf.

They ran up to the struggling man and quickly encircled

him. One had a large bow with an arrow notched, whilst the other two held metal-tipped spears over their heads. They were completely oblivious to the forester party and Raf glanced at the others who also stood there in surprise, unsure of what to do.

"Edokko," called Orikon to the leader. "What's going on?"

Edokko glanced over to them, his face glistening with sweat. If he was surprised to see them standing there, he didn't show it. "Nothing to do with you, forester. This *bhesanté* belongs to me."

Raf leaned over to Tarvil and asked, "What's a *bhesanté*, dad? I thought they were iMahlis?"

"*Bhesanté* are the largest tribe of iMahlis. Edokko and his men are from the other smaller tribe called *fetumu*."

"But what are they doing to that guy?"

"I think we need to stay out of this," replied his father. "The man is probably a thief or something."

"Pah, rubbish," muttered Bolyai. "More like he's their slave. *Fetumu* deal in slave-trading. Their favorite prey are their fellow iMahlis."

The iMahli on the ground gave up trying to undo the ropes tangled around his ankles and twisted to face Tarvil, yelling, "Please! I a-"

He keeled over as the butt-end of a spear was rammed into his head. The *fetumu* standing behind him knelt down and tried to tie his arms together, but the man struggled away from him, his free arm moving to his leather belt to whip out something that he held up for them to see. The *fetumu* immediately swung his spear at the outstretched hand, knocking something hard to spin through the air and disappear into some bushes near the foresters.

"What was that?" said Bolyai, craning to see over the side of the wagon.

"I couldn't see," replied Orikon. "A necklace or something?"

206

The *bhesanté* groaned and cradled his hand against his chest before two of the iMahlis swooped in to wrestle him physically to the ground.

Fergus sprang away to the bushes and within seconds had picked up something and returned it to Tarvil. "Here."

Tarvil held it up in surprise. "I know this talisman. It's Abuniah's! How did he get it? Maybe the man *is* a thief." He cast a hesitant look at the iMahli.

Fergus was staring at the scene with wide eyes. "Is that man *really* a slave, Mr. Gency? I thought they only had those in Miern, like the ones in the Pits."

"I don't know, Fergus, but I think we need to have a talk with that *bhesanté* and find out what's going on here." Tarvil straightened his belt and stepped up toward the group of men with his hands held up.

As soon as Edokko saw him, he lunged forward waving the notched arrow at Tarvil's chest. "Back!"

"I want to speak to this man," said Tarvil.

"No! He is mine."

"Not according to our laws, iMahli. I must insist that you let me talk to him."

Edokko stepped forward between Tarvil and the *bhesanté* and one of the others jumped to his feet and whipped his spear into the air. Tarvil moved back defensively until Orikon appeared at his side, his bow and arrow also drawn and notched. The hunter was a tall and powerfully built man, but the iMahlis showed little fear. However, when there was a metallic click from the wagon behind, the iMahlis paused and looked past him nervously. Raf turned to see Bolyai standing over a chunky crossbow that was resting on the rail, two thick ironwood bolts loaded, and his finger curled casually around the trigger.

Edokko barked a quick order to his men and the two behind the *bhesanté* immediately hauled him to his feet and shuffled backward with their weapons still trained on the foresters.

With a roar and a shove, the *bhesanté* broke free of his guards and sprinted through Edokko and the other man, knocking them sideways. Edokko reacted instantly and brought his bow up in one swift motion to unleash an arrow at the back of the fleeing man. It whizzed through the air, narrowly missing him and pierced one of the *saanen* behind them with a wet thud. The animal bleated in agony and stumbled over onto the ground. The iMahli next to Edokko took a step forward and started to throw his spear, but stalled halfway through as an arrow suddenly thudded into his shoulder. He dropped to the ground, roaring in pain. Seeing Orikon setting another arrow to his bow, Edokko shouted something back at the others and they turned as one and fled.

The foresters stood their ground and watched as the iMahlis sprinted away, one stumbling as he cradled his injured shoulder. They didn't look back once as they ran down the path. The left fork of the path...

Raf stood up on the wagon back, stuttering, "Isn't that -"

"Wait!" shouted Tarvil, running forward. "Don't go that wa-"

It was too late. A cracking noise rumbled through the ground, interrupting him. The iMahlis skidded to a halt and stared around in confusion. With a ripping sound, the ground around them split open and the iMahlis were sucked downward, disappearing in a cloud of dust. Their screams faded very quickly.

"We must move!" urged Bolyai, watching as the ground continued to buckle and crumble outward.

Orikon whipped out his hunting knife and in two quick slices cut the cord binding the *bhesanté's* hands, and then did the same to the tether harnessing the dead *saanen*. He took the animal's body and hoisted it onto the back of the wagon as Bolyai shouted loudly and flicked the reins. The three remaining goats tugged hard and the wagon jerked forward along the path.

They traveled for half a mile or so before finally slowing down. Fergus crept around the area and came back to report that he couldn't smell anything bad around them, so they relaxed on the ground and caught their breath.

The iMahli crouched down on his heels and rubbed the back of his head gently.

"You got a bit of a knock there," said Tarvil.

The *bhesanté* shrugged and then said, "My thanks." He patted his chest. "I am Tiponi."

"And how is it that you came by this, Tiponi?" Tarvil held up Abuniah's talisman.

"Your griot, he gave it to me. He said if I need help, to show that."

"Griot?" Raf looked at Tarvil.

"Their word for a musician," said Tarvil. He turned back to Tiponi. "Have you met our griot before?"

"Those *fetumu* who died there," began Tiponi, "they were taking me somewhere in the forest. Your griot knew who I was and gave me this gift. I escaped this morning."

"What do you mean he knew who you were?" asked Raf. "Who are you, Tiponi? Someone important?"

Tiponi gave a scowl, as if angry with himself, and then turned away. Bolyai had sat up, giving the iMahli a strange, intense look.

"We're all friends here, Tiponi," encouraged Tarvil. "You have nothing to fear from us."

Tiponi shook his head firmly. "It is not fear, forester. I owe you my life, but it is not for me to say who I am. Please, do not ask me to do this thing."

Not for him to say who he is? Raf thought. *What's that supposed to mean?*

As if echoing Raf's thoughts, Orikon gave a half-smile and said, "Who but *you* can say who you are, iMahli?"

Tiponi ignored him.

"He's not allowed to say who he is because it puts certain other people in danger. Am I right, Tiponi?" Bolyai sounded uncharacteristically excited and the others turned to look at him. "I've never met one before. Excellent!" Bolyai broke into a delighted smile. "Tiponi is a go-between!"

The iMahli's expression turned to utter dismay. "How do you know this?" he spat. His whole body tensed, and it seemed to Raf that he was steeling himself to either attack them or run away.

"Just a good guess."

"This is..." Tiponi's voice cracked with emotion. "This cannot happen! No-one can know this! I cannot betray my Trust!" He held out his hands imploringly to the group, his breathing ragged.

"Calm down, go-between. Your secret is safe with us," replied Bolyai.

"Safe? How can I trust you?"

"Well, for one thing, we saved your life. You owe us a debt, my friend. Secondly, I am a Forest Elder."

"You? You are *ishranga*? This is how you know these things?"

Bolyai nodded and Tiponi touched his fingers to his forehead in an oddly reverent way.

"Elder, what is an *ishranga*?" asked Tarvil.

Raf closed his mouth, relieved his father had beaten him to asking the question.

"An iMahli Elder. Tiponi is the link between the tribe and their *ishranga*. The reason he's so worried is because no other iMahlis, apart from the go-betweens, know where these *ishrangas* are. Being hidden keeps them safe from harm."

"Why would someone want to hurt an Elder?" asked Fergus, horrified.

"Well, boy," replied Bolyai, "in iMahliland, *ishrangas* are the carriers of the tribes' lore and traditions. They are important and dearly respected."

"It is so," agreed Tiponi.

"*Ishrangas* are also very powerful," continued Bolyai. "I've heard that they can do mysterious things, and have access to ancient knowledge, but their secrets are closely guarded - that's what this 'Trust' is. And that's why I want to speak to a certain *ishranga* I've heard of about a cure. I feel sure they will have the answer."

"Have you met one before?" asked Raf.

Bolyai shook his head. "They are well hidden and fiercely protected. Perhaps that is why they have lasted this long."

"It is so," repeated Tiponi. "Until now. A month ago, two go-betweens were taken. A week later, their *ishrangas* were dead. I must warn all the others, which is why I must return home to Dandari."

"Dandari, you say?" said Bolyai intently. "Now there's a coincidence. I'm seeking an *ishranga* quite near Dandari. One called Shima'sidu."

Tiponi's eyes widened completely at the name. "I...I cannot talk of this!" He scrambled to his feet and stood staring up the path, his body absolutely rigid.

. . . .

Far behind the forester party, where the paths had forked, silence finally settled again and the dust from the collapsed ground was cleared away by the afternoon breeze. A herd of wild *saanen* wandered out through the undergrowth and onto the path, nibbling away at shoots growing around a thick banyan.

One of them lifted its head, eyes flickering to the gaping crevice further up the path; a soft rustling could be heard coming from inside. It edged closer to the noise, short tail twitching nervously behind it. A particularly loud crack was heard, and as one, the entire herd's heads sprang up, all eyes turning to stare intently at the hole.

Nearest them, some long roots went taut over the side of the dark pit and then quivered slightly in the dirt. In a flash, the *saanen* erupted in panic and scrambled backward to disappear into the safety of the brush.

"**O**y, time to go."

Raf woke up at a nudge from his father. His eyes had grown too heavy to resist a quick nap after a massive meal – something he wasn't used to having in the middle of the day. The Luanchester Foreman had returned from the Overcouncil the evening before, and when the little Eirdale group had arrived late that morning, they were greeted by an enthusiastic crowd singing the *gretanayre,* before being ushered to a feast prepared in their honor. Yawning, he walked with Tarvil to where the others waited and slung his bag up onto the back of the wagon.

Orikon patted his shoulder. "Good luck. Bring back a cure."

Fergus pushed past to wrap Raf in a tight hug and then stepped aside to let Tarvil by.

"Try not to get yourself into too much trouble and we'll see you in a few days, yeah?" Raf smiled nervously at him. "You'll be fine. You may not get a sojourn after this, so make the most of it." A flicker of a smile crossed Tarvil's face. "And try to stay in the Elder's good books."

Bolyai picked something out of his teeth. "Come on," he muttered. "We have miles to go before sunset."

Orikon passed Raf a small wooden container. "Here's some shea butter. It's what the canopy farmers use when they work in the direct sun. Make sure you put it on every day until –"

"– you start looking like Tiponi," chuckled Tarvil.

"– until you're used to it," said Orikon.

213

Raf laughed, despite himself and then took a breath. "All right, then."

Bolyai clicked his tongue and, with the addition of a replacement goat from a Luanchester farmer, the team of *saanen* moved forward slowly. Raf turned one last time to wave at the group standing behind, and then jumped up on the back of the wagon with Tiponi. The sound of the *farwelayre* drifted up to them from behind and faded as they rolled out of earshot.

. . . .

Knock knock knock.

"Foreman!"

The Foreman got up from his desk and opened the Council room door. He stared down at the sweating face of a familiar student who was standing there, ashen-faced.

"What is it, Cisco?"

The boy was holding a tiny birch paper note in his hand. "Foreman, I've been looking after the dovecote since Orikon left and a message has just come through from someone called Tunit in Three Ways."

"The apprentice carpenter? What does it say? Is it about the Festival? Or the crossroads?"

"No, sir. It's about something that's happened with a villager. Stan Dawsley's been arrested."

"Dawsley? What do you mean 'arrested'?"

"Sir, he says that Miernan soldiers did it."

"What?" said the Foreman. "Arresting a Council member? Miernan soldiers can't do that!" He paced back and forth. "What *is* Allium up to? And Stan Dawsley of all people?" He clenched his fists behind him and stared out the window at the fading sunset.

"Foreman?"

"Ring the chimes, Cisco; I need my Council here right now."

The *saanen* jostled into each other, bleating urgently as they tried to get out of the way of the two approaching men. Tarvil and Orikon marched quickly up through the darkening village to the sequoia chambers and paused outside the entrance as they heard an argument in full swing inside.

Tarvil gave the tall hunter standing next to him a wry look. "Another cheerful meeting, it seems."

Orikon grunted and pressed forward through the doorway. The Council looked up as they entered and the bear-like Foreman Manyara instantly launched into the *gretanayre* with enthusiasm. When the singing had finished, he gestured for them to take their seats around the table in the room.

"Evening. I know you've only just arrived back from Luanchester, but I'm afraid there's more news from up north."

Tarvil smiled faintly at him. "With all that has happened this past week, I don't suppose we should be surprised at more gripping developments."

Leiana gave him a brief hug and then angrily said, "Even though the coterie up there has apparently been closed, we've had a message snuck through from Three Ways telling us that Stan Dawsley has been arrested."

"It would seem," added the Foreman, "that Councilman Dawsley was attempting to make his way here when he was stopped by Miernan soldiers and forcibly returned to the village. The message doesn't give us much more information other than that."

"So do we think that Allium has somehow hired himself some military heavies from Miern?" asked Tarvil. "Just to make sure his Festival is a success? It seems a little extreme."

"Of course it is," said Dalton from the other table end. "It's more likely that this is all a huge misunderstanding. Allium wouldn't think of bringing Miernan soldiers into all this."

Leiana and Dr. Allid challenged him on this before the Foreman raised his hands and shouted, "Quiet!"

They stopped and sullenly turned to him.

"Personally, as much as I want to wring Allium's neck with my own bare hands, I believe we must give him the benefit of the doubt until we see something more solid than a pigeon message. Relationships are strained enough between Eirdale and Three Ways as it is."

"But Miernan soldiers? Arresting foresters?" said Leiana. "They have no authority here! We need to confront him!"

"But we must be careful," urged Tarvil. "This letter says that Dawsley has been 'arrested'? But what does that mean? And it seems a poor reason to arrest someone just for traveling south. Maybe he was stopped from doing something unlawful? We can't rule that out, as unlikely as it is. We must know more about it!"

The Foreman cupped his chin pensively. "I think I have to agree with you on this. We mustn't presume too much, despite Allium's Festival betrayal and this nonsense with cutting down the *Ancient*. Travel is hazardous now, and for all we know he may have sent messengers to us who couldn't get here. Perhaps the barricade was erected for that reason."

"Without any evidence, that seems the most obvious explanation," agreed Dalton. "We can hardly base everything on some brief note from a young boy. Personally, I'm more worried about finding a cure for the trees. I've had three more reports of new rotten patches since yesterday!"

The Foreman pinched the bridge of his nose and sighed. "Everything rests on this expert the Elder knows. If their journey is unsuccessful, all our other troubles - including these hassles with Three Ways – are going to be obsolete."

Tarvil nodded. "Well, they'll be back in a few days. Until then, there's nothing we can do about that, so let's try to get word to this Tunit in Three Ways and see if we can find out more details."

. . . .

Voices woke Raf up and he realized he'd fallen asleep again from the gentle rocking motion of the wagon. He opened his eyes to see Bolyai and Tiponi deep in discussion in front.

"– but it left this wound to remind me," finished the *bhesanté,* tapping his shoulder.

"Wait, how did you get that?" asked Raf.

"Ah, the energetic youth awakes from his second nap of the exhausting afternoon riding on a wagon," said Bolyai dryly.

Raf smiled and stretched. "No seriously, how did you get it, Tiponi?"

The iMahli reached around to run his hand along the pretty savage wound on his shoulder. "I was hunting with some others from my village when the *fetumu* attacked us. I, alone, escaped and hid in a tree. The branch I was in, it broke underneath me. The edge of the branch made this."

"Oooh," groaned Raf, shuddering.

"It is not a good injury. I tried to find the healer in Dombonyoka, but the *fetumu* tracked me and caught me. They took me through the forest. To your village, first. Lucky for me."

"Oh." Raf lay back and gazed around idly at the scattered rays of hot sun piercing the canopy, before reaching over and taking the *paodrin* from its pouch next to Bolyai. He held it to his lips, put his fingers in place along the various holes, and played. He stared, mesmerized, at his fingers which danced in front of his eyes as if they had taken on a life of their own.

He couldn't say how long he had played for, but some time later he finally stopped and returned it distractedly to the pouch, stretching his cramped neck.

"You are good," said Tiponi. He nodded his head at the *paodrin.* "What is that instrument?"

217

"Um…it's the Elder's," replied Raf. "And I'm not that good, really."

Bolyai watched him out of the corner of his eye as he lounged against the side of the driver's bench, running his fingers through his thin wisps of beard. Glancing at the path in front of them, he looked out at the sinking sun and then, with a tug on the reins, called the goats to a halt.

"Dinner," he said in response to Raf's questioning look. "An early night, and then tomorrow we will set off at dawn and hopefully reach Dandari by nightfall."

He dismounted from the wagon and dug around in a sack attached to the railing. From inside, he pulled out two dead wood pigeons and threw them down at Raf's feet. "Prepare these."

"I don't think my knife's sharp enough, Elder. I blunted it quite badly recently." He realized that the Elder probably didn't know about the incident with Wesp and quickly continued. "I normally sharpen it using Dad's whetstone, but I didn't bring it with me, sorry."

"What are you on about?" said Bolyai. "Just use any stone."

"A stone? But I told you, I didn't bring anything. I nor-" Raf stopped. The Elder was pointing a finger at the ground.

"A stone from… Are we… do you mean…" Raf stared down at the ground in bewilderment. There were stones scattered everywhere! Then he looked up and saw that all around them, stretching away as far as he could see in any direction were trees. *Small* trees. There wasn't an *Ancient* in sight. They were out of the Forest.

"You are now standing on the border with iMahliland," said Bolyai.

"Over there are the Dombonyoka Hills. Past them, you will be in my land," said Tiponi.

Raf stood and stared at them, a blush creeping up his face. His hand shook as he lifted it up to wipe a sudden sheen from his forehead. "I didn't even realize," he mumbled faintly.

"You *were* playing the *paodrin* for an age," said Bolyai. "But enough now. We need food and water. You will have plenty of time to get used to being out of the Forest."

He moved off to relieve himself behind some bushes as Tiponi strolled up the path, scanning the ground, before kneeling down and unearthing a fist-sized rock from the dirt. He walked back to Raf, dusting the rock down, and gave it him.

Raf took his knife out and set to running the blade carefully up and down the side of the rock, absorbing himself in the task to calm down and settle his thoughts.

OK. I'm out of the Forest. Actually on solid ground. No Ancients *anywhere, just…little trees. This is… incredible.*

By the time he managed to get the knife sharp enough to prepare the birds, Tiponi had set up a small fire and Bolyai was cleaning some strange potatoes he had found. Rather than the small round ones that they ate in the Forest, these were huge – a foot long each - and a pale red color.

"If you're thirsty," said Bolyai, "I'm sure Tiponi can show you how to find some waterwort nearby. You should learn how to do that now because after the mountains, water will become a problem."

Raf could only purse his lips in confusion and look at Tiponi blankly. The iMahli gestured for him to follow. They walked down the path until Tiponi grunted and pointed at a tiny purple flower growing up through some dry grass.

"*Shuji.* If you find it, there is water under." As he was explaining, he demonstrated by scooping dirt away in a circle around the flower. "Take this out."

Under the flower was a huge round turnip-like root that Tiponi pulled up. It was surprisingly big - head-sized - and when he cut into it, a succulent cream-colored flesh was exposed. Taking Raf's knife, he scraped it sideways along the inner flesh of the root until he had a handful of soggy splinters. He squeezed them in his hand over his tilted head, and a line of water trickled into his open mouth.

He passed the knife back to Raf. "Now you."

It was quite easy to do - although you didn't get a huge amount of liquid out of the handfuls; but it was cool and had the slightest suggestion of sweetness to it.

It's not a watervine, but at least it does the job, Raf thought.

He stood up when he'd finished, and after making sure he could recognize the flower in the future, walked back to the others with the other half of the root for Bolyai. Not long after, Raf was finishing a crispy wing as Bolyai put the fire out and ground up some of the waterwort.

"How is your shoulder, Tiponi?"

The iMahli shrugged. "There is pain, but it will heal."

"Maybe we can speed it up with some aloe and a few herbs," said the Elder. "Don't want it to get infected."

He retrieved a small bag from the wagon which had an assortment of leaves folded inside it. Crushing a succulent piece of aloe in his hands, he began rubbing it softly onto Tiponi's wound. "I know it hurts at first, but this will make it better quicker." He glanced at Raf. "Do you remember the *haelanayre*?"

Raf nodded vaguely as he stared at Tiponi's shoulder, failing to notice the peculiar look that Bolyai gave him. The Elder started singing softly and Raf accompanied him, watching the Elder's hands move gently along the wound. It was an easy, lilting melody and he found his eyes closing as he sang along.

Even in the glare of the setting sun, he found the sudden glimmer of colors in his mind dazzling. He didn't flinch from it though, and let it swell around him in its now familiar way.

He focused in on where the wound was and saw that, while it wasn't as intensely black as the mass of threads he'd seen in Jan, there was definitely a small streak of darkness. And as with before, he could make out a subtle drifting of blue mist toward the dark patch. He also felt a peculiar sense of someone else there with him, another connection to the colors.

220

So, it was the Elder! He definitely knows how to use it, too.

He watched as the colors moved toward the patch, inch by inch. It was very slow though, so Raf concentrated and threw himself wading forward into the color. A flood of energy filled him and brought a wave of goose-bumps as he felt himself connect with the colors, becoming one with them. He had hardly even started thinking about trying to heal the wound when a sapphire streak crystallized out of the surrounding mist and swept in, as thick as syrup. It poured over the blackness where the wound was, completely filling and saturating it. In seconds, he could see that the dark patch was no longer there; it had been completely erased.

Raf smiled to himself with satisfaction. And then for a brief moment his awareness switched to a more external one and he heard himself singing alone.

Not again...

He opened his eyes and saw the Elder not two feet from him. His face bore an expression of disbelief that made Raf's heart leap into his throat.

"*You,*" whispered Bolyai. The haggard old man was crouched with one knee on the ground, pointing a finger at him. He stood up slowly and stepped closer to him, pushing the finger hard into Raf's chest. "What color was it, boy?"

"I don't know wh-"

"What *color* was it?" hissed the Elder.

"I... blue, I think? I don't know what you m..." stammered Raf desperately. "How did you know? Did you see it, too?"

The Elder gaped at him, his mouth quivering slightly. His arm slowly lowered until it lay against his side again. "I knew it," he whispered. "I *knew* there was one there. It was you in the tree, wasn't it? And you with the sick woodsmith."

Then, to Raf's astonishment, the Elder tilted his head back and erupted into a husky laugh, clenching his gnarled fists in front of him and pumping them up and down.

Raf tried to quickly get up, but as he did he came face to

face with Tiponi who was staring at him wildly, one arm hooked back rubbing his shoulder.

Bolyai bent over to catch his breath, wheezing, and then beckoned to Raf. "Listen to me," he said slowly. "Your Bard - the one who was banished?"

"What about him?"

"When you went to speak to him, did he tell you anything about music? *Old* music?"

"No...."

"He never mentioned *anything* to you about music? That's a pity." Bolyai looked away deep in thought. "It was lucky I came when I did. So old already. But, never mind, it's still... after so long... to find one..."

"What are you talking about?" begged Raf.

"I don't even know where to start, boy," said Bolyai. "If you learned nothing from your Bard -"

"He's an idiot!" said Raf. "He was always drunk and going on about crazy stuff. Some music, yeah, but most of it was rubbish about it being food for plants or something! And he called it menfi...meg...- well, something about foraging, or -"

Bolyai interrupted Raf by laughing again, his head tilting back up to the sky. "Indeed! Coincidence? I think not. The boy already knows of melforging and -"

"Melforger! That's it!" cut in Raf. "I remember now, a melforger! But, what *is* it?"

Nodding slowly to himself, Bolyai looked up at Raf. "That, boy, is what you are."

Raf tenderly rubbed some shea butter on the back of his neck, grimacing at the sharp sting of the exposed reddened skin above his shirt.

"No good putting it on *now*, boy. You should have done it yesterday afternoon when we first left the Forest."

Raf ignored the Elder and stretched his neck, feeling the onset of a dull headache. They'd been traveling for hours now since they'd left at dawn, and without an *Ancient* in sight, there was hardly any cover to block the brutal sun when it slid up over the horizon.

"Should we continue our chat, then?"

Raf shook his head irritably. "It's no good, Elder. It's just pointless."

Bolyai looked up at the skies and muttered, "First one in over a hundred years and it *would* be a whiny teenager."

He turned to Raf with feigned patience. "Maybe a different song would be better? If you'd only try what I was saying, y-"

"I don't know what you mean, though," interrupted Raf. "You talk about *holding* the color? That's not really how it works for me."

"Well, how do you use it, boy? Explain to me, then I can try to help you."

"I don't know!" replied Raf. "It's complicated. I don't *use* it, I sort of move with it. I don't know…" He groaned. "It's so hot. I just want to be cool for a bit."

"Oh, stop feeling sorry for yourself," said the Elder. "You must learn to harness it, even if you have to start with small steps. It's a skill that hasn't been seen for generations and I haven't met many other Elders, even, who were melforgers. There's only me and a few others, and none of us could do what you did to Tiponi's shoulder as quickly, or even half as well."

At hearing his name, the iMahli glanced back at them. He hadn't said a word to Raf since the incident, although when he looked at him, it was with an odd, unreadable expression.

Probably thinks I'm some sort of freak, Raf thought.

He found his eyes drawn yet again to the dark man's shoulder, and searched for any evidence of the vicious injury that had been there only the night before. There was absolutely nothing. If there was even a scar, it was so faint as to be almost invisible.

He chewed his lip and forced himself to look up at the path, noting wearily that there didn't seem to be an end in sight of the shallow rolling hill-tops. Another thing that was becoming more and more common was a short, wiry tree that Bolyai told him was called an acacia.

A pretty name for an unfriendly looking tree.

From a distance, they looked like soft green umbrellas, but up close, their branches and leaves were laden with countless small thorns. He was staring at a little copse of them in the distance when he noticed some movement underneath. Squinting, he stared hard, not believing his eyes - until they got close enough to get a clear view, and his mouth fell right open. They were birds. But huge! With thick feathered bodies on top of long, gangly legs and a neck that almost doubled their height, all of them would have towered at least a foot above Tiponi.

The iMahli had also spotted them. "There. We change for these." He nodded at the goats pulling the wagon

"What?" Raf sat up, his face twisting with suspicion. "What's he saying?"

Bolyai looked at him and the tiniest smile creased his

224

mouth. "You heard him. The goats won't do well in these conditions, let alone once we get out into the real plains, so we must change them at this farmstead for some ostriches."

"Wait," said Raf standing up. "Wait. We're going to travel into the plains, the dangerous plains I've heard about? Pulled by these 'ostriches', as you call them? You're not just pulling my leg here because I've never left the Forest before?" Bolyai sighed and gave Tiponi a dry look. "I mean, seriously, Elder, I'm really going to travel in a wagon pulled by some *birds*?"

"I suppose you could try to ride one yourself, if you wanted," said Bolyai. "But they can kick quite fiercely and their talons are razor sharp."

Raf slouched down heavily on the floor and rubbed his temples. "Too much sun. I've just had too much sun. Dad was right."

They reached the pen with the ostriches and a small group of iMahlis emerged from the shade of some acacias, walking up to greet Tiponi. They clapped their hands in front of their chests a few times and spoke to him in a way that seemed deferential, and Raf was reminded again that their friend was an iMahli of some stature.

The meeting didn't take long and after a few glances past Tiponi to the wagon, the deal appeared to be done. Tiponi untied the goats and led them into a pen, whilst the other iMahlis selected two ostriches and led them out by the thin harnesses they wore.

Raf noted that the two they had picked were larger than the rest, and their plumage completely different to the others. While most of the birds in the pen were a dull mottled brown, these two had a mix of tightly packed black feathers over the majority of their bodies, with startling flashes of white peeking out from under their wings and also atop the small fan of tail feathers.

He watched warily as they were harnessed to the wagon, taking in their talons which did indeed look capable of causing serious damage, and the large beaks from which there was an occasional low hissing. Their eyes were dark brown and stared impassively at Raf as the cords were all tightened. He decided he would keep his distance from the monstrous beasts and tried to inconspicuously move to the back of the wagon.

With another round of short claps, the iMahlis bid them farewell and Tiponi jumped up to take the reins. With a powerful heave from the birds, the wagon lurched into motion back toward the path. Tiponi clicked his tongue when they reached it and directed the birds to cross over into the dry grassland that covered the whole area.

"They can certainly move," muttered Raf, holding on to the sides as the wheels bounced over the uneven terrain. The ostriches' long necks were taut as their legs pumped furiously, kicking up sand and debris from the path.

Bolyai gave a grunt as they hit a tree root and then scowled briefly at the back of Tiponi. "This noise will make it hard for us to take up where we left off."

"With the music thing again?"

Bolyai's reply was cut off as he had to dodge a low hanging acacia branch that scraped over the side of the wagon.

"Well, that's a pity," said Raf, carefully looking up the path. The Elder watched him for a bit. "Do your parents know?"

Raf spun around. "No!" He hesitated and bit his lip. "Nobody knows. Not even my friends. I mean, I don't even know what I'd tell them."

"Your parents will want to know about this, trust me, boy."

"Will they? I don't think so," Raf replied. "I've never heard anyone say anything about this sort of thing before. Besides, then my mother'd probably make me sing *all* the time. It was bad enough she wanted me to perform in the stupid Festival."

Bolyai frowned at him. "You don't like music?"

"Of course I like music. I just don't like standing up and...you know..."

"You're afraid you'll embarrass yourself?"

"No, that's not it," replied Raf. "Well, I don't know. Maybe it is."

"If you practice and get good enough, though, I think you will find pleasure in it. This is a gift. You have a duty to use it, don't you see that?"

Raf looked skeptical and then reached down to get the shea butter again.

"There is so much we've lost over the years. So much." Bolyai stared pensively at the wagon floor. "If I cannot help you, then we must find someone who can. There is tell of people in Miern –"

"Melforgers?" Raf looked up in interest.

Bolyai shook his head. "That would be very unlikely. But I have heard that there are some with the talent amongst them. If we are to find someone to help you, it will be there, I feel sure."

"In Miern?" said Raf. "I was going to sojourn there. You're welcome to talk to my mother though, because she isn't interested in the idea."

"Oh, she's probably right, boy. Don't be mistaken, Miern is a dangerous place."

"Great, you sound *just* like her."

Bolyai stared at Raf, an eyebrow raised. "I…" Even in the blazing heat, Raf could feel his cheeks glow red. "Sorry, Elder."

Bolyai grunted softly and then reached down to seize a stick of dried meat to chew on.

"Besides," Raf continued, "we've got to fix the Forest before we can do anything else, right? My family's stuck in there. How long till we get to this *ishranga* person?"

Tiponi leaned back from the bench and replied, "Whole day."

"And to the escarpment?" asked Bolyai.

"Not long," replied Tiponi.

Raf scanned ahead of them through the trees and saw nothing that stood out from the rolling plains of dry grass.

"What's this escarpment?"

Bolyai smiled. "A treat for the eyes. We've been climbing steadily for a while now and will soon reach the top. It's quite something. We'll rest there before we head down onto the plains."

. . . .

Raf looked up at the sound of Tiponi whistling at the ostriches. The wagon drew to a stop and with the halt in its noisy progress, a peace fell. The wind whistled softly through the grass and then a few seconds later, a few staccato blasts of chirruping came from crickets hidden in the undergrowth. Somewhere in the distance, a lone hornbill blew a shrill trumpeting call.

Getting up from the uncomfortable position he'd had to adopt with all the bouncing, Raf stretched and looked around. Behind them to the left and right was the same rolling plain of grass sprinkled with acacia trees, but in front of them was a small rise that seemed to disappear into the sky.

"Go have a look," said Bolyai.

Raf jumped down off the wagon and, keeping a wide berth of the ostriches, stepped his way through the dry grass toward the top of the slope. As he got closer, he realized that hidden in the grass were some things that made him draw up, a crooked smile appearing on his face.

"Rocks." He sounded the word out and his smile broadened into a wide grin. It wasn't anything like the whetstones they used in the Forest and until you actually saw a 'rock', it was difficult to imagine the textured hardness and mottled grey color of these huge natural objects. And they were just sitting here!

A soft breeze brought a moment of coolness to his burned cheeks and he looked up to find himself facing a vista that took his breath away. Directly in front of him, for a mile perhaps, the mountain side sloped down at a sharp angle until it leveled out far below. From there, as far as the eye could see, a vast plain was laid out like a sandy brown tablecloth, scattered with lumpy hills and granite knolls, and dotted here and there with tiny acacia trees. The landscape rolled away and just kept rolling and rolling until it faded from view in the shimmering distance.

"Impressive, isn't it?" came the quiet voice of Bolyai behind him. Raf nodded, lost for words. "Well, come on then."

Tiponi steered the wagon toward a break in the rocks and they found themselves at the beginning of a path which set off at an angle down the slope. Shading his eyes, Raf followed it and saw that it veered left a few hundred feet down, then right, and so on, moving like a snake between the clumps of rock all the way down to the bottom.

An awful long way to go when it'd probably be quicker just to go straight down, surely, he mused.

As he was about to voice this opinion, he watched a small rock, dislodged from its place by an ostrich's talons, tumble forward and then pick up speed rolling down the escarpment. Bouncing high in the air, it only took a matter of seconds before it reached the bottom of the slope, where it hurtled hard into another rock. The sharp clatter of the impact was loud enough to drift all the way up to Raf. He winced and looked at Tiponi who was on foot, slowly leading the ostriches along the path.

I'm glad he knows what he's doing.

. . . .

It took an age, but the wagon made its way down the treacherous incline and eventually the path leveled out into a less precipitous slope and Tiponi climbed back up on the driver's bench.

The heat had intensified more and more as they descended, and now, without the breeze that had given them some respite higher above, everything seemed to roast. Even as he looked around, the trees and grass as close as fifty yards away swayed eerily in the searing haze. It was too hot for anything else other than sitting silently on the wagon, staring out at the plains. Nobody said a word. Not even when they stopped and Tiponi found some *shuji* to dice up for water for the ostriches, squeezing the moisture into a wooden bowl which they drank in seconds.

Raf found himself rocking to the motion of the wagon, unable to sleep for the heat; his skin was dry and itched as the sun sucked every last particle of water from it. He started imagining things, seeing things, and twice sat up in shock as he thought he saw people walking next to them, only to find it was a dead tree, or a clump of grass. There finally came a time though, when he kept seeing the same odd thing again and again and finally gathered enough energy to sit up.

"Tiponi?" The iMahli, seemingly unaffected by the heat, turned and looked at him. "What's wrong with those trees? The acacias?" Raf pointed at a fairly large specimen they were traveling past.

Tiponi looked over at it. "Wrong?"

"Yeah, there's that weird bump thing on it, see?" About half way up the trunk of the acacia, there was a round, knobbly shape about the same size as a large pumpkin.

Bolyai added in a hoarse voice, "Looks like a beehive from all the holes covering it." He squinted up at Tiponi. "I didn't think there were bees this far into the plains."

"But you can see leaves sticking out of the top of it," cut in Raf. "It's a plant, isn't it?"

"These things you find often in my land," said Tiponi. "It grows from a seed left by birds."

"Like banyans?" asked Bolyai.

Tiponi shrugged. "I don't know those. But inside that plant is full of ants."

"Ants inside the plant?" asked Raf. "You mean they've eaten into it?"

Tiponi tilted his head at Raf suspiciously and then seeing no sign that he was joking, heaved on the reins and pulled the wagon to a stop.

"It is not for eating. They live inside. Like you in your trees."

Raf frowned. "What do you mean?"

"You live in your trees, in your space. The ants live in these plants, in their space."

"Do they eat the plant to make their space?"

"They do not."

"So the plant is like that already? Inside, I mean? With space for the ants to live?"

Tiponi nodded and gestured with his fingers. "Small holes everywhere. These ants, they protect the plant; it gives them a house."

"You're saying it's natural? But how? How can it possibly grow like that?"

Tiponi shrugged.

Bolyai gave a thoughtful look. "It's similar to how our *Ancients* have grown, I suppose."

Raf squinted curiously at the plant and then pushed himself off the wagon to the ground. He made his way up to the tree and scrutinized the plant up close; there were indeed hundreds of tiny ant-sized holes covering the surface of the plant.

"Where are the ants, Tiponi?"

The iMahli tied the ostriches to a small branch, and joined them at the tree. "Inside," he said, and rapped the plant with the back of his knuckles.

Nothing happened. Tiponi beat the plant hard with a fist.

"Maybe they're asleep in this heat?" suggested Bolyai.

Tiponi shook his head. "They always protect the plant. Strange." He peered at the holes closely and then spotted the leaves. "Ah," he muttered. "Dead."

They saw that the leaves that sprouted from the top end of the plant were shriveled and yellow.

"Can I cut it open? To see the inside?" asked Raf.

Tiponi nodded, so Raf used his knife and dug it deep into the side of the plant, pivoting it in one smooth slice downward. Then he levered it sideways with a yank to break off the outside half.

All three of them suddenly stepped backward as a sharp rotten smell filled their noses. Tiponi hissed while Bolyai and Raf looked on, horrified at what they saw.

"That's the smell, Elder," said Raf quietly, wafting his hand in front of his nose. "This has the tree disease from the Forest! It must have."

"It *can't*," muttered Bolyai. He stared around the vicinity, taking in the few trees nearby. "It's too dry and hot – and too far – to have caught it from anything in the Forest."

Nobody said anything. Tiponi took one last grim look and then walked back to the wagon. For the next hour they traveled quickly, covering a lot of ground, stopping only a few times to dig up *shuji*. They also checked a few other ant-plants, but all of them were dead and rotten. The escarpment disappeared into the hazy horizon behind them and the land turned into a rolling sea of rocky hills and desolate valleys. The grass and acacias became scarcer, replaced by sandy dunes and occasional patches of small thorny shrubs.

The sun was almost touching the horizon on its descent and Raf could feel the temperature plummeting when Tiponi finally pulled the ostriches to a stop and stood up, stretching his neck and arms.

"Are we there?"

Tiponi shook his head. "First we eat, then I take you. It is close now."

"Where is it, though? I can't see anything."

"Only if you know where to look, you will find it. I will take you, but you must never tell its place to anyone. You must promise me this."

Raf joined Bolyai in offering assurances they would never tell anyone. Then he scanned their location. The only thing that looked remotely capable of concealing a hiding place was a small rocky knoll half a mile ahead of them.

"Is that it? Is the *ishranga* up there?" Tiponi looked up, saw where he was looking, and nodded before climbing down off the wagon. "Really?" Raf was disappointed.

Seems a bit of a stupid place to hide. I mean, on top of a small hill in this flat place? Pretty easy to spot. So much for it being well-protected. And it must be tiny up there!

Hidden in the dim dusk light, he watched his quarry packing up the small fire. Edokko lifted himself nimbly off the ground and crept back around the small ridge to where the others were waiting.

A tall, clean-shaven man looked up from cleaning his knife. "Well?" He nodded and the man snorted. "That's good news for you, little chief. It means I don't have to punish you for losing him the first time round."

Edokko held back his temper, aware of the pepperbox strapped to the man's belt. Dealing with Miernans was always tricky, and he'd found these soldiers to be ruthless. Besides, now that he'd found the go-between, they'd catch him and Edokko would get paid - and without having to take the *bhesanté* all the way to the Pass. Almost better that the idiot had escaped, really. Although it was a pity to have lost his men in the strange ground collapse.

He pointed over the ridge. "They are heading toward Dandari, that way."

The man tapped his belt thoughtfully. "Well that's no good. We'll have to cut them off before they get to reinforcements."

One of the other men looked up. "But, Johin, if we chase them, they'll hear us coming, won't they?"

"I'm not chasing anybody. We can make it to that hill over there before them and then ambush them. But remember, we need the iMahli alive."

"*Bhesanté*," corrected Edokko.

"Whatever." Johin shifted his belt and then slung himself up onto the camel behind. "Come on then, chief. Lead on. And quickly, but not too close."

Edokko dipped his head and turned to walk away. The other man pulled himself up onto the other camel and followed along behind Johin. As soon as they were on flatter ground, Edokko picked up his pace and jogged off through the darkening night, giving their prey a wide berth. By the time they had reached the far side of the small hill, the temperature had fallen considerably, the last sliver of amber sun disappearing below the horizon.

The two men dismounted and tied the camels' reins to a stake that they drove into the ground. The gangly animals immediately settled themselves down on the sand, heads tilted back, their tongues lolling comically out of their mouths.

Edokko removed a bundle of rope from his shoulder bag and carefully unraveled it, looping it around his wrist so that the little solid weights attached to it didn't get tangled with each other. Then he slung it across his shoulders and armed himself with a short iMahli bow while the Miernans loaded their pepperboxes. When they were all ready, they crawled up to the crest of the small dune and peeked over. The fading sunset painted the plains with a dull orange which made it just possible to make out a small, dark shape moving toward them.

"Well done," whispered Johin, patting Edokko's shoulder. "Now let's move. We need to be ready for them."

They scrambled around the side of the dune and ran, stooped low, to the foot of the hill. It was quite stony, and the shorter Miernan stumbled once, eliciting a curse from Johin. But they soon came across a small slope that took them out of view of the party ahead. At the top of the slope, there were some rocks overgrown with wiry shrubs, and the three men hid themselves behind these.

"Don't do anything until I say so," said Johin tersely. He peered ahead. "How many can you see with the go-between, little chief?"

Edokko took a moment and then murmured, "Two others."

"Perfect." Johin turned to the other Miernan. "As soon as they pass us, I'll take the left one, you got the right. Okay?" The other man nodded, his teeth gleaming in the dim light. "No mistakes. As soon as they're down, we get the iMahli. Use that sling of yours, chief. Go for his legs. If he runs, I'll stop him. Just remember, I want him alive."

They settled into their positions, weapons at the ready, and waited. The sounds of the wagon drifted closer and they could hear some muffled conversation above the hissing and stomping of the ostriches.

"Wait," mouthed Johin, his pepperbox resting against the side of the rock. The wagon rolled closer. He held a finger up in the air. "Wait…"

The wagon turned slightly on its path and seemed to aim straight for them. Johin smirked and gently eased his pepperbox down to point forward. Beside him, Edokko crouched low, holding the sling balanced in his throwing arm.

"Wait…"

. . . .

Raf and Bolyai stood in the murky evening light, and watched Tiponi expectantly. The iMahli was staring up the slope of the hill, his lips moving soundlessly.

"This is too important to back out now, Tiponi. We need to find a cure," urged Bolyai.

"Even so." Tiponi rubbed his head with his hands.

"If you can't take us with you, then can you at least go by yourself?" asked Raf

"But you have *seen* it," said Tiponi. "I have betrayed the Trust."

"Nonsense," muttered Bolyai. "You've seen how bad the Forest is. And your *ishranga* is the only one I've heard of who

236

might be able to help. Also, we saved you! You have a debt."

Tiponi nodded reluctantly.

Bolyai turned to point at Raf, "And not only that, but he healed you! The *ishranga* will want to meet him. You know that."

The iMahli took a deep breath and exhaled slowly, looking at Raf. He reached up in the darkness and rubbed his hand over his shoulder. "Yes..." Then, nodding more assuredly, he said, "It is so."

He walked past them. "Come. But be careful to stay behind me; very important. And say nothing!"

Raf frowned at the iMahli's anxious expression before filing in behind Bolyai as they made their way up the stony gravel path.

. . . .

Edokko watched the figures disappear up the hill. Beside him, Johin was motionless, his pepperbox still resting on the rock. The other Miernan was fidgeting with his own weapon, eyes darting between Johin and the slope.

"Johin," he hissed, "why didn't we shoot? I could've got the small one near me easy!"

Johin held his finger up to his lips, slipping his pepperbox under his belt. Then he crawled backward, keeping a careful eye on the hill. The other two followed him and they made their way soundlessly back to where their camels lay. When they arrived, Johin stood gazing at the hill top above them, a hungry look on his face.

It was other Miernan who broke the silence. "They've got away again! Why d'you let them escape?"

"They won't leave without their wagon." Johin smiled. "Besides, we've only gone and struck gold."

"Why?"

Johin rubbed his hands together absently. "Tell me, why do we want the go-between?"

"Because Captain Djennik will pay us?"

"But why does *he* want a go-between?"

"Who cares? All I want is the reward."

"You're a fool. This man knows where one of the tribes' leaders is; *that's* why they need him. Isn't that right, Edokko?"

The short iMahli nodded.

Johin put his arm around the other Miernan and pointed up the hill. "Well, up there, on that hill, is a leader. I'll bet anything that's who they were talking about." He shook his head. "And I'm thinking the reward for a leader would be ten, maybe twenty, times bigger than just a go-between."

"You think so?" The other's face lit up. "Well let's get them now! They won't expect us."

Edokko grabbed Johin's arm.

"Get your hand off me, iMahli, unless you want it cut off."

Edokko obliged and then said, "They are not alone."

"There are more people up there?"

"Very dangerous." Edokko glanced up at the hill, the whites of his eyes showing.

Johin frowned at him. "Well, I'm not wasting this opportunity to capture a tribal leader, little chief."

"So what do we do?" asked the other Miernan.

"We wait," replied Johin. "Then we'll take them when they least expect it. Our pepperboxes will easily deal with any resistance these primitive fools offer."

"Tiponi, are you sure th-"

"Shhhh!"

Raf rolled his eyes impatiently. From their vantage point, he was convinced Tiponi had got it wrong. They had reached the summit of the small hill and found themselves above a ten foot deep, round depression - but it was empty. Dark, rocky walls formed the sides and even with the pale sheen of moonlight falling on every surface, there was no sign of life of any sort anywhere.

He sighed and shook his head, keeping a close eye on where he was putting his feet. Tiponi led them sideways along the outcropping rocks that formed a rough ledge curving above the pit. Ahead of them, as they inched their way around, there was a rough ramp that sloped downward to the bottom of the pit, and when they reached it Tiponi looked back at them to make sure they followed him down.

The three of them stepped quietly down into the pit, and it was only then that Raf noticed a thin crack in the opposite wall – wide enough for a person to fit through if they stooped, and in a position that made it impossible to spot from above.

Clever, he mused.

He lifted his waterskin to his mouth and took a deep draught - but then dropped it in fright as there was a sharp whirring sound in the air and something long and thin suddenly burst through it. Tiponi hissed and quickly threw his arms up into the air, hands splayed open. A voice hidden in the rocks above cut through the night, shouting something in a language Raf didn't understand. Tiponi responded urgently in the same language. The voice barked something else – something very unfriendly - and Tiponi waved his hands protectively in the air, rattling off a flurry of frantic responses.

Raf felt his heart pounding in his chest as he looked down at the waterskin, a flat shadow on the floor. An arrow shaft was sticking out and the glint of feathers at the end caught the dim light.

That almost hit me!

Tiponi cautiously lowered his arms and started to say something, stepping forward toward the voices, when there were more whirring sounds through the air. This time, they flew in from either side of the group and three arrows suddenly ricocheted off the ground not a yard away from their feet. He leaped backward and shrieked up at them, pointing desperately in Raf's direction.

"Tiponi, what are they saying?" hissed Bolyai, eyeing the darkness above them.

"That I should never have brought you!"

At another shout from the hidden archers, he flung his hands back in the air and yelled over his shoulder, "Get down! On your knees!"

Raf and Bolyai sank onto their knees, arms raised like Tiponi's.

"But who are they?" urged Bolyai. "Where is the *ishranga*? Have you told them about the disease?"

"Yes!" whined Tiponi.

Bolyai looked up at the ledge above and called, "I want to speak with Shima'sidu!"

There was silence and then a terse response.

"What did he say?" The Elder nudged Tiponi's shoulder. "What?"

"He…he wants to how you know the *ishranga*."

Tiponi was about to say more, but flinched as there was a commotion above and six iMahlis stepped into the pale

240

moonlight. Each was wielding a huge, body-length bow, loaded and tightly drawn. Raf tried to swallow, but found his mouth was bone-dry. At a sound behind him, he twisted nervously to watch as, from the dark crack, a shape emerged. It was an iMahli. An absolutely, gigantic one. He was wearing a worn leather skirt, but was otherwise unclothed, exposing an enormous muscled torso and a completely bald head. The most disturbing aspect to Raf was his skin which was a pale, almost milk-white color in the moonlight.

The giant lit two small torches set on either side of the crack and then turned back. Raf flinched as a startling pair of blue eyes were illuminated in the torchlight, peering at him with undisguised hostility. Between the flickering torches emerged three more of the freakish warriors. Any one of them would have stood head and shoulders above Eirdale's Foreman, and they looked strong enough to crush the foresters with their bare hands – although they wouldn't need to resort to that from the look of the long blades that each held out in front of them.

The four warriors spread out to flank the group; lithe and powerful, every movement emanated danger. It was terrifying and Raf felt his body shaking as he took in the fearsome sight of the brutes, anticipating a charge at any moment that he'd be helpless against. But once they had spread out, they stood patiently watching the three of them. Raf registered the archers behind them who were also standing still, at the ready.

But, ready for what?

His question was answered when, from inside the crack, a piercing shout cut through the night. All the iMahlis seemed to tense in anticipation, and Tiponi collapsed onto his knees on the ground, his head tucked tightly to his chest. Raf felt his shoulders hunch up, convinced that something awful was about to happen, when there was a loud rattling and into the torchlight stepped the strangest looking person he'd ever seen.

It was a very thin iMahli woman with an immense bush of

241

almost orange hair that sprouted out in all directions from her head. She was dressed in a faded brown tunic with a huge net of beads arranged in intricate patterns around her neck, and matching ankle-bracelets. She had a more normal colored skin for an iMahli – a little darker than Tiponi's – and it was oddly young skin, smooth and unwrinkled, although there was something about her that exuded age. Perhaps it was her eyes which, also sky-blue like her iMahli guards, seemed to stare right through him.

For no apparent reason, her eyes rolled backward until only the whites showed and she tilted her head up and ululated wildly into the night air. It was a frightening sound and Raf closed his eyes in discomfort. When he opened them again, he found her staring at him coldly, taking in his clothes, moving on to Bolyai and then finally to Tiponi. At the sight of the latter, her eyes opened very wide and she started vibrating her hands which were heavily adorned with beads and small pieces of metal. They rattled softly at first, and then more and more violently as she continued her piercing glare at the prostrate man.

She suddenly flung her hands into the air, stopping the rattling, and hissed something at Tiponi which he reacted to with an instant garbled response, still keeping his chin on his chest. As he gibbered on, she turned to look at Bolyai and then, with one click of her tongue, Tiponi went silent.

"You are from the forest," she said slowly, in a thick accent. Bolyai, who throughout the entire event had remained kneeling and watchful, nodded. "You have come a long way. Why?"

Bolyai started to stand up, but no sooner had he made the tiniest motion when the four pale warriors burst forward with astounding agility and the Elder found himself staring at the pointed end of four blades. To his credit, the Elder didn't flinch and Raf was impressed as he continued moving slowly until he was standing up.

"My name is -"

"- Bolyai. I know this."

If he was surprised at this, the Elder didn't show it, and instead dipped his head. "You are Shima'sidu?"

She flicked all her fingers open and at the gesture, the warriors stepped back in perfect unison, their blades still drawn. "It is so."

To Raf's surprise, Bolyai started to softly sing the *gretanayre*. He was *so* taken aback, in fact, that it took him until half way through the song to summon the courage to join in. It was difficult, and his voice cracked more than once with the wave of adrenalin that held him in its grip.

When they had finished, the *ishranga* stared at them with a calculating frown and then, without even looking at him, snapped, "Tiponi!"

The iMahli scrambled to his feet and stood next to Bolyai. Raf felt a pang of guilt and empathy for the man as he spotted a sheen of sweat all over his body. Even standing, he was unable to meet her eyes and stood staring at the ground between them.

"Why have you broken the Trust?"

Tiponi swallowed loudly. "*Ishranga*, there is a problem with their trees."

Shima'sidu rattled her wrists again and ululated, making Raf jump. "You come here to tell me about this? With these others? These strangers?" She opened her mouth and made a strange sound like the hiss of a wildcat. "You think I do not know this thing? I am *ishranga*; I know!"

Tiponi quailed under her glare. "Also, the boy, he...he is *ishranga* too. A powerful *ishranga*."

Shima'sidu gave a choking sound and then ululated again. "This young boy? This *child*? What is this nonsense?" She suddenly looked up at the ledges. "A trick!"

As if reading her emotions, the warriors instantly closed together in front of her to form a human wall.

"It's true," said Bolyai quietly. "I've seen it. He healed your go-between when he was injured. More quickly and completely than I have ever seen."

Tiponi nodded desperately and tapped his shoulder. Shima'sidu made the hissing noise again and then crept through the warriors who danced out the way fluidly to their former positions. She walked up and poked Raf in his chest. Raf felt his hands sweating profusely and tried to subtly rub them dry on his top. She moved close to him, her nose almost touching his, looking into his eyes. Above them, Raf heard the creak of bows being drawn.

She moved her head next to his and whispered, "Are you *ishranga*?"

"I don't know..." he mumbled. "I think so."

"Do you."

She stepped back and then ululated again, her eyes rolling back in her head. Raf stood shaking, watching as she drew out the noise to an excruciating volume, and then snapped her head back to down to stare at him. With one of her hands, she plucked something from her necklace and Raf noted that it was actually a seed, rather than a wooden bead. She held it in the palm of her hand and then, closing her eyes, started humming a pattern of notes that sounded very unfamiliar and outlandish to Raf.

He watched as the seed twitched in her hand and suddenly split open. Then slowly, a small green shoot appeared and two delicate leaves unfolded themselves as a tiny white root grew out and wriggled like a worm on her palm. It only lasted a few seconds before the leaves turned yellow and wilted, shriveling into a crumpled heap. He frowned at it and, when nothing else happened, looked up to see her glaring at him coldly.

"Show me," she said.

"Sorry? What do you mean?"

"Show me!"

"What now? Here?" Raf flinched as the guards moved in

closer behind her, their blue eyes boring into him. "I...I don't think I can just make it happen like you did. It's all new to me and, and...I don't really understand what I'm doing yet."

Shima'sidu hissed in the animal-like way again and threw her head back to ululate. Turning to Tiponi, she shook her wrists and spat out a short sentence in their language. His face tightened and his arms slowly dropped to hang at his sides.

"You waste my time!"

Bolyai shook his head in frustration.

The *ishranga* pointed over their shoulders. "Go. And take this foolish *bhesanté* with you."

"Do you have an answer about our rotting trees?" asked Bolyai. "People will die if we fail. You must help us, please!"

The *ishranga* ululated yet again and then looked up at the skies. "This I cannot do." A faint troubled expression creased her moonlit face. "It is a sickness of all people. Of the land. And of your forest. It is not one disease, it is every disease. All disease."

Bolyai's bushy eyebrows knitted together cynically. "There *must* be a way to cure it, though. I would have thought you'd want to help. Obviously the things I've heard about you are wrong."

The *ishranga* turned around to face away from them. "You will find no answers here." She issued an order to the guards and then disappeared without another word through the crack in the wall. The iMahlis joined ranks and then bore down on them slowly.

"Come on." Bolyai took Tiponi's arm and dragged him back toward the slope, Raf following quickly.

They climbed up, stumbling along the way and then sidled past the archers who stood menacingly with their bows still taut. One of them grunted something offensive and Tiponi flinched as if he'd been hit. Raf helped the Elder support Tiponi's weight and they made their way clumsily to the path that led back down to their wagon, descending as quickly as

245

they could. As they reached the wagon and leaned against it, panting heavily, there was a noise from the top of the path and a voice shouted down something.

"What did he say?" asked Raf. He felt nervous not being able to see the archers and kept expecting arrows to come flying through the darkness at them. Tiponi's head was flopped down onto his chest and he muttered something that was too indistinct for them to hear.

"Come on, boy," snapped Bolyai, also staring up into the darkness. "Help me get him on the wagon and we'll move a little away to get some distance between us and those arrows. I think we may have worn out our welcome here."

Later that evening, Bolyai sat looking pensively into the small flames of the fire he had built. Raf was leaning back against the wagon wheel opposite the Elder, gazing up at the stars which were out in their millions, smothering the night sky with pinpricks of white. His heart had finally calmed down and with the panic of the incident on the hill top over, he felt the twin blow of exhaustion and the icy cold night taking hold. On the ground near them, the dark form of Tiponi was hunched facing away from them. He hadn't said a word since they had come down.

"Elder," said Raf quietly. "What do we do now?"

Bolyai took a long, tired breath. "I suppose we'll sleep here overnight, and then tomorrow morning, we'll try to work out the quickest way to the Pass."

"The *Pass*?" repeated Raf. "Why are we going to the Pass when we need to get back?"

"But we need to find someone who can help you. Don't you understand, boy?"

"My family are the ones who need help!"

"The best help you can give them is to find a cure. With that dismal *ishranga* being of no use to us, Miern is the best option now. We can also try to find someone there who can teach you how t-"

"Elder, you said yourself that you aren't even sure there'll be someone there who can help me. That's so far to go!"

"I'm hopeful. Miern is full of surprises and exactly the sort of place that we'd find unusual help." He leaned forward so that the flickering flames lit his face. "Don't worry about the Forest for now. It will stand for a while longer, despite what that woman said. Personally, I think she's gone a bit nutty out here in the middle of nowhere. But if she *is* on to something about the diseases we've seen recently, if this is even more widespread and perilous than I thought, then your gift is probably all the more important."

Raf picked up a stone from the dirt next to him and threw it into the darkness. "I don't know why you call it a gift, Elder. Nobody gave it to me, and I certainly didn't ask for it."

Suddenly, Tiponi turned, the blanket he had been huddled under slipping off as he growled, "Selfish!"

Raf felt a flush of discomfort. "But, Tiponi... I don't know what you... I..."

"You are *ishranga!*"

"But I don't know how to do it, Tiponi, I tried -"

"You did not try!" snapped the iMahli. "You could have showed just something, *anything*, and then...." A whimper escaped him and Raf realized with a pang of guilt that the iMahli was on the verge of tears.

"I'm sorry, Tiponi. I would've done it, honest, I just don't know how, when....there was just so much pressure, and -"

"But my shoulder?"

"I didn't really know what I was doing, though -"

"You have the *gift!*" he repeated, his hands raised in front of him. "If you had just shown it, then, -" he shook his head, "- I would not be banished."

Bolyai looked up from the fire. "Is that what happened? That's what they said up there?"

Tiponi nodded his head dejectedly. "I no longer have the Trust. I am not a go-between. I am shamed." He sank back into mourning and a silence fell over the group.

Raf looked out of the corner of his eye at the Elder as a hot flush of guilt weighed down on him, but Bolyai ignored him and stoked the fire. He got to his feet and walked past the ostriches out of the reach of the firelight.

It's not my fault, Raf thought bitterly. *What did he expect? I can't just sing when someone makes me. It's just like the stupid Festival all over again. And doing it right in front of those iMahli guards pointing their swords at me? Forget it.*

His thoughts returned to the scene and he felt a pang of embarrassment as he realized how pathetic he'd actually been.

I couldn't even move, I was so scared! Maybe she can just sing and make things grow on the spot, but she didn't have people standing around shooting stupid arrows at her! I've never been so frightened in my life.

He kicked a stone down the slope of a dune and then sat down on the sand with his arms wrapped around his knees. Apart from the wind and their small fire, he couldn't hear a single noise in all this openness. It was silent. Too silent. He felt as if the vast silence was crowding him, forcing him to face his thoughts. So he closed his eyes, humming the first song that came to him, the *gretanayre*. It took a little while, but as he sang and listened to the music, he felt a calmness come over him and the colors came rolling in out of the darkness.

He immediately registered that there was something unusual. Normally, there was a kind of dark fog that hovered on the edges of his mind's vision. Here though, there was an area off to his right which was strangely distinct. It seemed to be made up of many different colors woven intricately together. He had no idea how far away it was exactly - and even less idea of *what* it was – but he stopped humming and, opening his eyes, he stood up and walked toward where he'd seen it.

As he peered into the darkness, he realized that he had no idea of what he was looking for. With his eyes open, he was blind. So, he started humming again and closed his eyes.

Hands held cautiously in front of him, he shuffled carefully toward the strange weaving of colors over the uneven ground. It was difficult as he kept stumbling in the sand and over small rocks, but he made slow headway. As he neared the colors, they sharpened into beautiful webbing, forming a rough round shape, behind which the web stretched out in a cylindrical stream. Without understanding how, Raf recognized it as somehow…musical – or to do with music, at least.

Fascinated, he opened his eyes and took a moment to let them adjust to the darkness from the dazzling colors. He found himself standing at the foot of a small dune that was sprinkled with boulders.

Well, I know it was right in front of me when I stopped, he thought, squinting forward. All he could see was a large jagged rock set in amongst other smaller rocks, with a few scraggly shrubs growing around them. He touched the rock and tried to see if there was anything odd about it, but found nothing unusual. It was heavy and although he tried to push it, it didn't budge.

Maybe it's covering something?

Climbing up the sandy slope, he positioned himself above the rock and placed his feet on top, digging his hands into the thick sand for purchase. Then, he bent a leg back and kicked down hard on the top of the rock. He felt it shift a tiny amount, so he got both feet ready and, with a small jump, pounded down as hard as he could.

He wasn't prepared for what happened next, and as the rock gave way and toppled downward, he fell with it, only managing to stop himself plunging down the slope by throwing his arms out behind him and grasping for anything solid. His right hand caught hold of something firm and he clung on desperately, swinging sideways into the shrubs. The rock rolled over once more and then slid to a stop in the soft sand at the bottom of the slope.

Raf looked back up at what he had grabbed hold of and saw that it was the stone edging of a hole in the dune that he'd uncovered. He hoisted himself up and then used his hands to scoop out some of the sand that had trickled in from above.

Ducking, he peered into the blackness behind the entrance. In the dim light he could just make it out extending gently downward, oddly regular and uniform in width.

It's like a pipe of stone, he thought. *And large enough to be a tunnel. That's what the colors were! But how? What does it mean? And where does it go?*

He clambered up the dune and peered over the top, biting his lip thoughtfully as he lined its direction up.

Straight toward the hill with the ishranga *and her stupid guards. Just brilliant.*

He sighed and, making his mind up, closed his eyes and started singing softly again. There were too many unanswered questions, and feeling the need for something to distract him from reflecting on the situation with Tiponi, Raf stepped into the tunnel and tried to narrow his thoughts down to just the simple task of following the stone pipe downward.

Following the colors in his mind, he moved carefully and managed not to stumble too often as he made his way down. After a few minutes, his feet scuffed against something giving him just enough warning to avoid hitting his head. On opening his eyes, he found that there wasn't the slightest bit of light to help him, but feeling around with his hands, he realized he was standing in front of a rough wall. It wasn't made of rock though, and scratching at the surface, he guessed it was just compacted mud.

The colors definitely carry on past this. And I've been right up till now...

He crouched down, bunched his right arm up and butted his shoulder against the wall. It didn't give, but there was a crumbling sound from the other side and Raf guessed it to be only a foot thick, maybe less. Another two blows and a section of it gave way with a crunch. Raf's torso punched half way through the wall in a little landslide of dirt and stones that left him spluttering.

He looked up and noticed that there was a faint source of

light somewhere nearby which brought to life dim outlines of things closest to him. There was also an unexpected damp, acrid smell that he couldn't identify. Hauling the rest of his lower body through the small opening in the wall, he stepped forward cautiously, aware of a looming shape directly in front of him that sloped up toward the ceiling. He sidled around it, taking small steps, things slowly coming into focus as his eyes adjusted. His soft footsteps gave rise to surprisingly loud echoes that fluttered back and forth, painting a picture in his head of a *very* large room.

What is *this place?*

His eyes followed an uneven wall that materialized to his left, bending around in front of him a good fifty yards before closing in and looping back to his right. He could see two small flickering candles placed in holes in the wall that provided the meager light supply.

Well, those have been put there recently by someone.

His eyes opened in excitement as he scanned the middle of the chamber and spotted what he thought were trees disappearing into the blackness far above – almost big enough to be *Ancients*; but on closer inspection, they turned out to be large rocks. They were oddly shaped though, with wide round bases that extended upward, tapering, a bit like some of the huge ant-hills they had spotted on the plains. They were very smooth and slightly damp. Raf ran his hands distractedly over one. They were peculiarly situated in this room, and he felt the tingle of goose-bumps as a strange realization occurred to him: there was something purposeful about them. Something he couldn't quite grasp. He moved into the middle of the chamber, turning this way and that, trying to figure it out. Just like it had with the *Ash-knell* and Orfea and the *paodrin*, there was something about these giant rocks that he recognized, something that made sense to him…

And then it hit him.

They're instruments!

He felt light-headed as he turned around slowly on the spot, feeling it all fit into place in his mind. But how had it been done? They looked completely natural.

More importantly, he thought, *how do they work?*

He frowned in the gloom. *Definitely not like the Ash-knell. They didn't feel hollow at all, which meant they couldn't be drums, either.*

Seeking inspiration, he drew a calming breath and closed his eyes. It was the *gretanayre* again that came to mind and he started singing it softly.

The storm that exploded into his mind almost knocked him over. Countless colors streaked back and forth in frantic spirals, forming a seething vortex that filled the room. With no effort, he sank straight into them and become part of them and felt his awareness, his presence, grow. As it did, the room shimmered into perfect clarity and he realized that it wasn't the individual rocks that were instruments – the whole room was an instrument! The tunnel he'd come through was also part of it, some sort of channel for the sound. Every one of the rocks suddenly had a different character that he could now understand, a tone or timbre that set it apart from the others, but would blend together perfectly with the rest.

He reeled as the pure energy of the room filled him. He could feel the frenzy of colors spinning and curling through the air, like a thousand sparkling butterflies. He dived into them and felt himself spreading through the room, soaking it in colors, immersing the rocks in different hues as he danced and wheeled around them.

A part of him registered that the rocks themselves were now emitting a noise, a deep humming sound, serving only to intensify the colors as they boiled with energy. Faster and faster they moved, creating a giant whirlpool in the middle of the room, with Raf at its center. The sheer volume of the sound threatened to crush him to the floor and a glimmer of unease streaked through his mind at the raw power which was swelling to bursting point around him. He struggled against the fierce desire to continue, nervous about losing control, and inch by inch, detached himself from the connection, feeling the roar of sound dwindle.

He realized he was still singing and reluctantly quietened to a whisper before stopping altogether. Peeling open his tightly shut eyes, he stared up at the darkness above him, aware of pounding echoes still reverberating around the room, bouncing off every surface. They were beautiful sounds, and their fading away brought a sinking feeling of emptiness. All that was left was a deep, almost inaudible, throbbing from the floor. Raf also heard something else underneath it all though, a whimpering noise behind him. He tried to find the source and when he turned around, had to bite back a gasp of shock. The *ishranga* was standing not ten feet from him.

She was leaning against the wall, her head tilted backward, the dull light catching and illuminating her eyes which were completely rolled back in her head. Her throat was moving oddly and for a moment, Raf thought that she was choking. Casting nervous glances around the room for her guards, who were nowhere to be seen, he stepped up to her and softly tapped her shoulder. Her head dropped down and he jumped back, watching as her eyes gradually, in fits and starts, revolved downward until they were looking at him. Her breathing was fast and irregular and, even in the half-light, he could see that her skin was covered in goose-bumps.

She slowly calmed down, her eyes not leaving his for a second. When she spoke, it was a strained rasp. "How are you here?"

Raf quickly held his hands up. "I'm sorry! I was trying to help Tiponi, but followed the col-... er... I found this place."

Shima'sidu broke her gaze and glanced past him to the rock pillars behind. "The stones. How? I have never... I have heard stories, but never have I heard them sing so."

"I...don't know," replied Raf, biting his lip. "I told you, I don't really understand it. I just kind of saw how they worked and…and then I tried to…"

"You…you are truly *ishranga*." She held up a thin fingered hand, the thick bangle of beads rattling gently against her ebony skin. "The go-between did not lie."

"Well, I think I *did* heal his shoulder, *ishran-*"

"You must not call me this!" she whispered. "No more. To you, I am Shima'sidu," she lowered her head, "*ishranga.*"

Raf drew a sharp breath. She was bowing to him!

"Do not be afraid," she said, her eyes gleaming in the candlelight. "You are safe here, *ishranga.*" She suddenly raised her arms in the air and ululated wildly, the cry echoing around the room before grabbing his hand. "You must come with me! I must know you more."

She pulled him toward the opposite end of the room and he relented, letting her lead him through a small archway in the rock that led up a long, winding flight of stone stairs before opening out into a large, murky room. There was a sole candle on the floor. One side of the room's stone walls was completely covered in animal hides and hunting trappings, and in the middle of the room was laid out an enormous black and white striped carpet – some sort of animal hide – with rough pillows strewn around. The rest of the room extended back into darkness.

"*Ishr-*… Shima'sidu," said Raf hesitantly, "is it true that you banished Tiponi?"

She made the cat-like hissing noise again. "A go-between must keep the Trust. It is forbidden to bring strangers here, he knows this!"

"But that's not really fair," replied Raf. "We were trying to get a cure for the disease and, I suppose it's also my fault then because there was that whole thing with Tiponi's shoulder. And *that* was only after we saved him from those other iMahlis."

"What is this?" she said, her eyes narrowing.

"Some…fit…fet-"

"*Fetumu?*"

"Yeah, that's it. Some *fetumu* had captured him and we managed to rescue him."

Shima'sidu shook her bangles violently and stood up. "Did these *fetumu* know *what* he was?" Raf started to shake his head but she cut him off. "Of course they knew!" She hissed again furiously.

"He was trying to warn you when they got him," said Raf. "I think that maybe you're being too hard on him."

Shima'sidu hissed at him. But then her expression changed and she dipped her head. "Of course. *Ishranga.*"

She suddenly shouted out a phrase in iMahli. Raf almost fell backward when, a second later, one of the huge pale guards bounded out of the shadows at the back of the room.

He's been just there all this time!

Raf could feel his heart thumping in his throat. The guard was simply immense. In the candlelight, his powerful torso seemed to be hewn from rock, and the blade in his hands gleamed dangerously as he whipped it out, a look of fury at the sight of Raf standing next to Shima'sidu. She offered him no time to think though, and immediately snapped off a string of orders. Without hesitation, the guard turned on his heel and bounded soundlessly out the door.

"Where's he gone?" asked Raf nervously.

"*Ishranga*, do not fear. I will bring your Elder and the go-between. Then we talk."

"I seem to have been doing a lot of that recently," said Raf wryly. "To be honest, I was hoping you'd be able to tell me a few things."

"Yes?"

"Well…what did you mean about the disease? What you said before."

Her face grew serious and she made a half-hearted hiss. "It is everywhere, this disease. Here on the plains, in your forest, in the mountains. Everywhere."

"What is it? Is there a cure? Or can *you* cure it?"

Shima'sidu hissed again, shaking her head. "Not Shima'sidu." She pointed and rattled her beads at him. "But you, *ishranga,* you can do this thing."

"Me?"

"You are strong. I will teach you." She tilted her head back and let out another grating ululation.

Stan Dawsley stared down at the floor of the room. He could hear the guards talking in low voices outside the locked doors, and beyond them, in the distance, loud music. The fact that the Festival was up and running here in Three Ways contributed no small amount to his simmering anger. His thoughts returned to young Derril Robson, who had last been seen leading a party of soldiers to the crossroads. Stan refused to believe that he'd fallen into a collapsed hole as the Miernan captain had reported. Derril was as sure-footed a forester as anyone. Not to mention that the edges of the 'collapse' that Stan had glimpsed before his arrest were suspiciously neat.

Standing up, he started pacing again, only to stop as the doors were flung open. He turned and crossed his arms to face the gaudily dressed man who had entered.

"Dawsley. The Foreman wants to see you," said Brinchley.

Stan glared at him. "Does he? Well I think I'll just stay right here if you don't mind." He stepped forward. "When the other Foremen hear about this, -"

Brinchley clicked his jeweled fingers and two brawny Miernan soldiers stepped in through the door and marched up to Dawsley. They grabbed his shoulders and hauled him toward the door. Once outside, they marched Stan through a throng of soldiers seated at tables, straight into another office. Here, the fat, richly dressed Miernan sat talking with Three Ways' Foreman.

Allium looked up. "Perfect timing." He nodded at Brinchley who bowed and left.

258

"Thank you, gentlemen," he said to the soldiers, who released Dawsley and stood to the side.

Allium took a grape from a bowl on the tabletop and ate it, looking at Dawsley. "You have forced me to make a difficult decision, Councilman. Despite my orders to avoid the southern passage, y-"

"Orders? Since when is a Councilman answerable to orders about where he can travel?"

"Since the southern Forest started falling apart," snapped Allium in his high-pitched voice. "Reports of collapses cover my desk, as well as the story about this Robson boy falling through one at the crossroads. And what do you do but go wandering down there, despite me stationing soldiers there for our safety! It's lucky you didn't trigger another collapse and bring down more *Ancients*."

"Safety? The only collapse I saw was a huge hole that had been made by these Miernans! If only we'd known you would go on to hire foreign thugs to do your dirty work when you were elected!"

Allium's face tightened. "These 'thugs' you talk of are our future business partners. Honestly, Dawsley, how you made it to the Council I have no idea. You should be thankful that I, at least, have the vision to elevate Three Ways to its proper place."

"By stealing the Festival from Eirdale?"

"Eirdale couldn't possibly have catered for this sort of event. Not only are they too small, but they're struggling the most with these collapses. They're grateful that we've stepped in to rescue it."

"Interesting then that when I last spoke with Foreman Manyara, he still seemed to believe it was being hosted there this year. He was very much looking forward to the opportunity, I remember, as was everyone else, including our Three Ways folk."

Allium looked at Dawsley frostily and reached for another grape.

The Miernan suddenly chuckled, clapping his hands together. "You were right about him, Allium. Stubborn and foolish." The smile faded. "If he has this opinion, it's likely others will, too, yes?"

Allium nodded irritably. "But the Festival will be over soon. We can deal with the rest afterward."

"How can you be so...flippant?" snarled Dawsley. "These villagers trusted you with -"

"Actually," interrupted Allium, turning around. "I think that's enough of you, Dawsley. I've no need of you anymore."

"Your days as Foreman are numbered, Allium! I'll see to that. When the Council hear about -"

"Quite so, quite so. I agree, it would be a nuisance," interrupted Allium with a nod. Dawsley paused, confused. "I think it best if we kept you alone with your unhelpful thoughts until after the Festival. Perhaps longer." He glanced at the soldiers. "If you please, gentlemen?"

The guards looked at Nabolek who nodded and then they seized Dawsley's arms.

"You can't do this!" stuttered Dawsley. "I am a member of the Three Ways Council!"

"Not for very long." Allium jerked his head toward the door dismissively.

. . . .

As Dawsley was dragged out of the room shouting, Allium picked through the bowl of grapes and, finding one to his satisfaction, popped it into his mouth.

Nabolek stood up, his pendulous belly swinging as he walked toward the door. "What was all that about collapses?"

"A stroke of luck. The southerners have had some sort of tree disease problem."

"A *problem*?" said Nabolek. "The ground collapsing is not a problem, Allium; it is a catastrophe! I had always understood the forest platform to be completely stable. Why haven't I been told about this issue before?"

Allium smiled. "Don't let it worry you, Nabolek. It doesn't affect us up here. It's probably just a weak patch they've over-farmed, or where someone's built a fire illegally. It happens occasionally. This was perfectly timed, though, to make for a useful scapegoat that we could use to ensure our people remain here instead of traveling down to Eirdale. Brinchley has been talking to the Council members, making sure they all start to worry about the ground opening underneath them. Nothing *too* panicky, but enough to keep them - and the rest of Three Ways - uninterested in venturing south. With any luck, it'll also play straight into our hands when the Festival is over. That is, in the unlikely event of there being any opposition to my plan."

"Luck? I prefer to be in control of situations, Allium. And I do not like the idea of people becoming argumentative here in Three Ways. Especially not with what you plan afterward. It has ramifications for my own plans as well. If enough of them become unhappy like that man, it could be a completely different sort of problem to deal with."

"Quite," replied Allium peering into the distance. "After the Festival the real challenge begins. But with your men around, most will hold their tongues. They're not a very confrontational lot, this Three Ways lot." He turned to the Miernan. "You're absolutely sure nothing can get through the crossroads?" Nabolek smiled confidently. "Because our success relies on maintaining this communications gap between us and the Eirdalers until the Festival has been savored to our satisfaction and the senators are satisfied."

"And afterward? If the idea of you being appointed Baron is as unpopular as Dawsley leads me to believe?" Nabolek stroked his beard. "It seems to me, Foreman, that the southern forest holds little value for the moment. My soldiers will

261

certainly extinguish any interest in the short term, and Captain Lethar assures me that access to and from the south is impossible for the indefinite future."

"Yes, well I hope he has skills other than cutting down our trees." Allium ignored the flicker of irritation on Nabolek's face. "However, once the Festival finishes, I will deliver my plan to the Overcouncil and convince them that this is the best thing for the Forest."

"And if there are any violent attempts to get past the blockade? It seems to me that it might be necessary for my men to take a more persuasive role, yes? I don't want to go to all the trouble of winning over the senators and building this valuable trading link only to have it ruined by this southern rabble. We must protect our interests for the long term, as well. As the potential future Baron, you really should have thought this through already. You need to consider how you will run the forest, and how you will *control* it."

Allium looked at him. "You have some ideas?"

"It is almost certain that these southerners will persist in making their point afterward, and with increasing organization. It's obvious to anyone with military experience. But, whereas you seem content to just wait and see if unwanted problems flourish, like an ostrich burying its head in the sand, I am not. As I said, I like to be in control of the situation."

"Control?" Allium asked. "Well, I would obviously welcome advice from you before you leave. And, assuming the senators endorse me, once I am Baron I can request military assistance if absolutely necessary, correct?"

"You are too slow, Foreman, too reactive. I could foresee these sorts of issues long ago. I took the liberty of calling for a few reinforcements from my garrison in the Pass. They should arrive here in less than a week."

"That's very generous of you, Nabolek. I appreciate your trust in me, although I'm not completely sure that I need more men, to be honest. I mean, I have almost eighty men at my disposal already. I would have thought that was sufficient to handle things once you leave."

"Leave? With these new problems? Not a chance, Foreman; I have too much invested in this venture. Besides, as disciplined as my soldiers are, I'd rather not test their loyalty so far from home with a stranger. I will remain here, temporarily, to assist you in any way I can and ensure everything goes well. These southerners - and the locals – will quickly learn to behave."

Tiponi waited until the small pot of water started boiling on their tiny fire, before lifting it off and filling the mug. In the bitterly cold night air, the steam slowly drifted upward, a solid swirling mass in the crisp moonlight. With the pit to shelter them from the crosswinds, it was only when it reached above the stony sides that the steam was whisked away to dissolve into the darkness beyond.

Giving it a stir, Tiponi held the mug up, a coy smile playing on his face.

Raf took it and glared at him. "Enough, Tiponi. You're being stupid."

Bolyai clicked his tongue. "It's not every day a go-between is banished. And even less common that he's unbanished. Add in finding out that it was all because of *your* intervention, and I can understand why he's a bit relieved and somewhat grateful."

Tiponi nodded. "It is so."

Raf grunted in annoyance and took a sip from the mug, savoring the odd flavor of herbs that the water had been infused with.

"You like it, *ishranga*?"

"Look, you can stop calling me that," said Raf. "We've traveled together and you know me. Simply Raf. Just because she -" he nodded his head back toward the opening in the rocks behind him, "- calls me that, doesn't mean anybody else has to."

Tiponi dipped his head and then crouched down on his

haunches again. Around the ledge, the warriors who had terrified Raf so much before stood silently in the shadows, facing out toward the dark plains. Behind them, inside in her rocky lair, the *ishranga* had turned in for the night a while ago. Invisible up in the blackness of the jumble of rocks opposite them, he knew that the iMahli archers were stationed there as well. It was an unsettling place.

As if reading his mind, Bolyai muttered, "How does it feel, boy? Knowing they work for you, now?" Raf shrugged. "Notorious iMahli deathguards and archers watching over you... You've certainly come a long way from home." Bolyai gave a brief, dry chuckle, and then stared at the flickering flames. "You're not going to tell me what happened in there?"

Raf fiddled with a fingernail. "It's difficult to explain, El-"

"Of course it is," mumbled Bolyai. He looked back at the dark crevice. "I've no idea how you got past the deathguards, but you certainly made quite a racket once you got in there. Gave me a blinding headache and we almost lost one of the ostriches at one point, but Tiponi's got some quick reactions, fortunately." He rubbed his hands together for warmth. "Whatever it was, it must have been impressive to have her fawning all over you like that. You'd think she'd have a little more dignity."

Raf squirmed on the cold stone and sipped from the mug again. "Elder..."

"Hm?"

"What she said about the disease being everywhere, about it being 'all diseases', what does that even mean?"

Bolyai shook his head. "No idea. I still think she's off her rocker. It doesn't make sense in the slightest. Besides, she's wrong as well."

"How?"

"The disease in the Forest is something only affecting the banyans, as far as I can make out."

"Is that why it's so dangerous?"

"Of course. Banyans are crucial for our Forest villages; they help tie all the plants and trees together and make it a strong and stable platform." He frowned. "Maybe there's *something* in what she says, though. The disease we saw in the plains with the ant-plants was not the same thing. And what she was talking about in the mountains has to be a completely different disease as well. But it doesn't make sense that there are so many diseases occurring at once. I've never heard of anything like it." He gave the fire a sharp prod. "I was *sure* that she would be able to help; she's ancient and highly respected."

Raf mumbled, "She said…" He paused and then looked down as Bolyai glanced at him curiously. "She said she thought that maybe…I would be able to do something."

"To cure it?"

Raf nodded. "Maybe."

"How?"

"She said we'd talk about it tomorrow and she'll try to help me figure it out. She didn't understand how I didn't know." He gave a chuckle. "Sounded a bit like you, Elder."

Bolyai grunted and looked over at the dark entrance to her lair. "Well, good luck to her. I'm glad she thinks she can help, because I'll be skinned if I understand how you do it. And I've seen a fair few things in my time."

Raf looked at the Elder's weather-worn face. "Elder, how old are you?"

Bolyai looked at him suspiciously. "Why?"

"Are you as old as the *ishranga*?"

"Not likely. She is truly *old*." Bolyai laughed out loud. "I know she was already a respected *ishranga* when I was only just a twinkle in my mother's eye. She must have fifty years on me at least."

Raf thought about it and then said, "Doesn't that make you almost a hundred or something?"

"No need to rub it in."

Tiponi coughed and then quietly added, "Shima'sidu is the

oldest." They looked at him. "In the city, there is tell of others. Maybe as old, but I do not know this for sure."

"In Miern?" asked Bolyai. Tiponi nodded.

"Miern?" repeated Raf. "Odd place for an *ishranga*, don't you think?"

"Well, Miern was once renowned for its music. Its Festival in particular. That's where ours comes from, a long, long time ago. People used to come from all over the known world and it was a great meeting place, a cross-over for people to share cultures and knowledge. If we are to find answers, Miern is our best bet."

"Doesn't it happen anymore there? The Festival, I mean."

"Unfortunately, there are probably other priorities now."

"Like what?"

"Gold."

"And stones," added Tiponi.

Bolyai saw Raf's confused expression. "He means gems. Diamonds, emeralds and the like. There are mines sprouting up all over the Miernan countryside."

Raf tapped his head. "That's what the slaves are for that the *fetumu* capture, right? I get it. They kidnap *bhesanté* so that they can take them as slaves to work in the mines."

Tiponi shook his head. "Not only for this thing. The *bhesanté* live all over the plains, but not many in one place. It is our way. But we are more than the *fetumu*. Now, we are starting to fight. The *fetumu* are not happy, so they want to take the *ishrangas*."

"To punish you?"

Tiponi shook his head. "They are our leaders. Without them we are not one. We cannot fight as one people."

"But then why don't they just kill the *ishrangas*? Why take them?" Raf frowned. "And take them where, anyway? Not to the mines, surely?"

Tiponi shook his head. "I do not know. I have heard stories. Bad things." He stoked the fire, sending a small burst of sparks skyward. Then he moved over to lie on the ground under a blanket, ending the conversation rather abruptly.

Bolyai yawned again loudly and then put his hand on Raf's shoulder. "Come on then, young Eirdale *ishranga,* time to get some sleep."

· · · · · · ·

The wind picked up and Raf slept fitfully, tossing and turning on the stone floor, the blanket providing poor protection from both the lumpy ground and the biting temperatures. To add to his misery, the sunburn from the day's travel was awful. It itched and stung from the icy dry air and from chafing against the rough blanket. Eventually, he gave up and lay on his back, staring up at the cloudless night sky. The breeze whistled over the sides of the pit constantly, but it wasn't quite loud enough to drown out the sound of Bolyai's thick snores.

There was a sudden soft rattling sound. Raf tilted his head backward toward the cave opening behind.

She's up, he mused.

At more rattling, Raf sat up and turned, leaning on an arm. Then he heard something that sounded metallic.

Something's not right.

He turned back and his breath caught in his throat as he saw one of the deathguards staring at him. He seemed uneasy with Raf's sudden interest in the door.

He can't have heard it from up there, though, with all that wind. I think I'll just have a quick peek and make sure.

He shrugged off the blanket and got to his feet, moving quietly across the rocky floor toward the entrance, aware of the deathguard's eyes on him. He reached the opening and tilted his head to listen inside. Beside him, he felt an odd draught and turned to see the guard suddenly standing right next to him, his blue eyes regarding him uncertainly. Raf swallowed nervously and touched his ear to explain his actions. Then he dipped his head and edged through the thin black opening in the rock-face, feeling a looming presence trailing him. The entrance led straight into Shima'sidu's main room, and Raf walked cautiously up to the doorway and peered into the dark.

There was a flurry of movement toward the back of the room and Raf saw a murky figure straighten up from a mound on the floor and shout something. He ducked back instinctively as a sharp explosion erupted and flashes of white blinded him completely. A sharp pain tore into his left shoulder and he fell back into the wall behind him. Only, it turned out to not be a wall at all; it was the deathguard. With a soft sigh, his giant frame slid down the wall to the floor where he lay, gurgling and twitching, a dark patch spreading over his chest.

Raf winced at the throbbing in his shoulder and shouted for help. Noises from outside, muffled by the piercing ringing in his ears, grew louder and suddenly there were deathguards crowding the entrance. They stared at Raf and then down at the limp body on the floor, their faces wild with shock.

Raf lifted a hand to point, feeling something warm running down his arm. "In there! The *ishranga!*"

The deathguards flew past him, followed swiftly by the troop of iMahli archers who had made their way down, too. Behind them, Tiponi and Bolyai staggered in groggily.

"What's happened, boy?" hissed the Elder.

"Someone's got the *ishranga*, Elder!" He grunted in pain. "I was hit. I think it was a pepperbox."

Bolyai knelt down quickly and felt around Raf's shoulder. "It's passed straight through…but it wasn't close to the bone. Good." He looped an arm under Raf's armpit. "Help me, Tiponi."

But the iMahli didn't hear him. His eyes were glued to the scene inside the room in shock, so Bolyai hoisted Raf up by himself and they made their way inside.

It was a mess, with the large carpet in the middle scrunched up to one side. The opposite stone wall was empty, the animal hides having been torn down. At the far end, the iMahlis were grouped around the tiny doorway at the top of the steps. They were frantic, and the drawn blades caught the remaining candle's light, sending flashes around the room.

Tiponi dashed over to seize a huge spear from a rack on the wall. The deathguards were speaking urgently in their language, staring intently into the darkness.

Raf coughed in pain and then tried to lift his voice. "Go! Help her!"

Tiponi turned. "They are trapped in the cave. We will find them. And kill them!"

Raf felt a shudder of fear as a horrible realization dawned on him. "Tiponi, you must go now! Please hurry!"

"There is no way out, *ishranga* -"

"But there is! At the back, there is a tunnel," urged Raf through clenched teeth. "Hurry!"

Tiponi spun around. "What tunnel? The only way in is -"

"There's another entrance outside!" replied Raf. "It's hidden. I found it; that's how I g-"

Tiponi barely considered what he was saying before he yelled out in iMahli and the deathguards rounded on him. As he relayed what Raf had said, their faces filled with dismay, and with howls, they charged through the doorway down the steps beyond.

Raf held on to Bolyai, listening to the echoes of the iMahlis descending into the great cavern with the huge stony mounds. They hobbled along behind, Raf cradling his injured arm as they walked down the steep stone steps. Ahead of them, there were shouts as the iMahlis raced around the rocks in the cave, trying to find the tunnel, and both Raf and Bolyai jumped in fright as another blast ripped through the air and filled the cave with booming reverberations. There was a scream and then a roar from the deathguards.

Raf, holding his left arm bent against his chest, scrambled his way over the stony ground behind Bolyai and pulled up behind the Elder when he paused to peer down at a body on the ground.

"Is it one of the iMahlis?" asked Raf.

"No," replied Bolyai. "It's one of them. Whoever they are."

With a grim look at the body he continued through the darkness toward the other side of the cave where the deathguards were. As the two of them made it around the stone mound that Raf had first encountered in the cavern, there was the body of an iMahli archer lying in a mangled heap on the floor. Beyond him, they were just in time to see the last archer disappear through the hole that Raf had made in the mud wall of the stone tunnel. Tiponi was the only one remaining and he had slung the bow from the fallen archer around his shoulders, his hands shaking as he tried to strap on the small quiver of bows around his waist.

"Tiponi, -"

"They have taken her! The tunnel..." he gibbered. "What have you done? My *ishranga*...taken!"

Bolyai gripped Raf's shoulder as Tiponi managed to finally tie the strap, after which he ducked down into the jagged hole. The bow stuck on the top and with an impatient hiss, he yanked it through.

Raf watched him disappear into the tunnel, a rising panic setting in that made his breaths come short and quick.

I must have led them straight to her...

"Don't worry, boy," said Bolyai, "the deathguards will get them. Their sole purpose in life is to protect her and they are built perfectly for it. You should have told them about the tunnel sooner, perhaps."

Raf nodded and turned to say something, but a huge rumbling sound shook the ground. It was followed immediately by a deafening explosion of debris that burst out of the tunnel and knocked them backward to the ground. They staggered to their knees coughing in thick, hot smoke. From the entrance to the tunnel right in front of them came a muffled howl.

"Tiponi!" croaked Bolyai, rubbing ash out of his eyes.

From out of the heap of sand and broken fragments of rock, protruded the iMahli's flailing arm. Working together quickly, they took hold of it and heaved, kicking away the larger stones, until Tiponi's torso slid into view. He was covered in dirt and bleeding from numerous cuts, and fell clumsily to the floor in a fit of coughing. Behind him, the solid stone roof of the entrance had collapsed, and sharp fragments of rock had filled the space beyond, completely blocking it up. The tunnel was no more.

"Tiponi!"

The iMahli stopped in the gloom of the cave and looked back at Bolyai, his lacerated face distraught.

"You can't go chasing them in the dark."

Tiponi held his hands out imploringly, fingers curled into claws. "They have taken the *ishranga!* I must protect her! It is my Trust, my duty!"

"Tiponi," urged Bolyai, "they'll shoot you at first sight. They're obviously well-armed if they bring down a tunnel like that. And we don't even know how many of them there are."

"But, we cannot just leave her!"

"Of course we won't," replied Bolyai. "We'll rest and follow at first light in the morning. These people are armed and we don't want to walk into another trap like the others did." He gestured at the mess of rocks behind them.

"But, we will lose them! In the morning, the tracks will be gone," said Tiponi bitterly. He tried to rub dirt away from his face with equally dirty hands. "There should never have been this tunnel!"

"They could be going to the mines, right?" said Raf desperately. "To make her a slave?"

Bolyai shook his head. "The dead one over there is a Miernan soldier. I think they're taking the *ishranga* to the Pass. They have garrisons there so they'll probably head straight for the closest outpost."

"The Pass? We can't go all the way back to get to the entrance - it'll take too long!"

"Of course it will," replied Bolyai. Deep lines creased his forehead as he stared at the wall. "There are one or two other smaller entrances along the Pass that we'll have to try to find. We don't really have a choice. We'll have to head through the desert and try to cut them off further up."

Through the desert?

Raf swallowed. The desert was supposed to be a guaranteed death-trap. Hot, lifeless and waterless. It was the reason everyone traveled down the Pass to get across it.

Bolyai nodded to himself as if coming to a decision. "Let's head for Kastiyya. I know it's out of the way and will make the journey longer, but we can get supplies there and then angle up to try to cut them off. We can't let them reach Miern."

"Kastiyya?" asked Raf.

"An oasis. One of the very few this side of the Pass. It's half a day's travel from here, though, so we'll leave at first light to make it there before noon. We won't be able to travel for a few hours after that."

"Why?"

"If you think the plains were hot, boy, there's a nasty surprise coming when the desert sun makes its presence known."

. . . .

If Raf thought the Elder was being dramatic, he was proved wrong within a few hours of wagon-travel the next morning. They had left the deserted hilltop as soon as the first subtle wave of violet washed over the sky, and made steady progress until the sky lightened. Then, with an almost tangible force, the sun peeked over the horizon. And since that moment, the temperature, initially chilly enough for them to see their breath, rose with stunning speed.

Raf smothered himself with shea butter almost as soon as the sun appeared, keen to protect his burned skin as much as possible, but the heat seemed to scrape it away and make it itch unbearably. There was also the matter of his injured shoulder which, on inspection, revealed the bullet to have fortunately passed close to the outside of the top of his arm, leaving a scabby wound. As he was sitting sweating in the back of the jostling wagon, an idea suddenly popped into his head.

Humming gently, he closed his eyes tightly to cut out the sun and watched the colors sway faintly in front of him. Then, he tried to seek out his shoulder injury. It was impossible. As much as he tried to turn his attention around, he couldn't focus inward on himself - only outward.

"Don't bother, boy," said Bolyai. "Can't use it on yourself. It doesn't work like that."

The Elder closed his eyes and began to sing the same *haelanayre* that he had sung with Jan, and Raf suddenly felt an odd tingle that ran along his arm, and goose-bumps covered him. After a while, Bolyai stopped, and although the pain was still mostly there, the wound seemed less swollen and Raf found he could move his arm a little more freely.

"Thanks."

Lying listlessly against the side of the wagon, he stared out at the hostile landscape. The rolling, rocky hills and acacias of the plains had disappeared to be completely replaced by a flatter, sandy terrain. It extended on and on into the wavering distance, almost too bright to look at, and the only life of any kind anywhere was the occasional thorny shrub that twisted up from cracks in the parched ground. He lay back with a shirt covering his face. It made it stuffy, but the direct light of the sun was just too intense.

Tiponi changed direction slightly and the wagon turned to a more northerly setting. Instantly, the shirt was blown off Raf's face onto the floor as a strong gust of wind flew through the wagon, no longer impeded by the sides.

"So windy!" muttered Raf in irritation, pulling the shirt around his head and lying the loose ends, careful not to bump his arm.

Tiponi shook his head. "These winds, they are not strong, *ishranga*. Much worse in the desert."

"Well, they're already stronger than what *I'm* used to," replied Raf. "And besides, I told you not to call me that. Especially aft-"

"Now, now," said Bolyai. "It's too hot for that. Let's just save our energy, shall we? We have a long way to go and it's going to get much harder – and hotter - than this."

. . . .

Raf was in the middle of a disturbingly real dream when he felt a tap on his leg. He removed the shirt and opened his eyes to see Tiponi looking down at him. "What's wrong?"

"Kastiyya," the iMahli replied, nodding over the side of the wagon

Raf sat up and squinted in the fierce sunlight, shading his eyes. To their left, perhaps half a mile away, was a small sprouting of dunes and rocks in the vast, featureless land they had been traveling through. "Doesn't look like much to me."

Bolyai wiped the sweat off his forehead. "It's the entrance at the top of the valley. We'll have to travel down into it, but at the bottom, there's a large settlement around the spring. We can get supplies there from the locals and head off tomorrow morning. The next part of the journey will be longer, so it's important we get plenty of food and water. I've never tried this before, only the iMahli have; and even they don't stray off the caravan routes through the desert unless they absolutely have to."

"Great," muttered Raf.

Tiponi clicked his tongue to get the ostriches back into action and they made their way toward the outcrop of rocks. When they reached it, Tiponi dismounted and led the ostriches around a thin path that meandered amidst the rocks and sandy mounds until they reached a line of boulders that formed a sort of natural wall. The iMahli kept the ostriches moving though, guiding them toward two enormous rocky mounds that joined together. As they neared them, Raf made out a dark gap beneath the rocks, big enough for them to pass through; it was for this that Tiponi was heading. It was a wonderful feeling to enter the shade underneath for a brief period, and the absence of the sun beating down roused Raf's spirits enough that he found the energy to dismount and walk alongside Tiponi.

They emerged from the little passage and Raf couldn't help but ogle at the sight that met his eyes. Rocks of all sizes lay strewn on the ground which angled downward dramatically in front of them, leading to a round valley. And in the middle of the valley was water! A light-green pool, the surface rippling gently and sparkling in the sunlight, sat comfortably in the middle of the rocky basin. It was fringed by trees and bushes and streaks of grassy mounds which gave it the appearance of a giant, emerald eye. Raf felt a smile crease his sunburned cheeks and looked over in excitement at Bolyai who was nodding with relief at the oasis. He caught Raf's glance and smiled.

"Kastiyya," he said quietly. "And not a moment too soon. This sun's quite unbearable. And I haven't been for a dip in quite a while."

"A dip?"

Bolyai pointed down at the water's edge. "Can't you see? People are swimming down there at the side."

"What?" Raf squinted at the water. "Oh, yeah..."

There were some people, iMahlis from the look of them, who were sitting by the water and a few of them were splashing in the water. "Can we go in the water, too, Elder?"

Bolyai smiled at him and nodded.

"Only," Raf bit his lip wistfully, "I don't really know how to swim. I've never even been to Sayenham."

"You don't need to worry, boy; the water's only chest-high here."

Raf beamed and then jerked his hand at Tiponi. "Come on! Let's get down there!"

He climbed down from the wagon and took off along the path before having to pause and wait for the ostriches which stumbled their way along the stony path. The stupid things were taking their time!

Toward the bottom of the path, Raf noticed that there were more people in the shade of the palm trees along the sides, mostly iMahlis, but also a few groups of other, indistinguishable travelers, too. There were some large tents and thatched awnings that were attached around some of the bigger trees, and toward the back of the valley there was even a huge wooden building built up against a rocky cliff.

They made their way along the side of the pool and Raf walked along the edge, staring down in fascination at the clear water. "Look! Tadpoles! And what are those small, long things over there?"

"Fish," replied Tiponi.

"You're kidding!" laughed Raf. He flicked a foot into the water, watching the fish dart away. "Can we go in here?"

"No," replied Tiponi. "There only." He pointed to where the people were in the water on the other side.

"Why?"

"Just wait, boy," chided Bolyai. "This water here is clean; it's come right out of the bedrock under the ground. You only swim over there where the water flows out of this pool into the river. This part is where we get drinking water from, so you keep your dirty, sweaty body out of it, thank you very much."

"Oh."

They walked up toward the shaded area where most of the locals were. Tiponi seemed wary and stopped the wagon short of the main area, choosing to tie it to a twisted palm tree on the periphery.

"Why don't we go in closer, Tiponi?" asked Raf. "It's much more shaded."

Tiponi said nothing and continued to adjust the ostriches' harnesses, his face tight. Raf frowned at the iMahli's back and looked back up at where the other visitors were. It was only then that he noticed they were being watched. All the iMahlis, standing or seated, were staring at them. Some with badly-disguised hostility.

"Is there going to be a problem, Tiponi?" asked Bolyai quietly. "There are more travelers here than I've ever seen before. And if I'm not mistaken, those are *fetumu* over there, aren't they?"

"No trouble. *Bhesanté* run Kastiyya." Tiponi took some empty water bags and swung them onto his shoulder, turning to walk in the direction of a large tent by the wooden building.

"Come on, boy," said Bolyai.

Raf turned from where he had been staring at the water. "Oh... sorry, Elder. The water's beautiful. I don't understand how it stays above the ground, though. Do you -" He looked up and saw that Bolyai was too far away to hear so he jogged to catch up.

The three of them made their way toward the tent, their movements scrutinized by the milling iMahlis. If Tiponi was put off by the stares, he showed no sign of it and marched up to knock on a thick pole at the entrance. A voice answered and he lifted the tent flap and ducked inside, followed by Raf and Bolyai. It was quite dark inside the tent and Raf's eyes took a few seconds to adjust. When they did, he saw a long counter ahead of them with an assortment of goods on the shelves behind. Standing directly in front were two iMahlis, one of whom was busy speaking to some men who had their back turned to them. The other looked over at them inquiringly.

Tiponi clapped his hands in greeting and asked a lengthy question in iMahli. The man shook his head and mumbled a response, casting a nervous glance at the group on their left.

"He says we cannot take water," said Tiponi over his shoulder, keeping his voice low.

"Why not?" asked Raf. "There's so much of it. A whole pool! There's enough for everybody, surely?"

At his voice, one of the men turned around and looked at them. He leaned across and whispered something to the tall man beside him, who turned to look at Raf. His gaze fell on Raf's injured shoulder and then he slowly straightened up, his hands moving to his belt.

"Perhaps we should leave," said Bolyai, taking hold of Raf's arm and pulling him toward the entrance.

The men moved forward quickly after them. Bolyai shouted at Tiponi who spun around and charged back through the entrance. As he did, he barged into another man who was ducking inside, knocking him backward. Bolyai and Raf followed rapidly on his footsteps and emerged into the bright daylight, squinting as they scrambled toward their wagon. Tiponi only took a few steps though, before stopping, staring back at the man he had knocked down. Raf saw that it was a short iMahli.

"You!" hissed Tiponi.

Raf gasped with shock as the iMahli got to his feet, brushing himself off, and stared coolly at Tiponi. "It's Edokko!" he hissed to Bolyai. "The iMahli from the path by Luanchester. He's alive!"

Tiponi barked something at him and whipped out a hunting knife from his belt, waving it threateningly at Edokko. To Raf's astonishment, the short *fetumu* laughed at Tiponi's threat and then yelled something loudly into the air. Raf barely had time to turn around before there was a sudden jostling crowd of armed iMahlis surrounding them, cutting off their escape.

The tent flap was raised and the three men from inside casually walked out and surveyed the scene.

"Edokko," the tallest one said, "is this your go-between?" Edokko smiled and dipped his head. "So, first, the boy leads us to that tunnel, and now they follow us here? How convenient. It looks like I've paid you in full now, little chief."

Bolyai stepped forward. "Look here, whatever problem you h-"

To Raf, it seemed as if time slowed as one of the men standing to the side suddenly lifted a crossbow he was holding and rammed the end of it into Bolyai's face. With a groan, the Elder crumpled to the ground and lay still.

"I look forward to hearing from you in the future," said the man calmly, as if nothing had happened. "Sell these two and you can keep all the money."

"I get nothing for them, Johin," complained Edokko. He pointed at the Elder. "Too old."

"Well, get rid of them, then. I don't care. We leave in two hours. Captain Djennik will be *most* happy to see us with our latest catch." He tapped his head in farewell. "Till the next time, little chief."

Raf stared at Bolyai's face, unable to drag his eyes away from the Elder's cheek which was already being disfigured by dark purple swelling. He felt his eyes well up and didn't even try to resist when rough hands trussed him up and dragged him away.

Raf tried to wriggle his wrists loose, but the coarse rope bound his hands too tightly, so he pulled a leg underneath his body and tried to change positions to relieve the numbness. Twisting his head around awkwardly, he looked back at Bolyai who was sprawled in the sand a few feet away. Over the course of the night, the right side of the Elder's face had swollen horribly, pulling the corner of his mouth up into a disturbing half-grin.

"Bolyai?" he whispered.

He glanced back up at the doorway of the room they were being kept in. The guard on duty at the door yawned loudly and adjusted his leather chest-armor. A small table next to him held the remains of some fruit and an empty mug.

"You must help him, *ishranga*," came a voice from behind Raf.

"But what can I do, Tiponi?" he whispered. "They w-"

The guard at the door looked up and snapped, "Quiet, you two!"

Raf leaned back against the stake he and Tiponi were tied to and sighed. It had been a long night and he'd hardly slept; it was too uncomfortable sitting with his arms above his head, and the shoulder that had been wounded was aching. The temperature had also dropped right down once the sun had set so that in the early hours of the morning, he found himself huddling up as best he could, knees to chest, his breaths visible as puffs of pale smoke.

There was a noise at the entrance and the guard stepped

aside to let in an iMahli girl carrying a tray. She was short and had a necklace of wooden beads and carved ivory pieces that hung from her neck. Dipping her head to the guard, she carefully placed a tray down so as not to spill the full mug and food laid out on top.

"That's all I get?" muttered the guard. "Warm camel-milk and some hard bread?"

The iMahli girl dipped her head again and made to leave with the dirty tray but stopped as, to Raf's surprise, Tiponi suddenly addressed her in iMahli.

"Shhh!" Raf urged, trying to tilt his head behind. "What are you doing?"

"Oy!" yelled the guard, pointing angrily at them. "None of that, now! You hear me, iMahli? Shut up unless you want a beating."

Tiponi took no notice and spat out a flurry of sentences at the girl who paused and listened. The guard seized a wooden bludgeon leaning against his chair and came storming toward them. The iMahli girl looked straight at Raf as Tiponi said the word '*ishranga*', before the guard dealt him a vicious blow on his upper arm with the wooden club.

"You listen to me, slave!" he snarled. "If I tell you to stop, you stop right away! You hear me?"

Tiponi flinched, hunching up his shoulder to protect his face. "I hear," he replied quickly.

The guard lowered his arm. "You do that again and I'll make sure you can't speak anymore. You don't need your tongue in the mines." He walked back to sit down at the small table as the girl disappeared through the door without a backward glance.

. . . .

The guard ate his breakfast noisily and looked up when Raf's stomach suddenly made a grumbling sound. He held up a small piece of crust toward Raf.

"Hungry?" He let it drop onto the sand and laughed. Standing up from the table, he belched loudly and then stomped on the bread as he left the room.

The second he had gone, Tiponi whispered, "Now! Your Elder."

Raf knew what he meant and quickly closed his eyes. Humming softly, he tried to ignore the pain in his arms, the pain in his shoulder, the numbness in his legs and backside, and the empty gurgling of his stomach. It wasn't easy. And neither was it easy to remove the memory of Bolyai being knocked to the floor the day before. He persisted though, and by forcing himself to close his mind to everything but the tune he was humming, a small wave of blue quavered into view out of the corner of his eye.

Quickly, he tried to seize it and urge it toward Bolyai, but it wouldn't work. It seemed thick and unyielding and moved around him sluggishly. The harder he tried, the more it seemed to turn syrupy. He tried singing a bit louder.

"Oy! Now *you* as well?"

Raf was startled and jerked back, hitting his head against the post behind him, the colors disappearing in a flash of pain.

The guard stood at the door staring at him. "Do you want the same treatment as that stupid iMahli there, singer-boy?"

Raf shook his head.

"Good," replied the guard. He stepped into the room and turned to let two other men enter behind him.

Edokko casually stepped into view and looked down at Raf and then peered behind him at the Elder. He gestured to the man who had accompanied him. "Those two."

The second man was overweight and had a flat nose that had obviously been broken many times. He turned a set of cold, blue eyes on Raf and snorted. "Young and small." He turned to peer down at Bolyai on the ground. "And that one looks dead. Are you trying to pull a fast one on me?"

Raf looked at Bolyai and saw, with a sinking feeling, that

284

there was no improvement with his injured face.

"He should still be alive. I checked this morning," said the guard uncertainly.

The man grunted and then gave a short whistle. Through the door stepped three armed men. "Get these two to the wagon."

"You're taking them?" said the guard. "I thought they were coming with us?"

"I just bought them from our iMahli friend here," replied the man. "They're going to join the staff at my mine."

Raf's bonds were untied and his arms dropped to his sides, heavy and weak. He struggled to his feet under the watchful eye of one of the armed men while the other two pulled Bolyai up and, taking an arm each, dragged him out of the room.

He looked back as the tall man addressed Tiponi who had a fierce expression on his face. "Where are the other *ishrangas?*"

"I don't know," snarled Tiponi, pushing himself up against the post behind him. "I only know mine."

"And the other go-betweens? I'm sure you lot stick together. Tell me where to find them."

Tiponi let forth a ferocious tirade in iMahli. At the man's side, Edokko smiled and reached behind him to pick up the bludgeon from the table. Raf was shoved forward and he stumbled out of the room, hearing a muffled thud and a grunt of pain behind him.

He was marched through another room piled high with crates, and then out into the morning sun. He squinted in the bright light as they were lead to a small party of armed men waiting around two hefty wagons. Harnessed at the front were two huge animals that Raf assumed were camels. Some iMahlis were loading small crates and sacks onto the back as another man watched them, a pepperbox cradled under his arm.

He looked up as the group approached and, seeing Raf and Bolyai, scoffed, "That's all you could find, Ullet?"

"A pair of foresters, I'm guessing. Better than nothing,"

replied the man leading them. "Johin already took all the iMahlis he could get his hands on."

"Johin? We should've done him in an' taken the iMahli hag to Captain Djennik for the reward ourselves."

Ullet grunted sourly. He looked over the wagons with a careful eye. "Where're the water sacks? And where's the meat? We can't be traveling across the bleeding desert without them! I leave you with one simple job…"

"I sent the boys over there to get them ages ago! Maybe things're just taking longer now. Them iMahlis don't seem best pleased we taken over."

"Well, tough. 'Bout time we took control of the oasis and ran it properly. iMahlis don't understand business." Ullet swung his pepperbox to rest on his shoulder. "I'll go help them negotiate."

Raf stood and watched him walk off, his mind spinning. So the *ishranga* was being taken to this Captain Djennik? A Miernan soldier? What did he want with her? And what foul luck that the kidnappers had come this way! Raf found himself staring at the back of the huge wagon in front, and in particular, at the sets of heavy metal hoops that were attached along the inside. He had a horrible suspicion that he'd found where he and the Elder would be sitting for their journey. A journey to be slaves in a mine. The thought gave him shivers and he looked down at the Elder who had been dumped unceremoniously on the ground. He felt his throat tighten as the realization of what was happening dawned on him.

This is real. This is actually happening; it isn't a dream. The Elder's probably going to die, and I'm about to be taken to a mine somewhere far away. And I'll never see my family or the Forest again. Ever.

He felt his eyes well up. A picture of how his mother would take the news pushed itself into his thoughts and a burning sensation suddenly bubbled up from inside him. He found himself weeping. He flopped down next to Bolyai and hung

286

his head between his knees as he was overcome by great sobs.

I'm sorry, Elder... It's all my fault!

A scuffling behind them made him jump and looked up to see the man called Ullet standing behind him.

"Awh, don't cry, little forester boy. Things could be much worse."

Raf scowled at him and Ullet laughed, tossing a large sack to one of the other men. "Better improve that attitude before we get to my mine."

"Please," begged Raf, "just let us go!"

Ullet snorted loudly. "You probably wouldn't want that, boy. You'll be better off with me. You'll work hard, but at least in the mine you'll be fed and no soldiers will be unloading pepperboxes at you."

Raf wiped his eyes and frowned. "What do you mean?"

"Word is, the Gerent's sent an army to your little forest to take control of it."

"What?"

"My guess is that there are far too many resources there going to waste." Ullet clicked his fingers and gestured to the men to get the wagons ready to depart, and then turned back to Raf. "So while your villages will probably be wrapped up in some ugly fighting, your people dropping like flies all over the place, you'll be safely working for me. And if you work hard, life will be good."

Ullet looked up as another soldier jumped up onto the driver's bench. "Come on, then. Might as well get going now. We got a lengthy trip in front of us."

He nodded to the other men and climbed up to take a seat on the bench, letting out a sharp whistle. Two men hoisted Bolyai onto the back of the wagon, and then he and Raf were both tied firmly to the metal rings on the sides.

The two wagons set off and trundled their way toward the steep, rocky path that led up out of the basin to the desert.

Raf stared numbly at the supplies around them in the

wagon. From the amount of water, they seemed to be prepared for a very long trip. One which would be brutal if the last day's travel was anything to go by. Too brutal for the Elder who was in a very bad way, although still alive from the tiny movements of his ribs.

If he dies, I'll never forgive myself, thought Raf. *Even if we die in the mines that would be better. Just not now, not here. Not in this horrible place with these people around. Not when I can do something about it.*

He glanced around at the men walking beside the wagon and shook his head to clear his thoughts. He could feel his hands shaking.

No time for nerves now. I'm the only one who can help.

He took a deep breath and then dropped his head to stare at the wagon floor. And he began singing. The *haelanayre* was the first song that came to mind and he focused on the tune, closing himself from everything around him. He knew people were watching, knew they could hear him. But it wasn't important. He closed his eyes and sang louder, lifting his head up. In the darkness, the colors came to life.

The second he joined with them, he felt a soothing rush of freshness pour through him, invigorating him. And when he brought to mind the idea of healing the Elder, a deep azure wave swept into view, crashing out of the dim mist at the edges of his vision. He let himself embrace it all, soaking up the awareness, the beautiful connection, and then directed it all at the Elder. He flowed toward him, delved into his head, pooled the color into the dark mess of his injured face, filling it completely. He was relentless, pouring more and more of himself into the song, into the colors and into the healing.

"How...?"

Raf's eyes snapped open at the voice, his head reeling from the jarring severance from the colors, and he saw Ullet staring at him in bewilderment from the bench. "You just... How did you *do* that?"

Raf looked over to the Elder and saw that his cheek had changed from a swollen purple-black mound, to a healthy pink. No sign of the swelling could be seen at all. The bubble of sheer delight – and relief - was quickly stifled though, when Ullet stepped off the bench and climbed down into the back of the wagon, an intense and hungry look on his face.

"What did you just do to him, boy? Tell me!" His eyes were wide as he pointed at the Elder.

Raf swallowed and tried to speak, but his throat felt tight and nothing came out. One of the Miernans in the wagon ahead of them shouted something to Ullet. With a quick, frustrated look at Raf, Ullet returned to the driver's bench and stood up, craning his head around, trying to see what the commotion was. Raf wiped his eyes and leaned over the side to see a line of iMahlis come jogging down the rocky bend from the exit to the desert, shouting excitedly. Ullet stood on tiptoes, peering in a westerly direction. He lifted an arm up and whistled loudly to stop the wagons.

"What is it?" said Bolyai. "Can you see anything?"

Raf shook his head. "Maybe someone's attacking us or s-" He stopped as his breath caught. "Bolyai...! You're all right! And you're awake!"

"Your powers of observation haven't deserted you, I see," replied the Elder, moving himself up into a sitting position. "And I see our situation has deteriorated a little since, since..." He looked thoughtfully at the floor and then up at Raf. "What happened?"

Raf filled him in on what had occurred since the evening before.

"Odd," said Bolyai, rubbing his cheek. "It doesn't feel broken. Or even particularly sore." He looked questioningly at Raf who blushed and looked away.

"Ah." Bolyai nodded slowly. "Well, thank you."

Raf shrugged and stared out to where Ullet was pointing and shouting something at the wagon in front.

"Elder, it never rains in the desert, right?"

"Here? Never."

"Well, I can see dark, grey clouds on the horizon. They're pretty big. And I mean *huge.* Looks like we're going to get some serious rain."

Bolyai shuffled to his knees and pulled against the bindings to peer over the rocks to their left. His face fell.

"What? This is good news, right?" said Raf.

"It isn't rain, boy; it's a sand-storm! They're dangerous and move lightning fast. We need to get back to the shelter of the oasis quickly."

It seemed Ullet had had the same thought and he shouted out instructions to the wagon drivers in front. With some difficulty, they guided the camels around and followed Ullet's wagon at pace back down the path. Raf held on to the wagon's side, watching wisps of sand being whipped up on the ground as the breeze strengthened around them.

"Quick!" shouted Ullet, jumping down from the wagon as it finally reached a patch where the path leveled out. "Get these wagons secured. All supplies inside, now!"

The camels were led to some palm trees, their harnesses fastened around the trunks. Ullet's men removed the cargo from the back of the wagon to the entrance of the storage building as quickly as they could. Around them in the basin, iMahlis moved swiftly, hammering pegs into the ground to erect tents. These weren't like tents Raf had ever seen, though. They had thick hemp ropes pulling the leather sheets low and tight to the ground so that the highest point was only about two feet off the sand.

As he watched the hive of activity, Raf realized that the wind was actually subsiding. Even as the Miernans removed the last few sacks from the wagon, the breeze died completely. The men paused, arms laden with supplies, and stared around at the surrounding walls of the basin as a strange shroud of silence fell over everything. It seemed to Raf as if his ears had been suddenly covered with wads of wool. However, the horizon continued to darken ominously and he looked questioningly at Bolyai. The Elder was staring up at the rocky walls west of them with a grim expression.

"What is it, Eld-"

"Shhh!"

Whereas before, the sky had been dark in the west, it now seemed even darker in the east, and as the Elder tilted his head back to look directly upward, he drew a sharp breath. Raf followed his gaze. The sky above was quickly thickening and turning into one single whirling mass of clouds. Huge mountains of dark brown and grey seemed to form out of nothing as they watched, and the whole sky began turning to form a giant spiral above their heads as if being stirred slowly by some unseen hand. A flicker of sheet lightning suddenly tore through the churning furrows of cloud, sending a sharp crash echoing around the oasis.

"We have to get inside," murmured Bolyai. "We're going to get caught right in the middle!"

The standstill in the basin was broken by the iMahlis who flew into an almost berserk flurry of activity at the sight of the brooding clouds above. One of the *fetumu* who was unloading the wagon dropped what he was carrying and started running away, but Ullet leaped forward and hauled him back by his arm.

"Where are you going?" he hissed angrily.

The iMahli didn't seem to hear him, and was mumbling distractedly, eyes fixed on the skies. Ullet scowled in irritation as the man snatched his arm free and sprinted away toward one of the tents.

From all around them, a deep groaning noise was filling the basin. And then, with no warning at all, the wind flared up again and came pouring over both rocky sides of the basin in a deafening torrent. It wasn't just noise this time; the wind had substance to it, a physical force, and it slammed into everything. It whipped Raf's hair back and yanked his shirt violently against his skin. Sand and dirt were sucked up into the air making it thick and murky so that he had to squint to make out Bolyai in the wagon.

"What do we do?" he shouted.

Bolyai jerked his arms in vain against the bindings. "We *have* to find shelter!"

Raf tried to undo his own hands but the ropes were fastened too well to the metal rings. He lifted his head over the side of the wagon and shouted, "Help us!"

There was no reply other than the wind which grew to a terrifying roar. Its sheer force was making the wagon shake, rocking it back and forth on the spindly wheels. Powerful gusts seemed to attack them from every direction, and there were now small stones flying through the air, striking them painfully.

Raf flinched as a particularly strong blast of wind covered him with debris, and he buried his head under his arms, spitting out a mouthful of sand. The wind-surge continued until suddenly the floor moved and he felt the whole wagon topple sideways, dumping him painfully onto the ground, his arms tangling with the bindings. Next to him, he heard muffled groans from Bolyai and tried to call out, but the wind swallowed his shrieks with ease. He pulled as hard as he could at the ropes, feeling them cut into his wrists. Twisting back and forth desperately, he could sense the dust-storm closing in around them, battering the wooden slats of the wagon. There was a ripping sound and the panel at the back was suddenly torn from its hinges and flew away, bouncing wildly into the swirling banks of dust.

Something pulled at Raf's hands and he forced open his eyes just enough to see a dark form hovering in front of him. He tried to shout but the wind howled even louder and he had to duck his head under his arm as another stinging spray of stones bombarded the wagon. Instinctively, he tried to raise his hand – and found that it was loose! A flash of metal in front of him and his other hand was free. Raf used his hands to protect his eyes and peered into the gloom to see Tiponi beckoning to him as he helped Bolyai to his feet.

The howling winds pummeled them and it was all Raf could do to keep his eyes open enough to see the indistinct figures of the other two in front of him. They staggered toward the building against the cliff into which Ullet had escaped, but pulled up behind a group of iMahlis who were screaming at the closed door and pounding desperately on it. As they arrived and tried to take stock of the situation, there was a sharp explosion and an iMahli nearest the door jerked backward and fell to the ground.

Raf turned to find Tiponi suddenly grabbing his arm. "Come! We must go!"

He coughed painfully into his hands and staggered after the others. The wind now was so strong that the three of them were walking forward at a steep angle to avoid being thrown backward, and having to dodge projectiles which continually came hurtling through the air. Ahead of them, a tall shape materialized out of the foggy gloom and they joined Tiponi in collapsing to the ground against what turned out to be a palm tree. They simply couldn't walk any further. The three of them huddled together against the trunk and tried to shelter their faces from the wind. It wasn't so much wind anymore as monstrous swirling sheets of sand that lashed horizontally across the ground, filling the air and blocking out everything, including the sky above. The storm thundered and resonated throughout the basin and rendered any communication impossible.

From off to their right where the large wooden building was, a wall of wind came blasting through the valley and Raf heard a sharp cracking sound – loud enough to rise above the clamor. The area where the cliff had been seemed to lighten slightly, and there was a strange shaking of the ground underneath them. Raf stared in horror as an enormous boulder, as wide as an *Ancient,* suddenly emerged into view and rolled ponderously past them down into the water.

That must have crushed the building! All those people inside…

He closed his eyes tightly and clenched his teeth. How could it end now? After all that had happened? Leaving the Forest for the first time? The things he had done with music. Jan… Bhothy… Tiponi… And the *ishranga!* He felt the cutting blade of guilt as he acknowledged that she was probably well on her way to some equally horrible ending because of him.

Raf felt a molten surge of emotion charge through his body. It wasn't fear, though; more anger and frustration. It *couldn't* end now! They needed to find shelter. If they stayed here, they'd risk being suffocated or even crushed by one of these rocks like tiny ants.

Ants…

The noise was now so loud that it formed an impenetrable wall that closed in tightly around them. It cut him off, isolating him. A tiny speck of awareness in a sea of raging chaos. Even covering his ears made no difference, so he clamped his arms tightly around his head, and tunneled into his thoughts, finding solace there, seizing on a desperate idea.

He started singing.

There was nothing he could hear – but he didn't expect to, and it didn't matter. He could *feel* it. In the darkness of his mind, the song took flight and blossomed into colors that spun anxiously around him, mimicking the dust-storm that threatened to consume them. He plunged himself into the colors and threw his thoughts back to that moment in the plains when they'd first found the ant-plant on the acacia. Instantly, the colors transformed into a deep burgundy. He focused on the palm tree they were all huddled against and watched the color flow into the tree, a thick river of rich purple, until it was completely infused. He summoned an image of the ant-plant, remembering how it had looked when he cracked it open. And *why* it had been like that. He watched as the color come to life and whirled in front of his eyes of its own accord, feeding on his thoughts, sharing his will through their connection. The trunk writhed and groaned as it changed.

And then the wild winds seemed to die. With a soft scraping noise, the chaos waned and then was cut off completely. All Raf could hear was a muffled roar that raged on. *Outside.*

A soft voice took Raf by surprise and the connection was extinguished.

"Well done, boy."

Behind him, Tiponi muttered in a hoarse voice, *"Ishranga."*

Raf reached out blindly in front of him and felt his fingers touch hard, rough wood a mere foot away from his face, tracing it as it curved around him. In the darkness, he smiled faintly to himself.

He had no idea how much time had passed. It could have been minutes, it could have been hours. There had been nothing to measure it by, just the dull, monotonous drone from outside that had slowly subsided until a dead silence was left. In fact, the silence was so complete that their breathing sounded uncannily loud and filled the blackness with echoes.

"Tiponi?" he whispered.

"*Ishranga?*"

"Do you think the storm's over? Would it be safe to go outside now?"

"Outside, *ishranga?* Where are we?"

Raf heard a cough between them and then Bolyai muttered, "I thought I'd seen everything." There was pause and a questioning grunt from the iMahli. "I believe the young *ishranga* here wrapped us inside a tree somehow. That about right, boy?"

Raf was glad for the darkness around them to hide his face. "Pretty much, Elder."

Bolyai laughed quietly. "I have absolutely no idea how you did it. But you saved us. That storm... I've never seen one so fierce. And for a tree to grow so quickly!"

"But how are we supposed to get out, though?" muttered Raf. "Speaking of which, how did *you* get out of that room, Tiponi? I was worried what Edokko would do when we left."

"The girl helped."

"That slave you spoke to?"

Tiponi grunted affirmatively. Then there was a shuffling

sound from where the iMahli was sitting. Raf heard some scraping and then a soft pounding for a few seconds until there was a shark cracking noise.

"Careful with the knife, Tiponi," warned Bolyai. "We'll struggle to get out of here without it."

Raf anxiously patted his belt and realized with a jolt that he didn't have his own precious knife. It must have been taken when they were tied up. Strangely, the thought didn't distress him as much as it would have a week ago.

There was a grunt of effort and a loud crunch.

"Did you break the blade?"

"No." There was a worried tone to Tiponi's voice and Raf suddenly picked up a strange sound, like a trickle of water.

"What's that?"

"Sand. The hole is underneath."

"The sand's built up that high?" said Bolyai. "Try further up. Here, step on my hands."

There was shuffling noise and a grunt. "I can't hold your weight, Tiponi. Raf, you'll have to do it. Come, take the knife and we'll lift you."

"Elder, I -"

"Boy, every moment we wait is another that the kidnappers are getting away with the *ishranga*. Come on."

Raf groaned and then used his hands to locate Bolyai. Tiponi's hand found his shoulder and then his fingers into which he put the long knife. Carefully supporting Raf's feet, they hoisted him up in the darkness.

The trunk narrowed quickly and Raf had to duck to leave enough room to move in. Carefully positioning the blade in a cleft in the wood, he hit the handle hard with the palm of his hand. It took some effort, but eventually, he felt the blade pierce through to the other side. Giving it a twist and levering it to open the wood as much as possible without breaking the blade, he yanked it out again.

His heart sank at a soft pouring sound. More sand trickled

through the new hole down onto the men below and he heard Bolyai cursing. They lowered him back down to the ground and the three of them moved against the outside of the trunk to avoid the sand.

"Now what?" said Raf. He felt a lump in his throat and bit back a whimper. "I've trapped us under the sand. We're *buried...*"

"You saved us, boy. We'd be dead if it wasn't for what you just did, don't forget that." There was a pause. "Can you tell me how you did this? Melforging doesn't happen by accident, you *meant* for this to happen."

Raf groaned and slumped back down on to his haunches. "Elder, I told you, I don't -" He stopped, embarrassed at himself. "I...I suppose I was remembering the ant-plants we saw. You remember the ones in the plains? I thought that if those could grow for the ants, then maybe I could make this tree grow to protect us in the same way."

"You just...'remembered' that? You thought about it and that's all it took?" Bolyai grunted. "It doesn't make sense in the slightest. But *you* know how it works and can use it; that much is clear."

"We could starve here, though! I don't know what to do about the sand. It's going to fill the tree up!"

"It's not an immediate threat, so don't worry," said the Elder. "You can't do anything with the sand as it's not alive. So it's got to be the tree you deal with."

Raf chewed his lip as a flicker of hope ignited inside him. He stared unseeing in the darkness, as the beginnings of another idea grew in his head. "Elder, I need you and Tiponi to be still."

There was shuffling and he felt them settle. Then, only silence remained punctuated by the soft hiss of falling sand. Sitting down and wrapping his arms around his knees in the darkness, Raf closed his eyes. He ignored the pounding of his heart and started humming the *gretanayre.*

The colors were there instantly, flickering and pulsing vigorously, and he let the panic of their predicament slip away to a corner of his mind. He relaxed and let himself sink into the melody and become one with the music, one with the colors. They seemed to welcome him, filling him with energy.

And then he thought of home. Memories from the Forest came slowly and grudgingly, but with all that had happened recently, and what with being buried under the sand, it was hardly surprising. However, he steadfastly summoned to mind his family's home, drew on all his memories, and pieced together the huge sycamore *Ancient* until he could almost see it in front of him.

As he had done with the ant-plant idea, he focused on the image and guided the thick rush of purple that bubbled out of the darkness back into the palm tree. It drenched every part of it from the roots that had now grown far below the ground, right up to the fronds at the very top. The images of his home and the palm occupied the same space and became one, and he urged the palm to grow, willed it to expand into the other – to *become* the other.

It was more difficult as he persisted and the colors seemed to be absorbed quickly as they arrived at the edges; but he focused and mustered thicker purples, concentrating them out of the surrounding mist until the tree gleamed with an almost incandescent blaze. Wave after wave he sent, picturing his home constantly, tracing it in all the detail he could remember.

After a while, Raf found that he was flagging a bit and his efforts were becoming clumsy. The colors weakened and he seemed to be losing connection with it all, less and less able to control it. So, he stopped humming; and everything calmed down and became still again. The connection dissipated, broke apart, and he sighed wearily as he was suddenly overcome with an empty, listless feeling. Around him, there were residual flashes and flickers in the darkness at the edge of his vision, and he felt a throbbing in his temples. For a moment or two, he slumped with his head against his chest, sapped of all energy.

"*Ishranga?*"

"It's the best I could do," replied Raf. "I'm bushed." He reached back to the trunk behind him and leaned against it.

"Did it work? Whatever you just tried to do?"

Raf turned to where the voice had come from. "What are you doing over there, Elder?"

"Avoiding the sand. It came pouring in half way through what you were doing. I don't know what's changed with this palm, but it feels very different in here now. Definitely a bit bigger."

"I made it grow."

"Again?"

Raf scratched his head and tried to get his bearings. "Elder, is there a space over there? An opening or something?"

"An opening? Possibly, but sand is piled up here and blocking anything that might be behind it. I don't really want to dig around in case I set it off and it buries us completely." He paused. "What did you do?"

"I tried to make it grow like home, like our *Ancient*."

"You must be careful, boy. There are limits to melforging. Some things cannot be done, and everything is bound by the laws of nature."

Raf mulled this over. "Let me check for the other opening."

"Another one?"

"Well, my home has two branches. The blocked one by you leads to my bedroom, but mom and dad's is over here. It's a bit higher than ours, so maybe…"

Raf crawled backward carefully in the blackness. His groping hands ran over the wooden wall until they suddenly found the lip of an opening.

"No sand," he whispered. He moved forward and peered up into the inky blackness. There was the faintest glimmer of light above and he could just make out the outline of a passageway as it extended up and spiraled out of view. His heart fluttered in his chest.

Well, it definitely grew loads more, then. That's something.

He got slowly to his feet, and then flinched as he knocked his head into the top of the passage.

"What was that?"

"Nothing, Elder. The ceiling's much higher at home."

Raf also noticed that the passageway was narrower and twisted much more severely as it went up - which sent a stab of panic through his stomach.

Why isn't it exactly the same as my home? Didn't it work? It looks like it'll be too small to fit through higher up...

He ducked his head down and continued to climb, hearing the sounds of the others following behind him.

"What *is* this?" asked Bolyai in disbelief.

Raf continued around the twisting bend, speeding up as hope and dread fought with each other in his mind. Every step brought more light, but it was also getting narrower and narrower. After two full circles of the spiraling passage, the walls on either side were so close that he had to edge along sideways and Raf realized that it would soon taper to a dead-end. A few yards later, he let out a loud gasp of relief as the passage ended abruptly at an opening which was *just* big enough to squeeze through. It led out into a much larger, brightly lit space.

Sunlight!

He eased himself out and stretched his cramped neck before looking around in recognition at what was a strangely familiar space. He felt a smile force its way onto his face.

It's a small version of my parents' bedroom. Brilliant!

Looking to the right, there was an oval window that let in piercing sunlight as well as a warm breeze. Behind him, the other two emerged, murmuring in astonishment at the room.

"It's a wonder," said Bolyai softly. "You truly have the gift, boy."

Shading their eyes, they moved forward past him to the window. Tiponi took one look outside and then hissed through his teeth. Raf's proud smile faded and he went up nervously to join them. They had a commanding view of their surroundings as the window was set high above the ground. Peering out into the blazing sunlight, he understood Tiponi's reaction.

The palm tree had been in the middle of the oasis valley, right next to the water's edge. Now, looking around, there was absolutely nothing to suggest an oasis had ever been here. No water. No plants. No rocks. And no people.

"It's tragic," said Bolyai.

The entire area, as far as the eye could see in every direction, was a flat, unbroken sea of sand. Kastiyya had been buried alive.

The three of them hoisted themselves over the window and carefully climbed down the overlapping links of palm bark, dropping to the sand. To their left, the other shorter palm trunk, mirroring Raf and Rio's side of the home, poked out from the sand at a sharp angle away from them, and ended abruptly against the backdrop of a clear sky where green fronds sprouted from the top.

Raf stood awkwardly in the shade, watching as Bolyai stepped back and stared up at the palm tree, muttering to himself. Tiponi, meanwhile, had immediately wandered a short distance away to scan the horizon north of them.

"Can you see anything, Tiponi?" Raf's voice sounded strangely muted out in the open. The iMahli shook his head.

Bolyai walked slowly over the fine sand to stand next to Raf. "We should leave. I don't have any idea how long we were buried in there, but every second counts now."

"To go after the *ishranga*? Elder, we need to get back to the Forest! That Miernan told me an army of soldiers are on their way there!"

302

Bolyai frowned and looked away before turning back. "And?"

"*And?* Elder, you remember what they did up in Three Ways, don't you? Soldiers destroyed the crossroads and cut down an *Ancient!* Who knows what else they're going to do! I mean, Eirdale could be under attack right now!"

"So, tell me, what exactly do you think you could do about it?"

"What do...? I mean, we could..." Raf's mouth closed and he looked hopelessly at the Elder.

"Exactly. You're just one boy, and you'd be powerless to do anything," replied Bolyai. "It'd also take us over a week to get back without transport."

"But -"

"After which time it'll be far too late to do anything, anyway. *If* we make it back alive."

"Eld-"

"And what about the problem with the trees?" There was suddenly a tinge of fear in Bolyai's voice. "If we don't find a way to cure it, it won't matter what any soldiers are doing." He let the thought sink in and softened his tone. "Reaching the Pass from here will be incredibly difficult, but the Forest is dying, boy. And the only people who can help - the *only* ones - are the three of us." He looked over at Tiponi who had his back to them. "And his *ishranga*. She said she could teach you to cure it, but at this very moment she's being dragged to the Pass by the mercenaries *you* led straight to her."

Raf bit his lip at the cutting accusation and looked down at his feet.

Bolyai looked away. "We can send word to your parents as soon as we reach the Pass so at least they don't worry – assuming, like you say, they don't have bigger problems to deal with."

He said nothing more but turned to watch Raf from under his bushy eyebrows. After a few moments, he walked away to join Tiponi who stood brooding impatiently.

Raf stared out at the shimmering sand that stretched to the horizon. Westward lay his home, his family and the Forest. To the north lay the Pass, the *ishranga*, and…possibly a cure.

Every instinct urged Raf to go home as fast as possible, to leave behind the searing heat and endless sand, and curl up safe and secure inside their sycamore *Ancient*.

But Bolyai's right, if we don't find a cure, then the whole Forest will die.

He sighed and shook his head.

The foresters will just have to look after themselves.

He took a deep breath of the warm air and walked up to Tiponi and Bolyai.

The Elder turned to look at him out of the corner of his eye. "Well?"

Raf nodded resolutely. Without another word, Tiponi set off, the other two following closely behind him, their sandals kicking up sprays of fine sand.

The palm tree stood silently watching them depart, its two armored trunks extending majestically into the sky, the sole reminder of what was once the sprawling oasis of Kastiyya. The bright green fronds at the very top rustled and swayed coyly, as the desert breeze welcomed the first new *Ancient* in centuries.

End of Book 1

APPENDIX

ALLIUM, Fahrag: Foreman of Three Ways.

ALMIA: Miern's smaller sister-city, it is found to the north at the foothills of the Ka'toan mountains, built along the Almia River.

ANCIENT: A tree of enormous size found in the Aeril Forest. Anywhere from two hundred to three hundred yards in height, these giants are the backbone of the Forest, scattered every few hundred feet, with their first branching layer forming the natural platform on which the foresters live. They also provide accommodation for the foresters inside their own trunks. However, it is unknown exactly how this impressive woodwork was achieved as the architecture seems organic rather than cut/sawn, and hasn't diminished the *Ancients'* stability or their structural integrity in any way, which would seem impossible.

AYRES: Traditional songs found throughout the Forest and beyond, remnants of a bygone era. *Farwelayre* – the parting song, *Metanayre* – the meal-time song, *Haelanayre* – the song of healing, *Gretanayre* – the song of greeting.

BANYAN: A type of strangler fig. Seeds are deposited along branches of a tree and then germinate, sending roots down. When they reach the ground, they grow deep into the earth and slowly start thickening and spreading on and around the branch, eventually enveloping and killing – or strangling – the host tree. Using these roots that are now thick, supportive columns, the banyan can grow laterally and cover huge areas – joining with others to form a single entity comprised of many banyans.

BARD: A mostly disbanded position within the Forest, the role was a musical one, teaching and maintaining musical traditions. Some of the older literature implies there were other, mysterious and powerful aspects to the role, but time has eroded any clearer understanding.

BRINCHLEY: Allium's deputy.

BRUNNOW, Cisco: Eirdale boy.

CANOPY FARMS: Set high up in the third layer of the *Ancients*, often a hundred yards or more above the inhabited platform layer, these farms are staggered along the wide branches, linked by wooden walkways.

DAWSLEY, Stan: Councilman of Three Ways.

DESERT: The sandy bed of what was once a great sea. Almost completely devoid of life, the desert stretches from the edge of the

Aeril Forest two hundred miles across to the plains near Miern. The desert is a death-trap for travelers with its lack of water – other than a few scattered oases, constant gusting winds, searing heat and occasional devastating sand storms.

DUME, Allid, Dr.: Councilman of Eirdale.

ELDERS: Little is known about this rare group of foresters. They lead hermit-like lives in seclusion, far from the villages, and are seldom, if ever, seen. Some are rumored to be well in excess of a hundred years old. Anecdotal evidence puts forward that they are well-versed in Forest-lore, and there is even some evidence to suggest they may have been descendants of Bards.

FERTHEN, Jan: master woodsmith from Eirdale.

FESTIVAL: The annual celebration of music to which most foresters travel. Hosting the event is a great honor for the village concerned and offers the chance for trade, entertainment and socializing on a scale impossible at other times.

FOREMAN: The leader of the village Council. Responsible for the running of the village and representing the village at an Overcouncil.

FOREST PLATFORM: The second layer of the Forest, hundreds of feet above the actual ground, upon which the foresters live. The first main branches from the *Ancients* form the major supports for this platform. Joining them and tying them together are creepers, vines, roots from the plentiful normal-sized trees on top, and banyans. These are solid and support the weight of the solid compacted earth above, on which the foresters live.

GENCY, Leiana: Councilwoman of Eirdale, Raf's mother.

GENCY, Tarvil: Councilman of Eirdale, Raf's father.

GENCY, Raf: Eirdale boy.

GERENT (JEH-rint): The current ruler of Miern, Sanatos II, took over the role when his father died 7 years ago. Known by his official title as 'Ayah', he has one six-year-old son, his heir, Áthas. His first wife died giving birth to Áthas, after which he married Mesathinia, a member of the Siminutrian royal family, in a political union to attempt to put a halt to the growing hostilities between the two nations. Known for being an astute and ambitious ruler, keen on growing trade and developing Miern into a successful, safe, thriving metropolis, he has unfortunately been distracted of late by the mysterious kidnapping of his son.

GO-BETWEEN: The chosen iMahli whose sacred duty it is to act as a liaison, conveying the *ishranga's* orders to the tribe, keeping them up to date with events - and protecting their identity and location from everyone at all costs – known as the Trust.

iMAHLI (ih-MAH-lee): nomadic tribes that inhabit the plains south and east of the desert, comprised of two main groups, the *fetumu* and the *bhesanté*.

- The *bhesanté* culture is one of gregariousness, strong family ties and steeped in musical tradition. They travel in close-knit communities of family units and, as they are hunter-gatherers by nature, they move around the plains following resources and trading, generally staying within certain territories. Each community is autocratically run by an iMahli Elder known as an *ishranga,* whose role is to maintain their way of life, fend off detrimental outside influences, and safeguard the tribe's lore.

- The *fetumu* were once similar to the *bhesanté*, but over the centuries they lost touch with their traditions and cultural inheritance, turning to a more mercenary, often barbaric, way of life. With the addition of a *fetumu* senator in Miern, their presence has become more evident throughout the gerency and allegations toward them abound: of violence, bribery, theft, murder and various other crimes. According to numerous sources, their harshest treatment is saved for their iMahli cousins, the *bhesanté* – whom they have been known to kidnap - a situation which resulted in the *ishranga* all moving to secret locations for their protection.

ISHRANGA (ee-SHRUNG-gah): An iMahli Elder. Hidden away in their secret lairs, guarded by a group of deathguards from the *fetumu* bandits, these reclusive leaders are reported to possess strange powers. They are the holders of the tribe's lore and history, communicating with the tribe through their trusted go-between.

JOVER: (Old Jover) Senor Eirdale farmer.

KASTIYYA (kuss-TEE-ya): The only oasis south of the Pass, a thriving center for trade.

KA'TOANS (kuh-TOE-ins): Known colloquially as 'cavers', these wary and enigmatic people live in the mountains beyond Almia. Skilled miners, they produce the majority of the gold in circulation from cave-mines deep in the mountains – in which, it is rumored, many of them live.

MANYARA, Eliath: Foreman of Eirdale.

MIERN (MEE-air'n): Largest city in the known world. Population: approximately 140,000. Forged centuries ago when various nomadic tribes settled together between two large lakes. The main river was split to flow around the city, feeding a network of canals and sewers. The city flourished on farming, mining and trade.

NABOLEK: Cousin to the Gerent, he has been sent to the Forest to oversee the annual Festival and host the senators who are judging Foreman Allium's application to become a Baron.

ORIKON: Head hunter of Eirdale.

OTTERY, Resma: Councilwoman of Eirdale.

OVERCOUNCIL: a meeting of all the Foremen. The highest authority in the Forest.

THE PASS: The dry ravine down which an ancient river used to flow – itself the remnant of the once huge sea that covered the desert plains. At over 150 miles long, it connects the Aeril Forest with the eastern cities of Miern and Almia. Travel through the Pass is considered the safest way to traverse the desert as it affords some protection from the brutal elements. Miernan soldiers control and patrol the Pass, and travelers gather in the safety of 'communes' which provide some security against *fetumu* bandits and marauding eastern tribes.

PERENESON, Dalton: Councilman of Eirdale.

POLLATH, Luka: Foreman of Marondale, father of Leiana Gency.

SHIMA'SIDU: ancient and revered *ishranga*.

SHUJI (SHOO-jee): A small purple flowering plant found in the desert plains, notable for its enlarged roots which can be mashed and squeezed to extract water. (Also known as: *waterwort*)

SIMINUTRIA: A nation to the north-west of the mountains. Historic enemies, a relative peace has been found since the Gerent married Mesathinia, a member of their royal family.

SOJOURN: At the end of their schooling, according to tradition, foresters travel to experience life outside of their village – often out of the Forest. Anywhere from a few weeks to as much as a year, it should offer them the opportunity to get work experience, to find an apprenticeship and to broaden their horizons from what is an appreciably claustrophobic and sheltered life in the Forest.

THRAEN, Ryp: Foreman of Picorham. An enormous man, he is rumored to have once killed a bear with his bare hands.

TOVIER, Nathyn: Councilman of Eirdale. Nedrick's father.

TOVIER, Nedrick: Eirdale boy.

TUNIT: woodsmith apprentice under Jan Ferthen in Three Ways.

WATERVINE: A type of vine found throughout the Forest which, when cut open, produces a stream of potable water.

ACKNOWLEDGEMENTS

There are many people to whom I am indebted for their help in writing Melforger, whether it was for their feedback, their patience, their encouragement or their practical help.
Most of all, though, I'd like to just thank them for believing in me. Those of us in life who are surrounded by wonderful, inspiring people, as I am, are the lucky ones.

www.melforger.com

41115551R00188

Printed in Poland
by Amazon Fulfillment
Poland Sp. z o.o., Wrocław